THE WITCH
by A. E. van Vogt
Was she a harmless granny come home to spend her final days, or a creature of ancient evil bent on stealing souls away?

WIZARD'S WORLD
by Andre Norton
Condemned on his own world, he fled to another through time and space only to find his battle with mind magic was just beginning. . . .

THE WITCHES OF KARRES
by James H. Schmitz
When a kind-hearted space captain rescued three young girls from their hostile owners, he was headed for a spell of triple trouble that would change his whole future. . . .

OPERATION SALAMANDER
by Poul Anderson
Could a gorgeous witch professor and a handsome undergraduate werewolf find happiness while trying to stop an escaped salamander from burning the campus down around them?

Witches and warlocks, babes, beauties, and ugly old hags—these are just a few of the denizens you will meet in—

WITCHES

Asimov's

Magica

WITCHES

Isaac Asimov's Magical Worlds of Fantasy #2

EDITED BY

Isaac Asimov
Martin H. Greenberg
and Charles G. Waugh

A SIGNET BOOK

NEW AMERICAN LIBRARY

NAL BOOKS ARE AVAILABLE AT QUANTITY DISCOUNTS
WHEN USED TO PROMOTE PRODUCTS OR SERVICES.
FOR INFORMATION PLEASE WRITE TO PREMIUM MARKETING DIVISION,
NEW AMERICAN LIBRARY, 1633 BROADWAY,
NEW YORK, NEW YORK 10019.

ACKNOWLEDGMENTS

"My Mother Was a Witch" by William Tenn. Copyright © 1966 by William
Tenn. Reprinted by permission of the author and his agent, Virginia Kidd.

"A Message From Charity" by William Lee. Copyright © 1967 by Mercury
Press, Inc. From *The Magazine of Fantasy and Science Fiction*. Reprinted
by permission of the agents for the author's estate, the Scott Meredith
Literary Agency, Inc., 845 Third Avenue, New York, N.Y. 10022

"The Witch" by A. E. van Vogt. Copyright © 1942 by Street & Smith Publications, Inc., renewed 1970 by A. E. van Vogt. Reprinted by permission
of Forrest J Ackerman, 2495 Glendower Avenue, Hollywood, CA 90027.

"The Witches of Karres" by James H. Schmitz. Copyright © 1949 by Street
& Smith Publications, Inc. Reprinted by permission of the agents for the
author's estate, the Scott Meredith Literary Agency, Inc., 845 Third
Avenue, New York, N.Y. 10022.

"Spree" by Barry N. Malzberg. Copyright © 1984 by Barry N. Malzberg.
By permission of author.

"Devil's Henchman" by Murray Leinster (writing as Will F. Jenkins).
Copyright © 1952 by Will F. Jenkins. Reprinted by permission of the
agents for the author's estate, the Scott Meredith Literary Agency, Inc.,
845 Third Avenue, New York, N.Y. 10022.

"Malice in Wonderland" by Rufus King. Copyright © 1957 by Davis
Publications, Inc. Reprinted from the book *Malice in Wonderland* by Rufus
King by permission of Doubleday & Company, Inc.

(The following page constitutes an extension of the copyright page.)

SIGNET TRADEMARK REG. U.S. PAT. OFF. AND FOREIGN COUNTRIES

REGISTERED TRADEMARK—MARCA REGISTRADA

HECHO EN CHICAGO, U.S.A.

SIGNET, SIGNET CLASSIC, MENTOR, PLUME, MERIDIAN AND NAL BOOKS
are published by New American Library,
1633 Broadway, New York, New York 10019

First Printing, April, 1984

3 4 5 6 7 8 9

PRINTED IN THE UNITED STATES OF AMERICA

Contents

Introduction

WITCHES
by Isaac Asimov

In Anglo-Saxon times, a magician was called a "wicca." At least, a male magician was. A female magician was a "wicce," the feminine form of the word. In modern English, the word became "witch." You might think that we would use the modern English system for deriving a female from a male noun and speak of a male magician as a "witch" and a female magician as a "witchess." After all, we talk of "enchanters" and "enchantresses"; of "sorcerers" and "sorceresses."

But it doesn't work for "witch." That term is always used for a female magician. We simply don't think of males as "witches."

On the other hand, a "wizard" is always a male magician, and no one uses the term "wizardess."

For that reason, in modern English we think of "wizard" and "witch" as the male and female version, respectively, of the same word. After all, we don't have to have every female word formed by adding the "-ess" suffix. We may have "prince/princess," and "count/countess," but we don't have "king/kingess." Instead we have "king/queen" and, for that matter, "gentleman/lady," "boy/girl," "bull/cow." Why not, then, "wizard/witch"?

You can use each word in the original meaning of magician, or in a modern diluted meaning. A wizard can be merely some man who is extraordinarily clever or good at his task. A witch can be merely some woman who is so roguishly lovely that men cannot resist her. Both are so good at what they do that they seem to use magic.

Yet there is an important difference, too, an asymmetry. If we consider the words in the original meaning of someone who makes use of magic to accomplish some aim, that aim might be either a good or an evil one in intention and in fact. In the case of a wizard, it is liable to be good (to our casual thinking) as often as bad. The greatest wizard in literature is the one in the Arthurian legends—Merlin. And he is certainly considered to be on the side of good. The most popular wizard in modern children's literature is the Wizard of Oz, and he is also on the side of good.

Witches, too, might be either good or evil, and in the Oz books, Glinda is a good witch. However, that is quite exceptional. We almost always think of witches as evil. In the movie *The Wizard of Oz*, we tend to forget the pale, washed-out Billie Burke as the wholly improbable good witch, and remember only the magnificent performance of Margaret Hamilton as the Wicked Witch of the West. In literature generally, the most memorable witches are the three weird sisters in *Macbeth*, and they, too, are clearly evil phenomena.

Why, then, are witches so much more likely to be viewed as evil than wizards are? There, the fault might lie with the Bible. Witches, wizards, and all varieties of enchanters and magicians were thought to use the powers of demons and devils, and therefore to be working in opposition to God, so that they were considered to be evil virtually as a matter of course. Their tampering with the supernatural was held to be a capital offense in the Bible. The Hebrew word for such tamperers was translated into the English of the King James Bible as "witch," so that we have the verse: "Thou shalt not suffer a witch to live" (Exodus 22:18). A word equivalent to "witch" was used in the translation of that verse into other European languages.

As a result, during the first century or so after the Protestant Reformation, when Europe was torn by religious wars, and everyone was tense over religious differences, a virtual witch-hunting mania swept over Europe, and thousands of essentially innocent people were tortured and killed. A few men were, but the vast majority who suffered were women.

Though educated people no longer believe in witches (in the sense of thinking that there are people who can truly manipulate supernatural entities), the aura of evil remains in connection with witches rather than with wizards.

A woman may be a witch at any age. After all, what's to stop a young woman from dealing with demons? (Thus, in this anthology of stories about witches, there are young as well as old witches.)

Nevertheless, when we think of witches, we generally think of old women. What's more, in the sad days when witches were being hunted down by the hundreds, old women suffered in numbers far out of proportion to their occurrence in the general population.

The witches in *Macbeth* are always pictured as old women; the traditional witches with which we are presented in Halloween illustrations are always old women. Why old?

Here's what I think—

Up to about a century and a half ago, the average life expectancy was only thirty-five at the most, and old people generally made up a considerably smaller percentage of the population than they do now. What's more, in addition to the causes of death that dealt with either sex indiscriminately, women frequently died in childbirth, too. For that reason, there were fewer old women than old men.

The face changes with age. For one thing, it becomes wrinkled and withered. For another, teeth disappear. In the days when teeth weren't cleaned and were certainly never cared for properly, it was probably a rare human being who had any teeth left after the age of forty.

In the case of old men, the wrinkled face and the toothless gums were hidden by the beard which almost all men wore. Old women, however, had no beards, and the few that existed must have looked very odd, and even frightening, with their faces so different from those of younger people. And since difference is often equated with evil, old women were easy to think of as evil.

Look at the old witches of Halloween. Invariably, they have pointed noses and chins that approach each other. That is virtually the trademark of the witch. However, when there are no teeth in the mouth, the nose and chin naturally approach each other more closely than when teeth serve as a barrier. The Halloween witch is merely a toothless old woman.

I wonder if modern dentistry may not have done more to wipe out fear of witches than any amount of education. That and the fact that with the general extension of the life span, old people—and old women, in particular—have grown too common to chill one.

—But in stories, they still exist, and they can still frighten, so welcome to this anthology.

My Mother Was a Witch

by William Tenn

"William Tenn" is a pseudonym for Philip Klass, a professor of English at Penn State University. He was one of the most important writers associated with the social/satirical science fiction of the 1950s, a man both funny and bitter, with the ability to step back from the society in which he lived and see its dark side. His total output has been disappointingly small, but his major stories (he has produced very little since 1970) can be found in a half-dozen of the best collections in the field, including The Human Angle *(1956),* The Square Root of Man *(1971), and* The Wooden Star *(1968). A* Lamp for Medusa *is a delightful short novel first published in 1968. In addition, Mr. Klass is one of the best before/during/after-dinner speakers in science fiction.*

I spent most of my boyhood utterly convinced that my mother was a witch. No psychological trauma was involved; instead, this belief made me feel like a thoroughly loved and protected child.

My memory begins in the ragged worst of Brooklyn's Brownsville—also known as East New York—where I was surrounded by witches. Every adult woman I knew was one. Shawled conventions of them buzzed and glowered constantly at our games from nearby "stoops." Whenever my playmates swirled too boisterously close, the air turned black with angry magic: immense and complicated curses were thrown.

"May you never live to grow up" was one of the simpler, cheerier incantations. "But if you do grow up, may it be like a radish, with your head in the ground and your feet in the air." Another went: "May you itch from head to foot with scabs that drive you crazy—but only after your fingernails have broken off so you can't scratch."

These remarks were not directed at me; my mother's counter-magic was too widely feared, and I myself had been schooled in every block and parry applicable to little boys. At bedtime, my mother spat thrice, forcing the Powers with whom she was in constant familiar correspondence to reverse curses aimed at me that day back on their authors' heads threefold, as many times as she had spit.

A witch in the family was indeed a rod and a staff of comfort.

My mother was a Yiddish witch, conducting her operations in that compote of German, Hebrew, and Slavic. This was a serious handicap: she had been born a Jewish cockney and spoke little Yiddish until she met my father, an ex-rabbinical student and fervent Socialist from Lithuania. Having bagged him in London's East End on his way to America, she set herself with immediate, wifely devotion to unlearn her useless English in place of what seemed to be the prevailing tongue of the New World.

While my father trained her to speak Yiddish fluently, he cannot have been of much help to her and their firstborn in that superstitious Brooklyn slum. He held science and sweet reason to be the hope of the world; her casual, workaday necromancy horrified him. Nary a spell would he teach her: idioms, literary phrases and fine Yiddish poetry, by all means, but no spells, absolutely no spells.

She needed them. A small boy, she noted, was a prime target for malice and envy, and her new neighbors had at their disposal whole libraries of protective cantrips. Cantrips, at first, had she none. Her rank on the block was determined by the potency of her invocations and her ability—when invoked upon—to knock aside or deftly neutralize. But she sorely lacked a cursing tradition passed for generations from mother to daughter; she alone had brought no such village lore to the United States wrapped in the thick bedspreads and sewed into goosedown-stuffed pillows. My mother's only weapons were imagination and ingenuity.

Fortunately her imagination and ingenuity never failed her— once she had gotten the hang of the thing. She was a quick study too, learning instruments of the occult as fast as she saw them used.

"Mach a feig!" she would whisper in the grocer's as a beaming housewife commented on my health and good looks. Up came my fist, thumb protruding between forefinger and middle-finger in the ancient male gesture against the female evil eye. *Feigs* were my reserve equipment when alone: I could make them at any cursers and continue playing in the serene confidence that all unpleasant wishes had been safely pasteurized. If

an errand took me past threatening witch faces in tenement doorways, I shot *feigs* left and right, all the way down the street.

Still, my mother's best would hardly have been worth its weight in used pentagrams if she had not stood up worthily to Old Mrs. *Mokkeh*. *Mokkeh* was the lady's nickname (it is Yiddish for plague or pestilence) and suggested the blood-chilling imprecations she could toss off with spectacular fluency.

This woman made such an impression on me that I have never been able to read any of the fiercer fairy tales without thinking of her. A tiny, square female with four daughters, each as ugly and short as she, Mrs. *Mokkeh* walked as if every firmly planted step left desolated territory forever and contemptuously behind. The hairy wart on the right side of her nose was so large that behind her back—only behind her back; who knew what she'd wish on you if she heard you?—people giggled and said, "Her nose has a nose."

But that was humor's limit; everything else was sheer fright. She would squint at you, squeezing first one eye shut, then the other, her nose wart vibrating as she rooted about in her soul for an appropriately crippling curse. If you were sensible, you scuttled away before the plague that might darken your future could be fully fashioned and slung. Not only children ran, but brave and learned witches.

Old Mrs. *Mokkeh* was a kind of witch-in-chief. She knew curses and spells that went back to antiquity, to the crumbled ghettoes of Babylon and Thebes, and she reconstructed them in the most novel and terrible forms.

When we moved into the apartment directly above her, my mother tried hard to avoid a clash. Balls must not be bounced in the kitchen; indoor running and jumping were strictly prohibited. My mother was still learning her trade at this time and had to be cautious. She would frequently scowl at the floor and bite her lips worriedly. "The *mokkehs* that woman can think up!" she would say.

There came a day when the two of us prepared to visit cousins in the farthest arctic regions of the Bronx. Washed and scrubbed until my skin smarted all over, I was dressed in the good blue serge suit bought for the High Holy Days recently celebrated. My feet were shod in glossy black leather, my neck encircled by a white collar that had been ultimately alloyed with starch. Under this collar ran a tie of brightest red, the intense shade our neighborhood favored for burning the sensitive retina of the Evil Eye.

As we emerged from the building entrance upon the stone

stoop, Mrs. *Mokkeh* and her eldest, ugliest daughter, Pearl, began climbing it from the bottom. We passed them and stopped in a knot of women chatting on the sidewalk. While my mother sought advice from her friends on express stops and train changes, I sniffed like a fretful puppy at the bulging market bags of heavy oilcloth hanging from their wrists. There was onion reek, and garlic, and the fresh miscellany of "soup greens."

The casual, barely noticing glances I drew did not surprise me; a prolonged stare at someone's well-turned-out child invited rapid and murderous retaliation. Staring was like complimenting—it only attracted the attention of the Angel of Death to a choice specimen.

I grew bored; I yawned and wriggled in my mother's grasp. Twisting around, I beheld the witch-in-chief examining me squintily from the top of the stoop. She smiled a rare and awesomely gentle smile.

"That little boy, Pearlie," she muttered to her daughter. "A darling, a sweet one, a golden one. How nice he looks!"

My mother heard her and stiffened, but she failed to whirl, as everyone expected, and deliver a brutal riposte. She had no desire to tangle with Mrs. *Mokkeh*. Our whole group listened anxiously for the Yiddish phrase customarily added to such a compliment if good will had been at all behind it—*a leben uff em,* a long life upon him.

Once it was apparent that no such qualifying phrase was forthcoming, I showed I had been well-educated. I pointed my free right hand in a spell-nullifying *feig* at my admirer.

Old Mrs. *Mokkeh* studied the *feig* with her narrow little eyes. "May that hand drop off," she intoned in the same warm, low voice. "May the fingers rot one by one and wither to the wrist. May the hand drop off, but the rot remain. May you wither to the elbow and then to the shoulder. May the whole arm rot with which you made a *feig* at me, and may it fall off and lie festering at your feet, so you will remember for the rest of your life not to make a *feig* at me."

Every woman within range of her lilting Yiddish malediction gasped and gave a mighty head-shake. Then stepping back, they cleared a space in the center of which my mother stood alone.

She turned slowly to face Old Mrs. *Mokkeh*. "Aren't you ashamed of yourself?" she pleaded. "He's only a little boy—not even five years old. Take it back."

Mrs. *Mokkeh* spat calmly on the stoop. "May it happen ten times over. Ten and twenty and a hundred times over. May he wither, may he rot. His arms, his legs, his lungs, his belly. May he vomit green gall and no doctor should be able to save him.''

This was battle irrevocably joined. My mother dropped her eyes, estimating the resources of her arsenal. She must have found them painfully slender against such an opponent.

When she raised her eyes again, the women waiting for action leaned forward. My mother was known to be clever and had many well-wishers, but her youth made her a welterweight or at most a lightweight. Mrs. *Mokkeh* was an experienced heavy, a pro who had trained in the old country under famous champions. If these women had been in the habit of making book, the consensus would have been: even money she lasts one or two rounds; five to three she doesn't go the distance.

"Your daughter, Pearlie—'' my mother began at last.

"Oh, momma, no!'' shrieked the girl, suddenly dragged from noncombatant status into the very eye of the fight.

"Shush! Be calm,'' her mother commanded. After all, only green campaigners expected a frontal attack. My mother had been hit on her vulnerable flank—me—and was replying in kind. Pearl whimpered and stamped her feet, but her elders ignored this: matters of high professional moment were claiming their attention.

"Your daughter, Pearlie,'' the chant developed. "Now she is fourteen—may she live to a hundred and fourteen! May she marry in five years a wonderful man, a brilliant man, a doctor, a lawyer, a dentist, who will wait on her hand and foot and give her everything her heart desires.''

There was a stir of tremendous interest as the kind of curse my mother was kneading became recognizable. It is one of the most difficult forms in the entire Yiddish thaumaturgical repertoire, building the subject up and up and up and ending with an annihilating crash. A well-known buildup curse goes, "May you have a bank account in every bank, and a fortune in each bank account, and may you spend every penny of it going from doctor to doctor, and no doctor should know what's the matter with you.'' Or: "May you own a hundred mansions, and in each mansion a hundred richly furnished bedrooms, and may you spend your life tossing from bed to bed, unable to get a single night's sleep on one of them.''

To reach a peak and then explode it into an avalanche—that is the buildup curse. It requires perfect detail and even more perfect timing.

"May you give your daughter Pearlie a wedding to this wonderful husband of hers, such a wedding that the whole world will talk about it for years." Pearlie's head began a slow submergence into the collar of her dress. Her mother grunted like a boxer who has been jabbed lightly and is now dancing away.

"This wedding, may it be in all the papers, may they write about it even in books, and may you enjoy yourself at it like never before in your whole life. And one year later, may Pearlie, Pearlie and her wonderful, her rich, her considerate husband—may they present you with your first grandchild. And, *masel tov*, may it be a boy."

Old Mrs. *Mokkeh* shook unbelievingly and came down a step, her nose wart twitching and sensitive as an insect's antenna.

"And this baby boy," my mother sang, pausing to kiss her fingers before extending them to Mrs. *Mokkeh*, "what a glorious child may he be! Glorious? No. Magnificent! Such a wonderful baby boy no one will ever have seen before. The greatest rabbis coming from all over the world only to look upon him at the *bris*, so they'll be able to say in later years they were among those present at his circumcision ceremony eight days after birth. So beautiful and clever he'll be that people will expect him to say the prayers at his own *bris*. And this magnificent first grandson of yours, just one day afterward, when you are gathering happiness on every side, may he suddenly, in the middle of the night—"

"Hold!" Mrs. *Mokkeh* screamed, raising both her hands. "Stop!"

My mother took a deep breath. "And why should I stop?"

"Because I take it back! What I wished on the boy, let it be on my own head, everything I wished on him. Does that satisfy you?"

"That satisfies me," my mother said. Then she pulled my left arm up and began dragging me down the street. She walked proudly, no longer a junior among seniors, but a full and accredited sorceress.

A Message from Charity
by William M. Lee

*The late William Lee published only a few stories in the
science fiction magazines, most for* The Magazine of
Fantasy and Science Fiction. *In addition to the present
selection, "Sea Home" (F&SF, June 1968), and
"Trouble on Kort" (F&SF, April 1969) are both well
worth reading.*

That summer of the year 1700 was the hottest in the memory of
the very oldest inhabitants. Because the year ushered in a new
century, some held that the events were related and that for a
whole hundred years Bay Colony would be as torrid and steamy
as the Indies themselves.

There was a good deal of illness in Annes Towne, and a score
had died before the weather broke at last in late September. For
the great part they were oldsters who succumbed, but some of
the young were sick too, and Charity Payne as sick as any.

Charity had turned eleven in the spring and had still the figure
and many of the ways of thinking of a child, but she was tall and
strong and tanned by the New England sun, for she spent many
hours helping her father in the fields and tryng to keep some sort
of order in the dooryard and garden.

During the weeks when she lay bedridden and, for a time,
burning up with the fever, Thomas Carter and his good wife
Beulah came as neighbors should to lend a hand, for Charity's
mother had died abirthing and Obie Payne could not cope all
alone.

Charity lay on a pallet covered by a straw-filled mattress
which her father, frantic to be doing something for her and
finding little enough to do beyond the saying of short fervent
prayers, refilled with fresh straw as often as Beulah would allow.
A few miles down Harmon Brook was a famous beaver pond
where in winter the Annes Towne people cut ice to be stored
under layers of bark and chips. It had been used heavily early in

18

the summer, and there was not very much ice left, but those families with sickness in the home might draw upon it for the patient's comfort. So Charity had bits of ice folded into a woolen cloth to lay on her forehead when the fever was bad.

William Trowbridge, who had apprenticed in medicine down in Philadelphia, attended the girl, and pronounced her illness a sort of summer cholera which was claiming victims all up and down the brook. Trowbridge was only moderately esteemed in Annes Towne, being better, it was said, at delivering lambs and foals than at treating human maladies. He was a gruff and notional man,, and he was prone to state his views on a subject and then walk away instead of waiting to argue and perhaps be refuted. Not easy to get along with.

For Charity he prescribed a diet of beef tea with barley and another tea, very unpleasant to the taste, made from pounded willow bark. What was more, all her drinking water was to be boiled. Since there was no other advice to be had, they followed it and in due course Charity got well.

She ran a great fever for five days, and it was midway in this period when the strange dreams began. Not dreams really, for she was awake though often out of her senses, knowing her father now and then, other times seeing him as a gaunt and frightening stranger. When she was better, still weak but wholly rational, she tried to tell her visitors about these dreams.

"Some person was talking and talking," she recalled. "A man or perchance a lad. He talked not to me, but I could hear or understand all that he said. 'Twas strange talk indeed, a porridge of the King's English and other words of no sense at all. And with the talk I did see some fearful sights."

"La, now, don't even think of it," said Dame Beulah.

"But I would fen both think and talk of it, for I am no longer afeared. Such things I saw in bits and flashes, as 'twere seen by a strike of lightning."

"Talk and ye be so minded, then. There's naught impious in y'r conceits. Tell me again about the carriages which traveled along with nary horse."

Annes Towne survived the Revolution and the War of 1812, and for a time seemed likely to become a larger, if not an important community. But when its farms became less productive and the last virgin timber disappeared from the area, Annes Towne began to disappear too, dwindling from twoscore of homes to a handful, then to none; and the last foundation had crumbled to rubble and been scattered a hundred years before it could have been nominated a historic site.

In time dirt tracks became stone roads, which gave way to black meanderings of macadam, and these in their turn were displaced by never-ending bands of concrete. The crossroads site of Annes Towne was presently cleared of brambles, sumac and red cedar, and overnight it was a shopping center. Now, for mile on spreading mile the New England hills were dotted with ranch houses, salt boxes and split-level colonial homes.

During four decades Harmond Brook had been fouled and poisoned by a textile bleach and dye works. Rising labor costs had at last driven the small company to extinction. With that event and increasingly rigorous legislation, the stream had come back to the extent that it could now be bordered by some of these prosperous homes and by the golf course of the Anniston Country Club.

With aquatic plants and bullfrogs and a few fish inhabiting its waters, it was not obvious to implicate the Harmon for the small outbreak of typhoid which occurred in the hot dry summer of 1965. No one was dependent on it for drinking water. To the discomfort of a local milk distributor, who was entirely blameless, indictment of the stream was delayed and obscured by the fact that the organisms involved were not a typical strain of *Salmonella typhosa*. Indeed they ultimately found a place in the American Type Culture Collection, under a new number.

Young Peter Wood, whose home was one of those pleasantly situated along the stream, was the most seriously ill of all the cases, partly because he was the first, mostly because his symptoms went unremarked for a time. Peter was sixteen and not highly communicative to either parents or friends. The Wood Seniors both taught, at Harvard and Wellesley respectively. They were intelligent and well-intentioned parents, but sometimes a little offhand, and like many of their friends, they raised their son to be a miniature adult in as many ways as possible. His sports, tennis and golf, were adult sports. His reading tastes were catholic, ranging from Camus to Al Capp to science fiction. He had been carefully held back in his progress through the lower grades so that he would not enter college more than a year or so ahead of his age. He had an adequate number of friends and sufficient areas of congeniality with them. He had gotten a driver's license shortly after his sixteenth birthday and drove seriously and well enough to be allowed nearly unrestricted use of the second car.

So Peter Wood was not the sort of boy to complain to his family about headache, mild nausea and other symptoms. Instead, after they had persisted for forty-eight hours, he telephoned for an appointment on his own initiative and visited the family doctor. Suddenly, in the waiting room, he became much worse, and was given a cot in an examining room until Dr. Maxwell was free to drive him home. The doctor did not seriously suspect typhoid, though it was among several possibilities which he counted as less likely.

Peter's temperature rose from 104° to over 105° that night. No nurse was to be had until morning, and his parents alternated in attendance in his bedroom. There was no cause for alarm, since the patient was full of wide-spectrum antibiotic. But he slept only fitfully with intervals of waking delirium. He slapped at the sheet, tossed around on the bed and muttered or spoke now and then. Some of the talk was understandable.

"There's a forest," he said.

"What?" asked his father.

"There's a forest the other side of the stream."

"Oh."

"Can you see it?"

"No, I'm sitting inside here with you. Take it easy, son."

"Some deer are coming down to drink, along the edge of Weller's pasture."

"Is that so?"

"Last year a mountain lion killed two of them, right where they drank. Is it raining?"

"No, it isn't. It would be fine if we could have some."

"It's raining. I can hear it on the roof." A pause. "It drips down the chimney."

Peter turned his head to look at his father, momentarily clear-eyed.

"How long since there's been a forest across the stream?"

Dr. Wood reflected on the usual difficulty of answering explicit questions and on his own ignorance of history.

"A long time. I expect this valley has been farm land since colonial days."

"Funny," Peter said. "I shut my eyes and I can see a forest. Really big trees. On our side of the stream there's a kind of a garden and an apple tree and a path goes down to the water."

"It sounds pleasant."

"Yeah."

"Why don't you try going to sleep?"

"OK."

The antibiotic accomplished much less than it should have done in Peter's case, and he stayed very sick for several days. Even after diagnosis, there appeared no good reason to move him from home. A trained nurse was on duty after that first night, and tranquilizers and sedatives reduced her job to no more than keeping a watch. There were only a few sleepy communications from her young patient. It was on the fourth night, the last one when he had any significant fever, that he asked.

"Were you ever a girl?"

"Well, thanks a lot. I'm not as old as all that."

"I mean, were you ever inside a girl?"

"I think you'd better go back to sleep, young man."

He uttered no oddities thereafter, at least when there was anyone within hearing. During the days of his recovery and convalescence, abed and later stretched out on a chaise longue on the terrace looking down toward Harmon Brook, he took to whispering. He moved his lips hardly at all, but vocalized each word, or if he fell short of this, at least put each thought into carefully chosen words and sentences.

The idea that he might be in mental communication with another person was not, to him, very startling. Steeped in the lore of science fiction whose heroes were, as like as not, adepts at telepathy, the event seemed almost as an expected outcome of his wishes. Many nights he had lain awake sending out (he hoped) a mental probe, trying and trying to find the trick, for surely there must be one, of making a contact.

Now that such a contact was established he sought, just as vainly, for some means to prove it. How do you know you're not dreaming, he asked himself. How do you know you're not still delirious?

The difficulty was that his communication with Charity Payne could be by mental route only. Had there been any possibility for Peter to reach the girl by mail, by telephone, by travel and a personal visit, their rapport on a mental level might have been confirmed, and their messages cross-checked.

During their respective periods of illness, Peter and Charity achieved a communion of a sort which consisted at first of brief glimpses, each of the other's environment. They were not—then— seeing through one another's eyes, so much as tapping one another's visual recollections. While Peter stared at a smoothly plastered ceiling, Charity looked at rough-hewn beams. He, when his aching head permitted, could turn on one side and watch a television program. She, by the same movement, could see a small smoky fire in the monstrous stone fireplace, where water was heated and her beef and barley broth kept steaming.

Instead of these current images, current for each of them in their different times, they saw stored-up pictures, not perfect, for neither of them was remembering perfectly; rather like pictures viewed through a badly ground lens, with only the objects of principal interest in clear detail.

Charity saw her fearful sights with no basis for comprehension —a section of dual highway animated by hurtling cars and trucks and not a person, recognizable as a person, in sight; a tennis court, and what on earth could it be; a jet plane crossing the sky; a vast and many-storied building which glinted with glass and the silvery tracings of untarnished steel.

At the start she was terrified nearly out of her wits. It's all very well to dream, and a nightmare is only a bad dream after you waken, but a nightmare is assembled from familiar props. You could reasonably be chased by a dragon (like the one in the picture that St. George had to fight) or be lost in a cave (like the one on Parish Hill, only bigger and darker). To dream of things which have no meaning at all is worse.

She was spared prolongation of her terror by Peter's comprehension of their situation and his intuitive realization of what the experience, assuming a two-way channel, might be doing to her. The vignettes of her life which he was seeing were in no way disturbing. Everything he saw through her mind was within his framework of reference. Horses and cattle, fields and forest, rutted lanes and narrow wooden bridges were things he knew, even if he did not live among them. He recognized Harmon Brook because, directly below their home, there was an immense granite boulder parting the flow, shaped like a great bearlike animal with its head down, drinking. It was strange that the stream, in all those years, had neither silted up nor eroded away to hide or change the seaming of the rock, but so it was. He saw it through Charity's eyes and knew the place in spite of the forest on the far hill.

When he first saw this partly familiar, partly strange scene, he heard from somewhere within his mind the frightened cry of a little girl. His thinking at that time was fever-distorted and incoherent. It was two days later after a period of several hours of normal temperature when he conceived the idea—with sudden virtual certainty—these pastoral scenes he had been dreaming were truly something seen with other eyes. There were subtle perceptual differences between those pictures and his own seeing.

To his mother, writing at a table near the windows, he said, "I think I'm feeling better. How about a glass of orange juice?"

She considered. "The doctor should be here in an hour or so. In the meantime you can make do with a little more icewater. I'll get it. Drink it slowly, remember."

Two hundred and sixty-five years away, Charity Payne thought suddenly, "How about a glass of orange juice?" She had been drowsing, but her eyes popped wide open. "Mercy," she said aloud. Dame Beulah bent over the pallet.

"What is it, child?"

"How about a glass of orange juice?" Charity repeated.

"La, 'tis gibberish." A cool hand was laid on her forehead. "Would ye like a bit of ice to bite on?"

Orange juice, whatever that might be, was forgotten.

Over the next several days Peter Wood tried time and again to address the stranger directly, and repeatedly failed. Some of what he said to others reached her in fragments and further confused her state of mind. What she had to say, on the other hand, was coming through to him with increasing frequency. Often it was only a word or a phrase with a quaint twist like a historical novel, and he would lie puzzling over it, trying to place the person on the other end of their erratic line of communication. His recognition of Bear Rock, which he had seen once again through her eyes, was disturbing. His science fiction conditioning led him naturally to speculate about the parallel worlds concept, but that seemed not to fit the facts as he saw them.

Peter reached the stage of convalescence when he could spend all day on the terrace and look down, when he wished, at the actual rock. There for the hundredth time he formed the syllables. "Hello, who are you?" and for the first time received a response. It was a silence, but a silence reverberating with shock, totally different in quality from the blankness which had met him before.

"My name is Peter Wood."

There was a long pause before the answer came, softly and timidly.

"My name is Charity Payne. Where are you? What is happening to me?"

The following days of enforced physical idleness were filled with exploration and discovery. Peter found out almost at once that, while they were probably no more than a few feet apart in their respective worlds, a gulf of more than a quarter of a thousand years stretched between them. Such a contact through time was a greater departure from known physical laws, certainly, than the mere fact of telepathic communication. Peter reveled in his growing ability.

In another way the situation was heartbreaking. No matter how well they came to know one another, he realized, they could never meet, and after no more than a few hours of acquaintance he found that he was regarding this naïve child of another time with esteem and a sort of affection.

They arrived shortly at a set of rules which seemed to govern and limit their communications. Each came to be able to hear the other speak, whether aloud or subvocally. Each learned to perceive through the other's senses, up to a point. Visual perception became better and better especially for direct seeing while, as they grew more skillful, the remembered scene became less clear. Tastes and odors could be transmitted, if not accurately, at least with the expected response. Tactile sensations could not be perceived in the slightest degree.

There was little that Peter Wood could learn from Charity. He came to recognize her immediate associates and liked them, particularly her gaunt, weather-beaten father. He formed a picture of Puritanism which, as an ethic, he had to respect, while the supporting dogma evoked nothing put impatience. At first he exposed her to the somewhat scholarly agnosticism which prevailed in his own home, but soon found that it distressed her deeply and he left off. There was so much he could report from the vantage of 1965, so many things he would show her which did not conflict with her tenets and faith.

He discovered that Charity's ability to read was remarkable, though what she had read was naturally limited—the Bible from cover to cover, *Pilgrim's Progress*, several essays and two of Shakespeare's plays. Encouraged by a schoolmaster who must have been an able and dedicated man, she had read and reread everything permitted to her. Her quite respectable vocabulary was gleaned from these sources and may have equaled Peter's own in size. In addition she possessed an uncanny word sense which helped her greatly in underatanding Peter's jargon.

She learned the taste of bananas and frankfurters, chocolate ice cream and Coke, and displayed such an addiction to these delicacies that Peter rapidly put on some of the pounds he had lost. One day she asked him what he looked like.

"Well, I told you I am sixteen, and I'm sort of thin."

"Does thee possess a mirror?" she asked.

"Yes, of course."

At her urging and with some embarrassment he went and stood before a mirrored door in his mother's bedroom.

"Marry," she said after a dubious pause, "I doubt not thee is comely. But folk have changed."

"Now let me look at you," he demanded.

"Nay, we have no mirror."

"Then go and look in the brook. There's a quiet spot below the rock where the water is dark."

He was delighted with her appearance, having remembered Hogarth's unkind representations of a not much later period and being prepared for disappointment. She was in fact very much prettier by Peter's standards than by those of her own time, which favored plumpness and smaller mouths. He told her she was a beauty, and her tentative fondness for him turned instantly to adulation.

Previously Peter had had fleeting glimpses of her slim, smoothly muscled body, as she had bathed or dressed. Now, having seen each other face to face, they were overcome by embarrassment and both of them, when not fully clothed, stared resolutely into the corners of the room.

For a time Charity believed that Peter was a dreadful liar. The sight and sound of planes in the sky were not enough to convince her of the fact of flying, so he persuaded his father to take him along on a business flight to Washington. After she had recovered from the marvels of airplane travel, he took her on a walking tour of the Capitol. Now she would believe anything, even that the American Revolution had been a success. They joined his father for lunch at an elegant French restaurant and she experienced, vicariously, the pleasures of half of a half bottle of white wine and a chocolate eclair. Charity was by way of getting spoiled.

Fully recovered and with school only a week away, Peter decided to brush up his tennis. When reading or doing nothing in particular, he was always dimly aware of Charity and her immediate surroundings, and by sharpening his attention he could bring her clearly to the forefront of his mind. Tennis displaced her completely and for an hour or two each day he was unaware of her doings.

Had he been a few years older and a little more knowledgeable and realistic about the world, he might have guessed the peril into which he was leading her. Fictional villainy abounded, of course, and many items in the news didn't bear thinking about, but by his own firsthand experience, people were well intentioned and kindly, and for the most part they reacted to events with reasonable intelligence. It was what he expected instinctively.

A first hint of possible consequences reached him as he walked home from one of his tennis sessions.

"Ursula Miller said an ill thing to me today."

"Oh?" His answer was abstracted since, in all truth, he was

beginning to run out of interest in the village gossip which was all the news she had to offer.

"Yesterday she said it was an untruth about the thirteen states. Today she avowed that I was devil-ridden. And Ursula has been my best friend."

"I warned you that people wouldn't believe you and you might get yourself laughed at," he said. Then suddenly he caught up in his thinking. "Good Lord—Salem."

"Please, Peter, thee must stop taking thy Maker's name."

"I'll try to remember. Listen, Charity, how many people have you been talking to about our—about what's been happening?"

"As I have said. At first to Father and Aunt Beulah. They did believe I was still addled from the fever."

"And to Ursula."

"Aye, but she vowed to keep it secret."

"Do you believe she will, now that she's started name-calling?"

A lengthy pause.

"I fear she may have told the lad who keeps her company."

"I should have warned you. Damn it, I should have laid it on the line."

"Peter!"

"Sorry. Charity, not another word to anybody. Tell Ursula you've been fooling—telling stories to amuse her."

" 'Twould not be right."

"So what. Charity, don't be scared, but listen. People might get to thinking you're a witch."

"Oh, they couldn't."

"Why not?"

"Because I am not one. Witches are—oh, no, Peter."

He could sense her growing alarm.

"Go tell Ursula it was a pack of lies. Do it now."

"I must milk the cow."

"Do it now."

"Nay, the cow must be milked."

"Then milk her faster than she's ever been milked before."

On the Sabbath, three little boys threw stones at Charity as she and her father left the church. Obadiah Payne caught one of them and caned him, and then would have had to fight the lad's father save that the pastor intervened.

It was on the Wednesday that calamity befell. Two tight-lipped men approached Obadiah in the fields.

"Squire wants to see thy daughter Charity."

"Squire?"

"Aye. Squire Hacker. He would talk with her at once."

"Squire can talk to me if so be he would have her reprimanded. What has she been up to?"

"Witchcraft, that's what," said the second man, sounding as if he were savoring the dread news. "Croft's old ewe delivered a monstrous lamb. Pointly pinched-up face and an extra eye." He crossed himself.

"Great God!"

" 'Twill do ye no good to blaspheme, Obadiah. She's to come with us now."

"I'll not have it. Charity's no witch, as ye well know, and I'll not have her converse with Squire. Ye mind the Squire's lecherous ways."

"That's not here nor there. Witchcraft is afoot again and all are saying 'tis your Charity at bottom of it."

"She shall not go."

First one, then the other displayed the stout truncheons they had held concealed behind their backs.

" 'Twas of our own good will we told thee first. Come now and instruct thy daughter to go with us featly. Else take a clout on the head and sleep tonight in the gaol house."

They left Obie Payne gripping a broken wrist and staring in numbed bewilderment from his door stoop, and escorted Charity, not touching her, walking at a cautious distance to either side, to Squire Hacker's big house on the hill. In the village proper, little groups of people watched from doorways and, though some had always been her good friends, none had the courage now to speak a word of comfort.

Peter went with her each reluctant step of the way, counting himself responsible for her plight and helpless to do the least thing about it. He sat alone in the living room of his home, eyes closed to sharpen his reading of her surroundings. She offered no response to his whispered reassurances and perhaps did not hear them.

At the door her guards halted and stood aside, leaving her face to face with the grim-visaged squire. He moved backward step by step, and she followed him, as if hypnotized, into the shadowed room.

The squire lowered himself into a high-backed chair. "Look at me."

Unwillingly she raised her head and stared into his face.

Squire Hacker was a man of medium height, very broad in the shoulder and heavily muscled. His face was disfigured by deep pock marks and the scar of a knife cut across the jaw, souvenirs of his earlier years in the Carib Islands. From the Islands he had also brought some wealth which he had since increased manyfold by the buying of land, share cropping and money lending.

"Charity Payne," he said sternly, "take off thy frock."

"No. No, please."

"I command it. Take off thy garments, for I must search thee for witch marks."

He leaned forward, seized her arm and pulled her to him. "If thee would avoid public trial and condemnation, thee will do as I say." His hands began to explore her body.

Even by the standards of the time, Charity regularly spent extraordinary hours at hard physical labor and she possessed a strength which would have done credit to many young men. Squire Hacker should have been more cautious.

"Nay," she shouted and drawing back her arm, hit him in the nose with all the force she could muster. He released her with a roar of rage, then, while he was mopping away blood and tears with the sleeve of his ruffled shirt and shouting imprecations, she turned and shot out the door. The guards, converging, nearly grabbed her as she passed but, once away, they stood no chance of catching her and for a wonder none of the villagers took up the chase.

She was well on the way home and covering the empty road at a fast trot before Peter was able to gain her attention.

"Charity," he said, "Charity, you mustn't go home. If that s. o. b. of a squire has any influence with the court, you just fixed yourself."

She was beginning to think again and could even translate Peter's strange language.

"Influence!" she said. "Marry, he is the court. He is the judge."

"Ouch!"

"I wot well I must not be found at home. I am trying to think where to hide. I might have had trial by water. Now they will burn me for surety. I do remember what folk said about the last witch trials."

"Could you make your way to Boston and then maybe to New York—New Amsterdam?"

"Leave my home forever! Nay. And I would not dare the trip."

"Then take to the woods. Where can you go?"

"Take to—? Oh. To the cave, mayhap."

"Don't too many people know about it?"

"Aye. But there is another across the brook and beyond Tom Carter's freehold. I do believe none know of it but me. 'Tis very small. We must ford the brook just yonder, then walk that fallen tree. There is a trail which at sundown will be tromped by a herd of deer.''

"You're thinking about dogs?"

"Aye, on the morrow. There is no good pack in Annes Towne.''

"You live in a savage age, Charity."

"Aye," she said wryly. " 'Tis fortunate we have not invented the bomb.''

"Damn it," Peter said, "I wish we'd never met. I wish I hadn't taken you on the plane trip. I wish I'd warned you to keep quiet about it.''

"Ye could not guess I would be so foolish.''

"What can you do out here without food?''

"I'd liefer starve than be in the stocks, but there is food to be had in the forest, some sorts of roots and toadstools and autumn berries. I shall hide myself for three days, I think, then seek out my father by night and do as he tells me.''

When she was safely hidden in the cave, which was small indeed but well concealed by a thicket of young sassafras, she said:

"Now we can think. First, I would have an answer from thy superior wisdom. Can one be truly a witch and have no knowledge of it?''

"Don't be foolish. There's no such thing as a witch.''

"Ah well, 'tis a matter for debate by scholars. I do feel in my heart that I am not a witch, if there be such creatures. That book, Peter, of which ye told me, which recounts the history of these colonies.''

"Yes?''

"Will ye look in it and learn if I came to trial and what befell me?''

"There'd be nothing about it. It's just a small book. But—''

To his parents' puzzlement, Peter spent the following morning at the Boston Public Library. In the afternoon he shifted his operations to the Historical Society. He found at last a listing of the names of women known to have been tried for witchcraft between the years 1692 and 1697. Thereafter he could locate only an occasional individual name. There was no record of any Charity Payne in 1700 or later.

He started again when the reading room opened next day, interrupting the task only momentarily for brief exchanges with Charity. His lack of success was cheering to her, for she overestimated the completeness of the records.

At close to noon he was scanning the pages of a photostated doctoral thesis when his eye caught a familiar name.

"Jonas Hacker," it read. "Born Liverpool, England, date uncertain, perhaps 1659, was the principal figure in a curious action of law which has not become a recognized legal precedent in English courts.

"Squire Hacker, a resident of Annes Towne (cf. Anniston), was tried and convicted of willful murder and larceny. The trial was posthumous, several months after his decease from natural causes in 1704. The sentence pronounced was death by hanging which, since it could not be imposed, was commuted to forfeiture of his considerable estate. His land and other possessions reverted to the Crown and were henceforward administered by the Governor of Bay Colony.

"While the motivation and procedure of the court may have been open to question, evidence of Hacker's guilt was clear cut. The details are these. . . ."

"Hey, Charity." Peter rumbled in his throat.

"Aye?"

"Look at this page. Let me flatten it out."

"Read it please, Peter. Is it bad news?"

"No. Good, I think." He read the paragraphs on Jonas Hacker.

"Oh, Peter, can it be true?"

"It has to be. Can you remember any details?"

"Marry, I remember well when they disappeared, the ship's captain and a common sailor. They were said to have a great sack of gold for some matter of business with Squire. But it could not be, for they never reached his house."

"That's what Hacker said, but the evidence showed that they got there—got there and never got away. Now here's what you must do. Late tonight, go home."

"I would fen do so, for I am terrible athirst."

"No, wait. What's your parson's name?"

"John Hix."

"Can you reach his house tonight without being seen?"

"Aye. It backs on a glen."

"Go there. He can protect you better than your father can until your trial."

"Must I be tried?"

"Of course. We want to clear your name. Now let's do some planning."

The town hall could seat no more than a score of people, and the day was fair; so it was decided that the trial should be held on the common, in discomforting proximity to the stocks.

Visitors came from as far as twenty miles away, afoot or in carts, and nearly filled the common itself. Squire Hacker's own armchair was the only seat provided. Others stood or sat on the patchy grass.

The squire came out of the inn presently, fortified with rum, and took his place. He wore a brocaded coat and a wide-brimmed hat and would have been more impressive if it had not been for his still swollen nose, now permanently askew.

A way was made through the crowd then, and Charity, flanked on one side by John Hix, on the other by his tall son, walked to the place where she was to stand. Voices were suddenly stilled. Squire Hacker did not condescend to look directly at the prisoner, but fixed a cold stare on the minister: a warning that his protection of the girl would not be forgiven. He cleared his throat.

"Charity Payne, is thee willing to swear upon the Book?"

"Aye."

"No mind. We may forgo the swearing. All can see that ye are fearful."

"Nay," John Hix interrupted. "She shall have the opportunity to swear to her word. 'Twould not be legal otherwise." He extended a Bible to Charity, who placed her fingers on it and said, "I do swear to speak naught but the truth."

Squire Hacker glowered and lost no time coming to the attack. "Charity Payne, do ye deny being a witch?"

"I do."

"Ye do be one?"

"Nay, I do deny it."

"Speak what ye mean. What have ye to say of the monstrous lamb born of Master Croft's ewe?"

"I know naught of it."

"Was't the work of Satan?"

"I know not."

"Was't then the work of God?"

"I know not."

"Thee holds then that He might create such a monster?"

"I know naught about it."

"In thy own behalf will thee deny saying that this colony and its neighbors will in due course make wars against our King?"

"Nay, I do not deny that."

There was a stir in the crowd and some angry muttering.

"Did ye tell Mistress Ursula Miller that ye had flown a great journey through the air?"

"Nay."

"Mistress Ursula will confound thee in that lie."

"I did tell Ursula that someday folk would travel in that wise. I did tell her that I had seen such travel through eyes other than my own."

Squire Hacker leaned forward. He could not have hoped for a more damning statement. John Hix's head bowed in prayer.

"Continue."

"Aye. I am blessed with a sort of second sight."

"Blessed or cursed?"

"God permits it. It cannot be accursed."

"Continue. What evil things do ye see by this second sight?"

"Most oftentimes I see the world as it will one day be. Thee said evil. Such sights are no more and no less evil than we see around us."

Hacker pondered. There was an uncomfortable wrongness about this child's testimony. She should have been gibbering with fear, when in fact she seemed self-possessed. He wondered if by some strange chance she really had assistance from the devil's minions.

"Charity Payne, thee has confessed to owning second sight. Does thee use this devilish power to spy on thy neighbors?"

It was a telling point. Some among the spectators exchanged discomfited glances.

"Nay, 'tis not devilish, and I cannot see into the doings of my neighbors—except—"

"Speak up, girl. Except what?"

"Once I did perceive by my seeing a most foul murder."

"Murder!" The squire's voice was harsh. A few in the crowd made the sign of the cross.

"Aye. To tell true, two murders. Men whose corpses do now lie buried unshriven in a dark cellar close onto this spot. 'Tween them lies a satchel of golden guineas."

It took a minute for the squire to find his voice.

"A cellar?" he croaked.

"Aye, a root cellar, belike the place one would keep winter apples." She lifted her head and stared straight into the squire's eyes, challenging him to inquire further.

The silence was ponderous as he strove to straighten out his thoughts. To this moment he was safe, for her words described every cellar in and about the village. But she knew. Beyond any question, she knew. Her gaze, seeming to penetrate the darkest corners of his mind, told him that, even more clearly than her words.

Squire Hacker believed in witches and considered them evil and deserving of being destroyed. He had seen and shuddered at the horrible travesty of a lamb in farmer Croft's stable yard, but he had seen like deformities in the Caribbee and did not hold the event an evidence of witchcraft. Not for a minute had he thought Charity a witch, for she showed none of the signs. Her wild talk and the growing rumors had simply seemed to provide the opportunity for some dalliance with a pretty young girl and possibly, in exchange for an acquittal, a lien upon her father's land.

Now he was unsure. She must indeed have second sight to have penetrated his secret, for it had been stormy that night five years ago, and none had seen the missing sailors near to his house. Of that he was confident. Further, shockingly, she knew how and where they lay buried. Another question and answer could not be risked.

He moved his head slowly and looked right and left at the silent throng.

"Charity Payne," he said, picking his words with greatest care, "has put her hand on the Book and sworn to tell true, an act, I opine, she could scarce perform, were she a witch. Does any person differ with me?"

John Hix looked up in startled hopefulness.

"Very well. The lambing at Master Croft's did have the taint of witchcraft, but Master Trowbridge has stated his belief that some noxious plant is growing in Croft's pasture, and 'tis at the least possible. Besides, the ewe is old and she has thrown runty lambs before.

"To quote Master Trowbridge again, he holds that the cholera which has afflicted us so sorely comes from naught but the drinking of bad water. He advises boiling it. I prefer adding a little rum."

He got the laughter he sought. There was a lessening of tension.

"As to second sight." Again he swept the crowd with his gaze. "Charity had laid claim to it, and I called it a devilish gift to test her, but second sight is not witchcraft, as ye well know. My own grandmother had it, and a better woman ne'er lived. I hold it to be a gift of God. Would any challenge me?

"Very well. I would warn Charity to be cautious in what she sees and tells, for second sight can lead to grievous disputations. I do not hold with her story of two murdered men although I think that in her own sight she is telling true. If any have aught of knowledge of so dire a crime, I adjure him to step forth and speak."

He waited. "Nobody? Then, by the authority conferred on me

by his Excellency the Governor, I declare that Charity Payne is innocent of the charges brought. She may be released.''

This was not at all the eventuality which a few of Squire Hacker's cronies had foretold. The crowd had clearly expected a day-long inquisition climaxed by a prisoner to bedevil in the stocks. The Squire's about-face and his abrupt ending of the trial surprised them and angered a few. They stood uncertain.

Then someone shouted hurrah and somone else called for three cheers for Squire Hacker, and all in a minute the gathering had lost its hate and was taking on the look of a picnic. Men headed for the tavern. Parson Hix said a long prayer to which few listened, and everybody gathered around to wring Obie Payne's good hand and to give his daughter a squeeze.

At intervals through the afternoon and evening Peter touched lightly on Charity's mind, finding her carefree and happily occupied with visitors. He chose not to obtrude himself until she called.

Late that night she lay on her mattress and stared into the dark.

''Peter,'' she whispered.

''Yes, Charity.''

''Oh, thank you again.''

''Forget it. I got you into the mess. Now you're out of it. Anyway, I didn't really help. It all had to work out the way it did, because that's the way it had happened. You see?''

''No, not truly. How do we know that Squire won't dig up those old bones and burn them?''

''Because he didn't. Four years from now somebody will find them.''

''No, Peter, I do not understand, and I am afeared again.''

''Why, Charity?''

''It must be wrong, thee and me talking together like this and knowing what is to be and what is not.''

''But what could be wrong about it?''

''That I do not know, but I think 'twere better you should stay in your time and me in mine. Goodbye, Peter.''

''Charity!''

''And God bless you.''

Abruptly she was gone and in Peter's mind there was an emptiness and a knowledge of being alone. He had not known that she could close him out like this.

With the passing of days he became skeptical and in time he might have disbelieved entirely. But Charity visited him again. It was October. He was alone and studying, without much interest.

"Peter."

"Charity, it's you."

"Yes. For a minute, please, Peter, for only a minute, but I had to tell you. I—" She seemed somehow embarrassed. "There is a message."

"A what?"

"Look at Bear Rock, Peter, under the bear's jaw on the left side."

With that, she was gone.

The cold water swirled around his legs as he traced with one finger the painstakingly chiseled message she had left: a little-girl message in a symbol far older than either of them.

The Witch

by A. E. van Vogt

A. E. van Vogt, along with Isaac Asimov, Robert A. Heinlein, and Theodore Sturgeon, was one of the major figures of science fiction's Golden Age—roughly 1939–1943. His inventive and complex novels like Slan *(1946),* The Weapon Makers *(1947),* The Book of Ptah *(1947), and* The World of A *(1948), all of which appeared earlier as serials, were highlights of this period and were tremendously influential in the development of the field. However, a long diversion into L. Ron Hubbard's Dianetics cost him many potentially productive years, and he never fully regained his earlier stature. His many short stories are equally inventive and outstanding, and can be found in some sixteen collections, including* The Best of A. E. Van Vogt *(1976).*

From where he sat, half hidden by the scraggly line of bushes, Marson watched the old woman. It was minutes now since he had stopped reading. The afternoon air hung breathless around him. Even here, a cliff's depth away from the sparkling tongue of sea that curled among the rocks below, the heat was a material thing, crushing at his strength. But it was the letter in his pocket, not the blazing sunlight, that weighed on Marson's mind. Two days now since that startling letter had arrived, and he still hadn't the beginning of the courage necessary to ask for an explanation. Frowning uncertainly—unsuspected—unsuspecting —he watched.

The old woman basked in the sun. Her long, thin, pale head drooped in sleep. On and on she sat, moveless, an almost shapeless form in her black sack of a dress. The strain of looking hurt his eyes; his gaze wandered; embraced the long, low, tree-protected cottage with its neat, white garage and its aloneness there on that high, green hill overlooking the great spread of

37

city. Marson had a brief, cozy sense of privacy—then he turned back to the old woman.

For a long moment, he stared at the spot where she had been. He was conscious of a dim, intellectual surprise, but there was not a real thought in his head. After a brief period he grew aware of the blank, and he thought: Thirty feet to the front door from where she had been sitting; and she would have had to cross his line of vision to get there. An old woman, capable of moving— well, thirty feet a minute.

Marson stood up. There was a searing pain where an edge of the sun had cut into his shoulders. But that passed. From his upright position, he saw that not a solitary figure was visible on the steeply mounting sidewalk. And only the sound of the sea on the rocks below broke the silence of that hot Saturday afternoon. Where had the old wretch disappeared to?

The front door opened, and Joanna came out. She called to him: "Oh, there you are, Craig. Mother Quigley was just asking where you were."

Marson came silently down from the cliff's edge. Almost meticulously, he took his wife's words, figuratively rolled them over in his mind, and found them utterly inadequate. The old woman couldn't have been *just* asking for him, because the old woman had *not* gone through that door and therefore hadn't asked anyone anything for the last twenty minutes.

At last he said, "Where's Mother Quigley now?"

"Inside." He saw that Joanna was intent on the flower box on the window beside the door. "She's been knitting in the living room for the last half hour."

Amazement in him yielded to sharp annoyance. There was too damn much old woman in his mind since that letter had come less than forty-eight hours before. He drew it out, and stared bleakly at the scrawl of his name on the envelope.

It was simple enough, really, that this incredible letter had come to him. After the old woman's arrival nearly a year before, an unexpected nightmare, he'd mentally explored all the possible reverberations that might accrue from her presence in his home. And the thought had come that if she'd left any debts in the small village where she'd lived, he'd better pay them. A young man, whose appointment to the technical school principalship had been severely criticized on the grounds of his youth, couldn't afford to have *anything* come back on him. And so a month before he'd leisurely written the letter to which this was the answer.

Slowly, he drew the note from its envelope and once more read the mind-staggering words:

Dear Mr. Marson:

As I am the only debtor, the postmaster handed me your letter; and I wish to state that when your great grandmother died last year I buried her myself and in my capacity as gravestone marker I carved a stone for her grave. I did this at my own expense, being a God-fearing man, but if there is a relative, I feel you should bear the cost of same, which is eighteen (18) dollars. I hope to hear from you, as I need the money just now.

Pete Cole.

Marson stood for a long moment, then he turned to speak to Joanna—just in time to see her disappearing into the house. Once more undecided, he climbed to the cliff's edge, thinking: The old scoundrel! The nerve of a perfect stranger of an old woman walking into a private home and pulling a deception like that.

His public situation being what it was, his only solution was to pay her way into an institution; and even that would require careful thought. Frowning blackly, he hunched himself deeper into his chair there on the cliff's edge and deliberately buried himself in his book. It was not until much later that memory came of the way the old woman had disappeared from the lawn. Funny, he thought then, it really was damned funny.

Blankly sat the old woman.

Supper was over; and, because for years there had been no reserves of strength in that ancient body, digestion was an almost incredible process, an all-out affair. She sat as one dead, without visible body movement, without thought in her brain, even the grim creature purpose that had brought her here to this house lay like a stone at the bottom of the black pool that was her mind. It was as if she had always sat there in that chair by the window overlooking the sea, like an inanimate object, like some horrible mummy, like a wheel that, having settled into position, seemed now immovable.

After an hour, awareness began to creep into her. The creature mind of her, the strange, inhuman creature mind behind that parchment-like, sharp-nosed mask of human flesh, stirred into life. It studied Marson at the living room table, his head bent thoughtfully over the next term curriculum he was preparing. Toothless lips curled finally into a contemptuous sneer.

The sneer faded as Joanna slipped softly into the room. Half-closed, letching eyes peered then, with an abruptly ravenous, beastlike lust, at the slim, lithe, strong body. Pretty, pretty body, soon now to be taken over. In the three-day period of the first new moon after the summer solstice . . . in nine days exactly—

Nine days! The ancient carcass shuddered and wriggled ecstatically with the glee of the creature. Nine short days, and once again the age-long cycle of dynamic existence would begin. Such a pretty body, too, capable of vibrant, world-ranging life. Thought faded as Joanna went back into the kitchen. Slowly, for the first time, awareness came of the sea.

Contentedly sat the old woman. Soon now, the sea would hold no terrors, and the blinds wouldn't have to be down, nor the windows shut. She would even be able to walk along the shore at midnight, as of old; and *they*, whom she had deserted so long ago, would once more shrink from the irresistible energy aura of her new, young body.

The sound of the sea came to her, where she sat so quietly; calm sound at first, almost gentle in the soft sibilation of each wave thrust. Farther out, the voices of the water were louder, more raucous, blatantly confident, but the meaning of what they said was blurred by the distance, a dim, clamorous confusion that rustled discordantly out of the gathering night. Night! She shouldn't be aware of night falling, when the blinds were drawn. With a little gasp, she twisted toward the window beside which she sat. Instantly, a blare of hideous fear exploded from her lips.

The ugly sound bellowed into Marson's ears, and brought him lurching to his feet. It raged through the door into the kitchen, and Joanna came running as if it were a rope pulling at her. The old woman screeched on; and it was Marson who finally penetrated to the desire behind that mad terror.

"Good Lord!" he shrugged. "It's the windows and the blinds. I forgot to put them down when dusk fell." He stopped, irritated, then: "Damned nonsense! I've a good mind to—"

"For Heaven's sake!" his wife urged. "We've got to stop that noise. I'll take this side of the room; you take the windows next to her."

Marson shrugged again, acquiescently. He was thinking: They wouldn't have this to put up with much longer. As soon as the summer holidays arrived, he'd make arrangements to put her in the Old Folks Home. And that would be that. Less than two weeks now.

His wife's voice broke almost sharply across the silence that came as Mother Quigley settled back into her chair. "I'm surprised at you forgetting a thing like that. You're usually so thoughtful."

"It was so damned hot!" Marson complained.

Joanna said no more; and he went back to his chair. But he was thinking suddenly: Old woman who fears the sea and the night, why did you come to this house by the sea, where the street lamps are far apart and the nights almost primevally dark? The gray thought passed. His mind returned with conscientious intentness to the preparation of the curriculum.

Startled sat the old woman! All the swift rage of the creature burned within her. That wretched man, daring to forget. And yet— "You're usually so thoughtful!" his wife had said. It was true. Not once in eleven months had he forgotten to look after the blinds—until tonight. Was it possible that he suspected? That somehow, now that the time for the change was so near, an inkling of her purpose had dripped from her straining brain? It had happened before. In the past, she had had to fight for her bodies against terrible, hostile men who had nothing but dreadful suspicion.

Jet-black eyes narrowed to pinpoints. With this man, there would have to be more than suspicion. Being what he was, practical, skeptical, cold-brained, not all the telepathic vibrations, nor the queer mind storms with their abnormal implications—if he had yet had any—would touch him or remain with him of themselves. Nothing but facts would rouse this man.

What facts? Was it possible that, in her intense concentration of thought, she had unwittingly permitted images to show? Or had he made inquiries? Her body shook, and then, slowly, purpose formed: She must take no chances. Tomorrow was Sunday, and the man would be home. So nothing was possible. But Monday—

That was it. Monday morning while Joanna slept—and Joanna always went back to bed for an hour's nap after her husband had gone to work—on Monday morning she would slip in and prepare the sleeping body so that, seven days later, entry would be easy. No more wasting time trying to persuade Joanna to take the stuff voluntarily. The silly fool with her refusal of home remedies, her prating of taking only doctor's prescriptions. Forcible feeding would be risky, but not half so risky as expecting this wretched, doting wreck of a body to survive another year.

Implacable sat the old woman.

In spite of herself, she felt the toll of the hours of anticipation. At Monday's breakfast, she drooled with the inner excitement of her purpose. The cereal fell from her misshaped mouth, milk and saliva spattered over the tablecloth—and she couldn't help it. Old hands shook, mouth quivered; in everything her being yielded to that dreadful anility of body.

With a start, she saw that the man was pushing clear of the table, and there was such a white look on his face that she scarcely needed his words, as he said:

"There's something I've been intending to say to Mother Quigley"—his voice took on a rasping note—"and right now, when I'm feeling thoroughly disgusted, is a darned good time to say it."

"For Heaven's sake, Craig"—Joanna cut in sharply, and the old woman snatched at the interruption, and began queasily to get to her feet—"what's made you so irritable these last few days? Now, be a good lover and go to school. Personally, I'm not going to clean up this mess till I've had my nap, and I'm certainly not going to let it get me down. 'By."

A kiss; and she was gone into the hallway. Almost instantly, she vanished into the master bedroom; and then, even as the old woman struggled desperately to get farther out of her chair, Marson was turning to her, eyes bleak and determined. Cornered, she stared up at him like a trapped animal, dismayed by the way this devilish body had betrayed her in an emergency, distorting her will. Marson said:

"Mother Quigley—I shall continue to call you that for the moment—I have received a letter from a man who claims to have carved a stone for the body he himself buried in your grave. What I would like to know is this: Who is occupying that grave?"

It was his own phrasing that brought Marson to startled silence. He stood strangely taut, struck rigid by a curious, alien horror, unlike anything he had ever known. For a long, terrible moment, his mind seemed to lie naked and exposed to the blast of an icy inner wind that whirled at him out of some nether darkness. Thoughts came, a blare of obscene mental vaporings, unwholesome, black with ancient, incredibly ancient evil, a very seething mass of unsuspected horrors. With a start he came out of that grisly world of his own imagination and grew aware that the old crone was pouring forth harsh, almost eager words:

"It wasn't me that was buried. There were two of us old ones in the village, and when she died, I made her face to look like mine, and mine to look like hers, and I took her money and . . . I used to be an actress, you know, and I could use makeup. That's how it was, yes, yes, makeup; and that's the whole explanation and I'm not what you think at all, but just an old woman who was poor. That's all, just an old woman to be pitied—"

She would have gone on endlessly if the creature-logic in her had not, with dreadful effort, forced her quiet. She stood then, breathing heavily, conscious that her voice had been too swift, too excited, her tongue loose with the looseness of old age, and her words had damned her with every syllable. It was the man who brought surcease to her desperate fear; the man saying explosively:

"Good heavens, woman, do you mean to stand there and tell me you did a thing like that—"

Marson stopped, overwhelmed. Every word the old woman had spoken had drawn him further back from the strange, unsettling morass of thoughts that had briefly flooded his mind, back into the practical world of his own reason, and his own ethics. He felt almost physically shocked, and it was only after a long moment that he was able to go on. He said finally, slowly:

"You actually confess to the ghoulish deed of disfiguring a dead body for the purpose of stealing money."

His voice collapsed before that abyss of unsuspected moral degradation. Here was a crime of the baser sort, an unclean, revolting thing that, if it were ever found out, would draw the censure of an entire nation, and ruin any school principal alive. He shuddered. He said hastily:

"I haven't time to go into this now." With a start, he saw that she was heading toward the hallway that led to her bedroom. More firmly, he called: "And there's another thing. Saturday afternoon, you were sitting out on the lawn—"

A door closed softly. Behind it, the old woman stood, gasping from her exertions, but with a growing conviction of triumph. The silly, stupid man still didn't suspect. What did she care what he thought of her? Only seven days remained, and if she could last them, nothing else mattered. The danger was that her position would become more difficult every day. That meant, when the time came, a quick entry would be absolutely necessary. That meant—the woman's body must be prepared now! Joanna, healthy Joanna, would be already asleep. So it was only a matter of waiting for that miserable husband to get out. She waited.

The sweet sound came at last from the near distance—the front door opening and then shutting. Like a stag at bay, the old woman quivered. Her body shook with the sick thrill of imminent action. She had made some preparation to offset disaster, but if she failed, if she were discovered—

The spasm of fear passed. With a final, reassuring fumble into the flat, black bosom of her dress, where the little bag of powder hung open, she glided forth. For the tiniest instant, she paused in the open doorway of Joanna's bedroom. Her gimlet eyes dwelt with a glitter of satisfaction on the sleeping figure. And then, she was in the room.

The morning wind from the sea struck Marson like a blow as he opened the door. He shut it with a swift burst of strength, and stood in the dully lighted hallway, indecisive. It wasn't that he wasn't going out. There were too many things to do before the end of the school year. It was just that the abrupt resistance of the wind had crystallized a thought: Ought he to leave without telling Joanna about the letter from the gravestone maker? After all, the old woman now knew that he knew. In her cunning eagerness to defend herself and the security she must consider threatened, she might mention the subject to Joanna, and Joanna would know nothing.

Still undecided, Marson took several slow steps, then paused again just inside the living room. Damn it, the thing could probably wait till noon, especially as Joanna would be asleep by now. Even as it was, he'd have to go by car or streetcar if he hoped to reach the school at his usual early hour.

His thought twisted crazily as the black form of the old woman glided ghostlike across the bedroom hallway straight into Joanna's room. Senselessly, a yell quivered on Marson's lips— senselessly, because there was in him no reasoned realization of alienness. The sound froze unuttered because abruptly that icy, unnatural wind out of blackness was blowing again in his mind. Abnormal, primordial things echoed and raged. He had no consciousness of running, but suddenly, there was the open bedroom door, and there was the old woman. And at that last instant, though he had come with noiseless speed, the creature sensed him.

She jumped with a sheer physical dismay that was horrible to see. Her fingers that had been hovering over Joanna's mouth jerked spasmodically, and a greenish powder in them sprayed partly on the bed, mostly on the little rug beside the bed.

And then, Marson was on top of her. That loathsome mind-wind was blowing stronger, colder; and in him was an utter, deadly conviction that demonic muscles would resist his strength to the limit. For a moment, that certainty prevailed even over reality. For there was nothing.

Thin, bony arms yielded instantly to his devastatingly hard thrust; a body that was like old, rotten paper crumbled to the floor from his murderous rush. For a moment, the incredibly easy victory gave Marson pause. But no astonishment could genuinely cancel that unnatural sense of unhuman things; no totality of doubt at this instant could begin to counterbalance his fury at what he had seen.

The old woman lay at his feet in a shapeless, curled-up blob. With a pitiless ferocity, a savage intent beyond any emotion he had ever known, Marson snatched her from the floor. Light as long-decayed wood, she came up in his fingers, a dangling, inhuman, black-clothed thing. He shook it, as he would have shaken a monster; and it was then, when his destroying purpose was a very blaze of unreasoning intensity, that the incredible thing happened.

Images of the old woman flooded the room. Seven old women, all in a row, complete in every detail from black, sacklike dress to semi-bald head, raced for the door. Three exact duplicates of the old woman were clawing frantically at the nearest window. The eleventh replica was on her knees desperately trying to squeeze under the bed. With an astounded gasp, Marson dropped the thing in his hands. It fell squalling, and abruptly the eleven images of the old woman vanished like figments of a nightmare.

"Craig!"

In a dim way, he recognized Joanna's voice. But still he stood, like a log of wood, unheeding. He was thinking piercingly: That was what happened Saturday on the lawn—an image of the old woman unwittingly projected by her furiously working mind as she sat in the living room knitting. Unwitting images had they been now, of a certainty. The old woman's desperately fearful mind seeking ways of escape. God, what was he thinking? There was—there *could* be nothing here but his own disordered imagination. The thing was impossible.

"Craig, what is all this anyway? What's happened?"

He scarcely heard; for suddenly, quite clearly, almost calmly, his mind was coordinating around a single thought, simple, basic, and terrible:

What did a man do with a witch in A. D. 1948?

The hard thought collapsed as he saw, for the first time, that Joanna was half-sitting, half-kneeling in the taut position she had jerked herself into when she wakened. She was swaying the slightest bit, as if her muscle control was incomplete. Her face was creased with the shock of her rude awakening. Her eyes, he saw, were wide and almost blank; and they were staring at the old woman. With one swift glance he followed that rigid gaze, and alarm struck through him. Joanna had not wakened till the old woman screamed. She *hadn't* seen the images at all. She would have only the picture of a powerful, brutal young man standing menacingly over the moaning form of an old woman— and by Heaven, he'd have to act fast.

"Look!" Marson began curtly, "I caught her slipping a green powder on your lips."

It was putting the thing into words that struck him dumb. His mind reeled before the tremendous fact that a witch had tried to feed dope to Joanna—*his* Joanna! In some incomprehensible way, Joanna was to be a victim, and he must convince her now of the action they must take. Before that purpose, rage fled. Hastily, he sank down on the bed beside Joanna. Swiftly, he launched into his story. He made no mention of the images or of his own monstrous suspicions. Joanna was even more practical than he. It would only confuse the issue to let her get the impression that he was crazy. He finished finally:

"I don't want any arguments. The facts speak for themselves. The powder alone damns her; the letter serves to throw enough doubt on her identity to relieve us of any further sense of obligation. Here's what we're going to do. First, I shall phone my secretary that I may not be in till late. Then I'll call up the Old Folks Home. I have no doubt under normal conditions there are preliminaries to entry, but money ought to eliminate all red tape. We're getting rid of her today and—"

Amazingly, Joanna's laughter interrupted him, a wave of laughter that ended in a sharp, unnormal, hysterical note. Marson shook her.

"Darling," he began anxiously.

She pushed him away, scrambled off the bed, and knelt with a curious excitement beside the old woman.

"Mother Quigley," she said, and her voice was so high-pitched that Marson half-climbed to his feet. He sank down again as she went on: "Mother Quigley, answer one question: That powder you were placing in my mouth—was it that ground seaweed remedy of yours that you've been trying to feed me for my headaches?"

The flare of hope that came to the old woman nearly wrecked her brain. How could she have forgotten her long efforts to make Joanna take the powder voluntarily? She whispered:

"Help me to my bed, dearie. I don't think anything is broken, but I'll have to lie down . . . yes, yes, my dear, that was the powder. I was so sure it would help you. We women, you know, with our headaches, have to stick together. I shouldn't have done it, of course, but—'' A thought, a blaze of anxiety, struck her. She whimpered, "You won't let him send me away, will you? I know I've been a lot of trouble and—''

She stopped, because there was a queer look on Joanna's face; and enough was enough. Victory could be overplayed. She listened with ill-suppressed content as Joanna said swiftly:

"Craig, hadn't you better go? You'll be late.''

Marson said sharply, "I want the rest of that weed powder. I'm going to have it analyzed.''

But he avoided his wife's gaze; and he was thinking, stunned: "I'm crazy. I was so dizzy with rage that I had a nightmare of hallucinations.''

Wasn't it Dr. Lycoming who had said that the human mind must have racial memory that extended back to the nameless seas that spawned man's ancestors? And that under proper and violent stress, these memories of terror would return? His shame grew as the old woman's shaking fingers produced a little canvas bag.

Without a word, he took the container and left the room.

Minutes later, with the soft purr of his car throbbing in his ears, eyes intent on the traffic, the whole affair seemed as remote and unreal as any dream. He thought: "Well, what next? I still don't want her around but—'' It struck him with a curious, sharp dismay that there was not a plan in his head.

Tuesday morning the old woman awakened with a start and lay very still. Hunger came, but her mind was made up. She would not dress or eat until after the man was gone to work, and she would not come out at noon, or after school hours, but would remain in this room, with the door shut, whenever he was around.

Six days before she could act, six days of dragging minutes, of doubts and fears.

Wednesday at 4:30 p.m., Marson's fingers relaxed on the shining knob of the front door as the laughter of women tinkled from inside. He recalled that he had been warned of an impending tea. Like an unwelcome intruder, he slipped off down the street, and it was seven o'clock before he emerged from the "movie" and headed homewards. He was thinking for the hundredth time: "I saw those old woman images. I know I saw them. It's my civilized instinct that makes me want to doubt, and so keeps me inactive.''

The evening paper was lying on the doorstep. He picked it up;

and later, after a supper of left-over sandwiches and hot coffee, he glanced through it. A paragraph from an anti-communist editorial caught, first his eyes, and then his mind.

The enemy has not really fooled us. We know that all his acts, directly or indirectly, have been anti-*us*. The incredible and fantastic thing is this knowing all we know and doing nothing.

If an individual had as much suspicion, as much evidence, that someone was going to murder him at the first opportunity, he would try to prevent the act from being committed; he would not wait for the full, bloody consummation.

The greater fact is that there will come a time when everything possible is too little, even all-out effort too late.

With a start, Marson allowed the paper to fall. The ideology of the editorial was already out of his mind. But the theme, the inmost meaning of that editorial was for him and for his problem. *Knowing what he knew and doing nothing.*

Uneasily, but with sudden determination, he climbed to his feet. "Joanna," he began, and realized that he was talking to an empty room. He peered into the bedroom. Joanna lay on the bed, fully dressed, sound asleep. Marson's grimness faded into an understanding smile. Preparing that afternoon tea had taken its toll. After an hour, she was still asleep, and so very quietly, very gently, he undressed her and put her to bed. She did not waken even when he kissed her good night.

Thursday: By noon, his mind was involved with a petty-larceny case, a sordid, miserable affair of a pretty girl caught stealing. He saw Kemp, the chemistry assistant, come in; and then withdraw quietly. In abrupt fever of excitement, he postponed the unwelcome case, and hastened after Kemp. He found the man putting on his hat to go to lunch. The young chemistry instructor's eyes lighted as they saw Marson, then he frowned.

"That green powder you gave me to analyze, Mr. Marson, it's been a tough assignment. I like to be thorough, you know."

Mr. Marson nodded. He knew the mettle of this man, which was why he had chosen him rather than his equally obliging chief. Kemp was young, eager; and he knew his subject.

"Go on," said Marson.

"As you suggested," Kemp continued, "it was ground weed. I took it up to Biology Bill . . . I mean, I took it up to Mr. Grainger."

In spite of himself, Marson smiled. There had been a time when he had said "Biology Bill" as a matter of course. "Go on," was all he said now.

"Grainger identified it as a species of seaweed known as *Hydrodendon Barelia*."

"Any special effects if taken into the human system?" Marson was all casualness.

"No-o! It's not dangerous, if that's what you mean. Naturally, I tried it on the dog, meaning myself, and it's rather unpleasant, not exactly bitter but sharp."

Marson was silent. He wondered whether he ought to feel disappointed or relieved. Or what? Kemp was speaking again:

"I looked up its history, and surprisingly, it has quite a story. You know how in Europe they make you study a lot of stuff about the old alchemists and all that kind of thing, to give you an historical grounding."

"Yes."

Kemp laughed. "You haven't got a witch around your place by any chance?"

"Eh!" The exclamation almost burned Marson's lips. He fought to hide the tremendousness of that shock.

Kemp laughed again. "According to *Die Geschichte der Zauberinnen*, by the Austrian Karl Gloeck, *Hydrodendon Barelia* is the modern name for the sinister witch's weed of antiquity. I'm not talking about the special witches of our Christian lore, with their childish attributes, but the old tribe of devil's creatures that came out of prehistory, regular full-blooded sea witches. It seems when each successive body gets old, they choose a young woman's body, attune themselves to it by living with the victim, and take possession any time after midnight of the first full-moon period following the 21st of June. Witch's weed is supposed to make the entry easier. Gloeck says . . . why, what's the matter, sir?"

His impulse, his wild and terrible impulse, was to babble the whole story to Kemp. With an effort, he stopped himself; for Kemp, though he might talk easily of witches, was a scientist to the depths of his soul. And what he—Marson—might have to do must not be endangered by the knowledge that some practical, doubting person suspected the truth. The mere existence of suspicion would corrode his will, and, in the final issue, undermine his decision to act.

He heard himself muttering words of thanks. Minutes later, on his way, he was thinking miserably: What could he say, how could he convince Joanna that the old woman must be gotten rid of? And there was one more thing that he had to clear up before he would dare risk everything in the only, unilateral action that remained. One more thing—

All Saturday morning, the sun shone brilliantly, but by afternoon black clouds rode above his racing car. At six in the evening it rained torrentially for ten minutes; and then, slowly, the sky cleared.

His first view of the village was from a hill, and that, he thought, relieved, should make it easier. From a group of trees he surveyed the little sprawl of houses and buildings. It was the church that confused him at first. He kept searching in its vicinity with his field glasses. And it was nearly half an hour before he was convinced that what he sought was not there. Twilight was thick over the world now, and that brought surging panic. He couldn't possibly go down to the village and inquire where the graveyard was. Yet—hurry, hurry! He walked deeper into the woods along the edge of the hill. There was a jutting point of ground farther along, from where he would be able to sweep the countryside. These villages sometimes had their graveyards a considerable distance away.

The little roadway burst upon him abruptly, as he emerged from the brush; and there, a few scant feet away, was a trellised gate. Beyond it, in the gathering shadows, simple crosses gleamed, an angel stood whitely, stiffly, poised for flight; and several great, shining granite stones reared rigidly from a dark, quiet earth.

Night lay black and still on the graveyard when his cautiously used flashlight at last picked out the headstone he sought. The inscription was simple:

Mrs. Quigley
Died July 7, 1945
Over 90 years old

He went back to the car, and got the shovel; and then he began to dig. The earth was strong; and he was not accustomed to digging. After an hour, he had penetrated about a foot and a half. Breathless, he sank down on the ground, and for a while he lay there under the night sky with its shifting panoply of clouds. A queer, intellectual remembrance came that the average weight of university presidents and high school principals was around one hundred eighty pounds, according to Young. But the devil of it was, he thought grimly, it was all weight and no endurance. Nevertheless, he had to go on if it took all night.

At least, he was sure of one thing. Joanna wasn't home. It had been a tough job persuading her to accept that week-end invitation alone, tougher still to lie about the duties that would take him out of the city until Sunday morning; and he had had to promise faithfully that he would drive out Sunday to get her. The simplest thing of all had been getting the young girl to look after the old woman over the week-end.

The sound of a car passing brought him to his feet in one jerky movement. He frowned. It wasn't that he was worried, or even basically alarmed. His mind felt rock-steady; his determination was an unshaken thing. Here in this dark, peaceful setting, disturbance was as unlikely as his own ghoul-like incursion. People simply didn't come to graveyards at night.

The night sped as he dug on and on, nearer to that secret he must have before he could take the deadly action that logic dictated even now. And he didn't feel like a ghoul. There was no feeling at all, only his purpose; and there was the dark night, the quietness, broken only by the swish of dirt thrown upward and outward. His life, his strength flowed on here in this little, tree-grown field of death; and his watch showed twenty-five minutes to two when at last the spade struck wood.

It was after two when his flashlight glowed eerily into the empty wooden box. For long seconds, he stared; and now that the reality was here, he didn't know what he had expected. Obviously, only too obviously, an image had been buried here—and vanished gleefully as the dirt began to thud in the filling of the grave. But why a burial at all? Who was she trying to fool? His mind grew taut. Reasons didn't matter now. *He knew;* that was what counted. And his actions must be cold and deadly as was the purpose of the creature that had fastened itself on his household.

His car glided onto the deserted early-morning highway. The gray dawn came out of the east to meet him as he drove; and only his dark purpose, firmer, icier each minute, an intellectualized thing as unquenchable as sun fire, kept him companion.

It was deep into the afternoon when his machine, in its iron-throated second gear, whirred up the steep hill and twisted into the runway that led to the garage. He went into the house and for a while he sat down. The girl whom Joanna had left in charge was a pretty, red-haired thing named Helen. She was quite fragilely built, he noted with grim approval; he had suggested her for the week-end with that very smallness in mind. And yes, she wouldn't mind staying another night if they didn't come home. And when was he leaving to get his wife?

"Oh, I'm going to have a nap first," Marson replied. "Had rather a hard drive. And you . . . what are you going to do while I sleep?"

"I've found some magazines," the girl said. "I'm going to sit here and read. I'll keep very quiet, I assure you."

"Thank you," Marson said. "It's just for a couple of hours, you know."

He smiled bleakly to himself as he went into the bedroom and closed the door. Men with desperate plans had to be bold, had to rely on the simplest, most straightforward realities of life—such as the fact that people normally stayed away from cemeteries at night. And that young women didn't make a nuisance of themselves by prowling around when they had promised not to. He took off his shoes, put on his slippers, and then he waited for five long minutes to give her time to settle down.

Finally, softly, he went through the bathroom door that led to the hallway that connected kitchen and bedrooms. The kitchen door creaked as he went out, but he allowed himself no qualms; not a trace of fear entered into the ice-cold region that was his brain.

The car was parked at the side of the house, where there was only one window. He took the five-gallon tin of gasoline out of the back seat, carried it through the kitchen down into the basement. He covered it with some old cloth, then he was up again through the kitchen. He reached the bedroom, thinking tensely: It was these details that must paralyze most people planning murder. Tonight when he came back, he wouldn't be able to drive the car up the hill, because it was to be a very special, unseen, ghostly trip. The car would be parked at least a mile away, and obviously, it would be fantastically risky, and tiring, to lug a five-gallon tin of gas a whole mile through back alleys. And what a nightmare it would be to blunder with such a tin through the kitchen and into the basement at midnight. Impossible, too, he had found, to get anything past Joanna without her seeing.

Murder had its difficulties; and quite simply, of course, murder it must be. And by fire. All that he ever heard about witches showed the overwhelming importance of fire. And just let lightly built Helen try to break down the old woman's door after the fire had started and he had locked that door from the outside.

He lay for a while quietly on the bed, and the thought came that no man would seem a greater scoundrel than he if all that he had done and all that he intended to do was ever found out. For a moment, then, a fear came black as pitch; and as if the picture was there before his eyes, he saw the great school slipping from him, the greater college beyond fading like the dream it was, fading into the mists that surrounded a prison cell.

He thought: It would be so easy to take half measures that would rid him and Joanna of the terrible problem. All he needed to do next day was to take her to the Old Folks Home while Joanna was still away, and ruthlessly face down all subsequent objections. The old woman would escape, perhaps, but she would never come back to them.

He could retreat, then, into his world of school and Joanna; existence would flow on in its immense American way—and somewhere soon there would be a young woman witch, glowing with the strength of ancient, evil life renewed; and somewhere too there would be a human soul shattered out of its lawful body, a home where an old woman had blatantly, skillfully, intruded.

Knowing what he did, and doing nothing short of everything!

He must have slept on that thought, the demanding sleep of utterly weary nerves, unaccustomed to being denied their rest. He wakened with a shock. It was pitch dark, he saw, and—

The bedroom door opened softly. Joanna came tiptoeing in. She saw him by the light that streamed from the hall. She stopped and smiled. Then she came over and kissed him.

"Darling," she said, "I'm so glad that you hadn't started out to get me. A delightful couple offered to drive me home, and I thought, if we met you on the way, at least it would have saved you that much, after your long, tiring week-end. I've sent Helen home. It's after eleven, so just undress and go straight to bed. I'm going to have a cup of tea myself; perhaps you'd like one too."

Her voice barely penetrated through the great sounds that clanged in his brain, the pure agony of realization. *After eleven*— less than an hour to the midnight that, once a year, began the fatal period of the witch's moon. The whole world of his plans was crashing about his ears.

He hovered about her while she put the kettle on. It was half-past eleven when they finished tea, and still he couldn't speak, couldn't begin to find the beginning that would cover all the things that had to be said. Wretchedly, he grew aware of her eyes watching him as she puffed at her cigarette.

He got up and started to pace the floor; and now there was dark puzzlement in her fine brown eyes. Twice, she started to speak, but each time cut herself off. And waited. He could almost feel her waiting in that quiet, earnest way of hers, waiting for him to speak first.

The impossibility, he thought, the utter impossibility of convincing this calm, practical, tender-hearted wife of his. And yet, it *had* to be done, now before it was too late, before even all-out effort would be too little. The recurrence of that phrase from the editorial started a streak of cold perspiration down his face. He stopped short, stopped in front of her; and his eyes must have been glaring pools, his rigid posture terrifying; for she shrank back.

"Craig—"

"Joanna, I want you to take your hat and coat and go to a hotel."

It needed no imagination to realize that his words must sound insane. He plunged on with the volubility of a child telling an exciting story. And that was the way he felt—like a child talking to a tolerant grown-up. But he couldn't stop. He omitted only his grim murder purpose. She would have to absorb the shock of that later when it was all over. When he had finished, he saw that her gaze was tender.

"You poor darling," she said. "So that's been bothering you. You were worried about me. I can just see how everything would work on your mind. I'd have felt the same, if it were you apparently in danger."

Marson groaned. So that was the angle she was taking—sweet understanding; humoring his natural alarm; believing not a word. He caught his mind into a measure of calm. He said in a queer, shaky voice:

"Joanna, think of Kemp's definite analysis of it as witch's weed, and the fact that the body is not in the grave."

Still there was no fire in her eyes, no flame of basic fear. She was frowning; she said:

"But why would she have to go to all that trouble of burying one of her images, when all she had to do was get on the train and come here? Physically, that is what she did; why that enormous farce of a burial?"

Marson flared, "Why the lie she told me about having put makeup on someone else who was buried there? Oh, darling, don't you see—"

Slowly, reasonably, Joanna said, "There may have been some connivance, Craig, perhaps between the man, Pete Cole, who wrote you the letter, and Mother Quigley. Have you thought of that?"

If she had been with him, he thought, when he opened that dark grave. If she had seen the incredible images— If, if, if—

He stole a glance at the clock on the wall. It was seventeen minutes to twelve, and that nearly twisted his brain. He shuddered, and fought for control of his voice. There were arguments he could think of, but the time for talk was past, far past. Only one thing mattered.

"Joanna," he said, and his voice was so intense that it shocked him, "you'll go to the hotel for three days, for my sake?"

"Why, of course, darling." She looked serene, as she stood up. "My night bag is still packed. I'll just take the car and—" A thought seemed to strike her. Her fine, clear brow creased. "What about you?"

"I'll stay here of course," he said, "to see that she stays here. You can phone me up at school tomorrow. Hurry, for Heaven's sake."

He felt chilled by the way that her gaze was appraising him. "Just a minute," she said, and her voice was slow, taut. "Originally, you planned to have me out of the way only until tomorrow. What—are you—planning to do—tonight?"

His mind was abruptly sullen, rebellious, his mouth awkward, as if only the truth could come easily from it. Lies had always been hard for him. But he tried now.

"All I wanted was to get you out of the way while I visited the grave. I didn't really figure beyond that."

Her eyes didn't believe him; her voice said so, but just what words she used somehow didn't penetrate. For an odd steadiness was coming to him, realization that the time must be only minutes away and that all this talk was worthless. Only his relentless purpose mattered. He said simply, almost as if he were talking to himself:

"I intended to lock her door from the outside, and burn the house, but I can see now that isn't necessary. You'd better get going, darling, because this is going to be messy, and you mustn't see it. You see, I'm going to take her out to the cliff's edge, and throw her to the night sea she fears so violently."

He stopped because the clock, incredibly, said eight minutes to twelve. Without a sound, without waiting for the words that seemed to quiver on her lips, he whirled and raced into the bedroom corridor. He tried the old woman's door. It was locked. A very fury of frustration caught at his throat.

"Open up!" he roared.

There was silence within the room. He felt Joanna's fingers tugging at his sleeve. And then he was flinging the full weight of his hundred and eighty pounds at that door. Two bone-wrenching thrusts, and it went down with an ear-splitting crash. His fingers fumbled for the light switch. There was a click, and then—

He stopped, chilled, half-paralyzed by what the light revealed: Twelve old women, twelve creatures snarling at him from every part of the room. The witch was out in the open. And ready.

The queerest thing of all in that tremendous moment was the sheer glow of triumph that swept him—the triumph of a man who has indisputably won an argument with his wife. He felt a crazy, incredible joy; he wanted to shout: "See! see! wasn't I right? Wasn't it exactly as I told you?"

With an effort, he caught hold of himself; and the shaky realization came that actually he was on the verge of madness. He said unsteadily:

"This is going to take a little time. I'll have to carry them one by one to the cliff; and the law of averages says that I'll strike the right one sooner or later. We won't have to worry about her slipping away in between, because we know her horrible fear of the night. It's only a matter of perseverance."

His voice faltered the faintest bit, for suddenly the ghastly reality of what was here struck his inner consciousness. Some of the creatures sat on the bed, some on the floor; two stood, their arms around each other; and half of them were gibbering in a fantastic caricature of terror. With a start, he grew aware of Joanna behind him. She was pale, incredibly pale for Joanna, and her voice, when she spoke, quavered. She said:

"The trouble with you, Craig, is that you're not practical. You want to do physical things like throwing her onto the rocks at the bottom of the cliff, or burning her. It proves that even yet your basic intellect doesn't believe in her. Or you'd know what to do."

She was pressing against him, staring wide-eyed over his shoulder at that whimpering, terrified group. Now, before he could realize her intention, she slipped under his arm, and was into the room. Her shoulder bumped him slightly in passing, and threw him off balance. It was only for a moment, but when he could look again, eight squalling crones had Joanna surrounded.

He had a brief glimpse of her distorted face. Six gnarled hands were clawing to open her mouth; a tangle of desperate old women's hands were clutching at her arms and her legs, trying to hold her flailing, furious body. *And they were succeeding!* That was the terrifying reality that drove him into the midst of that brew of old women with battering fists—and pulled Joanna clear.

Immense anger grew out of his fear. "You silly fool!" he

raged. "Don't you realize it must be after midnight?" Then, with an abrupt, fuller realization that she had actually been attacked, piercingly:

"Are you all right?"

"Yes." Shakily. "Yes."

But *she* would have said that too. He glared at her with mad eyes, as if by the sheer intensity of his gaze he would see through her face into her brain. She must have seen his terrible thought in his straining countenance, for she cried:

"Don't you see, darling? The blinds, the windows—pull them up. That's what I intended to do. Let in the night. Let in the things she fears. If she exists, then so must they. Don't you see?"

He took Joanna with him, kicking at the creatures with his fists and feet, with a grim merciless ferocity. He tore the blind from its hooks; one thrust of his foot smashed the whole lower pane of the window. And then, back at the door, they waited.

Waited!

There was a whisper of water splattering on the window sill. A shape without shape silhouetted abnormally against the blue-black sky beyond the window. And then, the water was on the floor, trickling from a misty shape that seemed to walk. A voice sighed, or was it a thought?

"You nearly fooled us, Niyasha, with that false burial. We lost sight of you for months. But we knew that only by the sea and from the sea could your old body draw the strength for the change. We watched, as we watched so long for so many of the traitors; and so at last you answer the justice of the ancient waters."

There was no sound but the sibilation of water trickling. The old women were silent as stones; and they sat like birds fascinated by a snake. And suddenly, the images were gone, snuffed out. One fragile, lonely-looking old woman sat on the floor directly in the path of the mist-thing. Almost primly, she gathered her skirts about her.

The mist enveloped her form. She was lifted into it, then instantly dropped. Swiftly, the mist retreated to the window. It was gone. The old woman lay flat on her back, eyes open and staring; her mouth open, too, unprettily.

That was the overall effect—the utter lack of anything beautiful.

The Witches of Karres

by James H. Schmitz

The late (1911–1981) James H. Schmitz became a full-time writer only in 1961, at the age of fifty, but he quickly established himself as an excellent craftsman, especially adept at depicting convincing aliens and their environments. He also developed a very popular tele-pathic female series character, Telzey Amberdon, who came along at just about the same time as the James Bond films, not a bad coincidence for a secret-agent-type protagonist. Her exploits are recorded in such books as The Universe Against Her *(1964),* The Lion Game *(1973), and* The Telzey Toy *(1973). "The Witches of Karres" is perhaps his most famous story.*

I

It was around the hub of the evening on the planet of Porlumma that Captain Pausert, commercial traveler from the Republic of Nikkeldepain, met the first of the witches of Karres.

It was just plain fate, so far as he could see.

He was feeling pretty good as he left a high-priced bar on a cobbly street near the spaceport, with the intention of returning straight to his ship. There hadn't been an argument, exactly. But someone grinned broadly, as usual, when the captain pronounced the name of his native system; and the captain had pointed out then, with considerable wit, how much more ridiculous it was to call a planet Porlumma, for instance, than to call it Nikkeldepain.

He proceeded to collect a gradually increasing number of pained stares by a detailed comparison of the varied, interesting and occasionally brilliant role Nikkeldepain had played in history with Porlumma's obviously dull and dumpy status as a sixth-rate Empire outpost.

In conclusion, he admitted frankly that he wouldn't care to be found dead on Porlumma.

Somebody muttered loudly in Imperial Universum that in that case it might be better if he didn't hang around Porlumma too long. But the captain only smiled politely, paid for his two drinks and left.

There was no point in getting into a rhubarb on one of these border planets. Their citizens still had an innocent notion that they ought to act like frontiersmen—but then the Law always showed up at once.

He felt pretty good. Up to the last four months of his young life, he had never looked on himself as being particularly patriotic. But compared to most of the Empire's worlds, Nikkeldepain was downright attractive in its stuffy way. Besides, he was returning there solvent—would they ever be surprised!

And awaiting him, fondly and eagerly, was Illyla, the Miss Onswud, fair daughter of the mighty Councilor Onswud, and the captain's secretly affianced for almost a year. She alone had believed in him!

The captain smiled and checked at a dark cross-street to get his bearings on the spaceport beacon. Less than half a mile away. He set off again. In about six hours, he'd be beyond the Empire's space borders and headed straight for Illyla.

Yes, she alone had believed! After the prompt collapse of the captain's first commercial venture—a miffel-fur farm, largely on capital borrowed from Councilor Onwud—the future had looked very black. It had even included a probable ten-year stretch of penal servitude for "willful and negligent abuse of intrusted monies." The laws of Nikkeldepain were rough on debtors.

"But you've always been looking for someone to take out the old *Venture* and get her back into trade!" Illyla reminded her father tearfully.

"Hm-m-m, yes! But it's in the blood, my dear! His great-uncle Threbus went the same way! It would be far better to let the law take its course," Councilor Onswud said, glaring at Pausert, who remained sulkily silent. He had *tried* to explain that the mysterious epidemic which suddenly wiped out most of the stock of miffels wasn't his fault. In fact, he more than suspected the tricky hand of young Councilor Rapport, who had been wagging futilely around Illyla for the last couple of years!

"The *Venture*, now—!" Councilor Onswud mused, stroking his long, craggy chin. "Pausert can handle a ship, at least," he admitted.

That was how it happened. Were they ever going to be surprised! For even the captain realized that Councilor Onswud was unloading all the dead fish that had gathered the dust of his warehouses for the past fifty years on him and the *Venture*, in a last, faint hope of getting *some* return on those half-forgotten investments. A value of eighty-two thousand maels was placed on the cargo; but if he'd brought even three-quarters of it back in cash, all would have been well.

Instead—well, it started with that lucky bet on a legal point with an Imperial Official at the Imperial capitol itself. Then came a six-hour race fairly won against a small, fast private yacht—the old *Venture* 7333 had been a pirate-chaser in the last century and could still produce twice as much speed as her looks suggested. From there on, the captain was socially accepted as a sporting man and was in on a long string of jovial parties and meets.

Jovial and profitable—the wealthier Imperials just couldn't resist a gamble; and the penalty he always insisted on was that they had to buy!

He got rid of the stuff right and left! Inside of twelve weeks, nothing remained of the original cargo except two score bundles of expensively built but useless tinklewood fishing poles and one dozen gross bales of useful but unattractive allweather cloaks. Even on a bet, nobody would take them! But the captain had a strong hunch those items had been hopefully added to the cargo from his own stocks by Councilor Rapport; so his failure to sell them didn't break his heart.

He was a neat twenty percent net ahead, at that point—

And finally came this last-minute rush-delivery of medical supplies to Porlumma on the return route. That haul alone would have repaid the miffel-farm losses three times over!

The captain grinned broadly into the darkness. Yes, they'd be surprised—but just where was he now?

He checked again in the narrow street, searching for the port-beacon in the sky. There it was—off to his left and a little behind him. He'd got turned around somehow!

He set off carefully down an excessively dark little alley. It was one of those towns where everybody locked their front doors at night and retired to lit-up, enclosed courtyards at the backs of the houses. There were voices and the rattling of dishes nearby, and occasional whoops of laughter and singing all around him; but it was all beyond high walls which let little or no light into the alley.

It ended abruptly in a cross-alley and another wall. After a moment's debate, the captain turned to his left again. Light spilled out on his new route a few hundred yards ahead, where a courtyard was opened on the alley. From it, as he approached, came the sound of doors being violently slammed, and then a sudden, loud mingling of voices.

"Yeeee-eep!" shrilled a high, childish voice. It could have been mortal agony, terror, or even hysterical laughter. The captain broke into an apprehensive trot.

"Yes, I see you up there!" a man shouted excitedly in Universum. "I caught you now—you get down from those boxes! I'll skin you alive! Fifty-two customers sick of the stomachache—YOW!"

The last exclamation was accompanied by a sound as of a small, loosely built wooden house collapsing, and was followed by a succession of squeals and an angry bellowing, in which the only distinguishable words were: ". . . threw the boxes on me!" Then more sounds of splintering wood.

"Hey!" yelled the captain indignantly from the corner of the alley.

All action ceased. The narrow courtyard, brightly illuminated under its single overhead bulb, was half covered with a tumbled litter of what appeared to be empty wooden boxes. Standing with his foot temporarily caught in one of them was a very large, fat man dressed all in white and waving a stick. Momentarily cornered between the wall and two of the boxes, over one of which she was trying to climb, was a smallish, fair-haired girl dressed in a smock of some kind, which was also white. She might be about fourteen, the captain thought—a helpless kid, anyway.

"What *you* want?" grunted the fat man, pointing the stick with some dignity at the captain.

"Lay off the kid!" rumbled the captain, edging into the courtyard.

"Mind your own business!" shouted the fat man, waving his stick like a club. "I'll take care of her! She—"

"I never did!" squealed the girl. She burst into tears.

"Try it, Fat and Ugly!" the captain warned. "I'll ram the stick down your throat!"

He was very close now. With a sound of grunting exasperation, the fat man pulled his foot free of the box, wheeled suddenly and brought the end of the stick down on the top of the captain's cap. The captain hit him furiously in the middle of the stomach.

There was a short flurry of activity, somewhat hampered by shattering boxes everywhere. Then the captain stood up, scowling and breathing hard. The fat man remained sitting on the ground, gasping about ". . . the law!"

Somewhat to his surprise, the captain discovered the girl standing just behind him. She caught his eye and smiled.

"My name's Maleen," she offered. She pointed at the fat man. "Is he hurt bad?"

"Huh—no!" panted the captain. "But maybe we'd better—"

It was too late! A loud, self-assured voice became audible now at the opening to the alley:

"Here, here, here, here, here!" it said in the reproachful situation-under-control tone that always seemed the same to the captain, on whatever world and in whichever language he heard it.

"What's all this about?" it inquired rhetorically.

"You'll all have to come along!" it replied.

Police Court on Porlumma appeared to be a business conducted on a very efficient, around-the-clock basis. They were the next case up.

Nikkeldepain was an odd name, wasn't it, the judge smiled. He then listened attentively to the various charges, countercharges, and denials.

Bruth the Baker was charged with having struck a citizen of a foreign government on the head with a potentially lethal instrument—produced in evidence. Said citizen had admittedly attempted to interfere as Bruth was attempting to punish his slave Maleen—also produced in evidence—whom he suspected of having added something to a batch of cakes she was working on that afternoon, resulting in illness and complaints from fifty-two of Bruth's customers.

Said foreign citizen had also used insulting language—the captain admitted under pressure to "Fat and Ugly."

Some provocation could be conceded for the action taken by Bruth, but not enough. Bruth paled.

Captain Pausert, of the Republic of Nikkeldepain—everybody but the prisoners smiled this time—was charged (a) with said attempted interference, (b) with said insult, (c) with having frequently and severely struck Bruth the Baker in the course of the subsequent dispute.

The blow on the head was conceded to have provided a provocation for charge (c)—but not enough.

Nobody seemed to be charging the slave Maleen with anything. The judge only looked at her curiously, and shook his head.

"As the Court considers this regrettable incident," he remarked, "it looks like two years for you, Bruth; and about three for you, captain. Too bad!"

The captain had an awful sinking feeling. He had seen something and heard a lot of Imperial court methods in the fringe systems. He could probably get out of this three-year rap; but it would be expensive.

He realized that the judge was studying him reflectively.

"The Court wishes to acknowledge," the judge continued, "that the captain's chargeable actions were due largely to a natural feeling of human sympathy for the predicament of the slave Maleen. The Court, therefore, would suggest a settlement as follows—subsequent to which all charges could be dropped:

"That Bruth the Baker resell Maleen of Karres—with whose services he appears to be dissatisfied—for a reasonable sum to Captain Pausert of the Republic of Nikkeldepain."

Bruth the Baker heaved a gusty sigh of relief. But the captain hesitated. The buying of human slaves by private citizens was a very serious offense in Nikkeldepain! Still, he didn't have to make a record of it. If they weren't going to soak him too much—

At just the right moment, Maleen of Karres introduced a barely audible, forlorn, sniffling sound.

"How much are you asking for the kid?" the captain inquired, looking without friendliness at his recent antagonist. A day was coming when he would think less severely of Bruth; but it hadn't come yet.

Bruth scowled back but replied with a certain eagerness: "A hundred and fifty m—" A policeman standing behind him poked him sharply in the side. Bruth shut up.

"Seven hundred maels," the judge said smoothly. "There'll be Court charges, and a fee for recording the transaction—" He appeared to make a swift calculation. "Fifteen hundred and forty-two maels—" He turned to a clerk: "You've looked him up?"

The clerk nodded. "He's right!"

"And we'll take your check," the judge concluded. He gave the captain a friendly smile. "Next case."

The captain felt a little bewildered.

There was something peculiar about this! He was getting out of it much too cheaply. Since the Empire had quit its wars of expansion, young slaves in good health were a high-priced article. Furthermore, he was practically positive that Bruth the Baker had been willing to sell for a tenth of what the captain actually had to pay!

Well, he wouldn't complain. Rapidly, he signed, sealed and

thumbprinted various papers shoved at him by a helpful clerk; and made out a check.

"I guess," he told Maleen of Karres, "we'd better get along to the ship."

And now what was he going to do with the kid, he pondered, padding along the unlighted streets with his slave trotting quietly behind him. If he showed up with a pretty girl-slave in Nikkeldepain, even a small one, various good friends there would toss him into ten years or so of penal servitude-immediately after Illyla had personally collected his scalp. They were a moral lot.

Karres—?

"How far off is Karres, Maleen?" he asked into the dark.

"It takes about two weeks," Maleen said tearfully.

Two weeks! The captain's heart sank again.

"What are you blubbering about?" he inquired uncomfortably.

Maleen choked, sniffed, and began sobbing openly.

"I have two little sisters!" she cried.

"Well, well," the captain said encouragingly. "That's nice— you'll be seeing them again soon. I'm taking you home, you know!"

Great Patham—now he'd said it! But after all—

But this piece of good news seemed to be having the wrong effect on his slave! Her sobbing grew much more violent.

"No, I won't," she wailed. "They're here!"

"Huh?" said the captain. He stopped short. "Where?"

"And the people they're with are mean to them, too!" wept Maleen.

The captain's heart dropped clean through his boots. Standing there in the dark, he helplessly watched it coming:

"You could buy them awfully cheap!" she said.

II

In times of stress, the young life of Karres appeared to take to the heights. It might be a mountainous place.

The Leewit sat on the top shelf of the back wall of the crockery and antiques store, strategically flanked by two expensive-looking vases. She was a doll-sized edition of Maleen; but her eyes were cold and gray instead of blue and tearful. About five or six, the captain vaguely estimated. He wasn't very good at estimating them around that age.

"Good evening," he said, as he came in through the door. The Crockery and Antiques Shop had been easy to find. Like

Bruth the Baker's, it was the one spot in the neighborhood that was all lit up.

"Good evening, sir!" said what was presumably the store owner, without looking around. He sat with his back to the door, in a chair approximately at the center of the store and facing the Leewit at a distance of about twenty feet.

". . . and there you can stay without food or drink till the Holy Man comes in the morning!" he continued immediately, in the taut voice of a man who has gone through hysteria and is sane again. The captain realized he was addressing the Leewit.

"Your other Holy Man didn't stay very long!" the diminutive creature piped, also ignoring the captain. Apparently, she had not yet discovered Maleen behind him.

"This is a stronger denomination—much stronger!" the store owner replied, in a shaking voice but with a sort of relish. *"He'll* exorcise you, all right, little demon—you'll whistle no buttons off him! Your time is up! Go on and whistle all you want! Bust every vase in the place—"

The Leewit blinked her gray eyes thoughtfully at him.

"Might!" she said.

"But if you try to climb down from there," the store owner went on, on a rising note, "I'll chop you into bits—into little, little bits!"

He raised his arm as he spoke and weakly brandished what the captain recognized with a start of horror as a highly ornamented but probably still useful antique battle-ax.

"Ha!" said the Leewit.

"Beg your pardon, sir!" the captain said, clearing his throat.

"Good evening, sir!" the store owner repeated, without looking around. "What can I do for you?"

"I came to inquire," the captain said hesitantly, "about that child."

The store owner shifted about in his chair and squinted at the captain with red-rimmed eyes.

"You're not a Holy Man!" he said.

"Hello, Maleen!" the Leewit said suddenly. "That him?"

"We've come to buy you," Maleen said. "Shut up!"

"Good!" said the Leewit.

"Buy it? Are you mocking me, sir?" the store owner inquired.

"Shut up, Moonell!" A thin, dark, determined-looking woman had appeared in the doorway that led through the back wall of the store. She moved out a step under the shelves; and the Leewit leaned down from the top shelf and hissed. The woman moved hurriedly back into the doorway.

"Maybe he means it," she said in a more subdued voice.

"I can't sell to a citizen of the Empire," the store owner said defeatedly.

"I'm not a citizen," the captain said shortly. This time, he wasn't going to name it.

"No, he's from Nikkel—" Maleen began.

"Shut up, Maleen!" the captain said helplessly in turn.

"I never heard of Nikkel," the store owner muttered doubtfully.

"Maleen!" the woman called shrilly. "That's the name of one of the others—Bruth the Baker got her. He means it, all right! He's buying them—"

"A hundred and fifty maels!" the captain said craftily, remembering Bruth the Baker. "In cash!"

The store owner looked dazed.

"Not enough, Moonell!" the woman called. "Look at all it's broken! Five hundred maels!"

There was a sound then, so thin the captain could hardly hear it. It pierced at his eardrums like two jabs of a delicate needle. To right and left of him, two highly glazed little jugs went *"Clink-clink,"* showed a sudden veining of cracks, and collapsed.

A brief silence settled on the store. And now that he looked around more closely, the captain could spot here and there other little piles of shattered crockery—and places where similar ruins apparently had been swept up, leaving only traces of colored dust.

The store owner laid the ax down carefully beside his chair, stood up, swaying a little, and came towards the captain.

"You offered me a hundred and fifty maels!" he said rapidly as he approached. "I accept it here, now, see—before witnesses!" He grabbed the captain's right hand in both of his and pumped it up and down vigorously. "Sold!" he yelled.

Then he wheeled around in a leap and pointed a shaking hand at the Leewit.

"And NOW," he howled, "break something! Break anything! You're his! I'll sue him for every mael he ever made and ever will!"

"Oh, do come help me down, Maleen!" the Leewit pleaded prettily.

For a change, the store of Wansing, the jeweler, was dimly lit and very quiet. It was a sleek, fashionable place in a fashionable shopping block near the spaceport. The front door was unlocked, and Wansing was in.

The three of them entered quietly, and the door sighed quietly shut behind them. Beyond a great crystal display-counter, Wansing was moving about among a number of opened shelves, talking softly to himself. Under the crystal of the counter, and in close-packed rows on the satin-covered shelves, reposed a many-colored gleaming and glittering and shining. Wansing was no piker.

"Good evening, sir!" the captain said across the counter.

"It's morning!" the Leewit remarked from the other side of Maleen.

"Maleen!" said the captain.

"We're keeping out of this," Maleen said to the Leewit.

"All right," said the Leewit.

Wansing had come around jerkily at the captain's greeting, but had made no other move. Like all the slave owners the captain had met on Porlumma so far, Wansing seemed unhappy. Otherwise, he was a large, dark, sleek-looking man with jewels in his ears and a smell of expensive oils and perfumes about him.

"This place is under constant visual guard, of course!" he told the captain gently. "Nothing could possibly happen to me here. Why am I so frightened?"

"Not of me, I'm sure!" the captain said with an uncomfortable attempt at geniality. "I'm glad your store's still open," he went on briskly. "I'm here on business—"

"Oh, yes, it's still open, of course," Wansing said. He gave the captain a slow smile and turned back to his shelves. "I'm making inventory, that's why! I've been making inventory since early yesterday morning. I've counted them all seven times—"

"You're very thorough," the captain said.

"Very, very thorough!" Wansing nodded to the shelves. "The last time I found I had made a million maels. But twice before that, I had lost approximately the same amount. I shall have to count them again, I suppose!" He closed a shelf softly. "I'm sure I counted those before. But they move about constantly. Constantly! It's horrible."

"You've got a slave here called Goth," the captain said, driving to the point.

"Yes, I have!" Wansing said, nodding. "And I'm sure she understands by now I meant no harm! I do, at any rate. It was perhaps a little—but I'm sure she understands now, or will soon!"

"Where is she?" the captain inquired, a trifle uneasily.

"In her room perhaps," Wansing suggested. "It's not so bad when she's there in her room with the door closed. But often she sits in the dark and looks at you as you go past—" He opened another drawer, and closed it quietly again. "Yes, they do move!'' he whispered, as if confirming an earlier suspicion. "Constantly—''

"Look, Wansing," the captain said in a loud, firm voice. "I'm not a citizen of the Empire. I want to buy this Goth! I'll pay you a hundred and fifty maels, cash.''

Wansing turned around completely again and looked at the captain. "Oh, you do?'' he said. "You're not a citizen?'' He walked a few steps to the side of the counter, sat down at a small desk and turned a light on over it. Then he put his face in his hands for a moment.

"I'm a wealthy man,'' he muttered. "An influential man! The name of Wansing counts for a great deal on Porlumma. When the Empire suggests you buy, you buy, of course—but it need not have been I who bought her! I thought she would be useful in the business—and then, even I could not sell her again within the Empire. She has been here for a week!''

He looked up at the captain and smiled. "One hundred and fifty maels!'' he said. "Sold! There are records to be made out—'' He reached into a drawer and took out some printed forms. He began to write rapidly. The captain produced identifications.

Maleen said suddenly: "Goth?''

"Right here,'' a voice murmured. Wansing's hand jerked sharply, but he did not look up. He kept on writing.

Something small and lean and bonelessly supple, dressed in a dark jacket and leggings, came across the thick carpet of Wansing's store and stood behind the captain. This one might be about nine or ten.

"I'll take your check, captain!'' Wansing said politely. "You must be an honest man. Besides, I want to frame it.''

"And now,'' the captain heard himself say in the remote voice of one who moves through a strange dream, "I suppose we could go to the ship.''

The sky was gray and cloudy; and the streets were lightening. Goth, he noticed, didn't resemble her sisters. She had brown hair cut short a few inches below her ears, and brown eyes with long, black lashes. Her nose was short and her chin was pointed. She made him think of some thin, carnivorous creature, like a weasel.

She looked up at him briefly, grinned, and said: "Thanks!''

"What was wrong with *him*?'' chirped the Leewit, walking backwards for a last view of Wansing's store.

"Tough crook,'' muttered Goth. The Leewit giggled.

"You premoted this just dandy, Maleen!'' she stated next.

"Shut up," said Maleen.

"All right," said the Leewit. She glanced up at the captain's face. "You been fighting!" she said virtuously. "Did you win?"

"Of course, the captain won!" said Maleen.

"Good for you!" said the Leewit.

"What about the takeoff?" Goth asked the captain. She seemed a little worried.

"Nothing to it!" the captain said stoutly, hardly bothering to wonder how she'd guessed the takeoff was the one operation on which he and the old *Venture* consistently failed to cooperate.

"No," said Goth, "I meant when?"

"Right now," said the captain. "They've already cleared us. We'll get the sign any second."

"Good," said Goth. She walked off slowly down the hall towards the back of the ship.

The takeoff was pretty bad, but the *Venture* made it again. Half an hour later, with Porlumma dwindling safely behind them, the captain switched to automatic and climbed out of his chair. After considerable experimentation, he got the electric butler adjusted to four breakfasts, hot, with coffee. It was accomplished with a great deal of advice and attempted assistance from the Leewit, rather less from Maleen, and no comments from Goth.

"Everything will be coming along in a few minutes now!" he announced. Afterwards, it struck him there had been a quality of grisly prophecy about the statement.

"If you'd listened to me," said the Leewit, "we'd have been done eating a quarter of an hour ago!" She was perspiring but triumphant—she had been right all along.

"Say, Maleen," she said suddenly, "you premoting again?"

Premoting? The captain looked at Maleen. She seemed pale and troubled.

"Spacesick?" he suggested. "I've got some pills—"

"No, she's premoting," the Leewit said scowling. "What's up, Maleen?"

"Shut up," said Goth.

"All right," said the Leewit. She was silent a moment, and then began to wriggle. "Maybe we'd better—"

"Shut up," said Maleen.

"It's all ready," said Goth.

"What's all ready?" asked the captain.

"All right," said the Leewit. She looked at the captain. "Nothing," she said.

He looked at them then, and they looked at him—one set each of gray eyes, and brown, and blue. They were all sitting around the control room floor in a circle, the fifth side of which was occupied by the electric butler.

What peculiar little waifs, the captain thought. He hadn't perhaps really realized until now just how *very* peculiar. They were still staring at him.

"Well, well!" he said heartily. "So Maleen 'premotes' and gives people stomachaches."

Maleen smiled dimly and smoothed back her yellow hair.

"They just thought they were getting them," she murmured.

"Mass history," explained the Leewit, offhandedly.

"Hysteria," said Goth. "The Imperials get their hair up about us every so often."

"I noticed that," the captain nodded. "And little Leewit here—she whistles and busts things."

"It's *the* Leewit," the Leewit said, frowning.

"Oh, I see," said the captain. "Like *the* captain, eh?"

"That's right," said the Leewit. She smiled.

"And what does little Goth do?" the captain addressed the third witch.

Little Goth appeared pained. Maleen answered for her.

"Goth teleports mostly," she said.

"Oh, she does?" said the captain. "I've heard about that trick, too," he added lamely.

"Just small stuff really!" Goth said abruptly. She reached into the top of her jacket and pulled out a cloth-wrapped bundle the size of the captain's two fists. The four ends of the cloth were knotted together. Goth undid the knot. "Like this," she said and poured out the contents on the rug between them. There was a sound like a big bagful of marbles being spilled.

"Great Patham!" the captain swore, staring down at what was a cool quarter-million in jewel stones, or he was still a miffel-farmer.

"Good gosh," said the Leewit, bouncing to her feet. "Maleen, we better get at it right away!"

The two blondes darted from the room. The captain hardly noticed their going. He was staring at Goth.

"Child," he said, "don't you realize they hang you without trial on places like Porlumma, if you're caught with stolen goods?"

"We're not on Porlumma," said Goth. She looked slightly annoyed. "They're for you. You spent money on us, didn't you?"

"Not that kind of money," said the captain. "If Wansing noticed— They're Wansing's, I suppose?"

"Sure!" said Goth. "Pulled them in just before takeoff!"

"If he reported, there'll be police ships on our tail any—"

"Goth!" Maleen shrilled.

Goth's head came around and she rolled up on her feet in one motion. "Coming," she shouted. "Excuse me," she murmured to the captain. Then she, too, was out of the room.

But again, the captain scarcely noticed her departure. He had rushed to the control desk with a sudden awful certainty and switched on all screens.

There they were! Two sleek, black ships coming up fast from behind, and already almost in gun range! They weren't regular police boats, the captain recognized, but auxiliary craft of the Empire's frontier fleets. He rammed the *Venture*'s drives full on. Immediately, red-and-black fire blossoms began to sprout in space behind him—then a finger of flame stabbed briefly past, not a hundred yards to the right of the ship.

But the communicator stayed dead. Porlumma preferred risking the sacrifice of Wansing's jewels to giving them a chance to surrender! To do the captain justice, his horror was due much more to the fate awaiting his three misguided charges than to the fact that he was going to share it.

He was putting the *Venture* through a wildly erratic and, he hoped, aim-destroying series of sideways hops and forward lunges with one hand, and trying to unlimber the turrets of the nova guns with the other, when suddenly—!

No, he decided at once, there was no use trying to understand it—there were just no more Empire ships around. The screens all blurred and darkened simultaneously; and, for a short while, a darkness went flowing and coiling lazily past the *Venture*. Light jumped out of it at him once, in a cold, ugly glare, and receded again in a twisting, unnatural fashion. The *Venture*'s drives seemed dead.

Then, just as suddenly, the old ship jerked, shivered, roared aggrievedly, and was hurling herself along on her own power again!

But Porlumma's sun was no longer in evidence. Stars gleamed and shifted distantly against the blackness of deep space all about. The patterns seemed familiar, but he wasn't a good enough navigator to be sure.

The captain stood up stiffly, feeling a heavy cloud. And at that moment, with a wild, hilarious clacking like a metallic hen, the electric butler delivered four breakfasts, hot, one after the other, right onto the center of the control room floor.

The first voice said distinctly: "Shall we just leave it on?"

A second voice, considerably more muffled, replied: "Yes, let's! You never know when you need it—"

The third voice, tucked somewhere in between them, said simply: "*Whew!*"

Peering about the dark room in bewilderment, the captain realized suddenly that the voices had come from the speaker of an intership communicator, leading to what had once been the *Venture*'s captain's cabin.

He listened; but only a dim murmuring came from it now, and then nothing at all. He started towards the hall, then returned and softly switched off the communicator. He went quietly down the hall until he came to the captain's cabin. Its door was closed.

He listened a moment, and opened it suddenly.

There was a trio of squeals:

"Oh, don't! You spoiled it!"

The captain stood motionless. Just one glimpse had been given him of what seemed to be a bundle of twisted black wires arranged loosely like the frame of a truncated cone on—or was it just above?—a table in the center of the cabin. Where the tip of the cone should have been burned a round, swirling, orange fire. About it, their faces reflecting its glow, stood the three witches.

Then the fire vanished; the wires collapsed. There was only ordinary light in the room. They were looking up at him variously—Maleen with smiling regret, the Leewit in frank annoyance, Goth with no expression at all.

"What out of Great Patham's Seventh Hell was that?" inquired the captain, his hair bristling slowly.

The Leewit looked at Goth; Goth looked at Maleen. Maleen said doubtfully: "We can just tell you its name—"

"That was the Sheewash Drive," said Goth.

"The what-drive?" asked the captain.

"Sheewash," repeated Maleen.

"The one you have to do it with yourself," the Leewit said helpfully.

"Shut up," said Maleen.

There was a long pause. The captain looked down at the handful of thin, black, twelve-inch wires scattered about the table top. He touched one of them. It was dead-cold.

"I see," he said. "I guess we're all going to have a long talk." Another pause. "Where are we now?"

"About three light-years down the way you were going," said Goth. "We only worked it thirty seconds."

"Twenty-eight!" corrected Maleen, with the authority of her years. "The Leewit was getting tired."

"I see," said Captain Pausert carefully. "Well, let's go have some breakfast."

III

They ate with a silent voraciousness, dainty Maleen, the exquisite Leewit, supple Goth, all alike. The captain, long finished, watched them with amazement and—now at last—with something like awe.

"It's the Sheewash Drive," explained Maleen finally, catching his expression.

"Takes it out of you!" said Goth.

The Leewit grunted affirmatively and stuffed on.

"Can't do too much of it," said Maleen. "Or too often. It kills you sure!"

"What," said the captain, "*is* the Sheewash Drive?"

They became reticent. People did it on Karres, said Maleen, when they had to go somewhere else fast. Everybody knew how there.

"But of course," she added, "we're pretty young to do it right!"

"We did it pretty good!" the Leewit contradicted positively. She seemed to be finished at last.

"But how?" said the captain.

Reticence thickened almost visibly. If you couldn't do it, said Maleen, you couldn't understand it either.

He gave it up, for the time being.

"I guess I'll have to take you home next," he said; and they agreed.

Karres, it developed, was in the Iverdahl System. He couldn't find any planet of that designation listed in his maps of the area, but that meant nothing. The maps were old and often inaccurate, and local names changed a lot.

Barring the use of weird and deadly miracle drives, that detour was going to cost him almost a month in time—and a good chunk of his profits in power used up. The jewels Goth had illegally teleported must, of course, be returned to their owner, he explained. He'd intended to look severely at the culprit at that point; but she'd meant well, after all! They were extremely peculiar children, but still children—they couldn't really understand.

He would stop off en route to Karres at an Empire planet with banking facilities to take care of that matter, the captain added. A planet far enough off so the police wouldn't be likely to take any particular interest in the *Venture*.

A dead silence greeted this schedule. It appeared that the representatives of Karres did not think much of his logic.

"Well," Maleen sighed at last, "we'll see you get your money back some other way then!"

The junior witches nodded coldly.

"How did you three happen to get into this fix?" the captain inquired, with the intention of changing the subject.

They'd left Karres together on a jaunt of their own, they explained. No, they hadn't run away—he got the impression that such trips were standard procedure for juveniles in that place. They were on another planet, a civilized one but beyond the borders and law of Empire, when the town they were in was raided by a small fleet of slavers. They were taken along with most of the local youngsters.

"It's a wonder," he said reflectively, "you didn't take over the ship."

"Oh, brother!" exclaimed the Leewit.

"Not that ship!" said Goth.

"That was an Imperial Slaver!" Maleen informed him. "You behave yourself every second on those crates."

Just the same, the captain thought as he settled himself to rest in the control room on a couch he had set up there, it was no longer surprising that the Empire wanted no young slaves from Karres to be transported into the interior! Oddest sort of children— but he ought to be able to get his expenses paid by their relatives. Something very profitable might even be made of this deal—

Have to watch the record entries though! Nikkeldepain's laws were explicit about the penalties invoked by anything resembling the purchase and sale of slaves.

He'd thoughtfully left the intership communicator adjusted so he could listen in on their conversation in the captain's cabin. However, there had been nothing for some time beyond frequent bursts of childish giggling. Then came a succession of piercing shrieks from the Leewit. It appeared she was being forcibly washed behind the ears by Maleen and obliged to brush her teeth, in preparation for bedtime.

It had been agreed that he was not to enter the cabin, because—for reasons not given—they couldn't keep the Sheewash Drive on in his presence; and they wanted to have it ready, in case of an emergency. Piracy was rife beyond the Imperial borders, and the *Venture* would keep beyond the border for a good part of the trip, to avoid the more pressing danger of police pursuit instigated by Porlumma. The captain had explained the potentialities of the nova guns the *Venture* boasted, or tried to. Possibly, they hadn't understood. At any rate, they seemed unimpressed.

The Sheewash Drive! Boy, he thought in sudden excitement, if he could just get the principles of that. Maybe he would!

He raised his head suddenly. The Leewit's voice had lifted clearly over the communicator:

". . . not such a bad old dope!" the childish treble remarked. The captain blinked indignantly.

"He's not so old," Maleen's soft voice returned. "And he's certainly no dope!"

He smiled. Good kid, Maleen.

"Yeah, yeah!" squeaked the Leewit offensively. "Maleen's sweet onthu-ulp!"

A vague commotion continued for a while, indicating, he hoped, that someone he could mention was being smothered under a pillow.

He drifted off to sleep before it was settled.

If you didn't happen to be thinking of what they'd done, they seemed more or less like normal children. Right from the start, they displayed a flattering interest in the captain and his background; and he told them all about everything and everybody in Nikkeldepain. Finally, he even showed them his treasured pocket-sized picture of Illyla—the one with which he'd held many cozy conversations during the earlier part of his trip.

Almost at once, though, he realized that was a mistake. They studied it intently in silence, their heads crowded close together.

"Oh, brother!" the Leewit whispered then, with entirely the wrong kind of inflection.

"Just what did you mean by that?" the captain inquired coldly.

"Sweet!" murmured Goth. But it was the way she closed her eyes briefly, as though gripped by a light spasm of nausea.

"Shut up, Goth!" Maleen said sharply. "I think she's very swee . . . I mean, she looks very nice!" she told the captain.

The captain was disgruntled. Silently, he retrieved the maligned Illyla and returned her to his breast pocket. Silently, he went off and left them standing there.

But afterwards, in private, he took it out again and studied it worriedly. His Illyla! He shifted the picture back and forth under the light. It wasn't really a very good picture of her, he decided. It had been bungled! From certain angles, one might even say that Illyla did look the least bit insipid.

What was he thinking, he thought, shocked.

He unlimbered the nova gun turrets next and got in a little firing practice. They had been sealed when he took over the *Venture* and weren't supposed to be used, except in absolute emergencies. They were somewhat uncertain weapons, though very effective, and Nikkeldepain had turned to safer forms of armament many decades ago. But on the third day out from Nikkeldepain, the captain made a brief notation in his log:

"Attacked by two pirate craft. Unsealed nova guns. Destroyed one attacker; survivor fled—"

He was rather pleased by that crisp, hard-bitten description of desperate space adventure, and enjoyed rereading it occasionally. It wasn't true, though. He had put in an interesting four hours at the time pursuing and annihilating large, craggy chunks of substance of a meteorite cloud he found the *Venture* plowing through. Those nova guns were fascinating stuff! You'd sight the turrets on something; and so long as it didn't move after that, it was all right. If it did move, it got it—unless you relented and deflected the turrets first. They were just the thing for arresting a pirate in midspace.

The *Venture* dipped back into the Empire's borders four days later and headed for the capital of the local province. Police ships challenged them twice on the way in; and the captain found considerable comfort in the awareness that his passengers foregathered silently in their cabin on these occasions. They didn't tell him they were set to use the Sheewash Drive—somehow it had never been mentioned since that first day; but he knew the queer orange fire was circling over its skimpy framework of twisted wires there and ready to act.

However, the space police waved him on, satisfied with routine identification. Apparently, the *Venture* had not become generally known as a criminal ship, to date.

Maleen accompanied him to the banking institution that was to return Wansing's property to Porlumma. Her sisters, at the captain's definite request, remained on the ship.

The transaction itself went off without a visible hitch. The jewels would reach their destination in Porlumma within a month. But he had to take out a staggering sum in insurance—"Piracy, thieves!'' smiled the clerk. "Even summary capital punishment won't keep the rats down." And, of course, he had to register name, ship, home planet, and so on. But since they already had all that information in Porlumma, he gave it without hesitation.

On the way back to the spaceport, he sent off a sealed message by radio-relay to the bereaved jeweler, informing him of the action taken, and regretting the misunderstanding.

He felt a little better after that, though the insurance payment had been a severe blow! If he didn't manage to work out a decent profit on Karres somehow, the losses on the miffel farm would hardly be covered now.

Then he noticed that Maleen was getting uneasy.

"We'd better hurry!" was all she would say, however. Her face grew pale.

The captain understood. She was having another premonition! The hitch to this premoting business was, apparently, that when something was brewing you were informed of the bare fact but had to guess at most of the details. They grabbed an aircab and raced back to the spaceport.

They had just been cleared there when he spotted a small group of uniformed men coming along the dock on the double. They stopped short and then scattered, as the *Venture* lurched drunkenly sideways into the air. Everyone else in sight was scattering, too.

That was a very bad takeoff—one of the captain's worst! Once afloat, however, he ran the ship promptly into the nightside of the planet and turned her nose towards the border. The old pirate-chaser had plenty of speed when you gave her the reins; and throughout the entire next sleep period, he let her use it all.

The Sheewash Drive was not required that time.

Next day, he had a lengthy private talk with Goth on the Golden Rule and the Law, with particular reference to individual property rights. If Councilor Onswud had been monitoring the sentiments expressed by the captain, he could not have failed to rumble surprised approval. The delinquent herself listened impassively; but the captain fancied she showed distinct signs of being rather impressed by his earnestness.

It was two days after that—well beyond the borders again— when they were obliged to make an unscheduled stop at a mining moon. For the captain discovered he had already miscalculated the extent to which the prolonged run on overdrive after leaving the capital was going to deplete the *Venture*'s reserves. They would have to juice up—

A large, extremely handsome Sirian freighter lay beside them at the Moon station. It was half a battlecraft really, since it dealt regularly beyond the borders. They had to wait while it was being serviced; and it took a long time. The Sirians turned out to be as unpleasant as their ship was good-looking—a snooty, conceited, hairy lot who talked only their own dialect and pretended to be unfamiliar with Imperial Universum.

The captain found himself getting irked by their bad manners—particularly when he discovered they were laughing over his argument with the service superintendent about the cost of repowering the *Venture*.

"You're out in deep space, captain!" said the superintendent. "And you haven't juice enough left even to travel back to the Border. You can't expect Imperial prices here!"

"It's not what you charged *them*!" The captain angrily jerked his thumb at the Sirian.

"Regular customers!" the superintendent shrugged. "You start coming by here every three months like they do, and we can make an arrangement with you, too."

It was outrageous—it actually put the *Venture* back in the red! But there was no help for it.

Nor did it improve the captain's temper when he muffled the takeoff once more—and then had to watch the Sirian floating into space, as sedately as a swan, a little behind him!

An hour later, as he sat glumly before the controls, debating the chance of recouping his losses before returning to Nikkeldepain, Maleen and the Leewit hurriedly entered the room. They did something to a port screen.

"They sure are!" the Leewit exclaimed. She seemed childishly pleased.

"Are what?" the captain inquired absently.

"Following us," said Maleen. She did not sound pleased. "It's that Sirian ship, Captain Pausert—"

The captain stared bewilderedly at the screen. There *was* a ship in focus there. It was quite obviously the Sirian and, just as obviously, it was following them.

"What do they want?" he wondered. "They're stinkers but they're not pirates. Even if they were, they wouldn't spend an hour running after a crate like the *Venture*!"

Maleen said nothing. The Leewit observed: "Oh, brother! Got their bow-turrets out now—better get those nova guns ready!"

"But it's all nonsense!" the captain said, flushing angrily. He turned suddenly towards the communicators. "What's that Empire general beam length?"

"`.0044,`" said Maleen.

A roaring, abusive voice flooded the control room immediately. The one word understandable to the captain was "*Venture.*" It was repeated frequently, sometimes as if it were a question.

"Sirian!" said the captain. "Can you understand them?" he asked Maleen.

She shook her head. "The Leewit can—"

The Leewit nodded, her gray eyes glistening.

"What are they saying?"

"They says you're for stopping," the Leewit translated rapidly, but apparently retaining much of the original sentence-structure. "They says you're for skinning alive . . . ha! They says you're for stopping right now and for only hanging. They says—"

Maleen scuttled from the control room. The Leewit banged the communicator with one small fist.

"Beak-Wock!" she shrieked. It sounded like that, anyway. The loud voice paused a moment.

"Beak-Wock?" it returned in an aggrieved, demanding roar.

"Beak-Wock!" the Leewit affirmed with apparent delight. She rattled off a string of similar-sounding syllables. She paused.

A howl of inarticulate wrath responded.

The captain, in a whirl of outraged emotions, was yelling at the Leewit to shut up, at the Sirian to go to Great Patham's Second Hell—the worst—and wrestling with the nova gun adjustors at the same time. He'd had about enough! He'd—

SSS-whoosh!

It was the Sheewash Drive.

"And where are we now?" the captain inquired, in a voice of unnatural calm.

"Same place, just about," said the Leewit. "Ship's still on the screen. Way back though—take them an hour again to catch up." She seemed disappointed; then brightened. "You got lots of time to get the guns ready!"

The captain didn't answer. He was marching down the hall towards the rear of the *Venture*. He passed the captain's cabin and noted the door was shut. He went on without pausing. He was mad clean through—he knew what had happened!

After all he'd told her, Goth had teleported again.

It was all there, in the storage. Items of half a pound in weight seemed to be as much as she could handle. But amazing quantities of stuff had met that one requirement—bottles filled with what might be perfume or liquor or dope, expensive-looking garments and cloths in a shining variety of colors, small boxes, odds, ends and, of course, jewelry!

He spent half an hour getting it loaded into a steel space crate. He wheeled the crate into the rear lock, sealed the inside lock and pulled the switch that activated the automatic launching device.

The outside lock clicked shut. He stalked back to the control room. The Leewit was still in charge, fiddling with the communicators.

"I could try a whistle over them," she suggested, glancing up. She added: "But they'd bust somewheres, sure."

"Get them on again!" the captain said.

"Yes, sir," said the Leewit surprised.

The roaring voice came back faintly.

"SHUT UP!" the captain shouted in Imperial Universum.

The voice shut up.

"Tell them they can pick up their stuff—it's been dumped out in a crate!" the captain told the Leewit. "Tell them I'm proceeding on my course. Tell them if they follow me one light-minute beyond that crate, I'll come back for them, shoot their front end off, shoot their rear end off, and ram 'em in the middle."

"Yes, SIR!" the Leewit sparkled. They proceeded on their course.

Nobody followed.

"Now I want to speak to Goth," the captain announced. He was still at a high boil. "Privately," he added. "Back in the storage—"

Goth followed him expressionlessly into the storage. He closed the door to the hall. He'd broken off a two-foot length from the tip of one of Councilor Rapport's overpriced tinklewood fishing poles. It made a fair switch.

But Goth looked terribly small just now! He cleared his throat. He wished for a moment he were back on Nikkeldepain.

"I warned you," he said.

Goth didn't move. Between one second and the next, however, she seemed to grow remarkably. Her brown eyes focused on the captain's Adam's apple; her lip lifted at one side. A slightly hungry look came into her face.

"Wouldn't try that!" she murmured.

Mad again, the captain reached out quickly and got a handful of leathery cloth. There was a blur of motion, and what felt like a small explosion against his left kneecap. He grunted with anguished surprise and fell back on a bale of Councilor Rapport's all-weather cloaks. But he had retained his grip—Goth fell half on top of him, and that was still a favorable position. Then her head snaked around, her neck seemed to extend itself; and her teeth snapped his wrist.

Weasels don't let go—

"Didn't think he'd have the nerve!" Goth's voice came over the communicator. There was a note of grudging admiration in it. It seemed that she was inspecting her bruises.

All tangled up in the job of bandaging his freely bleeding wrist, the captain hoped she'd find a good plenty to count. His knee felt the size of a sofa pillow and throbbed like a piston engine.

"The captain is a brave man," Maleen was saying reproachfully. "You should have known better—"

"He's not very *smart*, though!" the Leewit remarked suggestively.

There was a short silence.

"Is he? Goth? Eh?" the Leewit urged.

"Perhaps not very," said Goth.

"You two lay off him!" Maleen ordered. "Unless," she added meaningly, "you want to *swim* back to Karres—on the Egger Route!"

"Not me," the Leewit said briefly.

"You could still do it, I guess," said Goth. She seemed to be reflecting. "All right—we'll lay off him. It was a fair fight, anyway."

IV

They raised Karres the sixteenth day after leaving Porlumma. There had been no more incidents; but then, neither had there been any more stops or other contacts with the defenseless Empire. Maleen had cooked up a poultice which did wonders for his knee. With the end of the trip in sight, all tensions had relaxed; and Maleen, at least, seemed to grow hourly more regretful at the prospect of parting.

After a brief study, Karres could be distinguished easily enough by the fact that it moved counterclockwise to all the other planets of the Iverdahl System.

Well, it would, the captain thought.

They came soaring into its atmosphere on the dayside without arousing any visible interest. No communicator signals reached them; and no other ships showed up to look them over. Karres, in fact, had all the appearance of a completely uninhabited world. There were a larger number of seas, too big to be called lakes and too small to be oceans, scattered over its surface. There was one enormously towering ridge of mountains that ran from pole to pole, and any number of lesser chains. There were two good-sized icecaps; and the southern section of the planet was speckled with intermittent stretches of snow. Almost all of it seemed to be dense forest.

It was a handsome place, in a wild, somber way.

They went gliding over it, from noon through morning and into the dawn fringe—the captain at the controls, Goth and the Leewit flanking him at the screens, and Maleen behind him to do the directing. After a few initial squeals, the Leewit became oddly silent. Suddenly the captain realized she was blubbering.

Somehow, it startled him to discover that her homecoming had affected the Leewit to that extent. He felt Goth reach out behind him and put her hand on the Leewit's shoulder. The smallest witch sniffled happily.

" 'S beautiful!" she growled.

He felt a resurge of the wondering, protective friendliness they had aroused in him at first. They must have been having a rough time of it, at that. He sighed; it seemed a pity they hadn't got along a little better!

"Where's everyone hiding?" he inquired, to break up the mood. So far, there hadn't been a sign of human habitation.

"There aren't many people on Karres," Maleen said from behind his shoulder. "But we're going to The Town—you'll meet about half of them there!"

"What's that place down there?" the captain asked with sudden interest. Something like an enormous lime-white bowl seemed to have been set flush into the floor of the wide valley up which they were moving.

"That's the Theater where . . . *ouch*!" the Leewit said. She fell silent then but turned to give Maleen a resentful look.

"Something strangers shouldn't be told about, eh?" the captain said tolerantly. Goth glanced at him from the side.

"We've got rules," she said.

He let the ship down a little as they passed over "the Theater where—" It was a sort of large, circular arena, with numerous steep tiers of seats running up around it. But all was bare and deserted now.

On Maleen's direction, they took the next valley fork to the right and dropped lower still. He had his first look at Karres animal life then. A flock of large, creamy-white birds, remarkably Terrestrial in appearance, flapped by just below them, apparently unconcerned about the ship. The forest underneath had opened out into a long stretch of lush meadowland, with small creeks winding down into its center. Here a herd of several hundred head of beasts was grazing—beasts of mastodonic size and build, with hairless, shiny black hides. The mouths of their long, heavy heads were twisted up into sardonic, crocodilian grins as they blinked up at the passing *Venture*.

"Black Bollems," said Goth, apparently enjoying the captain's expression. "Lots of them around; they're tame. But the gray mountain ones are good hunting."

"Good eating, too!" the Leewit said. She licked her lips daintily. "Breakfast—!" she sighed, her thoughts diverted to a familiar track. "And we ought to be just in time!"

"There's the field!" Maleen cried, pointing. "Set her down there, captain!"

The "field" was simply a flat meadow of close-trimmed grass running smack against the mountainside to their left. One small vehicle, bright blue in color, was parked on it; and it was bordered on two sides by very tall, blue-black trees.

That was all.

The captain shook his head. Then he set her down.

The town of Karres was a surprise to him in a good many ways. For one thing, there was much more of it than you would have thought possible after flying over the area. It stretched for miles through the forest, up the flanks of the mountain and across the valley—little clusters of houses or individual ones, each group screened from all the rest and from the sky overhead by the trees.

They liked color on Karres; but then they hid it away! The houses were bright as flowers, red and white, apple-green, golden-brown—all spick and span, scrubbed and polished and aired with that brisk, green forest smell. At various times of the day, there was also the smell of remarkably good things to eat. There were brooks and pools and a great number of shaded vegetable gardens to the town. There were risky-looking treetop playgrounds, and treetop platforms and galleries which seemed to have no particular purpose. On the ground was mainly an enormously confusing maze of paths—narrow trails of sandy soil snaking about among great brown tree roots and chunks of gray mountain rock, and half covered with fallen needle leaves. The first six times the captain set out unaccompanied, he'd lost his way hopelessly within minutes, and had to be guided back out of the forest.

But the most hidden of all were the people! About four thousand of them were supposed to live in the town, with as many more scattered about the planet. But you never got to see more than three or four at any one time—except when now and then a pack of children, who seemed to the captain to be uniformly of the Leewit's size, would burst suddenly out of the undergrowth across a path before you, and vanish again.

As for the others, you did hear someone singing occasionally; or there might be a whole muted concert going on all about, on a large variety of wooden musical instruments which they seemed to enjoy tootling with, gently.

But it wasn't a real town at all, the captain thought. They didn't live like people, these Witches of Karres—it was more like a flock of strange forest birds that happened to be nesting in the same general area. Another thing: they appeared to be busy enough—but what was their business?

He discovered he was reluctant to ask Toll too many questions about it. Toll was the mother of his three witches; but only Goth really resembled her. It was difficult to picture Goth becoming smoothly matured and pleasantly rounded; but that was Toll. She had the same murmuring voice, the same air of sideways observation and secret reflection. And she answered all the captain's questions with apparent frankness; but he never seemed to get much real information out of what she said.

It was odd, too! Because he was spending several hours a day in her company, or in one of the next rooms at any rate, while she went about her housework. Toll's daughters had taken him home when they landed; and he was installed in the room that belonged to their father—busy just now, the captain gathered, with some sort of research of a geological nature elsewhere on Karres. The arrangement worried him a little at first, particularly since Toll and he were mostly alone in the house. Maleen was going to some kind of school; she left early in the morning and came back late in the afternoon; and Goth and the Leewit were just plain running wild! They usually got in long after the captain had gone to bed and were off again before he turned out for breakfast.

It hardly seemed like the right way to raise them! One afternoon, he found the Leewit curled up and asleep in the chair he usually occupied on the porch before the house. She slept there for four solid hours, while the captain sat nearby and leafed gradually through a thick book with illuminated pictures called "Histories of Ancient Yarthe." Now and then, he sipped at a cool, green, faintly intoxicating drink Toll had placed quietly beside him some while before, or sucked an aromatic smoke from the enormous pipe with a floor rest, which he understood was a favorite of Toll's husband.

Then the Leewit woke up suddenly, uncoiled, gave him a look between a scowl and a friendly grin, slipped off the porch and vanished among the trees.

He couldn't quite figure that look! It might have meant nothing at all in particular, but—

The captain laid down his book then and worried a little more. It was true, of course, that nobody seemed in the least concerned about his presence. All of Karres appeared to know about him, and he'd met quite a number of people by now in a casual way. But nobody came around to interview him or so much as dropped in for a visit. However, Toll's husband presumably would be returning presently, and—

How long had he been here, anyway?

Great Patham, the captain thought, shocked. He'd lost count of the days!

Or was it weeks?

He went in to find Toll.

"It's been a wonderful visit," he said, "but I'll have to be leaving, I guess. Tomorrow morning, early—"

Toll put some fancy sewing she was working on back in a glass basket, laid her thin, strong witch's hands in her lap, and smiled up at him.

"We thought you'd be thinking that," she said, "and so we— You know, captain, it was quite difficult to find a way to reward you for bringing back the children?"

"It was?" said the captain, suddenly realizing he'd also clean forgotten he was broke! And now the wrath of Onswud lay close ahead.

"Gold and jewel stones would have been just right, of course!" she said, "but unfortunately, while there's no doubt a lot of it on Karres somewhere, we never got around to looking for it. And we haven't money—none that you could use, that is!"

"No, I don't suppose you do," the captain agreed sadly.

"However," said Toll, "we've all been talking about it in the town, and so we've loaded a lot of things aboard your ship that we think you can sell at a fine profit!"

"Well now," the captain said gratefully, "that's fine of—"

"There are furs," said Toll, "the very finest furs we could fix up—two thousand of them!"

"Oh!" said the captain, bravely keeping his smile. "Well, that's wonderful!"

"And essences of perfume!" said Toll. "Everyone brought one bottle of their own, so that's eight thousand three hundred and twenty-three bottles of perfume essences—all different!"

"Perfume!" said the captain. "Fine, fine—but you really shouldn't—"

"And the rest of it," Toll concluded happily, "is the green Lepti liquor you like so much, and the Wintenberry jellies!" She frowned. "I forgot just how many jugs and jars," she admitted, "but there were a lot. It's all loaded now. And do you think you'll be able to sell all that?" she smiled.

"I certainly can!" the captain said stoutly. "It's wonderful stuff, and there's nothing like it in the Empire."

Which was very true. They wouldn't have considered miffel-furs for lining on Karres. But if he'd been alone he would have felt like he wanted to burst into tears.

The witches couldn't have picked more completely unsalable items if they'd tried! Furs, cosmetics, food and liquor—he'd be shot on sight if he got caught trying to run that kind of merchandise into the Empire. For the same reason that they couldn't use it on Nikkeldepain—they were that scared of contamination by goods that came from uncleared worlds!

He breakfasted alone next morning. Toll had left a note beside his plate, which explained in a large, not too legible script that she had to run off and fetch the Leewit; and that if he was gone before she got back she was wishing him good-bye and good luck.

He smeared two more buns with Wintenberry jelly, drank a large mug of cone-seed coffee, finished every scrap of the omelet of swan hawk eggs and then, in a state of pleasant repletion, toyed around with his slice of roasted Bollem liver. Boy, what food! He must have put on fifteen pounds since he landed on Karres.

He wondered how Toll kept that sleek figure.

Regretfully, he pushed himself away from the table, pocketed her note for a souvenir, and went out on the porch. There a tear-stained Maleen hurled herself into his arms.

"Oh, captain!" she sobbed. "You're leaving—"

"Now, now!" the captain murmured, touched and surprised by the lovely child's grief. He patted her shoulders soothingly. "I'll be back," he said rashly.

"Oh, yes, do come back!" cried Maleen. She hesitated and

added: "I become marriageable two years from now. Karres time—"

"Well, well," said the captain, dazed. "Well, now—"

He set off down the path a few minutes later, with a strange melody tinkling in his head. Around the first curve, it changed abruptly to a shrill keening which seemed to originate from a spot some two hundred feet before him. Around the next curve, he entered a small, rocky clearing full of pale, misty, early-morning sunlight and what looked like a slow-motion fountain of gleaming rainbow globes. These turned out to be clusters of large, vari-hued soap bubbles which floated up steadily from a wooden tub full of hot water, soap and the Leewit. Toll was bent over the tub; and the Leewit was objecting to a morning bath, with only that minimum of interruptions required to keep her lungs pumped full of a fresh supply of air.

As the captain paused beside the little family group, her red, wrathful face came up over the rim of the tub and looked at him.

"Well, Ugly," she squealed, in a renewed outburst of rage, "who you staring at?" Then a sudden determination came into her eyes. She pursed her lips.

Toll up-ended her promptly and smacked the Leewit's bottom.

"She was going to make some sort of a whistle at you," she explained hurriedly. "Perhaps you'd better get out of range while I can keep her head under. And good luck, captain!"

Karres seemed even more deserted than usual this morning. Of course, it was quite early. Great banks of fog lay here and there among the huge dark trees and the small bright houses. A breeze sighed sadly far overhead. Faint, mournful bird-cries came from still higher up—it could have been swan hawks reproaching him for the omelet.

Somewhere in the distance, somebody tootled on a wood-instrument, very gently.

He had gone halfway up the path to the landing field, when something buzzed past him like an enormous wasp and went *CLUNK!* into the hole of a tree just before him.

It was a long, thin, wicked-looking arrow. On its shaft was a white card; and on the card was printed in red letters:

STOP, MAN OF NIKKELDEPAIN!

The captain stopped and looked around slowly and cautiously. There was no one in sight. What did it mean?

He had a sudden feeling as if all of Karres were rising up

silently in one stupendous, cool, foggy trap about him. His skin began to crawl. What was going to happen?

"Ha-ha!" said Goth, suddenly visible on a rock twelve feet to his left and eight feet above him. "You did stop!"

The captain let his breath out slowly.

"What else did you think I'd do?" he inquired. He felt a little faint.

She slid down from the rock like a lizard and stood before him. "Wanted to say good-bye!" she told him.

Thin and brown, in jacket, breeches, boots, and cap of gray-green rock-lichen color, Goth looked very much in her element. The brown eyes looked up at him steadily; the mouth smiled faintly; but there was no real expression on her face at all. There was a quiverful of those enormous arrows slung over her shoulder, and some arrow-shooting gadget—not a bow—in her left hand.

She followed his glance.

"Bollem hunting up the mountain," she explained. "The wild ones. They're better meat—"

The captain reflected a moment. That's right, he recalled; they kept the tame Bollem herds mostly for milk, butter, and cheese. He'd learned a lot of important things about Karres, all right!

"Well," he said, "good-by, Goth!"

They shook hands gravely. Goth was the real Witch of Karres, he decided—more so than her sisters, more so even than Toll. But he hadn't actually learned a single thing about any of them.

Peculiar people!

He walked on, rather glumly.

"Captain!" Goth called after him. He turned.

"Better watch those takeoffs," Goth called, "or you'll kill yourself yet!"

The captain cussed softly all the way up to the *Venture*.

And the takeoff was terrible! A few swan hawks were watching but, he hoped, no one else.

V

There wasn't the remotest possibility, of course, of resuming direct trade in the Empire with the cargo they'd loaded for him. But the more he thought about it now, the less likely it seemed that Councilor Onswud was going to let a genuine fortune slip through his hands on a mere technicality of embargoes. Nikkel-depain knew all the tricks of interstellar merchandising; and the councilor himself was undoubtedly the slickest unskinned miffel in the Republic.

More hopefully, the captain began to wonder whether some sort of trade might not be made to develop eventually between Karres and Nikkeldepain. Now and then, he also thought of Maleen growing marriageable two years hence, Karres time. A handful of witch-notes went tinkling through his head whenever that idle reflection occurred.

The calendric chronometer informed him he'd spent three weeks there. He couldn't remember how their year compared with the standard one.

He found he was getting remarkably restless on this homeward run; and it struck him for the first time that space travel could also be nothing much more than a large hollow period of boredom. He made a few attempts to resume his sessions of small-talk with Illyla, via her picture; but the picture remained aloof.

The ship seemed unnaturally quiet now—that was the trouble! The captain's cabin, particularly, and the hall leading past it had become as dismal as a tomb.

But at long last, Nikkeldepain II swam up on the screen ahead. The captain put the *Venture* 7333 on orbit, and broadcast the ship's identification number. Half an hour later, Landing Control called him. He repeated the identification number, and added the ship's name, his name, owner's name, place of origin and nature of cargo.

The cargo had to be described in detail.

"Assume Landing Orbit 21,203 on your instruments," Landing Control instructed him. "A customs ship will come out to inspect."

He went on the assigned orbit and gazed moodily from the vision ports as the flat continents and oceans of Nikkeldepain II as they drifted by below. A sense of equally flat depression overcame him unexpectedly. He shook it off and remembered Illyla.

Three hours later, a ship ran up next to him; and he shut off the orbital drive. The communicator began buzzing. He switched it on.

"Vision, please!" said an official-sounding voice. The captain frowned, located the vision-stud of the communicator screen and pushed it down. Four faces appeared in vague outline on the screen, looking at him.

"Illyla!" the captain said.

"At least," young Councilor Rapport said unpleasantly, "he's brought back the ship, Father Onswud!"

"Illyla!" said the captain.

Councilor Onswud said nothing. Neither did Illyla. They both seemed to be staring at him, but the screen wasn't good enough to permit the study of expression in detail.

The fourth face, an unfamiliar one above a uniform collar, was the one with the official-sounding voice.

"You are instructed to open the forward lock, Captain Pausert," it said, "for an official investigation."

It wasn't till he was releasing the outer lock to the control room that the captain realized it wasn't Customs who had sent a boat out to him, but the police of the Republic.

However, he hesitated for only a moment. Then the outer lock gaped wide.

He tried to explain. They wouldn't listen. They had come on board in contamination-proof repulsor suits, all four of them; and they discussed the captain as if he weren't there. Illyla looked pale and angry and beautiful, and avoided looking at him.

However, he didn't want to speak to her before the others anyway.

They strolled back to the storage and gave the Karres cargo a casual glance.

"Damaged his lifeboat, too!" Councilor Rapport remarked.

They brushed past him down the narrow hallway and went back to the control room. The policeman asked to see the log and commercial records. The captain produced them.

The three men studied them briefly. Illyla gazed stonily out at Nikkeldepain II.

"Not too carefully kept!" the policeman pointed out.

"Surprising he bothered to keep them at all!" said Councilor Rapprt.

"But it's all clear enough!" said Councilor Onswud.

They straightened up and then and faced him in a line. Councilor Onswud folded his arms and projected his craggy chin. Councilor Rapport stood at ease, smiling faintly. The policeman became officially rigid.

Illyla remained off to one side, looking at the three.

"Captain Pausert," the policeman said, "the following charges—substantiated in part by this preliminary investigation—are made against you—"

"Charges?" said the captain.

"Silence, please!" rumbled Councilor Onswud.

"First: material theft of a quarter-million value of maels of jewels and jeweled items from a citizen of the Imperial Planet of Porlumma—"

"They were returned!" the captain protested.

"Restitution, particularly when inspired by fear of retribution, does not affect the validity of the original charge," Councilor Rapport quoted, gazing at the ceiling.

"Second," continued the policeman. "Purchase of human slaves, permitted under Imperial law but prohibited by penalty of ten years to lifetime penal servitude by the laws of the Republic of Nikkeldepain—"

"I was just taking them back where they belonged!" said the captain.

"We shall get to that point presently," the policeman replied. "Third, material theft of sundry items in the value of one hundred and eighty thousand maels from a ship of the Imperial Planet of Lepper, accompanied by threats of violence to the ship's personnel—"

"I might add in explanation of the significance of this particular charge," added Councilor Rapport, looking at the floor, "that the Regency of Sirius, containing Lepper, is allied to the Republic of Nikkeldepain by commercial and military treaties of considerable value. The Regency has taken the trouble to point out that such hostile conduct by a citizen of the Republic against citizens of the Regency is likely to have an adverse effect on the duration of the treaties. The charge thereby becomes compounded by the additional charge of a treasonable act against the Republic—"

He glanced at the captain. "I believe we can forestall the accused's plea that these pilfered goods also were restored. They were, in the face of superior force!"

"Fourth," the policeman went on patiently, "depraved and licentious conduct while acting as commercial agent, to the detriment of your employer's business and reputation—"

"WHAT?" choked the captain.

"—involving three of the notorious Witches of the Prohibited Planet of Karres—"

"Just like his great-uncle Threbus!" nodded Councilor Onswud gloomily. "It's in the blood, I always say!"

"—and a justifiable suspicion of a prolonged stay on said Prohibited Planet of Karres—"

"I never heard of that place before this trip!" shouted the captain.

"Why don't you read your Instructions and Regulations then?" shouted Councilor Rapport. "It's all there!"

"Silence, please!" shouted Councilor Onswud.

"Fifth," said the policeman quietly, "general willful and

negligent actions resulting in material damage and loss to your employer to the value of eighty-two thousand maels.''

"I've still got fifty-five thousand. And the stuff in the storage," the captain said, also quietly, "is worth half a million, at least!"

"Contraband and hence legally valueless!" the policeman said. Councilor Onswud cleared his throat.

"It will be impounded, of course," he said. "Should a method of resale present itself, the profits, if any, will be applied to the cancellation of your just debts. To some extent, that might reduce your sentence." He paused. "There is another matter—"

"The sixth charge," the policeman said, "is the development *and* public demonstration of a new type of space drive, which should have been brought promptly and secretly to the attention of the Republic of Nikkeldepain!"

They all stared at him—alertly and quite greedily.

So *that* was it—the Sheewash Drive!

"Your sentence may be greatly reduced, Pausert," Councilor Onswud said wheedlingly, "if you decide to be reasonable now. What have you discovered?"

"Look out, father!" Illyla said sharply.

"Pausert," Councilor Onswud inquired in a fading voice, "what is that in your hand?"

"A Blythe gun," the captain said, boiling.

There was a frozen stillness for an instant. Then the policeman's right hand made a convulsive movement.

"Uh-uh!" said the captain warningly.

Councilor Rapport started a slow step backwards.

"Stay where you are!" said the captain.

"Pausert!" Councilor Onswud and Illyla cried out together.

"Shut up!" said the captain.

There was another stillness.

"If you'd looked," the captain said, in an almost normal voice, "you'd have seen I've got the nova gun turrets out. They're fixed on that boat of yours. The boat's lying still and keeping its little yap shut. You do the same—"

He pointed a finger at the policeman. "You got a repulsor suit on," he said. "Open the inner port lock and go squirt yourself back to your boat!"

The inner port lock groaned open. Warm air left the ship in a long, lazy wave, scattering the sheets of the *Venture*'s log and commercial records over the floor. The thin, cold upper atmosphere of Nikkeldepain II came eddying in.

"You next, Onswud!" the captain said.

And a moment later: "Rapport, you just turn around—"

Young Councilor Rapport went through the port at a higher velocity than could be attributed reasonably to his repulsor units. The captain winced and rubbed his foot. But it had been worth it.

"Pausert," said Illyla in justifiable apprehension, "you are stark, staring mad!"

"Not at all, my dear," the captain said cheerfully. "You and I are now going to take off and embark on a life of crime together."

"But, Pausert—"

"You'll get used to it," the captain assured her, "just like I did. It's got Nikkeldepain beat every which way."

"Pausert," Illyla said, whitefaced, "we told them to bring up revolt ships!"

"We'll blow them out through the stratosphere," the captain said belligerently, reaching for the port-control switch. He added, "But they won't shoot anyway while I've got you on board!"

Illyla shook her head. "You just don't understand," she said desperately. "You can't make me stay!"

"Why not?" asked the captain.

"Pausert," said Illyla, "I am Madame Councilor Rapport."

"Oh!" said the captain. There was a silence. He added, crestfallen: "Since when?"

"Five months ago, yesterday," said Illyla.

"Great Patham!" cried the captain, with some indignation. "I'd hardly got off Nikkeldepain then! We were engaged!"

"Secretly . . . and I guess," said Illyla, with a return of spirit, "that I had a right to change my mind!"

There was another silence.

"Guess you had, at that," the captain agreed. "All right—the port's still open, and your husband's waiting in the boat. Beat it!"

He was alone. He let the ports slam shut and banged down the oxygen release switch. The air had become a little thin.

He cussed.

The communicator began rattling for attention. He turned it on.

"Pausert!" Councilor Onswud was calling in a friendly but shaking voice. "May we not depart, Pausert? Your nova guns are still fixed on this boat!"

"Oh, that—" said the captain. He deflected the turrets a trifle. "They won't go off now. Scram!"

The police boat vanished.

There was other company coming, though. Far below him but climbing steadily, a trio of revolt ships darted past on the screen, swung around and came back for the next turn of their spiral. They'd have to get a good deal closer before they started shooting; but they'd try to stay under him so as not to knock any stray chunks out of Nikkeldepain.

He sat a moment, reflecting. The revolt ships went by once more. The captain punched in the *Venture*'s secondary drives, turned her nose towards the planet and let her go. There were some scattered white puffs around as he cut through the revolt ships' plane of flight. Then he was below them, and the *Venture* groaned as he took her out of the dive.

The revolt ships were already scattering and nosing over for a counter-maneuver. He picked the nearest one and swung the nova guns towards it.

"—and ram them in the middle!" he muttered between his teeth.

SSS-whoosh!

It was the Sheewash Drive—but, like a nightmare now, it kept on and on!

VI

"Maleen!" the captain bawled, pounding the locked door of the captain's cabin. "Maleen—shut it off! Cut it off! You'll kill yourself. Maleen!"

The *Venture* quivered suddenly throughout her length, then shuddered more violently, jumped and coughed; and commenced sailing along on her secondary drives again. He wondered how many light-years from everything they were by now. It didn't matter!

"Maleen!" he yelled. "Are you all right?"

There was a faint *thump-thump* inside the cabin, and silence. He lost almost a minute finding the right cutting tool in the storage. A few seconds later, a section of door panel sagged inwards; he caught it by one edge and came tumbling into the cabin with it.

He had the briefest glimpse of a ball of orange-colored fire swirling uncertainly over a cone of oddly bent wires. Then the fire vanished, and the wires collapsed with a loose rattling to the table top.

The crumpled small shape lay behind the table, which was

why he didn't discover it at once. He sagged to the floor beside it, all the strength running out of his knees.

Brown eyes opened and blinked at him blearily.

"Sure takes it out of you!" Goth grunted. "Am I hungry!"

"I'll whale the holy, howling tar out of you again," the captain roared, "if you ever—"

"Quit your bawling!" snarled Goth. "I got to eat."

She ate for fifteen minutes straight, before she sank back in her chair, and sighed.

"Have some more Wintenberry jelly," the captain offered anxiously. She looked pretty pale.

Goth shook her head. "Couldn't—and that's about the first thing you've said since you fell through the door, howling for Maleen. Ha-ha! Maleen's *got* a boy friend!"

"Button your lip, child," the captain said. "I was thinking." He added, after a moment: "Has she really?"

"Picked him out last year," Goth nodded. "Nice boy from town—they get married as soon as she's marriageable. She just told you to come back because she was upset about you. Maleen had a premonition you were headed for awful trouble!"

"She was quite right, little chum," the captain said nastily.

"What were you thinking about?" Goth inquired.

"I was thinking," said the captain, "that as soon as we're sure you're going to be all right, I'm taking you straight back to Karres!"

"I'll be all right now," Goth said. "Except, likely, for a stomachache. But you can't take me back to Karres."

"Who will stop me, may I ask?" the captain asked.

"Karres is gone," Goth said.

"Gone?" the captain repeated blankly, with a sensation of not quite definable horror bubbling up in him.

"Not blown up or anything," Goth reassured him. "They just moved it! The Imperialists got their hair up about us again. But this time, they were sending a fleet with the big bombs and stuff, so everybody was called home. But they had to wait then till they found out where we were—me and Maleen and the Leewit. Then you brought us in; and they had to wait again, and decide about you. But right after you'd left . . . *we'd* left, I mean . . . they moved it."

"Where?"

"Great Patham!" Goth shrugged. "How'd I know? There's lots of places!"

*　　*　　*

There probably were, the captain admitted silently. A scene came suddenly before his eyes—that lime-white, arenalike bowl in the valley, with the steep tiers of seats around it, just before they'd reached the town of Karres—"the Theater where—"

But now there was unnatural night-darkness all over and about that world; and the eight thousand-some Witches of Karres sat in circles around the Theater, their heads bent towards one point in the center, where orange fire washed hugely about the peak of a cone of curiously twisted girders.

And a world went racing off at the speeds of the Sheewash Drive! There'd be lots of places, all right. What peculiar people!

"Anyway," he sighed, "if I've got to start raising you—don't say 'Great Patham' any more. That's a cuss word!"

"I learned it from you!" Goth pointed out.

"So you did, I guess," the captain acknowledged. "I won't say it either. Aren't they going to be worried about you?"

"Not very much," said Goth. "We don't get hurt often—especially when we're young. That's when we can do all that stuff like teleporting, and whistling, like the Leewit. We lose it mostly when we get older—they're working on that now so we won't. About all Maleen can do right now is premote!"

"She premotes just dandy, though," the captain said. "The Sheewash Drive—they can all do that, can't they?"

"Uh-huh!" Goth nodded. "But that's learned stuff. That's one of the things they already studied out." She added, a trace uncomfortably: "I can't tell you about that till you're one yourself."

"Till I'm what myself?" the captain asked, becoming puzzled again.

"A witch, like us," said Goth. "We got our rules. And that won't be for four years, Karres time."

"It won't, eh?" said the captain. "What happens then?"

"That's when I'm marriageable age," said Goth, frowning at the jar of Wintenberry jelly. She pulled it towards her and inspected it carefully. "I got it all fixed," she told the jelly firmly, "as soon as they started saying they ought to pick out a wife for you on Karres, so you could stay. I said it was me, right away; and everyone else said finally that was all right then—even Maleen, because she had this boy friend."

"You mean," said the captain, stunned, "this was all planned out on Karres?"

"Sure," said Goth. She pushed the jelly back where it had been standing, and glanced up at him again. "For three weeks, that's about all everyone talked about in the town! It set a perceedent—''

She paused doubtfully.

"That would explain it," the captain admitted.

"Uh-huh," Goth nodded relieved, settling back in her chair. "But it was my father who told us how to do it so you'd break up with the people on Nikkeldepain. He said it was in the blood."

"What was in the blood?" the captain said patiently.

"That you'd break up with them. That's Threbus, my father," Goth informed him. "You met him a couple of times in the town. Big man with a blond beard—Maleen and the Leewit take after him."

"You wouldn't mean my great-uncle Threbus?" the captain inquired. He was in a state of strange calm by now.

"That's right," said Goth. "He liked you a lot."

"It's a small Galaxy," said the captain philosophically. "So that's where Threbus wound up! I'd like to meet him again someday."

"We'll start after Karres four years from now, when you learn about those things," Goth said. "We'll catch up with them all right. That's still thirteen hundred and seventy-two Old Sidereal days," she added, "but there's a lot to do in between. You want to pay the money you owe back to those people, don't you? I got some ideas—"

"None of those teleporting tricks now!" the captain warned.

"Kid stuff!" Goth said scornfully. "I'm growing up. This'll be fair swapping. But we'll get rich."

"I wouldn't be surprised," the captain admitted. He thought a moment. "Seeing we've turned out to be distant relatives, I suppose it is all right, too, if I adopt you meanwhile—"

"Sure," said Goth. She stood up.

"Where you going?" the captain asked.

"Bed," said Goth. "I'm tired." She stopped at the hall door. "About all I can tell you about us till then," she said, "you can read in those Regulations, like the one man said—the one you kicked off the ship. There's a lot about us in there. Lots of lies, too, though!"

"And when did you find out about the communicator between here and the captain's cabin?" the captain inquired.

Goth grinned. "A while back," she admitted. "The others never noticed!"

"All right," the captain said. "Good night, witch—if you get a stomachache, yell and I'll bring the medicine."

"Good night," Goth yawned. "I will, I think."

"And wash behind your ears!" the captain added, trying to remember the bedtime instructions he'd overheard Maleen giving the junior witches.

"All right," said Goth sleepily. The hall door closed behind her—but half a minute later, it was briskly opened again. The captain looked up startled from the voluminous stack of "General Instructions and Space Regulations of the Republic of Nikkel-depain" he'd just discovered in one of the drawers of the control desk. Goth stood in the doorway, scowling and wide-awake.

"And you wash behind yours!" she said.

"Huh?" said the captain. He reflected a moment. "All right," he said. "We both will, then."

"Right," said Goth, satisfied.

The door closed once more.

The captain began to run his finger down the lengthy index of K's—or could it be under W?

Spree

by Barry N. Malzberg

*In an incredible burst of creativity, that extended through-
out the 1970s, Barry Malzberg produced several dozen
memorable science fiction novels and more than one
hundred short stories. No one had ever maintained this
kind of pace with consistently high quality before, at
least over so long a period. Particularly outstanding
were* Beyond Apollo *(1972 winner of the John W.
Campbell, Jr., Memorial Award),* Herovit's World
(1973), Guernica Night *(1974), and* The Destruction of
the Temple *(1974). These and other books extended the
genre, a field he has written about with great perception in* The Engines of the Night *(1982), a landmark
work of criticism. Many readers feel that he is even
better at the shorter lengths.*

At the International Artists & College Graduates Singles Mixer I
meet a registered nurse named Gloria Weinstein and decide to
tell her the truth. I am so sick of the secret, sick of it, it leaches
through the corridors of being, burbles with the blood, intersects
with the powers of speech; I have fought the revelation for all
this time and I can no longer do it. Will no longer do it. "I'm a
warlock," I say, holding a scotch on the rocks and facing her
squarely, her shoulders to the wall, her own drink bright in her
hand; her eyes drifting through the room to see if there might be
anyone more promising at the International Artists (there is not; I
can say this for a fact). "I can produce magical incantations. I
can change the scope and substance, the meaning and direction
of lives; I can even raise the dead, although this is one power I
have not yet explored."

She stares at me. If nothing else I have focused her intention.
"I've heard lines," she said, "I've been on this circuit for two
years now and I've aged before my time, but—"

"It's not a line," I say earnestly, "it's the truth. I just can't

99

hold back the truth anymore. I mean, I'm a graduate student on a fellowship and all that, I live a very ordinary life, to look at me you'd detect nothing strange at all, but truth is truth—''

"Graduate student where?"

"NYU,'' I say. I swallow the scotch convulsively; it mingles with the blood, spreads splinters of warmth and implication. "I'm afraid,'' I say, "afraid of the power, of the possibility—"

"So what are you saying to me?" Gloria Weinstein asks. She is moderately pretty, I suppose, five feet six or seven, dark hair, round full eyes, nurse's breasts ponderous through the thin sweater she wears, nurse's hands thin and charged with power as they surround the glass, although it is not these qualities which have attracted me to her so much as a certain vulnerability and accessibility, an openness to her posture, some small hints and breaks in her composure which have indicated to me, even before I began to talk, that she might listen, she might understand. "You're a warlock and you know magical incantations and I'm supposed to go to bed with you? To hear the spells and all that?" She shakes her head. "Yes indeed,'' she says, "that's a new one all right,'' but encouragingly she makes no move to leave, her posture against the wall remains easeful, her eyes, dense and accepting, rest now on mine. "I don't care,'' she says, "I've met them all. I've met interns and rapists and a truckdriver who was on the way to being an audited clear and a bartender who had been a trapeze artist with the circus. I've met a second violinist in the New York Philharmonic who was tone-deaf and a dancer with the New York City Ballet who had three knee operations, so I don't see why a warlock should be anything really special. That's a male witch, right? A warlock?"

"Something like that. It isn't quite that simple; it's a separate strain, a different archetype—"

"Hey,'' Gloria Weinstein says to me and puts her drink down on a ledge, then extends a hand to me, "I don't really need to hear about it, you don't have to tell me no more. Do you want to get out of here?"

"Yes,'' I say, "of course I'd like to get out of here. The only purpose of these things is to get out of them. Like life itself.''

"Then let's go,'' she says. "I have three roommates and there's always one of them off-shift sleeping, so you can forget that. You got a place?"

"I've got a furnished one-and-a-half on West 123rd Street,'' I say and think of the cluttered room, the incense, the piles of debris, the stones and magical books scattered on the shelves and the floor, "but I don't know if you'd want to go there, I haven't really cleaned it up."

"A warlock can't clean his room? You can't just point a finger and make a spell?"

"It isn't that simple," I say. "None of it is that simple. You're making fun of me, but I told you simply because I can't keep it secret anymore, I can't deal with it, I can't carry it all alone, there comes a time finally when you have to share—"

"It's all right," she says. She takes my hand. "I'm a *nurse*, remember. I'm big on sympathy. Let's get out of here." She leads me through the thin clumps of International Artists & Singles through the heavy odors of the room and through the doors; possessed, enchanted, I follow.

"A warlock," she says as we wait for our coats at the checkroom. "A warlock with magical spells and incantations. In a furnished room near Columbia University. Hey, why don't you live near NYU if you're going there?"

"They threw me out of Columbia in the fall," I said. "I just barely worked it out at NYU, but I've got all my things in the room; I couldn't just move."

"Why did they throw you out?"

"Why don't we just get our coats and go uptown?" I say.

Power fills me, the terrible rising power, scrolls and screed lurk in the darkness of consciousness as slowly I move upon her whispering the incantations, my dread choked off in the back of the throat emerges as small, hawklike cries in the darkness, then growing, mounting, spreading like blood, the blood rising, pulsing in the darkness, and the brisk collision is incidental to the rising of that blood, I bounce off stone, stone incident to circumstance, and move through, beating, beating, the smell of ozone suddenly high and hard in the air, dense, overtaking me—

"My God," she says as if from a far distance, "my God, you weren't kidding, were you?"

Falling, falling upon her I batter at the voice, there are more words, words fluttering like insects in the air, but I penetrate their center, move to the pool of darkness, now there are different sounds, flutelike, disparate, but I part them too, the collisions heavier, coming at me, walls tumbling, the splitting of the earth, and in the center of all of that a small chink of light. I concentrate upon one aspect of that light, working myself toward it, forcing it to expand, and slowly the darkness implodes, light leaching at the corridors, sounds all around, shrieks and the power comes from me then in an enormous incantation of speed and scurrying, I wedge myself all the way through and in the dazzle of circumstance am finally alone, free, in that high empty place which I have sought and which is at last mine, I seek purchase within it—

Inside the described pentagram the demon totters, falls to his haunches, crouches with difficulty, his taloned hands spread against the earth. "This has got to stop, you know," he says. "This can't go on. You're going to have to get hold of yourself, control the situation, find some kind of resolution, stop calling for help."

"I'm not calling for help," I say. Fires ring the demon; carefully I feed one of the magic parchments to the near flame, grant it sustenance. Within the ring of fire the demon cowers, but if the fire were ever to go out, if it were to go out, if it were—

"There is no help," the demon says, "there is only the flame over and again." His skin is damp against the heat; his sweat has the odor of sacred text. "Let me go," he says. "I'm in terrible pain."

"Pain from hell?" I try to laugh, but the hollow explosion of sound racks me. "What do you know of pain? Can pain feel pain? Give me the incantation," I say. "Give it to me now and you are free."

"You don't understand," the demon says. "There is no incantation, there is no magic, there is only yourself known over and again. Why do you think that I would have the answer?"

"From walking to and fro upon the earth and up and down within it; from the exile and the circumstance—"

"Oh come on," the demon says, "come on, come on, come on," his little voice beating and beating against the wall of flame, "come on, stop being a fool, demonology is not the answer, this is your *life*." His little shrieks and taunts inflame me. I put my hand through the fire to squeeze him and take what vengeance I can, but the pentagram resists my hand with sudden and awful power and I feel it open, feel the strength draining. The heat comes into the unprotected joints and I scream with the sudden pain, pull my hand out, retreat, stumble from that center and cower against a wall while the demon regards me with enormous, solemn eyes not untinged now with sympathy as I begin to understand what he has said: that even in hell, that in hell of all places and for its creatures, there must be the quality of pain.

*　　*　　*

In Washington Square Park, on a bench, watching the dere-licts assemble beyond one gate to compute the endless circum-stance of their lives while in other sections of the park more vigorous if useless attempts are made to come to terms with urban shock; in Washington Square Park on a bench I contem-plate my life and what has taken me to this condition and what if anything I can do about it. Unaware of my power until the age of fourteen, brought suddenly to terrible terms with it, attempting for a decade thereafter to deny it, finally accepting in my twenty-fourth year the dreadful circumstance: pursuit of the old texts, retreat into medievalism, the conversion of a degree in account-ing to an application for fellowship in philosophy, the months at Columbia, the disgraceful confrontation in the corridor with senior faculty and subsequent breakdown which brought me here, the circles of my life, the pit of my belief, the solemnity and terror of my obligation . . . I think and think of all of these things on the bench until I begin to tremble with implication; a warlock should not be in this position, I think, no warlock worthy of the name would be in a condition of this sort; he would invoke his powers and through spiritual decree free him-self . . . and yet the concept of the warlock entrapped overcomes me; in or out of time there is no end to the entrapment: *power achieved is only the power to further entrap,* and this insight bolts me upright from the bench. It is as if for the first time I see things clearly (I have had this illusion before), have some pur-chase on circumstance, have some true and final understanding of what I have achieved, and I move toward the gates rapidly, in haste to somehow commit this insight to action. It is only action that will save me now, only action that can at last bring me through this to some deeper understanding. One of the derelicts looks up, spits at me, I feel his saliva hitting my face like a blow, and I raise my hand, wheel on him, whisper the Word; his face caves in, he crumples upon himself, falls to the ground, the others stare at him, then at me, I raise my hand again. ''Don't do it,'' one of them cries, ''don't do it, sonny,'' and for just an instant I feel the pure and sentencing fire that will take me free but I hold back. This is not the way to do it, there will be another time and I will not waste my power upon derelicts. I turn and stalk from the park, they murmur behind me. High above I hear the birdlike cries of sustenance; from the cloudless and terrible sky the Elders have observed and once again have passed their judgment. In or out of time, in or out of power there is no end to judgment; to know this is to know it again and again and again.

*   *   *

In hunched and crowded sleep I dream of Gloria, the thin pressure of her body against me, the high and haunting sound of her voice as she took my measure, and I think in the dream that I perceive her with the mask torn and her pure witch's face glinting out at me. Gloria a witch then living under cover as I no longer can, Gloria living her terrible secret in the hospital corridors, in the International Artists Mixer, in the open and closed spaces of the city. "You've got to survive," she says to me, "don't you understand that, you can't tell them what you are. This is the end of the second millennium, the beginning of the third, technology, rationality, the machines, the terrible and barbarous circumstances of power, the knives and steel of the machines will kill if you tell them who you are.

"You must be like me," she says in the dream, rising then to confront me, her eyes dark and shrouded. "You must never tell, you must tell them nothing," and I enfold her with my arms, drag her down again to the sheets. "Don't tell," she says, "don't *tell tell tell*," and I want to scream to her that this is possible for her but not possible for me, that something has ripped, broken, the armament has been destroyed, and that absent of guile, stripped of concealment, I must not only invoke but describe my power. "Power denied turns against the bearer," I say to her, "power becomes then only the power to die," and hard and heavy against her I begin to scrapple in the motions of generation, still earnest even at this terrible time. Power does indeed seize me, in power I turn and I rise and I rise, it is as if in this elevation I will purchase at last an answer but instead am ripped free only of the fabric of the dream itself and come to consciousness in my cold room on a high floor in the tenement of life, staring out at the river, the cold frozen gray burning into sensibility, and Gloria dwindles, wraps the dream about herself and is destroyed. Alone and alone in the spaces of the room I look upon the texts and the bottles and the potions and the cryptograms which I have sped against the wall and think yes, the gleaming machinery, the steel and the knives will be the end of all of us if I emerge and yet if I were not to emerge they will kill us unbidden. One more try. One more try for the Pentagram. One more try at last for the Word which will strike not only at derelicts but at the hearts and souls of my countrymen, the living and the dead, the shallow and the spoken and bring them all to rise in that judgment which invoked awaits all of us, and I began once again with the paints to construct the circle . . .

* * *

Within which the demon poises chattering, his skin cold now, no more protective sweat as the fires shrivel him to stone. "You don't understand," he says, "you don't really understand any of this, do you?"

"Give me the word," I say. "Give it now."

"There is no word, there is no judgment—"

"I want it now," I say. Remorselessness fills me; I know that I have been denied for the last time. "Give it to me now or I will douse the fires and let the saints do with you what they will; I won't wait any longer, there's no time, there's never been any time from the beginning. Give it to me," I say.

The demon says, "You misunderstand, you misunderstand totally, don't you see—"

"Now," I say, "now or I'll call the father of hell himself to pronounce a judgment and if I do that then there will be nothing for any of us, all of it will be gone but you will pay and you will pay—"

The demon says, "You're a fool," and slowly stands within the circle. His eyes are enormous; the rest of him has contracted to that terrible stare. "I'll give you the word then but it won't make things any easier, it's only going to make them more terrible, don't you see that, don't you understand what you've done? You could have had it the easy way all your life, you could have used it to advantage but instead you allowed it to overtake—"

"The word," I say. "The Word."

The demon looks at me. He licks his lips; little wings sprout from his back, his eyes fill with luster and intensity.

"You fool," he says again.

He gives me the Word.

In hard embrace against Gloria I move into the splitting rock of circumstance waiting now for the proper time; the Word is within my possession and I can use it to advantage but only at the optimum point; it would be wrong to employ it when I cannot get the maximum effect. Poised, chattering, I hear her beginning to whisper once again, witch's secrets, ancient and debilitating oaths which will cut to the center of my power and—"Shut up, you bitch," I say, "shut up now." But she cannot stop, once unleashed a witch's confidences cannot so easily be denied, and rage fills me, rage at all of those forces which drove me toward revelation and then at last to demand the Word itself, and in the sudden, cool center of that rage I find the strength to do as I must. "I warned you," I say to her. "I warned you that it would be this way, *you made me do it.*" And then, stricken, I utter the Word itself, mumbling it at first under the tongue and then as her body begins to come to fire under its sound I say it again, louder, louder yet, begin to scream it, the syllables ripped out of my throat, great hawking cries. The room splits, it opens wings like a bird, and I am catapulted into a sudden open space where free at enormous height I seem to look down upon all of them, the knives and the steel, the poised machinery waiting below to consume. But I will not yield, I will not land. Instead I cry out the Word once more in all of its ancient and terrible powers and the seas and the cities collapse and run against one another, all mingles, all dwells . . .

And they come in the morning with solemn hands and solemn hearts and tell me what I did and wait politely while I assemble my clothing and join them at the door to be taken off. Because there is absolutely nothing left to do.

And because, with the word at last delivered, there is absolutely nothing left to say.

Devil's Henchman

by Murray Leinster

*Murray Leinster (1896–1975) was at one time the proud
possessor of the title "Dean of Science Fiction." His
was truly a remarkable and lengthy career, which began with his first sale in 1913 and continued almost
without interruption until his retirement in 1967. Although he worked in all genres, most of his production
was science fiction, where he is fondly remembered as
a pioneer of the "parallel world" story and the author
of the popular and award-winning "Med Service" series of stories.* The Best of Murray Leinster *(1978)
indeed shows him at his best. "Devil's Henchman"
was originally published under the author's real name,
Will F. Jenkins.*

When Joe Burchard wore the witch ring from the outland country
and fought with the devil in Ben Harper's body, the morning
didn't start out any different from any other. The sun rose over
the mountains, and the shadows were long and sprawling, and all
the spider webs shone like diamonds. The wind blew overhead,
going from yonder to some other place. Smoke from the cabins
all up and down the valley streaked out long and low. It was a
mighty nice day to be twenty-one years old in, like Joe was.
He'd licked every man but one in a day's walking, and he'd
courted and kissed every girl but two.

He didn't know a thing about the witch ring that morning,
though. He sat in his granny's cabin and ate the breakfast she'd
cooked him. He felt purely fine, like a body does when he's
twenty-one and tall and broad and hasn't got a care in the world.
He breathed in, and it felt good. He breathed out, and it felt even
better.

His granny looked at him sharp whilst he was eating his
breakfast. She'd been a witching woman once and she could see
more in a peek than most in a gape, and Joe was her only kin
and she loved him like nobody but a granny is able to. He had on

107

his store-going red wool shirt and his Saturday pants. That meant he'd be going down to Crowder's Store, where three roads crossed and the young men loafed around to show off to each other and the girls that came to the store with their mas.

"Huh!" says Joe's granny.

"Dressed up! You aim to be kissing some young girl and fighting some young man this morning. I know the signs."

He grinned at her. "Now," he says, "the fella ain't so young. He's Ben Harper. And the girl—I ain't sure, but Letty Smith asked me to stop by her folks' cabin for a letter she'd like to get mailed."

His granny thumped the floor with her stick, fretful.

"Foolish! Foolish! Foolish!" she says. "To you, it's fun, but Ben Harper's been craving Letty since she was old enough to look cornerways. He wouldn't fight no fist fight with somebody he thought she favored! He's got black eyes and no lobes to his ears, and that's a sign he ain't no fist-fighting man. He'll take to a knife or worse, he will!"

"Shucks!" says Joe. "There's the law, granny. Them days are long gone. He'd as soon take to witching."

"He might do that," says Joe's granny, peevish. "You're young yet, honey. You don't know what can happen inside a man when a girl he craves laughs at him. And if a man's heart is wrong and his cravings hot, there's ways of turning to witchery. But you, now—supposing you do kiss Letty at her folks' cabin and lick Ben Harper down to the store?"

Joe laughed, and he wiped his mouth.

"That's something I ain't figured out yet," he says.

His granny snapped, "There's Sally." Sally Walker was the only girl besides Letty in a day's walking that Joe hadn't courted and kissed, and Joe's granny thought a lot of Sally. But Joe didn't look up.

"No—o," says Joe. "I've known her all my born days. It wouldn't be no fun to court Sally or to kiss her. She's pretty enough. She's sweet. She's a right nice girl. But I just ain't got a mind to her."

His granny says, angry, "I was a witchin' woman once, before I got religion and married your grandpa. I know what's the matter. You're scared Sally wouldn't like you kissing her. You're—scared! I'd ought to do a little witchin'—"

Joe laughed and he got up and he went over and gave his granny a hug.

"You wouldn't witch me," he says.

"I wouldn't witch nobody," says his granny, peevish. "I promised your grandpa and I promised the Lord. Else I'd show you. Go along with you."

She gave him a shove and he laughed again and went over to the mirror that his granny kept tacked up on the wall. It was a sign and a reminder of what she'd given up, because a witching woman can't abide a mirror. Joe bent down to look in it, and he took a comb and he parted his straight black hair because he'd be stopping by Letty's folks' cabin, and she'd be there by her lone.

Then he went out of the cabin and striding on his way, and the sun was shining bright and a bobwhite called somewheres off in the woods, and the sky was so blue even a young man had to notice it. It felt purely good to be alive and young and a-walking to kiss a girl another man pined for, and fight that man and lick him after. Joe didn't take his granny's fussing serious. She'd got religion and married Joe's grandpa and he was waiting for her over Jordan and she wouldn't disappoint him. So Joe went on his way with nothing on his mind but the pleasure it was to be alive. He didn't think about the witching ring, that's sure. He didn't know there was such a thing.

But presently he thought about Sally. Her folks' cabin was the nearest to his granny's and when his own ma and pa died off while he was small he came to live with his granny. He could remember Sally from when neither of them was knee-high to a duck. And now he was grown-up, thinking of Sally gave him a queer kind of sad feeling, and a yearning feeling, and a scared feeling, too. So he backed down from thinking about her as much as he could.

The speckled shadows passed over as he walked. Birds chirped and katydids whirred all about. He went uphill and down, and all of a sudden he looked and there was Letty Smith's folks' cabin up above him and the gray rocks sticking out of the hillside all around. And sudden-like he knew that he didn't want to kiss Letty, but he was bounden to. He was going to fight Ben Harper, and Ben Harper craved Letty so bad that his eyes shone wild when they looked at her, and he'd never got religion. But she'd told Joe that her ma and her pa were going over the mountains to hear the new preacher and she'd have to stay home to look after the stock, and would he stop by to get a letter to mail for her down at Crowder's.

Joe stopped short and grunted to himself. He kind of fumed, because all of a sudden he didn't care a thing about kissing

Letty. And that wasn't natural, with him being twenty-one. He caught himself thinking. "If it was Sally, now—" and then he thought suspicious of his granny. She could make him feel this way if she liked. A spell muttered over a crumb of cornbread he'd eat the rest of out in the yard because of the mirror on the wall.

But he knew his granny wouldn't witch him even for his own good. She'd got religion years ago.

So Joe took a deep breath and climbed up the hillside, frowning to himself because it was funny he didn't want to kiss a pretty girl. But still he wasn't thinking about witchery, and least of all about the witch ring.

He stepped over the stile and went across the pasture to the cabin. There wasn't any noise but the chickens pecking and clucking and the wind above the Hollow. He opened his mouth to call, but the door opened and there was Letty looking at him. Her hair was straggly and she wasn't primped up. She looked white and scared and half crazy with crying and grief. She didn't say a word. Her hands were shaking.

"What's the matter?" says Joe, uncomfortable. "You sick?"

She didn't say a word, just looked at him imploring. And Joe felt queer.

He says, suspicious, "You sure act funny, Letty. You act like you was witched."

And that was what had to be said before Letty could speak. She put her face in her hands and she moaned.

"I *am* witched!" she cried. "That's it, Joe—I am!"

Now, Joe wasn't scared of witchery like some people, because his granny had told him—and she'd ought to know—that witchery hasn't got any power over a man unless his heart is wrong.

So Joe says, curious, "How does it take you, Letty? How does it feel?"

"I'm pins and needles all over," says Letty, pitiful, "and I itch and I ache to go to the one that's witched me, and nobody else can come near me without a pain in my heart and my breath stopping. So don't come near me, Joe. I'm witched and if you do I'll fall down dead." But she cried, heartbroken.

Joe shifted his weight from one foot to the other. Letty looked mighty pitiful, and she looked at him so pleading that it was right much of a dare for a young man that was twenty-one years old.

"My granny says," says Joe, "that witching ain't got any power if your heart's right."

Then Letty cried harder.

"I know," she says bitter. "I know all that. But I've had hate in my heart a long time. I hated Ben Harper because he craved me to love him and he wasn't the right one. I hated the girls you courted, because they wasn't me. There's no harm telling you because I'm witched, but I've laid awake nights thinking of you and I—I—" She says, heartbroke, "I've tried to witch you to dream love dreams of me and that's give witchery the power over me. And if you was to come near me now I'd have a pain in my heart and my breath would stop and I'd drop down dead."

Then she wrung her hands and cried desperate but her eyes went to him pleading. And Joe shifted his weight back to the foot he'd been standing on before. It's a mighty fine thing to be twenty-one, but Joe knew better than to fool with witchery. He thought hard, fidgeting. Letty'd been trying to witch him into loving her, and that was what gave witchery the power over her, so she was witched because of him.

She was a pretty girl, too, when she wasn't crying. Joe knew better than to look too close, but he did know that she was thin where a girl had ought to be thin, and where a girl oughtn't to be, she wasn't. She'd be nice to go buggy riding with or a-courting, but Joe hadn't ever thought of wanting to marry her.

"Who witched you?" says Joe, unhappy. "If I'm what made the trouble you're in, I'd ought to try to get you out."

"It's Ben Harper," says Letty. "He boiled a black cat in a kettle and threw the bones in a running stream, and he gave up crossing over Jordan and a man came and told him what to do. He told me. So I got to go to him, Joe. Please help me. So long as he's living, unless he takes the witching off, I'm suffering, and flesh and blood can't stand but so much!"

Then she twitched and she shivered and she gasped and she panted like she was going to have a fit.

Joe backed away, considerate, and he says, "I was figuring on seeing him down to the store today and he's the last man in a day's walking that I ain't licked. But if he's been fooling with a black cat's bones and started witching, it ain't no ordinary flesh and blood can lick him. My granny—"

"She won't help none," says Letty, a-wringing her hands. "She's got religion. And there ain't anything else can help me but Ben Harper dying or taking the witching off of me. But you could make him, Joe. There ain't anything I won't do for you, Joe, if only you'll do that for me!"

"You hold on," says Joe, "and I'll do it. You go stand on a

rock in a running stream. That'll weaken the witchery and I'll tend to Ben Harper.''

And he turned and he left her. And first off he started straight for Ben's cabin, figuring that Ben wouldn't be going to no store that Saturday morning if he'd put a spell on Letty so's she'd have to come to him. Ben would be waiting up in his cabin for his spell to work.

Then Joe began to realize that if Ben was a witch it wouldn't do no good to go after him alone, because, leaving out stronger witchery, there's just three things witching can't stand against. One's a purely good heart, and one's a bullet fired across still water, and one's the law and the Grand Jury. So Joe turned and headed back to talk to his granny. If it'd been Sally that had been itching and aching and crying and wringing her hands because Ben Harper'd witched her, Joe wouldn't have turned aside. He'd have gone straight to Ben Harper, and he'd have been raging, and somehow he'd've managed to kill Ben with his own bare hands before any spell could stop him. But this was Letty, so it was different.

The sky didn't look so blue to him, because he didn't see it. He thought about Letty, crying pitiful, and it was because of him that she'd been witched, and he thought about Sally Walker that may be Ben might turn his mind to witch some day.

He went tramping across the pasture and he went past the well. He stomped up on the porch and his eyes were hot and angry, and he went inside—and there was Sally Walker a-setting and talking with his granny. She'd seen him start off to Crowder's Store from her own folks' cabin up the mountainside, and she'd come over to visit.

The two of them, Sally and his granny, turned around and stared when Joe came stomping in.

He says, furious, ''Granny, Letty Smith's been witched!''

Then the words poured out as he told them, raging, all about it. His granny sniffed.

''Huh!'' she says. ''When I was a witching woman, before I got religion, *I* woulda handled this!''

Joe says, ''It's on account of me, Granny! He couldn't have witched her, but her heart ain't been right on account of me! She's been hating the girls I courted and she tried witching me to make me dream love dreams of her. She told me. And that gave witchery the power over her. I can't let Letty go be a witch's woman on account of me.''

His granny thumped her stick and looked at Sally, a-setting

there white and pale and twisting her fingers in her lap as she looked at Joe. Joe's granny says, "I told you he didn't have the sense he was born with!"

But she didn't move to do a thing. And Joe says, fierce, "I know you won't do no witching, Granny. So it looks like I got to get Ben Harper in my sights over still water. And I got to do it right away. I got to, Granny, because it's on account of me!"

His granny says, "What'll the law do? The sheriff don't pay no mind to witchin'. They'll hang you, and it'd serve you right for fooling around like you been doing."

"I'll go on a journey, after," says Joe. "They won't never catch me. But I'd never sleep nights thinking of Letty as a witch's woman and a-crying in the dark because she couldn't never pass over Jordan. I got to do it, Granny. I got to!"

"I promised," his granny says, peevish, "but Lord knows it's a temptation! Away back before there was any people living in this Hollow and before the ships come across the ocean to this land, the great-grandpappy of my grandpa was foolin' with witchery, and it's in the blood. But I promised—and I aim to cross over Jordan. I won't do a thing."

"Then," says Joe, "I'll get my rifle. Nothing else to do."

His granny thumped the floor with her stick. "You, Joe!" she says, angry, "I didn't say I wouldn't tell you what to do. This is a witchin' family, and there's things come down from long ago. Up in the attic there's one of them. When I burnt my witchin' things I wouldn't touch it because it couldn't be burnt, and after I got religion I wouldn't touch a witch thing excep' to burn it. And it's full of peril. But if your heart is right, you can take it an' fight Ben Harper and he won't never be able to witch nobody any more."

Joe, he says, miserable, "I don't know how right my heart is, but I don't want a thing from Letty, not even a thank you. All I want is to be able to sleep nights and not think of somebody cryin' in the dark because they won't never cross over Jordan, and it my fault."

Joe's granny sniffs and says, "Go up in the attic," she says. "High up where the bricks get narrow, and make a shelf. All the way in back there's a iron box. It's rusty and it's old. You fetch it here."

Joe went and climbed up to the attic. It was crowded with things from past times and long ago. There were boxes with quilts and comforters in them, and a spinning wheel Joe's granny had used when she was a girl, and what might've been a loom.

There was an old bed, all apart, and a flintlock musket, and all the things that pile up in a attic when folks live in the same house for generations. Joe had to step careful, but he got to the chimney, and he reached far back and up high, and he felt a little box all furry with cobwebs. Something ran over his fingers when he stirred it, but he brushed the cobwebs off and went back downstairs.

"There's a ring in that box," says Joe's granny, grim. "It's rusty because it's iron. There's paper in the box hand-writ, and there's no use tryin' to read it. You go outside and put on the ring. Then you can go fight Ben Harper and he can't do a thing to you by his witchin'. If you lick him, he won't never be able to witch no more. But I'm warnin' you, don't never let anybody you love see you while you wear that ring!"

Then Sally spoke, for the only time. Her voice was shaky. "If he—puts it on—can he cross over Jordan after?"

Joe's granny sniffed. "It's outland witchery," she says. "My grandma warned me—she that was never happy again after grandpa saw her wearin' the ring. There's witchery that meant turnin' your back to the Lord, and your heart has to be black to take pleasure in it. But there's witchery that has to be done with a good heart. It's full of peril, because to feel sure your heart is right is presumin' before the Lord. I trust I'm goin' over Jordan, but I know I'm a schemin' old woman and I wouldn't never dare to put on that ring. But Joe," she says, "he's bound and determined, and I wouldn't want to see him hung even for shootin' a witch."

She looked at Joe, stern, and he went out of the house. The box was iron, with designs on it, and he had to hit it a couple of licks with the axhead before the top opened up reluctant. And there was a ring in it, like his granny had said, and there was paper in it—only it wasn't paper but like rabbit skin with the fur off, and old and dry and yellow. He could read the writing, but it was spelled funny and it didn't make sense at all.

"By ye arte of alchymie," was what he made out, "I Thomas Dee, Doctor, have made ye ringe of veritie under ye signe of Saturne, but yt ys a sadde discouerie . . ."

Joe didn't try to read any more. He shut up the box and he put the ring on his finger. It fitted pretty good.

He didn't feel a mite different until he happened to look down at the ground. Then he was scared.

He shivered a minute and took the ring off fast. But then he thought about Letty all alone and itching and aching and crying because she knew she couldn't hold out forever. So he started off toward Ben Harper's cabin, holding the ring tight.

It wasn't far beyond where Letty lived, and the way was near. Tramping through the fallen leaves and pushing aside the bushes, it came to Joe Burchard that Letty'd be strengthened to fight the witchery if she knew his errand. So he turned aside a little and presently there were her folks' cabin on the hillside, with the gray rocks sticking up out of the earth all around. He stepped over the stile and up the sloping pasture, and when he was ten yards from the cabin he hollered.

There wasn't any answer. Not a sound but the clucking of the chickens and a bobwhite somewhere. Joe hollered again.

Still no answer. And then the sweat came out on Joe Burchard all over. It was plain enough. Letty was toilin' over the hills to Ben Harper, crying and wringing her hands as she went because she couldn't help herself.

Joe took out after her. He went fast. He carried the witch ring in his hand, not on his finger, and he vaulted the rail fence of the pasture, and he went running over the slanting ground, and once he stumbled and went crashing into a dead tree that crumbled to dust when he hit it, and then he knew that witchery was working on him to keep him from catching up to Letty to help her. The ring had fallen out of his hand.

It took him minutes to find it again, and Lord knows if he'd been thinking anything but good he wouldn't never have found it at all. He hunted and hunted desperate, and then he says, agonized, "Lord, help Your servant, because I don't want to do this for myself, being the only girl I purely care about is Sally. But I'm the cause of Letty bein' witched—" And there was the witch ring before him, laying on the ground in plain sight. He picked it up and put it on his finger and he run.

He flung through brushwood and he flung through briars. He climbed up steep ways and he slid down slopes. He waded waist-deep in hollows where the leaves had gathered, and he hauled himself up rockfalls by the vines that grew down over them. He came to a place where the path led to Ben Harper's cabin. He turned into that path and he run.

He hadn't gone a quarter of a mile when he saw Letty. She was moving along the path with her hands over her face, and she was crying bitter. There was sobbings that choked her, and sometimes she took down her hands from her face to wring them. And she was gasping, "I don't want to go. . . . I ain't goin'. . . . I'm goin' to stop when I get to that bush. . . . I'm a-goin' to set right down here an' not move a step. . . ."

But she went right on walking, slow and heavy and leaning back and crying, like somebody trying to walk in a freshet. Ben Harper's witching was strong!

Then Joe came up to her, panting, and he says, "Letty!"

And she turned her despairing eyes to him, and she fell down on the path and hid her face. She didn't know him. And Joe remembered that if he was to go near her she'd have a pain in her heart and her breath would stop. There couldn't nobody touch Letty but the one that had witched her. And she didn't know Joe. She lay on the ground, crying and shivering because she'd seen Joe Burchard with the witch ring on his finger, and she took on pitiful. So Joe began to realize how perilous it was to wear this ring, but he went on.

He run on down the path before her, and he brushed through briars and he pushed through brush, and there was Ben Harper's cabin. And Ben Harper sat on the steps before his door.

His eyes glittered and the sunshine seemed to dodge falling on him, and he was a strong, stout man and Joe had put him off to the last to lick, because licking Ben Harper without no witchery would be a hard job. But this was worse. Joe knew right away that he wouldn't have no chance at all without the witch ring.

Ben's eyes were glittering and his mouth was slobbering and he was an awful sight to look at. He'd turned his back on the Lord to have Letty for his own in this life, and he knew she was coming to him. He was waiting for his reward for turning witch, and it was terrible to see. But Joe knew, all of a sudden, that Ben wasn't alone, because right there in his body with him, a-gloating over what Ben thought, a-sharing everything he saw and knew and felt, there was the devil. He was right there in Ben's body, possessing it, and Ben didn't know. But Joe knew, for certain, and he felt almost sorry for Ben. So it was Ben he spoke to.

"Ben," he says, "look at my shadow."

Ben Harper looked—and the devil in his body looked, too. Then he screeched. And then he bounced up and come for Joe like a panther cornered in a henhouse will come for a man that opens the door. The devil in Ben Harper's body knew that he'd got power over any creature that casts a shadow except a man or woman whose heart is right. But he knew, and Ben knew, too, that when somebody that don't cast a shadow stands before him, it's time for the ending of evil and witchery, too. And with the witch ring on his finger, Joe didn't cast no shadow.

Ben Harper was a big man. He wasn't as tall as Joe, but he

was broader. His legs were like tree trunks and his arms were thick with muscle. His eyes glared hate, and his teeth showed like a snarling dog's, and he came panting to fight for his witchery and his meannesses and the pleasures he'd turned witch to have. And the devil stayed in his body to help him. Ben was fighting for Letty, wringing her hands and crying because she couldn't help herself from coming to him. He was fighting for the devil like a preacher fights for the Lord, only he fought with fists and boots and fingers and teeth, biting and gouging and frothing at the mouth because he was fighting for what he'd give up crossing over Jordan for.

And that was a fight! If it wasn't that the witch ring was a good fit on Joe Burchard's finger, Ben woulda got it off and trompled on it, and there would've been nothing left of Joe at all. They fought on the tromped clear space before Ben's cabin door, and they fought in the brush beyond the clearing. They fought into the rail fence around the pigsty, and they knocked it down and they fought in the mud and the mire and the hogs run squealing off into the pine thicket around.

Once Ben got both hands around Joe's throat, and the misty dark shapes all around grew thicker and crowded close. But Joe—with his eyes going black from lack of breath—managed to get hold of just one of Ben's fingers, and he bent it back and broke it, and Ben let go.

And presently they were up, beating at each other with their fists, gasping in each other's faces, and the blows they struck making smacking noises in the stillness that seemed to hold everywhere near by. And Joe felt his knees weakening, and he lurched ahead and gripped Ben around the waist and flung him to the ground, and then he pounded Ben's head on a mite of rock that stuck up out of the ground right there, and he hammered Ben's head on it, and he hammered and he hammered. And Joe must've been mighty dazed by the fighting he'd been through, because he sudden-like heard himself panting. "The Lord is my shepherd—" *Thump!* That was Ben's head on the rock. "I shall not want." *Thump!* "He leadeth me beside the still waters—" *Thump!*

And then Ben give a monstrous shudder and lay still.

He wasn't dead, because he was still breathing, but his eyes were closed and his arms were limp and his fingers hung loose and empty. There wasn't a quiver in him when Joe got up, panting.

He looked all around. The sunshine played over everything

plain and clear. It shone on Ben Harper, and there wasn't any more mistiness anywhere. Joe heard the birds singing. He heard Ben's hogs grunting a little way off, so he panted a while and then heaved Ben up off the ground and carried him into the cabin, so as not to leave him laying like dead for the hogs to find. And in the cabin he saw Something that the devil must've told Ben Harper to make, and Joe Burchard felt mighty sick at his stomach. But he kicked it to pieces and flung it in the fireplace and stirred up the embers to make it burn. And then he knew, from what his granny had told him, that Ben Harper couldn't never be a witch again, no matter what he did. So he'd better try mighty hard to get religion.

Then Joe went out of the cabin and down the path. He saw Letty Smith running away, swarming over fallen logs and running through the brush, with the witching off her so she didn't itch or ache or need to be fearful any more. And she was crying still, but it was with joy, and she'd get to somebody's cabin, crying with gladness, and get them to take her quick to a preacher so she could get religion and nevermore be like she'd been.

But Joe, he headed back to his granny's. It'd been a mighty hard fight. Where he wasn't scratched, he was black and blue. Where he wasn't sore, he stung, and where he didn't sting he ached pretty bad. And he was all wore out. But he started back for his granny's and there was something that his mind clung to. Letty'd seen him, she cried out and fell down an' hid her face. When Ben Harper saw him, he'd screeched and come despairing to fight. And his granny had said for Joe never to let anybody he cared about see him with the ring on his finger. That was a thing Joe had to find out about, being he was twenty-one.

When he came to his granny's cabin, he went past the well. He went up on the porch and he went in the door. And he turned to the mirror that his granny had tacked up on the wall for a proof and a reminder that she'd give up all her witching ways. He looked in that mirror to see what he looked like that he had scared Letty so bad, and made Ben Harper screech and fight. He figured he was going to see something mighty fearful.

But he didn't see a thing. He looked right through his own image and at the wall behind him. He was invisible in the mirror like he didn't cast a shadow in the sun. He stood there, staring at the mirror that didn't show him back at all.

Then his granny says, stern, "You Joe! Take off that there ring! Didn't I tell you not to let nobody see you with it on?"

Joe wrenched it off his finger, and he swallowed. He turned. And there was Sally Walker still setting in the chair where she'd been visiting with his granny. Joe groaned. He stumbled to a chair, and he put his face in his hands and felt like crying while his granny got up and went to get some rags and arnica for the beating he'd got whilst he was licking Ben. And Joe could've cried. He was twenty-one years old and he'd licked every man in a day's walking and he'd fought the devil besides, that day, and he'd won. But Sally Walker'd seen him with the witch ring on his finger and Joe didn't see any good in anything.

Then she said soft and anxious in his ear, "Joe, do you hurt bad anywheres?"

He jumped. He looked at her and she didn't look scared of him. She looked worried, but that was all. And Joe felt so good at seeing that, he went plain out of his head.

His granny's stick, thumping on the floor, brought him back to where he was and made him stop what he was doing.

"Huh!" says his granny, sniffing. "Now you licked every man in a day's walking and kissed every girl but one! Now what're you goin' to do?"

And Joe Burchard grinned like his throat would split, and he didn't mind the hurt at all. He held Sally Walker close and he says, "Granny, I reckon I'm going to settle down an' get married."

And he did. And it was a long time before he learned any more about the witch ring. His granny wouldn't talk about it, and Sally didn't know, but it stayed in Joe's mind. And one day his granny took sick and she looked triumphant because she'd kept her promise to Joe's grandpa and to the Lord, and she knew she'd be going over Jordan. So she lay in her bed, and Joe says:

"Granny," he says, "if you don't tell me I'll never know, and till I know I'll fret. When I was wearing that witch ring I scared Letty Smith and I scared Ben Harper, but when I looked in that mirror I looked right through my image and I couldn't see myself at all. How come?"

His granny grinned at him, laying there in the bed, waiting to pass over Jordan.

"Huh!" she says. "That ring is perilous, honey, because it makes folks see you like you really are. That's what Letty and Ben Harper saw. But no man can't never see himself like he really is, so you couldn't see a dawgoned thing!"

And Joe, he thought it over, and he says, "But you and Sally, you saw me with the witch ring on! You saw me like I really was, and it didn't scare neither of you."

But his granny just sniffed at him, while she looked at him soft—just as soft as Sally ever did. And she says, "You won't understand, honey. But we was two women that purely loved you. So it didn't matter a bit."

And Joe's granny was right. He didn't understand. Never till the day he died.

Malice in Wonderland

by Rufus King

The late (1893–1966) Rufus King was a major contributor to the pulp magazines in the 1920s and beyond. Although he worked primarily in the mystery field he also contributed stories to many other genre publications. He is best remembered for his novels about Lieutenant Valcour, a New York City detective of French Canadian origin. King wrote more than twenty mystery novels as well as four very good story collections, the last of which, The Faces of Danger, *appeared in 1964. He also worked as a playwright, scripting* Murder at the Vanities, *a musical comedy with music by John Green that was produced in New York in 1933.*

When Alice Wickershield was a little girl of nine and still believed in all the childhood wonderlands with their fantasy inhabitants, she was given a birthday party by an old woman whom she firmly considered to be a witch.

Alice frequently remarked to her best friend, Elsie Grunwald, "The tip of Mrs. Fleury's nose almost touches her chin, and that is a sign."

Elsie, who was of a similar age but completely disillusioned as to the fey, would answer practically, "That is because she hates wearing false teeth."

There the matter would drop until some later event would again bring Mrs. Fleury under scrutiny. Naturally, with Mrs. Fleury being the hostess, the birthday party brought the subject of her cabalistic specialty into focus once more.

Alive lived with her father (her mother was dead) in a house of Early-Boom design in the town of Halcyon, on the Florida coast to the north of Miami. Their neighbors on the west were the Grunwalds, whose only child, Elsie, was Alice's best friend; and on the other side was the sorceress with her old-fashioned, galleried home appropriately shrouded in dank grounds of somber tropical plantings.

The birthday party was in late June, and as school was over for the season, the festivities were able to get under way shortly after the noon hour with a series of mildly competitive games under the palm and ficus trees that smothered the grounds with their shade. It was at the conclusion of the games and the distribution of prizes, with each of the children miraculously having won one, that luncheon was served on the patio and Mrs. Fleury's witchery meshed into gear and determined, eleven years later, the question of Alice's fate.

Dessert for the luncheon was a delicious treat put up especially for Mrs. Fleury by a local company. It consisted of ice-cream tropical fish of various flavors and colors with each mold resting artistically on a foamy wave of spun sugar. At the side of each plate with its chill confection was a cracker bonbon, or snapper, that went bang when its ends were sharply pulled and which contained a favor and a strip of paper on which was printed a motto, that was presumed to shed a prophetic light on the puller's future.

"Children," Mrs. Fleury said, while these final temptations were being placed on the table, "I am going to command a test for your powers of self-control—Jefferson Hollingsworth, put down that cracker bonbon until you hear what I have to say."

"This is *it*," whispered Alice to Elsie. "Look at her chin."

Mrs. Fleury waited until Jefferson Hollingsworth, a handsome youngster with liquid chestnut eyes, reluctantly replaced his snapper beside a frozen version of a pistachio-and-raspberry carp.

"I am going to ask that each little guest take his or her cracker bonbon home, and that you do not tear it open until some moment of the most *desperate nature* may come to you during your lifetimes. As you know, the crackers conceal a printed motto and it is my wish for you—and for Alice in particular because it is her birthday anniversary—that the message conveyed in the motto shall guide you during this future crisis of either joy or sorrow to do the right, the happy thing."

"She is asking one hell of a lot from kids," Harold Grunwald said to his wife Sidonia after Elsie had returned from the party and reported the odd incident. "I'd say the old bat has lost her marbles."

"Well," Sidonia laughed, "it was too much for Elsie, and where that child gets her I.Q. from I wouldn't know. She produced a logical enough crisis out of a hat."

"She gets her I.Q. from me. At her age I had mastered the Morse code in preparation for becoming an international spy, and last month I merely mentioned the fact and Elsie picked out Mata Hari as her dream career in womanhood and can already take six words a minute in Morse. She uses her pal Alice as a receiving set."

"So that's why they've been tapping on things and looking remote."

"It is, and what's this about a logical crisis?"

"Just that Elsie opened her cracker bonbon before she even set foot in the house. She claimed the rich food at the party made her feel critically bilious, so she ripped out the motto."

"And what was the prophetic suggestion? Citrate of magnesia?"

"No, it was a rather horrid quotation from Shakespeare. *Open, locks, whoever knocks!*"

"What's so horrible in that?"

Sidonia, who was tons more intellectual than her husband (she had majored in English at Barry College), said, "It doesn't give the entire quotation. It's simply taken out of context."

"Put it back in again."

"It goes, *By the prickling of my thumbs, something wicked this way comes. Open, locks, whoever knocks!*"

Mr. Grunwald, becoming bored with the matter and wanting to get on with the Do-It-Yourself parakeet cage he was making, said, "All that superstitious rubbish is silly."

"I don't know. I honestly don't know, Hal. Sometimes I wonder."

Two weeks later Elsie, while presumably stitching up a ball costume for her favorite doll in the seclusion of the Grunwald's alamanda-draped gazebo, totally disappeared.

With the exception of Alice, all the children had followed Elsie's impulse and torn open their favors. They had read the time-weary little mottoes, been momentarily captivated by the tissue-paper hats, the modest souvenirs, and then had thrown the whole works into a wastebasket and out of their minds.

Not Alice.

Because she still believed in the wondrous, Alice had put her cracker bonbon in her treasure chest—a cardboard show box fancifully pasted over with Christmas wrappings—along with her diary, a dried toadstool highly favored as a parasol by elves, and sundry other articles of enduring sentiment.

It was only natural that being her most intimate companion, Alice should have been questioned more patiently and closely than any of the other children after Elsie had ''gone away''—that phrasing being considered as best suitable by their elders to cover the desperately serious reality. Alice bore the questioning stoically and only broke down once, when she asked Mrs. Grunwald whether she might keep the doll's ball gown that Elsie had been sewing on in the gazebo to remember Elsie by.

''But Elsie is coming back, dear,'' Sidonia said, restraining by the greatest willpower her own tears of torture and doubt.

''No, she isn't, Mrs. Grunwald. She was put under a spell by Mrs. Fleury and that's the end of her.''

''A spell, Alice?'' Sidonia repeated as her eyes narrowed speculatively that herein might lie some clue, however preposterous, to the fate of her lost child. ''What do you mean by a spell, dear?''

''Mrs. Fleury is a witch and Elsie disobeyed her *express command* by opening her cracker bonbon on such a silly excuse. A stomachache is not a crisis.''

Alice left the interview, taking with her the doll's unfinished ball gown with its needle and length of unused thread still stuck in lemonade-colored satin. She wrapped the dress around her own cracker bonbon, as both seemed to be linked in their special magical field, and returned them to the treasure chest where they were to lie fallow in their diablerie for many years to come.

When Hal Grunwald came home that night after a harrowing day spent with the police, the sheriff's deputies, and the road patrols, all of whom were searching for Elsie during this second day of her disappearance, Sidonia told him what Alice had said about Mrs. Fleury being a witch and he hit the ceiling.

He then collapsed dog-tired into a chair and held his hot head in his hands and said, ''Oh, my God, Sid, you could listen to childish drivel while we're moving heaven and earth to find her.''

''I'd listen to any sort of drivel if I thought it would do any good. After all, Hal, what *do* we know about Mrs. Fleury?''

''We know what she has told us.''

''That's exactly what I mean about our life here. The friends we make come from all over the country and we don't know a thing about them except what they tell us themselves.''

Sidonia, who had been holding her control by superhuman effort during the past tragical days and nights, grew hysterical, and her voice broke in odd high notes.

''We exercise more judgment about our servants than we do about our friends,'' she went on with those shrillish overtones. ''We check servants, look up references—why, they even have police cards of identity! But our friends? We let our children associate with them and we don't know *what they are.* Mrs. Fleury? From Cleveland, she says—widowed—her husband left her well off—and we smile and swallow it. She might be a mass poisoner for all we know! Alice claims she's a witch and you laugh. Well, a child's judgment might be better than our judgment. A child's eyes see things clearly, not through a fog of polite social conventions.''

"Sid, knock it off, will you? We're both carrying all the traffic will bear without getting sidetracked into black magic.''

The ransom note came that night.

With the vivid ears of childhood, Alice arranged all the fragments of overheard talks between her father and his friends into a factual whole. A ransom had been demanded, $50,000 had been paid, and Elsie still had not returned home.

"She can't," Alice said to Sidonia when they met by chance at the hibiscus border that divided the Wickershield and Grunwald properties. "She can't come back because she's dead.''

"Darling, don't say it. Oh, don't even think it!'' Sidonia plunged through the hedge and getting down on her knees gripped Alice's hands so hard that the bones felt all together. "You must tell me—I am begging this of you, Alice—isn't there something you know? Something real?''

"Witches are real.''

Sidonia looked at the child searchingly, half convinced in the torture-ridden uncertainties of her cracking mind that the fateful motto just might have had something to do with their loss.

"You really believe that, Alice, don't you?''

"It's dangerous not to.''

"Then destroy it. Burn your cracker bonbon. Get it now and burn it up.''

"I can't.''

"Why not?''

"Because it isn't time.''

So intense is the power of public opinion that Mrs. Fleury began feeling it on all sides—to the extent that she concluded the only answer lay in selling her place and leaving Halcyon.

The children beleaguered her with cries from a safe distance of *witch-witch-witch,* and the elders forming her circle of friends were electrically artificial in their greetings and perfunctory smiles.

Even the police thoroughly checked her whereabouts during the hour when Elsie had been sewing by herself in the gazebo. They handled the inquiry discreetly, of course, and no mention of it was made public officially; but the fact was shortly general knowledge that Mrs. Fleury had an ironclad alibi. She had been undergoing the rack of a hair and facial treatment at the shop of Halcyon's best and most talkative beautician.

In Alice's opinion this absolute alibi was futile for a witch, they being a breed notoriously famous for their astral ability to be in two different places at the same time, and she announced as much to the other children, who promptly stepped up their campaign of torment instead of dropping it.

Mrs. Fleury was unable to fight back, any more than she could have fought the invisible vapors from a swamp with her bare fists. Fortunately she found a ready buyer for her home in Dr. Jessup Hollingsworth, whose adopted son Jefferson had had to be cautioned at the birthday party against a premature snapping of his cracker bonbon.

Since coming to Halcyon over a year ago, Dr. Hollingsworth had been living with Jeff in the sterile splendor of a beach hotel. The doctor had reached the age of retirement and wanted to settle down.

"I want roots," he said to Haidee Glosser in her real estate office in town. "Not so much for myself as for Jefferson. My wife's tragic death made it impossible to continue living in our former home in New York."

"I understand," Miss Glosser murmured with sympathy while mentally pocketing a fat commission for the Fleury estate.

Within less than a week the deal was closed. Mrs. Fleury moved to the west coast and settled in St. Petersburg, which was, so far as east coast Floridians were concerned, as far away as the moon.

And Alice acquired a new best friend.

She and young Jeff Hollingsworth were classmates in elementary school, it was true, but there had been none of the special affinity that goes with a friendship on a next-door basis, once the initial ice of propinquity is melted—and at the age of nine the thaw comes fast.

"How do you like being adopted?" Elsie asked during the preliminaries.

"There's not much feeling about it," Jeff said.

"What happened to your adopted mother?"

"Foster mother."

"Foster. Thank you."

"Don't mention it. She was killed by a hit-and-run driver right after my adoption papers went through. I only remember her looks."

"What did she look like?"

"Like anybody."

"What are you going to be, Jeff, when you grow up?"

"A botanist."

"Why?"

"Because plants and trees and flowers are important. They can be like people, only nicer. I've got leaves and specimens of about almost everything around here. Each one is dried and labeled from where I found it."

"Have you ever met any elves while you were gathering them?"

"No."

"Do you believe in them, Jeff?"

"Maybe."

Inevitably, as the years of childhood and the ensuing 'teens dreamed by, Alice and Jeff drew more seriously toward each other in their affections, and only Sidonia Grunwald of the people who knew them tried to put a damper on the intimacy.

Sidonia had never given up, nor would she, no matter how earnestly Hal begged her to resign herself to the inevitable. Elsie was gone but they, he said, were left and had their lives together to be lived.

"She isn't gone," Sidonia would say with a kind of fierceness. "She's someplace."

Yes, Hal would think in his own emptiness, Elsie was some place all right, and a stomach-wrenching vision would come to him of their darling's small bones lying unshrived in some secret desolation of the everglades or under the water of rockpits or hyacinth-smothered canals, year after lonely year in their whitening.

"I cannot get it out of my head," Sidonia would say wildly, "that that place, that that woman had something to do with it."

"I wish you'd stop poking around over there. I know you do at night, and apart from the fact that I'm sure it annoys Doctor Hollingsworth, it just isn't healthy, Sid."

"You can't be healthy with an empty heart."

This fixed idea formed the basis for Sidonia's corroding reaction to the romance between Alice, whom she feverishly loved because there seemed to cling to the girl a lingering of her lost Elsie, and young Jeff. Actually, Sidonia was a little deranged on the subject, feeling herself constantly drawn to the old Fleury grounds (she never thought of it as the Hollingsworth place), and it was true, as Hal said, that she would steal over there and search around beneath its dank canopies especially when the moon was full.

She had convinced herself of the half-dented syllogism that the grounds were under a curse, therefore Jeff and his foster father, since they lived within the influence of their baleful star, were also accursed. Sidonia wanted no part of this disastrous magic to rub off on Alice, not even through the medium of young love.

The college years brought no hiatus in the serious intentions between Alice and Jeff. She went to Barry in Miami Shores and he attended the University of Miami in nearby Coral Gables. There Jeff delved deeply into the structure, physiology, and distribution of the members of the vegetable kingdom, with an ultimate aim of specializing in plant morphology. With this broadened knowledge Jeff, among later interests, had carefully emended his collections of boyhood specimens which were still methodically kept on file in the small laboratory he had equipped at home.

Rather because she wanted to be near him than from any curiosity about botany, Alice would often stay with Jeff in the laboratory while he worked, and one day when he was reclassifying some specimens of his childhood collection, her interest was caught by a closely set cluster of fine slender branches.

"It looks like a little broom, Jeff."

"It should. It's *hexenbesen*, more commonly known as witches'-broom."

The name aroused stirrings of many years ago.

"Did you find it here? When Mrs. Fleury owned the place?"

"Not actually."

He had picked it up, Jeff told her, from his foster father's bedroom floor in the beach hotel they had then been staying at. He imagined it must have fallen from a cuff of Dr. Hollingsworth's trousers when he had taken them off the night before.

"I remember asking him about it. It's an unusual find and I wanted to trace its source. It's an outgrowth caused by a plant parasite or fungus."

"Did you?"

"Did I what?"

"Trace its source?"

"Not until after we'd moved here."

Dr. Hollingsworth had told him, when questioned, that he might have picked it up while looking over the grounds with the real estate agent just before purchasing them.

"I finally located it," Jeff said, "after we'd moved in and I'd remembered that witches'-brooms sometimes appear on ferns—low enough to be caught in a cuff."

"So it did come from here. Funny."

"Why funny?"

"Don't you remember our thinking old Mrs. Fleury was a witch? At least I certainly did."

"All kids think crazy stuff."

"I know it and I realize now what a little fool I was about it. I'd like to see Mrs. Fleury again and tell her I'm sorry for having caused her to be pestered, for making her give up her home, really. Jeff—I wonder if she's still alive?"

"What makes you say that?"

"Just a feeling. A funny feeling, Jeff."

They were to be married shortly after graduation, and Mr. Wickershield, Alice's father, finally persuaded Sidonia in her self-assumed role of proxy mother to Alice to handle all the intricate arrangements for the wedding.

"I still feel," Sidonia said to Hal after she had reluctantly consented to Mr. Wickershield's urging, "that it is a mistake. It's—it's sinister, malign."

"Oh, please, Sid!"

Hal had grown stout and comfortable, and instead of continuing to be sympathetic he was getting irritated with what he thought of as Sidonia's perpetual mania and her occasional Ophelia-like nocturnal driftings around the old Fleury grounds. He had loved their lost Elsie with all his heart and he still loved her memory, but grief cannot live forever. If it did, he thought philosophically, all life on earth would die.

Dr. Hollingsworth, in his role of foster father, arranged the bachelor dinner for Jeff at a beach club of correct splendor, the groom's gift for the best man and the ushers being platinum cufflinks from Tiffany, the food and the wines compatible; and Jeff, whose familiarity with champagne was only on a nodding basis, got socked straight into left field. Unfortunately he remained on his feet, his talk was intelligible, and his good night to the doorman who brought his car sounded (as the doorman later testified) all right.

A milkman making his delivery shortly after sunup to the rear of Dr. Hollingsworth's house found Sidonia lying crumpled under the hibiscus that edged the driveway to the garage. He was not a man to panic, thanks to Korea, and having determined that she was still alive, he roused the house. All that is, but Jeff, who was still sprawled fully dressed across his bed in stuporous sleep.

. . . In the news of local interest [a Fort Lauderdale newscaster announced] the Halcyon police report an alleged drunk-driving accident on the grounds of Dr. Jessup Hollingsworth, formerly the old Fleury estate. The victim is a Mrs. Grunwald, a nearby neighbor whose daughter Elsie was kidnapped a decade ago and presumably killed by her abductor after a ransom of $50,000 had been paid. The old kidnapping case remains unsolved. According to her husband and her close friends, this tragedy continued to prey on Mrs. Grunwald and caused her to take walks at night around the Hollingsworth grounds which, they say, she associated in some fashion with her child's disappearance. The police believe that she was on such an excursion last night when Dr. Hollingsworth's adopted son Jefferson drove home from a bachelor dinner in a drunken condition and struck her. James Cray, 2714 Northeast Hempstead Court, who delivers the morning milk, found her lying under an hibiscus hedge where she had been flung by the impact. She is now at Memorial and her condition is critical . . .

The world came to an end but Alice did not break down. With Jeff released under a $5,000 bail bond, Sidonia's life spun on with a thread above the valley of death. Alice would make Jeff sit out the foreboding hours with her in the privacy of the Grunwalds' alamanda-draped gazebo where they were reasonably sheltered from the press and even from their friends. When evening fell each would go home to face the night with such courage as could be summoned.

"I don't suppose," Alice's father said to her, cupping the mouthpiece of a telephone on the second night following the accident, "that you would care to talk with her? She's peculiarly insistent."

"Who, Papa?"

"That woman who used to live next to us. You remember, a Mrs. Fleury. She's calling from St. Petersburg."

Alice rushed to the phone.

"Alice, dear child," Mrs. Fleury's (again) familiar voice came from the receiver, "I have been reading all about it and you will think me a silly old woman but I felt compelled to telephone. I want to ask you just one question."

"Yes, Mrs. Fleury?"

"Call me a superstitious old fool if you wish—I remember how you were childishly positive I was a witch," Mrs. Fleury paused to give a forgiving, paperish little laugh, "and perhaps I *am* one, because while I was reading about your fiancé's critical predicament, the most singular, almost clairvoyant vision popped into my mind. It made me feel exactly like one of the weird sisters and I simply leaped on my witch's broom and flew to call you up. Now tell me, Alice, do you remember the birthday party?''

"Of course, Mrs. Fleury."

"Do you recall the cracker bonbons and my nonsensically mysterious instructions about them?''

"Yes."

"Well, do you by the wildest chance still have yours?''

"Yes."

"Is it still unopened?''

"Yes."

"Then open it now."

And the wire went dead.

Alice felt her father still standing near the telephone, with Mr. Wickershield silently wondering just what the call had been all about in order to have affected his daughter in such an odd manner.

"I swear to you, Hal," he told Harold Grunwald afterward, "she positively drifted from the room as if she'd been put under a spell. . . ."

The cardboard treasure chest with its Christmas wrappings of holly gold and stars had for years been lying undisturbed in the bottom drawer of a dresser in Alice's room.

Alice got it out and put it on a desk where the shaft from a metal cone-shaded lamp made startling the colors' holiday brilliance. With a reluctance that combined the fear ever present when brushing the unnatural, and a hope that she did not dare feel too strongly because of the impossible qualities that draped it, she took out the cracker bonbon in its covering of the doll's ball gown, and pushed the treasure chest aside.

Then in her sudden eagerness Alice felt a finger pricked by the needle which was still caught in what had been Elsie's last stitch, and a drop of blood stained a pea-sized circle of red on the lemonade-colored satin of the little dress. Alice removed the dress and with no further ado took both ends of the cracker bonbon and pulled them sharply apart. The report, to her now more adult ears, produced but a trivial effect.

With a scissors she slit the white paper cover, and discarding a gay red paper hat and a miniature metal fire engine, she came at last to the strip of paper on which the motto was printed. An ugly wave of disappointment engulfed Alice as she read it. She had been expecting something truly prophetic—like Elsie's *Open*, *locks, whoever knocks!* which she later had learned had been out of dire context.

The motto dropped from her fingers and came to rest on the ball gown beside the needle. Beside the drop of blood. She had hoped so much, Alice now admitted to herself—she had been hoping all along with her desperate heart for some sign—and now all her hopes had come to this childlike ending of—of—

Her eyes darted from the motto to the blood drop, to the needle, to the line of stitches, in the last one of which the needle had been left. Clear under the cone-shafted light, they were visible in their good straight line. There was only one thing the matter with it, Alice decided critically. The line ran diagonally across the front panel of the gown and therefore, from a dressmaker's point of view, not only served no purpose but was the act of a seamstress gone suddenly mad.

Never would Elsie, as Alice remembered her lost best friend, with her fine capabilities in so many of the childhood arts, have been guilty of such botchery. Unless it were purposely done. And rarely had anything ever been done by Elsie that lacked purpose.

Alice's pulse quickened as a ripple of strange excitement caught her brain, and she examined more closely the misplaced line of stitching. Not only was the line misplaced but the stitches themselves were uneven in their spacing—another unthinkable thing for Elsie to have done.

Unless, again, it were *purposely* done.

So steeped was Alice in the flood made by the years rolled back that Elsie became real—with their best-friend loveship and all their secrets of shattering importance and their fearless preparations for facing the entrancing vistas of adult life to come. Yes, Alice remembered, their last projected career had been to become Mata Hari, with all her fascinating background of international intrigue.

And for which they had both learned the Morse code.

Her eyes flew to the line of unevenly spaced stitches. Dots and dashes, sewn in chartreuse thread on lemonade-colored satin. The pencil in her fingers automatically put the letters down on the spread-open white paper wrapper of the cracker bonbon. DRHOLCRZYHLPM—then nothing more.

So intense, so feverish, was Alice's excitement that little meant anything to her but that here was Elsie's last message on earth, and that within it undoubtedly lay a clue to her disappearance and, according to Mrs. Fleury, a help in Jeff's and Alice's present deadly crisis.

Taking the ball gown with her and leaving the rest of the

magical properties on the desk, with her heart going suffocatingly in hopeful thumps, Alice ran from her room and out of the house with no thought in her head other than to find and tell Jeff.

A lamp was lighted on the lower front gallery of the old Fleury house, and Dr. Hollingsworth was seated beside it in a wicker chair. He was smoking a cigar and reading.

"Alice, dear girl!" he said as she rushed up the steps and paused breathless before him. His professional training took a clinical look at her eyes, at the tremor in her fingers that held, as if with an ague, the edge of a piece of satin. "You have had a shock."

"Yes, Doctor—this."

He took it from her outstretched hand.

"It looks like—it's a doll's dress, isn't it?"

"It's the one Elsie was sewing on in the gazebo just before she disappeared."

"Elsie? Oh, of course—the little Grunwald girl."

"I must show it to Jeff!"

"But why?"

"There is a message stitched on it in Morse code. We had both learned the code together. It's Elsie's last message, Doctor—"

"Amazing!"

Alice took the gown from his fingers and said, "I'll go right in, if you don't mind, and tell Jeff."

"He isn't home."

Delay was a blow.

"Do you know where he is?"

"No. Jeff has been taking long walks these nights. Alone. Trying to knock himself out physically so that he can get some sleep. Alice, sit down. Since you can't tell Jeff, tell me."

This Alice did, from the birthday party down to the call from Mrs. Fleury and the motto and the stitches in Morse.

"What was your father's reaction? Is he getting in touch with the sheriff?"

"He knows nothing about it. It hit me so hard, Doctor, that I simply raced over here to tell Jeff. If I'd met Father on the way out I'd naturally have told him, but I didn't."

"What did the message say, Alice?"

"I haven't decoded it yet," Alice said, "because I'm waiting to do it with Jeff. I'm certain it will give us a clue to Elsie's kidnapping, and I know this sounds fantastic but I honestly believe that Mrs. Fleury is right and that it will help Jeff, too. Do you think that sentimental, Doctor?"

"Not that you feel that way, no. As I recall it, you were

firmly convinced that Mrs. Fleury was a witch. I'd simply say that your subconscious was getting in a few old licks.''

"I'm almost ready to believe in her sorcery again, Doctor. Take her telephoning, the cracker bonbon and the motto—she even *spoke* of a witch's broom—oh, it's not only Mrs. Fleury herself, it's the whole atmosphere of this place where she lived.''

"Witch's broom?''

"Yes. Witches'-broom is a growth that looks like a little broom. Of course you don't remember, but you caught some in the cuff of your trousers when you were looking over the grounds here with the real estate agent, and Jeff found it on the floor of your bedroom in the hotel.''

"Yes, now I do remember him asking me about it, and I remember that when he moved in here he located the spot it came from. A clump of ferns. Serpent ferns, I think he called them.''

"Do you remember where they are?''

"I believe so, in a general way. They're back quite a distance in this tropical jungle. Why?''

"I want to go there. Could we go there, Doctor? Now? While we're waiting for Jeff?''

"I suppose we could. But why?''

"I don't know why. This is crazy, but it's almost as if Mrs. Fleury were urging me to.''

Dr. Hollingsworth looked at Alice judicially, as if he were trying to determine a proper course of therapy for her very evident emotional state.

"You are overstrung, Alice. The walk might be good for you at that.''

"Then you'll show me?''

"I'll get a flashlight,'' Dr. Hollingsworth said.

Mr. Wickershield had been in the library selecting a book for a quiet hour's reading when he was conscious, as he thought, of a screen door slamming. Alice? Scarcely. Alice did not allow screen doors to slam. Still, that phone call from Mrs. Fleury had—just what had it done? Sort of knocked her for a loop, he decided.

Mr. Wickershield left the library and rapped on Alice's door, then went inside. She wasn't there. The only light on was the desk lamp with its cone of brilliance from the metal shade. Inescapably, his attention was drawn to the doll and to the flattened wrapper of the cracker bonbon. He went to the desk and he sat down. Clearly, vividly, as though it were today, recognition came and he recalled the whole grim episode, of the birthday party, the kidnapping of Elsie, and of that child of nine who had believed in the wondrous and was now his grown-up daughter Alice.

Something was missing. Of course, the doll dress that Elsie had been sewing and in which Alice had wrapped the cracker bonbon. Had she taken it with her when, judging from the screen door slam, she had pelted from the house? To show Jeff? Most likely.

The end of the motto strip was exposed beneath the cracker bonbon wrapper and he pulled it out. He reread it. Thoughtfully, he read it again.

Mr. Wickershield had served in Army Intelligence during the war, and his brain was experienced in appraisal and deduction well beyond that of an untrained man. Alice had found some clue in the doll's dress to Elsie's disappearance and had rushed over to discuss it with Jeff—that line of deduction was almost obvious.

He then recalled the children's plunge into Morse code—so the connection between the motto and some probable stitching on the doll dress and the penciled letters on the paper wrapper suggested itself at once.

His experience with decoding in Intelligence had been superficial, but he saw immediately that this message—that must, he thought, have been stitched with such haste and yet such care, and under God knew what a pall of terror—was scarcely a code at all.

Ice sluggished his blood as he read it, and as he started out at a brisk pace for the Grunwald house to pick up Hal.

The flashlight was powerful—one of those two-foot, heavy, cylindrical cases that could throw a beam an eighth of a mile, much farther than was needed for the job on hand.

"Well, there it is," Dr. Hollingsworth said. "The serpent ferns and the witches'-broom. Tell me, Alice, what really made you want to come here? I don't mind admitting that I am interested in extrasensory perception, but in all actuality I'm an out-and-out realist. Putting Mrs. Fleury's alleged witchery aside, why did you want to come?"

"Because there is something here."

"What?"

"Doctor, I don't know. That it is connected with Elsie I *do* know, even though I don't know the reason."

Alice parted the serpent ferns and took several hesitant steps within the large, lush clump.

"No need to be definite," Dr. Hollingsworth said. "Just tell me what you feel?"

"I feel a grave. I feel it is Elsie's, but I can't explain."

Dr. Hollingsworth moved the light shaft from the serpent ferns full upon Alice's face.

"That answer is simple, Alice," he said. "You are standing on it now."

Both Mr. Wickershield and Hal had wasted no time. To reach the steps of the old Fleury house front gallery was but a matter of minutes. Hal knocked on the screen door, through which they could see a dimly lighted stretch of empty hall. They waited a moment, then went inside.

"Anybody home?" Hal shouted, his voice unnaturally loud under the pressure of their dangerous urgency.

A door at the end of the hallway opened and Jeff came out.

"Who's shouting?" he said. "Oh—oh, hello. I've been working in my lab and I thought the house was coming down."

"Where is the Doctor?" Mr. Wickershield asked tensely.

"I left him reading on the gallery about an hour ago. I've been shut up in the lab since then. Why?"

"Where's Alice?"

"I've no idea. Why?"

"She ran over here to see you. Ten or fifteen minutes ago."

"Then where is she? I never heard a thing in the lab until your shout. What's the matter? What's happened?"

Mr. Wickershield explained tersely, while blood receded from Jeff's face in an ebbing tide.

"Where would he have taken her?" Mr. Wickershield asked.

"We'll search the grounds," Jeff said.

Pinned like a specimen bug in the harsh shaft of the flashlight, still having no knowledge of what Elsie's last message had meant, but no longer needing that knowledge now that the implication in Dr. Hollingsworth's statement about the grave was so plain, every muscle in Alice strained toward flight. But her control was gone. She stood like a statue among the serpent ferns, marbleized by shock and fright.

"You killed Elsie," she said, in someone else's voice.

"Yes."

"But you had everything. Money—position— Why?"

"I had no money. I had spent the small fortune I killed my wife for. I needed more."

"Your wife—then it wasn't a hit-and-run?"

"No. It was arranged."

"But Elsie—a little child—"

"I suggest you think of her rather in terms of fifty thousand dollars. A sum I have pyramided through legitimate business channels into a comfortable fortune. There was no need to continue with crime. Only Sidonia Grunwald's erratic prying around here offered a threat. Well, an appropriate opportunity presented itself and I took advantage of it."

"You involved Jeff. You are making him pay. Don't you love him? If you don't, if you never have, why did you adopt him?"

"For a front."

"Front?"

"Like the flower shops the Chicago gangsters used to run. Gave them a legitimate surface of respectability. Jeff did that for me."

"How?"

"As a son he gave me the desirable standing of being a family man, a good, kind father to a well-brought-up boy. A lone bachelor, or a widower, is always an object of speculative curiosity, whereas a father with a child is hardly ever suspected. Having reached my goal, however, Jeff became expendable."

"You arranged it so that they would believe he had hit Mrs. Grunwald."

"Of course. He stopped the car and passed out at the start of the driveway. Sidonia was going on with her act that night. I trailed her as I usually had, heard the car, saw Jeff's condition as he slumped over the wheel, and appreciated the perfect setup." Dr. Hollingsworth added matter-of-factly, "Before arranging her in the condition in which she was found I hit her with this flashlight."

Although the moon was at the full its blue-white brightness rinsed but sparsely through the tropical overhead as Jeff led the way.

"Move quietly so as not to startle him," Mr. Wickershield warned, the words thick from dread. "There may still be time."

Shortly, Jeff stopped.

"They're over there," he said. "Step here and you can see the beam from his flashlight—there, through that break in the shrubs."

Mr. Wickershield moved beside Jeff and saw it—saw it focused on Alice's rigid face.

Then saw it go out.

"Run for it!" he said.

It was Jeff who caught Dr. Hollingsworth's upraised arm before the torch could crash down again. . . .

The following evening, feeling somewhat like Madame Récamier with her famous levees à la chaise longue, Alice lay on a bamboo counterpart in the company of her father, Jeff, and Bill Duggan, chief investigator for the sheriff's department. Hal was at Memorial with Sidonia, who had passed the crisis and was given by the doctors a more than excellent chance for complete recovery.

Alice herself was fairly over the effects from the blow of the flashlight that had landed glancingly on her head before Jeff had put an end to the murderous attack.

"Evidence?" Duggan was saying. "We're glutted with it. The District Attorney looks like a canary-stuffed cat. That ransom note, the one the Grunwalds got eleven years ago, was still on file. The B.C.I. boys knew back then that it was written on a blank leaf torn from a book. From some particular book among the hundreds of thousands within the area, so that got them noplace. Now it does. Once the message stitched on the doll dress put the finger on him, Dr. Hollingsworth's library was inspected and the leaf was found to have been torn from a book on forensic medicine—a reference work he would have hesitated to throw away, even if he hadn't felt so sure of himself. Even the printing on the note, although he tried to disguise it, had been identified by an expert graphologist as being his."

"Did the witches'-broom help?" Alice asked. "The specimen Jeff kept?"

"Definitely. It puts him at the grave."

"Why do you suppose he picked that special spot?" Jeff asked.

"He told me. It's all down in his statement. He picked the Fleury grounds because, for one thing, they were handy. After a very bad attempt at trying to wheedle Elsie into going to a movie with him, and obviously frightening her enough by his manner and insistence into stitching her message for help, he killed her. Then he carried her from the gazebo, and the large clump of serpent ferns hid her nicely until he buried her in the center of them that night. Naturally, he could move about freely. There was no earthly reason why any suspicion would point to him."

"Wouldn't the everglades have been safer?" Mr. Wickershield asked. "Some far-off place?"

"He said he thought of that, then he thought that if the body ever were discovered under the ferns, Mrs. Fleury herself would provide an excellent suspect, what with her somewhat odd habits. Of course, he didn't know then that she had a perfect alibi. Nobody knew, until a couple of days later after we had turned up the fact that she was in the beauty shop."

"I can see why he bought the place as soon as it was put up for sale," Mr. Wickershield said. "He wouldn't want other tenants to have it. Their possible ideas on altering the landscaping could conceivably have uncovered the grave. I can even see how he might have got a perverted kick out of it, although Sidonia's prowlings must have kept him somewhat on edge."

"No, they kind of amused him for a while, but the night he fixed up the drunk-driving deal on Jeff was different. He felt it was time to call quits. You see, he'd been tailing her as usual and she did something that night she had never done before. Signed her own death warrant, you might say."

"What was it?"

"She went into the utility room by the garage and came out with a shovel."

Much later at night Duggan got home and told his wife all about it.

"Like a fairy tale," he said. "Only a damn grim one. Take that coded message, and the uncanny way the motto pointed toward the sewing on the doll dress. Here—here's a copy. Mr. Wickershield spotted it right off as simple contraction."

Mrs. Duggan looked at the slip of paper.

DRHOLCRZYHLPM

DR/HOL/CRZY/HLP/M

DOCTOR HOLLINGSWORTH

CRAZY HELP ME

"And the motto?" she asked.

"A stitch in time saves nine."

Operation Salamander

by Poul Anderson

*Poul Anderson has been entertaining readers of high-quality science fiction and fantasy for more than thirty-five years. He has consistently combined excellent writing with interesting ideas, and is still going strong. His many honors include six Hugoes, two Nebulas, and the Tolkien Memorial Award. He also served as President of the Science Fiction Writers of America and was Guest of Honor at the World Science Fiction Convention in 1959. He has worked effectively at all story lengths, but he excels at the novella. Among his fantasy works he is best known for two wonderful novels—*Three Hearts and Three Lions *(1961) and* A Midsummer's Tempest *(1974).*

The sky was full of broomsticks and the police were going nuts trying to handle the traffic. The Homecoming game always attracts an overflow crowd, also an overflow of high spirits. These I did not share. I edged my battered pre-war Chevvy past a huge 200-dragonpower Lincoln with sky-blue handle, polyethylene straw, and blatting radio. It sneered at me, but I got to the vacant rack first. Dismounting, I pocketed the runekey and mooched glumly through the mob.

The Weather Bureau kachinas are obliging about game nights. There was a cool crisp tang to the air, and dry leaves scrittled across the sidewalks. A harvest moon was rising like a big yellow pumpkin over the darkened buildings of Trismegistus University. I thought of Midwestern fields and woods, damp earthy smells and streaming mists, out beyond the city, and the wolf part of me wanted to be off and away after jackrabbits. But with proper training a were can control his reflexes, and polarized light doesn't have to cause more than a primitive tingle along his nerves.

For me, the impulse was soon lost in bleaker thoughts. Ginny, my darling! She should have been walking beside me, face lifted to the wind and long hair crackling in the thin frost; but the only consolation I had was an illegal hip-flask. Why the hell was I attending the game anyhow?

Passing Teth Caph Sameth frat house, I found myself on the campus proper. Trismegistus was founded after the advent of modern science, and its layout reflects that fact. The largest edifice houses the Language Department, because exotic tongues are necessary for the more powerful spells (which is why so many African and Asian students come here to learn American slang); but there are two English halls, one for the arts college and one for Engineering Poetics. Nearby is the Therianthropology Building, which always has interesting displays of foreign technique: this month it was Eskimo, in honor of the visiting agekok Dr. Ayingalak. A ways off is Zoology, carefully isolated inside its pentagonal fence, for some of those long-legged beasties are not pleasant neighbors. The medical school has a shiny new research center, courtesy of the Rockefeller Foundation, from which have already come such stunning advances as the polaroid filter-lenses that make it possible for those afflicted with the Evil Eye to lead normal lives.

Only the law school is unaffected. Their work has always been of the other world.

Crossing the Mall, I went by the grimy little Physical Sciences Building just in time for Dr. Griswold to hail me. He came puttering down the steps, a small wizened fellow with goatee and merry blue eyes. Somewhere behind their twinkle lay a look of hurt bafflement, as of a child who could never quite understand why no one else was really interested in his toys.

"Ah, Mr. Matuchek," he said. "Are you attending the game?"

I nodded, not especially wanting company, but he tagged along and I had to be sociable. Not that I was apple-polishing—I was in his chemistry and physics classes, but they were snaps. I simply didn't have the heart to rebuff a nice, lonely old geezer.

"Me too," he went on. "I understand the cheerleaders have planned something spectacular between halves."

"Yeh?"

He cocked his head and gave me a birdlike glance. "If there is any difficulty, Mr. Matuchek . . . if I can help you . . . it's what I'm here for, you know."

"It's OK," I lied. "Thanks anyway, sir."

"It can't be easy for a mature man, a combat veteran and a famous actor, to start in with a lot of giggling freshmen," he said. "I remember how you helped me in that . . . ah . . .

unfortunate incident last month. Believe me, Mr. Matuchek, I am grateful."

"Oh, hell, it's nothing. I came here to get an education." *And to be with Virginia Graylock—but that's impossible now.*

I saw no reason to load the details on him. It was simple enough. After we beat the kaftans off the Caliphate, I returned to Metro-Goldwyn-Merlin and resumed werewolfing for them. But the same exploit which introduced me to Ginny had left me bobtailed, and a brushpiece is a nuisance. I had medals, sure, but war heroes were a dime a coven—not that I claim an undue share of courage, events had merely flogged me into doing what I did. I couldn't get real conviction into my role in *Abbott and Costello Meet Paracelsus;* I don't look down on pure entertainment, but I discovered a newborn wish to do something more significant.

Ginny could get me into the Arcane Agency of which she was head witch, and I could work on that control of paranatural forces on which the whole world now depends. To be precise, I shared the common dream of taming Fire and Air enough to hitch them to a ship and reach the planets. But first I needed professional training. So Stephen Matuchek and MGM parted company with noises of mutual esteem, and I went to college on my savings and my G.I.

Ginny herself wanted a Ph.D.—she already had an M.A. from Congo—and Trismegistus offered her an instructorship while she took an extended leave of absence from the agency. Same school . . . we'd be together all our free hours, and I could probably talk her into an early marriage. Wonderful setup.

Like hell.

Griswold sighed, perhaps understanding my withdrawal. "There are times when I feel altogether useless," he said.

"Not at all, sir," I answered with careful heartiness. "How on Middle Earth would—oh, say alchemy—be practical without a grounding in chemistry and nuclear physics? You'd produce poisonous compounds, or blow up half a country."

"Of course, of course. You understand. You know something of the world—more than I, in all truth. But the students . . . well, I suppose it's only natural. They want to speak a few words, make a few passes, and get what they desire, just like that, without bothering to learn the Sanskrit grammar or the periodic table. They haven't realized that you never get something for nothing."

"They will. They'll grow up."

"Even the administration . . . this university just doesn't appreciate the need for physical science. Now at California,

they're getting a billion-volt Philosopher's Stone, but here—'
Griswold shrugged. "Excuse me. I despise self-pity."

We came to the stadium, and I handed over my ticket but
declined the night-seeing spectacles. They'd given me witch-
sight in basic training. My seat was on the 30-yard line, between
a fresh-faced coed and an Old Grad already hollering himself
raw. An animated tray went by, and I bought a hot dog and
rented a crystal ball. But that wasn't to follow the details of play.
I muttered over the globe and peered into it and saw Ginny.

She was seated on the 50, opposite side, the black cat Svartalf
on her lap, her hair a shout of red against the human drabness
around. That witchcraft peculiarly hers was something more old
and strong than the Art in which she was so adept. Even across the
field and through the cheap glass gazer, she made my heart
stumble.

The problem was simply this: Trismegistus' President Malzius
was a pompous mediocrity whose chief accomplishment had
been to make the trustees his yes-men. What he said, went. And
it was his arrogant idea to insist that all personnel take a geas to
obey every University regulation while their contracts were in
force. He had still corralled a pretty good faculty, for the salaries
were good and the rules the ordinary ones. Ginny had signed her
contract a month before I enrolled and not felt the kicker till too
late.

Students and faculty members, right down to the instructor
level, were not permitted to date each other.

Naturally I had stormed my way into Malzius' office and
demanded an exception. No use. He wasn't going to revise the
book for me—"bad precedent, Mr. Matuchek, bad precedent"—
and I agreed sulkily that it was, indeed, a bad president. The
rule would have had to be stricken completely, as the geas didn't
allow special dispensations. Nor did it allow for the case of a
student from another school, so it was pointless for me to
transfer. The only solution, till Ginny's contract expired in June,
would have been for me to drop out entirely, and with that
cold-iron determination of hers she wouldn't hear of that. Lose a
whole year? What was I, a wolf or a mouse? We had quite a
quarrel about it, right out in public. And when you can only
meet at official functions, it isn't just easy to kiss and make up.

Oh, sure, we were still engaged and still saw each other at
smokers, teas . . . really living it up. Meanwhile, as she pointed
out with that icy logic I knew was defensive but never could
break past, we were human. From time to time she would be

going out with some bachelor colleague, wishing he were me, and I'd squire an occasional girl around. . . .

Tonight she was with Dr. Alan Abercrombie, Assistant Professor of Comparative Nigromancy, sleek, blond, handsome, the lion of the tiffins. He'd been paying her a lot of attention while I smoldered alone.

Quite alone. I think Svartalf the cat considers my morals no better than his. I had every intention of fidelity, but when you've parked your broomstick in a moonlit lane and a cute bit of fluff is snuggled up against you . . . those round yellow eyes glowing from a nearby tree are remarkably style-cramping. I soon gave up and spent my evenings studying or drinking beer.

Heigh-ho. I drew my coat tighter about me and shivered in the wind. There was a smell of wrongness to the air . . . probably only my bad mood, I thought, but I'd sniffed trouble up in the future before now.

The Old Grad blasted my ears off as the teams trotted out into the moonlight, Trismegistus' Gryphons and the Albertus Magnus Wyverns. The very old grads say they can't get used to so many four-eyed runts wearing letters—apparently a football team was composed of dinosaurs back before the so-called Thaumaturgic Age. But of course the Art is essentially intellectual and has given its own tone to sports.

This game had its interesting points. The Wyverns levitated off and their skinny little quarterback turned out to be a werepelican. Dushanovitch, in condor shape, nailed him on our 20. Andrevski is the best line werebuck in the Big Ten, and held them for two downs. On the third, Pilsudski got the ball and became a kangaroo. His footwork was beautiful as he dodged a tackle (the guy had a Tarnkappe, but you could see the footprints advance) and passed to Mstislav. The Wyverns swooped low, expecting Mstislav to turn the ball into a raven for a field goal, but with lightning a-crackle as he fended off their counterspells, he made it into a pig . . . greased. (These were minor transformations, of course, a quick gesture at an object already sensitized, not the great and terrible Words I was to hear before dawn.)

A bit later, unnecessary roughness cost us 15 yards: Domingo accidentally stepped on a scorecard which had blown to the field and drove his cleats right through several of the Wyverns' names. But no great harm was done, and they got the same penalty when Thorsson was carried away by the excitement and tossed a thunderbolt. At the end of the first half, the score was Trismegistus 13, Albertus Magnus 6, and the crowd was nearly ripping up the benches.

I pulled my hat back off my ears, gave the Old Grad a dirty look, and stared into the crystal. Ginny was more of a fan than I; she was still jumping and hollering, hardly seeming to notice that Abercrombie had his arms around her. Or perhaps she didn't mind . . . ? I took a long resentful drag at my flask.

The cheering squad paraded out onto the field. Their instruments wove through an elaborate aerial maneuver, drumming and tootling, as they made the traditional march up to the Campus Queen. I'm told it's also traditional that she ride forth on a unicorn to meet them, but for some reason that was omitted this year.

The hair rose stiff on my neck and I felt the blind instinctive tug of Skinturning. Just in time I pulled myself back toward human and sat in a cold shudder. The air was rotten with danger. Couldn't *anyone* else smell it?

I focused my crystal on the cheering squad, looking for the source, only dimly aware of the yell—

> *Aleph, beth, gimel, daleth, he, vau,*
> *Nomine Domini, blow, wow, wow!*
> *Melt 'em in the fire and stick 'em with pins,*
> *Trismegistus always wins. . . .*
> MACILWRAITH!

"Hey . . . what's wrong, mister?" The coed shrank from me, and I realized I was snarling.

"Oh. Nothing . . . I hope." With an effort I composed my face and kept it human.

The fattish blond kid down among the rooters didn't look harmful, but there was a sense of lightning-shot blackness about his future. I'd dealt with him before, and—

I didn't snitch on him at the time, but it was he who had almost broken up Griswold's chemistry class. Pre-med freshman, rich boy, not a bad guy at heart but with an unfortunate combination of natural aptitude for the Art and total irresponsibility. Medical students are notorious for merry little pranks such as waltzing an animated skeleton through the girls' dorm, and he wanted to start early.

Griswold had been demonstrating the action of a catalyst, and MacIlwraith had muttered a pun-spell to make a cat boil out of the test tube. Only he slipped up quantitatively and got a saber-toothed tiger. Because of the pun, it listed to starboard, but it was still a vicious, panic-raising thing. I ducked into a closet, used my pocket moonflash, and transformed; as a werewolf I chased Pussy out the window and up a tree till somebody could call the Exorcism Department.

Having seen MacIlwraith do it, I looked him up and warned him that if he disrupted the class again I'd chew him out in the most literal sense. Fun is fun, but not at the expense of students who really want to learn and a pleasant elderly anachronism who's trying to teach them.

"TEAM!"

The cheerleader waved his hands and a spurt of many-colored fire jumped out of nothingness. Taller than a man it lifted, a leaping glory of red, blue, yellow, haloed with a wheel of sparks. Slitting my eyes, I could just discern the lizardlike form, white-hot and supple, within the aura.

The coed squealed. "Thrice blessed Hermes," choked the Old Grad. "What is it? A demon?"

"No, a fire elemental," I muttered. "Salamander. Hell of a dangerous thing to fool around with."

My gaze ran about the field as the burning shape began to do its tricks, bouncing, tumbling, spelling out words in long flamebands. Yes, they had a fireman down there in full canonicals, making the passes that kept the thing harmless. It ought to be all right. . . . I lit a cigaret, shakily. It is not well to call up Loki's pets, and the stink of menace to come was acrid in my nostrils.

A good show, but— The crystal revealed Abercrombie clapping, but Ginny with a worried frown between the long green eyes. She didn't like it any better than I. Switch the ball back to MacIlwraith, fun-loving MacIlwraith.

I was probably the only one in the stadium who saw it. The boy gestured at his baton. It sprouted wings. The fat fireman, swaying back and forth with his gestures, was a natural target for a good healthy goose.

"*Yeowp!*"

He rocketed heavenward. The salamander wavered. All at once it sprang up, thinning out till it towered over the walls. There was a spinning, dazzling blur, and the thing was gone.

My cigaret burst luridly into flame and I tossed it from me. Hardly thinking, I jettisoned my hipflask. It exploded from a touch of incandescence and the alcohol burned blue. The crowd howled, hurtling away their smokes, slapping at pockets where matches had kindled, getting rid of bottles. The Campus Queen shrieked as her thin dress caught fire. She got it off in time to prevent serious injury and went wailing across the field. Under different circumstances, I would have been very interested.

The salamander stopped its lunatic shuttling and materialized between goal posts that began to smoke—an intolerable blazing that scorched the grass and roared. The fireman dashed toward it, shouting the spell of extinguishment. From the salamander's mouth licked a tongue of fire. I heard a distinct Bronx cheer, then it was gone again.

The announcer, who should have been calming the spectators, screeched as it flickered before his booth. That touched off the panic! In one heartbeat, fifty thousand people were clawing and trampling, choking each other in the gates, blind with horror and trying only to fight their way out.

I vaulted across benches and an occasional head, down to the field. There was death on those jammed tiers. "Ginny! Ginny, come here where it's safe!"

She couldn't have heard me above the din, but came of herself, dragging a terrorized Abercrombie by one wrist. We faced each other in a ring of ruin.

The Gryphons came boiling out of their locker room. Boiling is the right word: the salamander had materialized down there and playfully wrapped itself around the shower pipes.

Sirens hooted under the moon and police broomsticks shot above us, trying to curb the stampede. The elemental flashed for a moment across one of the besoms. Its rider dove it low enough to jump off, and the burning stick crashed on the grass.

"God!" exclaimed Abercrombie. "It's loose!"

"Tell me more," I snorted. "Ginny, you're a witch. Can you do anything about this?"

"I can extinguish the brute if it'll hold still long enough for me to recite the spell," she said. Disordered ruddy hair had tumbled past her pale, high-boned face to the fur-clad shoulders. "That's our only chance—the binding charm is broken, and it knows that!"

I whirled, remembering friend MacIlwraith, and collared him. "Were you possessed?" I shouted.

"I didn't do anything—" he gasped. His teeth rattled as I shook him.

"Don't hand me that guff. I saw it!"

He collapsed on the ground. "It was just for fun," he whimpered. "I didn't know—"

Well, I thought grimly, that was doubtless true. It's the trouble with the Art—with any blind powerful force man uses, fire or dynamite or atomic energy or thaumaturgy. Any meathead can learn enough to begin something; these days, they start them in the third grade with spelling bees. But it's not always so easy to halt the something.

Student pranks were a standing problem at Trismegistus, as at all colleges. They were usually harmless enough—sneaking into the dorms with Tarnkappen, or 'chanting female lingerie out through the windows. Sometimes they could be rather amusing, like the time the statue of a revered and dignified former president was animated and went downtown singing bawdy songs. Often they fell quite flat, as when the boys turned Dean Hornsby into stone and it wasn't noticed for three days.

This one had gotten out of hand. The salamander was quite capable of igniting the whole city.

I turned to the fireman, who was jittering about trying to flag down a police broom. In the dim shifty light, none of the riders saw him. "What d'you figure to do?" I asked.

"I gotta report back for duty," he said harshly. "And then we'll need a water elemental, I guess."

"I have experience with the Hydros," offered Ginny. "I'll come along."

"Me too," I said at once.

Abercrombie glowered. "What can *you* do?"

"I'm were," I snapped. "In wolf shape I can't easily be harmed by fire. That might turn out useful."

"All right, Steve!" Ginny smiled at me, the old smile which had so often gone between us. Impulsively, I grabbed her to me and kissed her.

She didn't waste energy on a slap. I collected an uppercut that tumbled me on my tocus. "Not allowed," she clipped. That double-damned geas! I could see misery caged within her eyes, but her mind was compelled to obey Malzius' rules.

"It's . . . ah . . . no place for a woman—a lady as charming as you," murmured Abercrombie. "Let me take you home, my dear."

"I've got work to do," she said impatiently. "What the devil is wrong with those cops? We've got to get a lift out of here."

"Then I shall come too," said Abercrombie. "I am not unacquainted with blessings and curses, though—ha!—I fear that ever-filled purses are a trifle beyond my scope. In any event, the Treasury Department frowns on them."

Even in that moment, with riot thundering and hell let loose on earth, I was pleased to note that Ginny paid no attention to his famous wit. She scowled abstractedly and looked around. The Campus Queen was huddled near the benches, wearing somebody's overcoat. Ginny grinned and waved her wand. The Campus Queen shucked the coat and ran toward us. Thirty seconds later, three police broomsticks had landed. The fireman commandeered them and we were all whirled over the stadium and into the street.

During that short hop, I saw three houses ablaze. The salamander was getting around!

We gathered at the district police station, a haggard and sooty crew with desperate eyes. The fire and police chiefs were there, and a junior officer going crazy at the switchboard. Ginny, who had picked up her own broom and come via her apartment, arrived with Svartalf on one shoulder and the *Handbook of Alchemy and Metaphysics* under her arm. Abercrombie was browbeating the terrified MacIlwraith till I told him to lay off.

"My duty—" he began. "I'm a proctor, you know."

I suppose it's necessary to have witchsmellers on campus, to make sure the boys don't 'chant up liquor in the frat houses or smuggle in succubi. And every year somebody tries to get by an exam with a familiar under his coat whispering the answers from a crib-sheet. Nevertheless, I don't like professional nosy parkers.

"You can deal with him later," I said, and gave the boy a push out the door. "The salamander can fight back."

President Malzius huffed into the room. "What is the meaning of this?" he demanded. His pince-nez bobbed above full jowls. "I'll have you know, sir, I was preparing a most important address. The Lions Totem is holding a luncheon tomorrow, and—"

"Might not be any lunch," grunted the cop who had fetched him. "There's a salamander loose around here."

"Sala— No! It's against the rules! It is positively forbidden to—"

The man at the switchboard looked up. "It's just kindled the Methodist church at 14th and Elm," he said. "And my God, all our equipment is already working—"

"Impossible!" cried Malzius. "A demon can't go near a church."

"How stupid does a man have to be to get your job?" Ginny fairly spat it. "This *isn't* a demon. It's an elemental." Her temper was again sheathed in ice, and she continued slowly: "We haven't much hope of using a Hydro to put out the salamander, but we can raise one to help fight the fires. It'll always be three jumps behind, but at least the whole city won't be ruined."

"Unless the salamander gets too strong," cut in Abercrombie. His face was colorless and he spoke through stiff lips. "Then it can evaporate the Hydro."

"Call up two water beings," stammered Malzius. "Call up a hundred. I'll waive the requirement of formal application for permission to—"

"There's a limit, sir," Abercrombie told him. "The restraining force required is an exponential function of the total embodied mass. There probably aren't enough adepts in this town to control more than three at a time. If we raised four . . . we'd flood the city, and the salamander need only skip elsewhere."

"Alan—" Ginny laid her handbook on the desk and riffled its pages. Abercrombie leaned over her shoulder, remembering to rest one hand carelessly on her hip. I choked back my prize cuss-words. "Alan, just for a starter, can you summon one Hydro and put it to work?"

"Of course, gorgeous one," he smiled. "It is a—ha!—elemental problem."

She gave him a worried glance. "They can be as tricky as Fire or Air," she warned. "It's not enough just to know the theory."

"I have some small experience," he preened. "During the war— After this is over, come up to my place for a drink and I'll tell you about it." His lips brushed her cheek.

"Mr. Matuchek!" wailed Malzius. "Will you please stop growing fangs?"

I shook myself and suppressed the rage which had been almost as potent as moonlight.

"Look here," said the police chief. "I gotta know what's going on. You longhairs started this trouble and I don't want you making it worse."

Seeing that Ginny and Pretty Boy were, after all, legitimately busy, I sighed and whistled up a cigaret. "Let me explain," I offered. "I learned a few things about the subject, during the war. An elemental is not the same as a demon. Any kind of demon is a separate being, as individual as you and I. An elemental is part of the basic force involved: in this case, fire, or more accurately energy. It's raised out of the basic energy matrix, given temporary individuality, and restored to the matrix when the adept is through with it."

"Huh?"

"Like a flame. A flame exists only potentially till someone lights a fire, and goes back to merely potential existence when you put the fire out. And of course the second fire you light, even on the same log, is not identical with the first, so you can understand why an elemental isn't exactly anxious to be dismissed. If it ever breaks loose, as this one did, it'll do its damnedest to stay in this world and to increase its own power."

"But how come it can burn a church?"

"Because it's soulless, a mere physical force. Any true individual, human or otherwise, is under certain constraints of a . . . a moral nature. A demon is allergic to holy symbols. A man who does wrong has to live with his conscience in this world and face judgment in the next. But what does a fire care? And that's all the salamander is—a glorified fire. It's bound only by the physical laws of nature and paranature."

"So how do you, uh, put it out?"

"A Hydro of corresponding mass could do it—mutual annihilation. Earth could bury it or Air withdraw from its neighborhood. Trouble is, Fire is the swiftest of them all; it can flick out of an area before any other sort of elemental can injure it. So we're left without the dismissal spell. But that has to be said in the salamander's presence, and it takes about two minutes."

"Yeah . . . and when it hears you start the words, it'll burn you down or scram. *Very* nice. What're we gonna do?"

"I don't know, chief," I said, "except it's like kissing a sheep dog." I blew hard and smacked my lips. "You got to be quick. Every fire the critter starts feeds it more energy and makes it that much stronger. There's a critical point somewhere at which it becomes too powerful for anything to affect it."

"And then what happens?"

"Ragnarok."

I saw Ginny turn from the desk. Abercrombie was chalking a pentagram on the floor while a sputtering Malzius had been deputized to sterilize a pocket knife with a match—blood is a substitute for the usual powders, since it has the same proteins. The girl laid a hand on mine. "Steve, it'll take too long to get hold of all the local adepts and organize them," she said. "God knows what the salamander will be doing meanwhile. Are you game to track it down?"

"Sure," I agreed. "It can't hurt me—if I'm careful—till it gets big enough to burn up all the world's oxygen. But you're staying here!"

"Ever hear about the oath of my order? Come on."

As we went out the door, I gave Abercrombie a smug look. He had nicked his wrist and sprinkled the Signs; now he was well into the invocation. I felt cold dampness swirl through the room.

Outside, the night was still autumnally sharp, the moon high. Roofs were a sawtoothed silhouette against the leaping red glare at a dozen points around us, and sirens howled in the streets. Up overhead, across the small indifferent stars, I saw what looked like the whirl of dry leaves, refugees fleeing on their sticks.

Svartalf jumped to the front end of Ginny's Cadillac, and I took the saddle behind. We rode skyward.

Below us, blue fire sat and the station lights went out. Water poured into the street, a solid roar of it with President Malzius bobbing like a cork in the torrent.

"Unholy Sathanas!" I choked. "What's happened now?"

Svartalf ducked the stick low. "That idiot," groaned Ginny. "He let the Hydro slop all over the floor . . . short circuits . . ." She made a few rapid passes with her wand. The stream quieted, drew into herself, became a ten-foot-high blob glimmering in the moonlight. Abercrombie scuttled out and started it squelching toward the nearest fire.

I laughed. "Go on up to his place and listen to him tell about his vast experience," I said.

"Don't kick a man when he's down," Ginny snapped. "You've pulled your share of boners, Steve Matuchek."

Svartalf whisked the broom up again and we went low above the chimneypots. *Oof!* I thought. Could she really be falling for that troll? A regular profile, a smooth tongue, and proximity . . . I bit back an inward sickness and squinted ahead, trying to find the salamander.

"There!" Ginny yelled it over the whistle of cloven air. Svartalf bottled his tail and hissed.

The University district is shabby-genteel: old pseudo-Gothic caves of wood which have slipped from mansions to rooming houses, flyspecked with minor business establishments. It was burning merrily, a score of angry red stars flickering in the darkness between street lamps. As I watched, one of the stars exploded in a puff of steam—the Hydro must have clapped a sucker onto a fireplug and blanketed the place. I had a brief heretical thought that the salamander was doing a public service by eliminating those architectural teratologies . . . but of course lives and property were involved—

Tall and terrible, the elemental wavered beside the house on which it was feeding. It had doubled in size, and its core was too bright to look at. Flames whirled about the reptile head.

Svartalf braked and we hovered a few yards off, twenty feet in the air and level with the hungry mouth. Ginny was etched wild against night by that intolerable radiance. She braced herself in the stirrups and began the spell, her voice almost lost in the roar as the roof caved in. "*O Indra, Abaddon, Lucifer, Moloch, Hephaestos, Loki . . .*"

It heard. The seething eyes swung toward us and it leaped.

Svartalf squalled as his whiskers shriveled—perhaps it was only hurt vanity—and put the stick through an Immelmann turn and whipped away. The salamander bawled with the voice of a hundred blazing forests. Suddenly the heat scorching my back was gone, and the thing had materialized in front of us.

"That way!" I hollered, pointing. "In there!"

I covered Ginny's eyes and buried my own face against her back as we went through the plate-glass front of Stub's Beer Garden. The flame-tongue licked after us, recoiled, and the salamander ramped beyond the door.

We tumbled off the broom and looked around. The place was empty, full of a fire-spattered darkness. Everyone had fled. I saw a nearly full glass of beer on the counter and tossed it off.

"You might have offered me a drink," said Ginny. "Alan would have." Before I could recover enough to decide whether she was taunting or teasing me, she went on in a rapid whisper: "It isn't trying to escape. It's gained power—confidence—it means to kill us!"

Even then, I wanted to tell her that tousled red hair and a soot smudge across an aristocratic nose were particularly enchanting. But the occasion didn't seem appropriate. "Can't get in here," I panted. "Can't do much much more than ignite tthe building by thermal radiation, and that'll take a while. We're safe for the moment."

"Why . . . oh, yes, of course. Stub's is cold-ironed. All these college beer parlors are, I'm told."

"Yeh." I peered out the broken window. The salamander peered back, and spots danced before my eyes. "So the clientele won't go jazzing up the brew above 3.2—Quick, say your spell."

Ginny shook her head. "It'll just flicker away out of earshot. Maybe we can talk to it, find out—"

She trod forth to the window, and the thing crouched in the street extended its neck and hissed at her. I stood behind my girl, feeling boxed and useless. Svartalf, lapping spilled beer off the counter, looked up and sneered.

"Ohé, Child of Light!" she cried.

A ripple went down the salamander's back. Its tail switched restlessly, and a tree across the way kindled. I can't describe the voice that answered . . . crackling, bellowing, sibilant, it was

Fire given a brain and a throat. "Daughter of Eve, what have you to say to the likes of Me?"

"I command you by the Most High, return to your proper bonds and cease from troubling the world."

"Ho—oh, ho, ho, ho!" The thing sat back on its haunches (asphalt bubbled) and shuddered its laughter into the sky. *"You* command Me, combustible one?"

"I have at my beck powers so mighty they could wither your little spark into the nothingness whence it came. Cease and obey, lest worse befall you than dismissal."

I think the salamander was, for a moment, honestly surprised. "Greater than *Me?*" Then it howled so the tavern shook. "You dare say there are mightier forces than Fire? Than Me, Who am going to consume all the earth?"

"Mightier and more beautiful, O Ashmaker. Think—you cannot even enter this house. Water will extinguish you, Earth will smother you, Air alone can keep you alive. Best you surrender now—"

I remembered the night we had faced an afreet together. Ginny must be pulling the same trick—feeling out the psychology of the thing that raged and flared beyond the door—but what could she hope to gain?

"More beautiful!" The salamander's tail beat furrows in the street. It threw out bursting fireballs and a rain of sparks, red, blue, yellow, a one-being Fourth of July. I thought crazily of a child kicking the floor in a tantrum.

"More beautiful! Stronger! You dare say— Haaaaa—" Teeth of incandescence gleamed in a mouth that was jumping fire. "We shall see how beautiful you are when you lie a choked corpse!" Its head darted to the broken glass front. It could not pass the barrier of cold iron, but it began to suck air, in and out. A furnace wave of heat sent me gasping back.

"My God . . . it's going to use up all our oxygen. . . . Stay here!" Hardly thinking, I sprang for the door. Ginny shrieked, but I scarcely heard her "No!" as I went through.

Moonlight flooded me, cool and tingling between the unrestful guttering fires. I crouched to the hot sidewalk and felt a shudder as my body changed.

Wolf I was, and a wolf which only silver could kill . . . I hoped. My abbreviated tail thrust against the seat of my pants, and I remembered that some injuries are beyond the healing powers of even the were shape.

Pants! Hell and damnation! Have you ever tried being a wolf

while wrapped in shirt, trousers, underwear, and topcoat designed for a man?

I went flat on my moist black nose. My suspenders slid down and wrapped themselves about my hind legs. My tie tripped me up in front and my coat gleefully wrapped itself around the whole bundle.

Frantic, I snapped at the cloth, rolling over and tearing with my fangs. The salamander grew aware of me, and its tail slapped contemptuously across my back. For a moment of searing agony, hair and skin went up with the fabric . . . then I was free, and the fluid molecules rebuilt themselves. Hardly knowing what I did, I picked up a shoe which had dropped from my now smaller foot, laid it on the salamander's white-hot toe, and bore down.

It roared and swung about to attack me. Those jaws gaped wide enough to bite me in half. I skittered away. It paused, gauged the distance, flicked into nothingness, and materialized right on top of me.

I *think* I got a tooth-grip in the obvious place to bite a salamander when it is sitting on you, but the pain was too great for me to know. Then it was gone, the street lay bare and quiet between burning houses, and I gasped my way back toward wholeness.

Sanity returned. My shaggy head was in Ginny's lap, and she was stroking it and crying. Feebly, I licked her hand. Strength flowed back. As a man, I'd naturally have stayed where I was, but being a wolf with lupine instincts, I sat up and yipped.

"Steve . . . Almighty Father, Steve you saved our lives," whispered Ginny. "Another minute and we'd have been suffocating. My lungs still feel like mummy dust."

Svartalf trotted from the bar, looking as smug as a cat with singed whiskers can. He meowed. Ginny gave a trembling laugh and explained:

"But you owe Svartalf a pint of cream or something. He saved you too. A few more seconds and you'd have been dead—but he showed me how to drive the beast off."

I cocked my ears inquiringly.

"He manned the beer taps," she said. "I filled stein after stein and went out and threw them at the salamander. Not enough to do more than discommode it . . . but added to the trouble you were making, enough to make it skip."

Horrible waste of beer, I thought. But there was still work to do.

Penalties attach to everything. The trouble with being were is that in the other shape you have, essentially, an animal brain, with only a superficial layer of human personality. Or in plain language, as a wolf I'm a rather stupid man. I was only able to think I'd better reassume human form . . . and I did.

Ever see a cat grin? "Omi-gawd!" I groaned, and started to change back.

"Never mind that," said Ginny crisply, peeling off her fur coat. I broke all records donning it. Pretty tight fit around the shoulders, but it went low enough . . . if I was careful. The night wind nipped my shanks, but my face was of salamander temperature.

"Now where?" I asked quickly. "The damned critter could be anyplace."

"I think it will hang around the campus," she said. "Plenty of grazing, and it's not very smart. Let's get back on our stick."

She fetched it from the smoldering barroom and we lifted. "All we've done so far," I said, "is lose time."

"No, not entirely. I did get a line on its mind." Ginny turned her head back to face me as we cleared the rooftops. "I wasn't sure into just what form it had been conjured—you can mold the elemental forces into almost anything. But apparently the cheerleader was satisfied to give it a knowledge of English and a rudimentary intelligence. Add to that the volatile nature of Fire, and what have you got? A child."

"Some child," I muttered, hugging her coat to me.

"No, no, Steve, this is important. It has all the child's traits. Improvidence, complete lack of foresight . . . a wise salamander would lie low, gathering strength slowly, and would never think of burning the entire planet. Because what would it use for oxygen when that was finished? You'll note, too, its fantastic vanity; it went into an insane rage when I said there were powers stronger and more beautiful than it, and the crack about beauty hurt as much as the one about strength. Short span of attention . . . it could have smothered us easily before attending to as minor a nuisance as you provided. At the same time, within that span of attention, it focuses on one issue only, to the exclusion of everything else." She nodded thoughtfully, and the long blowing hair tickled my face. "I don't know just how, but some way its psychology must provide us with a lever."

My own vanity is not small. "I wasn't such a minor nuisance," I grumbled.

Ginny smiled and reached around to pat my cheek. "All right, Steve, all right. I love you just the same, and now I *know* you'll make a good husband."

That left me in a comfortable glow until I wondered precisely what she was thinking of.

We spotted the salamander below us, igniting a theater, but it flicked away even as I watched, and a mile off it appeared next to the medical research center. Glass brick doesn't burn very well. As we neared, I saw it petulantly kick the wall and vanish again. Ignorant and impulsive . . . a child . . . a brat from Hell!

Sweeping over the campus, we saw lights in the Administration Building. "Probably that's HQ for our side now," said Ginny. "We'd better report." Svartalf landed us on the Mall in front of the place and strutted ahead toward the steps.

A squad of cops armed with fire extinguishers guarded the door. "Hey, there!" One of them barred our path. "Where you going?"

"To the meeting," said Ginny, smoothing her tangled hair.

"Yeh?" The policeman's eye fell on me. "All dressed up for it, too, aren't you? Haw, haw, haw!"

I'd had about enough for one night. I wered and peeled off his own trousers. As he lifted his billy, Ginny turned it into a small boa constrictor. I switched back to human, we left the squad to its own problems and went down the hall.

The faculty meeting room was packed. Malzius had summoned all his professors. As we entered, I heard his orotund tones: ". . . disgraceful. The authorities won't even listen to me. Gentlemen, it is for us to vindicate the honor of Gown against Town." He blinked when Ginny and Svartalf came in, and turned a beautiful Tyrian purple as I followed in the full glory of mink coat and stubby chin. *"Mister* Matuchek!"

"He's with me," said Ginny curtly. "We were out fighting the salamander while you sat here."

"Possibly something more than brawn, even lupine brawn, is required," smiled Dr. Alan Abercrombie. "I see that Mr. Matuchek lost his pants in a more than vernacular sense."

Like Malzius, he had changed his wet clothes for the inevitable tweeds. Ginny gave him a cold look. "I thought you were directing the Hydro," she said.

"Oh, we got enough adepts together to use three water elementals," he said. "Mechanic's work. I felt my job was here. We can control the fires easily enough—"

"—if the salamander weren't always lighting fresh ones," clipped Ginny. "And every blaze it starts, it gets bigger and stronger, while you sit here looking beautiful."

"Why, thank you, my dear," he laughed.

I jammed my teeth together so it hurt. She had actually smiled back at him.

"Order, order!" boomed President Malzius. "Please be seated, Miss Graylock. Have you anything to contribute to the discussion?"

"Yes. I understand the salamander now." She took a place at the end of the table. It was the last vacant chair, so I hovered miserably in the background wishing her coat had more buttons.

"Understand it well enough to extinguish it?" asked Professor van Linden of Alchemy.

"No. But I know how it thinks—"

"We're more interested in how it operates," said van Linden. "How can we make it hold still long enough to hear a dismissal?" He cleared his throat. "Obviously, we must first know by what process it shuttles around so fast—"

"Oh, that's simple enough," piped up little Griswold timidly. He was drowned by van Linden's fruity bass:

"—which is, of course, by the well-known affinity of Fire for Quicksilver. Since virtually every home these days has at least one thermometer—"

"With all due respect, my good sir," interrupted Vittorio of Astrology, "you are talking utter hogwash. It is a simple matter of the conjunction of Mercury and Neptune in Scorpio—"

"You're wrong, sir!" declared van Linden. "Dead wrong! Let me show you the *Ars Thaumaturgica*." He glared around after his copy, but of course it had been mislaid and he had to use an adaptation of the Dobu yam-calling chant to find it. Meanwhile Vittorio was screaming:

"No, no, no! The conjunction, with Uranus opposing in the ascendant, as I can easily prove—" He went to the blackboard and started drawing a diagram.

"Oh, come now!" snorted Jasper of Metaphysics. "I don't understand how you can both be so wrong. As I showed in my paper read at the last A.A.A.S. meeting, the intrinsic nature—"

"That was disproved ten years ago!" roared van Linden. "The affinity—"

"*—Ding an sich—*"

"—up Uranus—"

I sidled over and tugged at Griswold's sleeve. He pattered into a corner with me. "Just how *does* the bloody thing work?" I asked.

"Oh . . . merely a question of wave mechanics." he whispered. "According to the Heisenberg Uncertainty Principle, a photon has a finite probability of being at any point of space. The salamander uses a simple diffraction process to change the spatial coordinates of psi squared, in effect going from point to point without crossing the intervening space, much like an electron making a quantum jump, though of course the analogy is not precise due to the modifying influence of—"

"Never mind," I sighed. "This confab is becoming a riot. Wouldn't we do better to—"

"—stick by the original purpose," agreed Abercrombie, joining us. Ginny followed. Van Linden blacked Vittorio's eye while Jasper threw chalk at both of them. Our little group went over near the door.

"I've already found the answer to our problem," said Abercrombie, "but I'll need help. A transformation spell—turn the salamander into something we can handle more easily."

"That's dangerous," said Ginny. "You'll need a really strong T-spell, and that sort can backfire. Just what happens then is unpredictable."

Abercrombie straightened himself with a look of pained nobility. "For you, my dear, no hazard is too great."

She regarded him with admiration. It does take guts to use the ultimate runes. "Let's go," she said. "I'll help."

Griswold plucked at my arm, "I don't like this, Mr. Matuchek," he confided. "The Art is too unreliable. There ought to be some method grounded in nature and nature's quantitative laws."

"Yeh," I said disconsolately. "But what?" I paddled out after Ginny and Abercrombie, who had their heads together over the handbook. Griswold marched beside me and Svartalf made a gesture with his tail at the Trismegistus faculty. They were too embroiled to notice.

We went out past an enraged but well-cowed squad of cops. The Physical Sciences hall was nearby, and its chemistry division held stuff that would be needed. We entered an echoing gloom.

The freshman lab, a long room full of workbenches, shelves, and silence, was our goal. Griswold switched on the lights and Abercrombie looked around. "But we'll have to bring the salamander here," he said. "We can't do anything except in its actual presence."

"Go ahead and make ready," the girl told him. "I know how to fetch the beast. A minor transformation—" She laid out some test tubes, filled them with various powders, and sketched her symbols on the floor. Those ball-point wands are useful.

"What's the idea?" I asked.

"Oh, get out of the way," she snapped. I told myself she was only striking at her own weariness and despair, but it hurt. "We'll use its vanity, of course. I'll prepare some Roman candles and rockets and stuff—shoot them off, and naturally it'll come to show it can do more spectacular things."

Griswold and I withdrew into a corner. This was big-league play. I was frankly scared, and the little scientist's bony knees were beating a tattoo in march time. Even Ginny—yes, there was sweat beading that smooth forehead. If this didn't work, we were probably all done for: either the salamander or the backlash of the spell could finish us. And we had no way of knowing whether the beast had grown too strong for a transformation.

The witch got her fireworks prepared, and went to an open window and leaned out. Hissing balls of blue and red, streamers of golden sparks, flew up and exploded.

Abercrombie had completed his diagrams. He turned to smile at us. "It's all right," he said. "Everything under control. I'm going to turn the salamander's energy into matter. E equals mc squared, you know. Just light me a Bunsen burner, Matuchek, and set a beaker of water over it. Griswold, you turn off these lights and use the polaroid bulbs. We need polarized radiation."

We obeyed—and I hated to see an old and distinguished man acting as lab assistant to this patronizing slickpaper adman's dream. "You *sure* it'll work?" I asked.

"Of course," he smiled. "I've had experience. I was in the Quartermaster Corps during the war, till they tapped me for the propaganda division . . . broadcasting nightmares, you know."

"Yeh," I said, "but turning dirt into K-rations isn't the same thing as transforming that hell-born monster. You and your experience!"

Suddenly and sickly, remembering how he had bungled with the Hydro, I realized the truth. Abercrombie was confident, unafraid—because he didn't *know* enough!

For a minute I couldn't unfreeze my muscles. Griswold stood fiddling unhappily with some metallic samples. He'd been using them only the other day for freshman experiments, trying to teach us the chemical properties—Lord, it seemed a million years ago . . .

"Ginny!" I stumbled toward her where she stood at the window throwing rainbows into the air. "My God, darling, stop—"

Crack! The salamander was in the room with us

I lurched back from it, half blinded. Grown hideously bigger, it filled the other end of the lab, and the bench tops smoked.

"Oh, so!" The voice of Fire blasted our eardrums. Svartalf shot up to a shelf top and began upsetting bottles of acid onto the varmint. It didn't notice. "So, small moist pests, you would try to outdo Me!"

Abercrombie and Ginny lifted their wands and shouted the few brief words of transformation.

Crouched back into my corner, peering through a sulfurous reek of fumes, I saw Ginny cringe and them jump for safety. She must have sensed the backlash. There was a shattering explosion and the air was full of flying glass.

My body shielded Griswold, and the spell didn't do more to me than turn me lupine. I saw Ginny nearby on her hands and knees, behind a bench, half unconscious . . . but unhurt, unhurt, praise all Powers forever. Svartalf—a Pekingese dog yapped on the shelf. Abercrombie was gone, but a chimpanzee in baggy tweeds scuttered wailing toward the door.

A fire-blast rushed before the ape. He whirled, screamed, and shinnied up a steam pipe. The salamander arched its back and howled with laughter.

"You would use your tricks on Me? Almighty Me, terrible Me, beautiful me? Ha, they bounce off like water from a hot skillet! And I, I, I am the skillet which is going to fry you!"

Somehow, the low-grade melodrama of its speech was not at all ridiculous. For this was the childish, vainglorious, senselessly consuming thing which was loose on earth to turn our broad fair home into one white blaze among the planets.

Under the polaroids, I switched back to human and stood up behind the bench. Griswold turned on a water faucet and squirted a jet with his finger. The salamander hissed in annoyance—yes, water still hurt, but there wasn't enough liquid here to quench it, you'd need a whole lake by this time. . . . It swung its head, gape-mouthed, and aimed at Griswold and drew a long breath.

All is vanity. . . .

I reeled over to the Bunsen burner that was heating a futile beaker of water. Ginny sat up and looked at me through scorched locks. The room shimmered in heat, my lungs were one great anguish. I didn't have any flash of genius, I acted on raw instinct and tumbled memories.

"Kill us," I croaked. "Kill us if you dare. Our servant is more powerful than you. He'll hound you to the ends of creation."

"Your servant?" Flame wreathed the words.

"Yeh . . . I mean yes . . . our servant, that Fire which fears not water!"

The salamander stepped back a pace, snarling. It was still not so strong that the very name of water didn't make it flinch. "Show Me!" it chattered. "Show Me! I dare you!"

"Our servant . . . small, but powerful," I rasped. "Brighter and more beautiful than you, and above taking harm from the Wet Element." I staggered to the jars of metal samples and got a pair of tongs. "Have you the courage to look on him?"

The salamander bristled. "Have I the *courage?* Ask rather, does it dare confront Me?"

I flicked a glance from the corner of my eye. Ginny had risen and was gripping her wand. She scarcely breathed, but her eyes were narrowed.

There was a silence. It hung like a world's weight in that long room, smothering what noises remained: the crackle of fire, Abercrombie's simian gibber, Svartalf's indignant yapping. I took a strip of magnesium in the tongs and held it to the burner flame.

It burst into a blue-white actinic radiance from which I turned dazzled eyes. The salamander was not so viciously brilliant. I saw the brute accomplish the feat of simultaneously puffing itself up and shrinking back.

"Behold!" I lifted the burning strip. Behind me, Ginny's rapid mutter came: *"O Indra, Abaddon, Lucifer . . ."*

The child mind, incapable of considering more than one thing at a time . . . but for how long a time? I had to hold its full attention for the hundred and twenty seconds required.

"Fire," said the salamander feverishly. "Only another fire, only a little piece of that Force from which I came."

"Can you do this, buster?"

I plunged the strip into the beaker. Steam puffed from the water, it boiled and bubbled—and the metal went on burning!

". . . abire ex orbis terrestris . . ."

"Mg plus H_2O yields Mg_1O plus H_2," whispered Griswold reverently.

"Keek-eek!" said Abercrombie.

"Yip-yip-yip!" said Svartalf.

"It's a trick!" screamed the salamander. "It's impossible! If even I cannot— *No!*"

"Stay where you are!" I barked in my best Army manner. "Do you doubt that my servant can follow you where you may flee?"

"I'll kill that little monster!"

"Go right ahead, chum," I agreed. "Want to have the duel fought under the sea?"

Whistles skirled above the racketing fire. The police had seen through our windows.

"I'll show you, I will!" There was almost a sob in the rear. I ducked behind the bench, pulling Griswold with me, as a geyser of flame rushed where I had been.

"Nyaah, nyaah, nyaah," I called. "You can't catch me! Scaredy cat!"

Svartalf gave me a hard look.

The floor trembled as the elemental came toward me, not going around the benches but burning its way through them. Heat clawed at my throat. I spun down toward darkness.

And it was gone. Ginny cried her triumphant *"Amen!"* and displaced air cracked like thunder.

I lurched to my feet. Ginny fell into my arms. The police entered the lab and Griswold hollered something about calling the fire department before his whole building went up in smoke. Abercrombie scampered out a window and Svartalf jumped down from the shelf. He forgot that a Pekingese isn't as agile as a cat, and his pop eyes bubbled with righteous wrath.

Outside, the Mall was cool and still. We sat on dewed grass and looked at the moon and thought what a great and simple wonder it is to be alive.

The geas held us apart, but tenderness lay on Ginny's lips. We scarcely noticed when somebody ran past us shouting that the salamander was gone, nor when church bells began pealing the news to all men.

Svartalf finally roused us with his barking. Ginny chuckled. "Poor fellow. I'll change you back as soon as I can, but there's more urgent business now. Come on, Steve."

Griswold, assured that his priceless hall was safe, followed us at a tactful distance. Svartalf merely sat where he was . . . too shocked to move, I guess, at the idea that there could be more important affairs than turning him back into a cat.

Dr. Malzius met us halfway, under one of the campus elms. Moonlight spattered his face and gleamed on the pince-nez. "My dear Miss Graylock," he began, "is it indeed true that you have overcome that menace to society? Most noteworthy. Accept my congratulations. The glorious annals of this great institution of which I have the honor to be president—"

Ginny faced him, arms akimbo, and nailed him with the chilliest gaze I have ever seen. "The credit belongs to Mr. Matuchek and Dr. Griswold," she said. "I shall so inform the press. Doubtless you'll then see fit to recommend a larger appropriation for Dr. Griswold's outstanding work."

"Oh, now, really," stammered the scientist. "I didn't—"

"Be quiet, you ninnyhammer," hissed Ginny. Aloud: "Only through his courageous and farsighted adherence to the basic teachings of natural law— Well, you can fill in the rest for yourself, Malzius. I don't think you'd be very popular if you went on starving his department."

"Oh . . . indeed . . . after all . . ." The president blew himself up. "I have given careful consideration to the matter. Was going to recommend it at the next meeting of the board, in fact."

"I'll hold you to that," said Ginny. "Now there is this stupid rule against student-faculty relationships. Mr. Matuchek is shortly going to be my husband—"

Whoosh! I tried to regain my breath.

"My dear Miss Graylock," sputtered Malzius, "decorum . . . propriety . . . why, he isn't even decent!"

I realized with horror that somehow, in all the excitement, I'd lost Ginny's expensive mink coat.

A pair of cops approached, dragging a small hairy form that struggled in their arms. One of them carried the garments the chimp had shed. "Begging your pardon, Miss Graylock." The tone was pure worship. "We found this monkey loose and—"

"Oh, yes." She laughed. "We'll have to restore him. But not right away. Steve needs those pants worse."

I got into them in a hurry. Ginny turned back to smile with angelic sweetness at Malzius.

"Poor Dr. Abercrombie," she sighed. "These things will happen when you deal with paranatural forces. Now I believe, sir, that there is no rule against faculty members conducting research."

"Oh, no," said the president shakily. "Of course not. On the contrary! We expect our people to publish—"

"To be sure. Now I have in mind a most interesting research project involving transformations. I'll admit it's just the least bit dangerous. It could backfire as Dr. Abercrombie's spell did." Ginny leaned on her wand and regarded the turf thoughtfully. "It could even . . . yes, there's even a small possibility that it could turn *you* into an ape, dear Dr. Malzius Or, perhaps, a worm. A long slimy one. But we mustn't let that stand in the way of Science, must we?"

"What? But—"

"Naturally," purred the witch, "if I were allowed to conduct myself as I wish with my fiancé, I shouldn't have time for research."

It took Malzius a bare fifty words to admit surrender. He stumped off in tottery grandeur while the last fire-glow died above the campus roofs.

Ginny gave me a long slow glance. "The rule can't officially be stricken till tomorrow," she murmured. "Think you can cut a few classes then?"

"Keek-eek-eek," said Dr. Alan Abercrombie. Then Svartalf showed up full of resentment and chased him up the tree.

Wizard's World

by Andre Norton

Andre Norton is one of the most popular of contemporary science fiction and fantasy writers, with a very high percentage of her more than one hundred books currently in print. She is also a highly honored writer, the recipient of two of the highest awards her field can offer: the Grand Master of Fantasy Award, bestowed by the World Fantasy Convention in 1977, and the Gandalf Award, given her by the World Science Fiction Convention in 1978. Although many of her novels are technically "juveniles," they can be enjoyed by readers of all ages. Appropriately, her most famous books are those of the "Witch World" series, including such outstanding works as Sorceress of the Witch World *(1968). She was also one of the first important sf writers to consistently feature female protagonists in her books.*

I

Craike's swollen feet were agony, every breath he drew fought a hot band imprisoning his laboring lungs. He clung weakly to a rough spur of rock in the canyon wall, swayed against it, raking his flesh raw on the stone. That weathered red and yellow rock was no more unyielding than the murderous wills behind him. And the stab of pain in his calves no less than the pain of their purpose in his dazed mind.

He had been on the run so long, ever since he had left the E-Camp. But until last night—no, two nights ago—when he had given himself away at the gas station, he had not known what it was to be actually hunted. The will-to-kill which fanned from those on his trail was so intense it shocked his Esper senses, panicking him completely.

Now he was trapped in wild country, and he was city-born.

Water—Craike flinched at the thought of water. Espers should control their bodies, that was what he had been taught. But there come times when cravings of the flesh triumph over will.

He winced, and the spur grated against his half-naked breast. They had a "hound" on him right enough. And that brain-twisted Esper slave who fawned and served the mob masters would have no difficulty in trailing him straight to any pocket into which he might crawl. A last remnant of rebellion sent Craike reeling on over the gravel of the long-dried stream bed.

Espers had once been respected for their "wild talents," then tolerated warily. Now they were used under guard for slave labor. And the day was coming soon when the fears of the normals would demand their extermination. They had been trying to prepare against that.

First they had worked openly, petitioning to be included in spaceship crews, to be chosen for colonists on the Moon and Mars; then secretly when they realized the norms had no intention of allowing that. Their last hope was flight to the waste spots of the world, those refuse places resulting from the same atomic wars which had brought about the birth of their kind.

Craike had been smuggled out of an eastern E-Camp, provided with a cover, sent to explore the ravaged area about the onetime city of Reno. Only he had broken his cover for the protection of a girl, only to learn, too late, she was bait for an Esper trap. He had driven a stolen speeder until the last drop of fuel was gone, and after that he had kept blindly on, running, until now.

The contact with the Esper "hound" was clear; they must almost be in sight behind. Craike paused. They were not going to take him alive, wring from him knowledge of his people, recondition him into another "hound." There was only one way, he should have known that from the first.

His decision had shaken the "hound." Craike bared teeth in a death's-head grin. Now the mob would speed up. But their quarry had already chosen a part of the canyon wall where he might pull his tired and aching body up from one hold to another. He moved deliberately now, knowing that when he had lost hope, he could throw aside the need for haste. He would be able to accomplish his purpose before they brought a gas rifle to bear on him.

At last he stood on a ledge, the sand and gravel some fifty feet below. For a long moment he rested, steadying himself with both hands braced on the stone. The weird beauty of the desert country was a pattern of violent color under the afternoon sun.

Craike breathed slowly; he had regained a measure of control. There came shouts as they sighted him.

He leaned forward and, as if he were diving into the river which had once run there, he hurled himself outward to the clean death he sought.

Water, water in his mouth! Dazed, he flailed water until his head broke surface. Instinct took over, and he swam, fought for air. The current of the stream pulled him against a boulder collared with froth, and he arched an arm over it, lifting himself, to stare about in stupefied bewilderment.

He was close to one bank of a river. Where the colorful cliff of the canyon had been there now rolled downs thickly covered with green growth. The baking heat of the desert had vanished; there was even a slight chill in the air.

Dumbly Craike left his rock anchorage and paddled ashore, to lie shivering on sand while the sun warmed his battered body. What *had* happened? When he tried to make sense of it, the effort hurt his mind almost as much as had the "hound's" probe.

The Esper "hound!" Craike jerked up, old panic stirring. First delicately and then urgently, he cast a thought-seek about him. There was life in plenty. He touched, classified and disregarded the flickers of awareness which mingled in confusion—animals, birds, river dwellers. But nowhere did he meet intelligence approaching his own. A wilderness world without man as far as Esper ability could reach.

Craike relaxed. Something had happened. He was too tired, too drained to speculate as to what. It was enough that he was saved from the death he had sought, that he was *here* instead of *there*.

He got stiffly to his feet. Time was the same, he thought—late afternoon. Shelter, food—he set off along the stream. He found and ate berries spilling from bushes where birds raided before him. Then, squatting above a side eddy of the stream, he scooped out a fish, eating the flesh raw.

The land along the river was rising, he could see the beginning of a gorge ahead. Later, when he had climbed those heights, he caught sight through the twilight of the fires. Four of them burning some miles to the southwest, set out in the form of a square!

Craike sent out a thought probe. Yes—men! But an alien touch. This was no hunting mob. And he was drawn to the security of the fires, the camp of men in the dangers of the night. Only, as Esper, he was not one with them but an outlaw. And he dare not risk joining them.

He retraced his path to the river and holed up in a hollow not large enough to be termed a cave. Automatically he probed again for danger. Found nothing, but animal life. He slept at last, drugged by exhaustion of mind and body.

The sky was gray when he roused, swung cramped arms, stretched. Craike had awakened with the need to know more of that camp. He climbed once again to the vantage point, shut his eyes to the early morning and sent out a seeking.

A camp of men far from home. But they were not hunters. Merchants—traders! Craike located one mind among the rest, read in it the details of a bargain to come. Merchants from another country, a caravan. But a sense of separation grew stronger as the fugitive Esper sorted out thought streams, absorbed scraps of knowledge thirstily. A herd of burden-bearing animals, nowhere any indication of machines. He sucked in a deep breath—he was—he was in another world!

Merchants traversing a wilderness—a wilderness? Though he had been driven into desert the day before, the land through which he had earlier fled could not be termed a wilderness. It was overpopulated because there were too many war-poisoned areas where mankind could not live.

But from these strangers he gained a concept of vast, barren territory broken only by small, sparse strips of cultivation. Craike hurried. They were breaking camp. And the impression of an unpeopled land they had given him made him want to trail the caravan.

There was trouble! An attack—the caravan animals stampeded. Craike received a startlingly vivid mind picture of a hissing, lizard thing he could not identify. But it was danger on four scaled feet. He winced at the fear in those minds ahead. There was a vigor of mental broadcast in these men which amazed him. Now, the lizard thing had been killed. But the pack animals were scattered. It would take hours to find them. The exasperation of the master trader was as strong to Craike as if he stood before the man and heard his outburst of complaint.

The Esper smiled slowly. Here—handed to him by Fate—was his chance to gain the good will of the travelers. Breaking contact with the men, Craike cast around probe webs, as a fisher might cast a net. One panic-crazed animal and then another—he touched minds, soothed, brought to bear his training. Within moments he heard the dull thud of hooves on the mossy ground, no longer pounding in a wild gallop. A shaggy mount, neither pony nor horse of his knowledge, but like in ways of each, its dull hide marked with a black stripe running from the root of shaggy mane to the base of its tail, came toward him, nickered questioningly. And then fell behind Craike, to be joined by another and another, as the Esper walked on—until he led the full train of runaways.

He met the first of the caravan men within a quarter of a mile and savored the fellow's astonishment at the sight. Yet, after the first surprise the man did not appear too amazed. He was short, dark of skin, a black beard of wiry, tightly curled hair clipped to a point thrusting out from his chin. Leggings covered his limbs, and he wore a sleeveless jerkin laced with thongs. This was belted by a broad strap gaudy with painted designs, from which hung a cross-hilted sword and a knife almost as long. A peaked cap of silky white fur was drawn far down so that a front flap shaded his eyes, and another, longer strip brushed his shoulders.

"Many thanks, Man of Power—" the words he spoke were in a clicking tongue, but Craike read their meaning mind to mind.

Then, as if puzzled on his closer examination of the Esper, the stranger frowned, his indecision slowly turning hostile.

"Outlaw! Begone, horned one!" The trader made a queer gesture with two fingers. "We pass free from your spells—"

"Be not so quick to pass judgment, Alfric—"

The newcomer was the Master Trader. As his man, he wore leather, but there was a gemmed clasp on his belt. His sword and knife hilt were of precious metal, as was a badge fastened to the fore of his yellow and black fur head gear.

"This one is no local outlaw." The Master stood, feet apart, studying the fugitive Esper as if he were a burden pony offered as a bargain. "Would such use his power for our aid? If he is a horned one—he is unlike any I have seen."

"I am not what you think—" Craike said slowly, fitting his tongue to the others' alien speech.

The Master Trader nodded. "That is true. And you intend us no harm; does not the sun-stone so testify?" His hand went to the badge on his cap. "In this one is no evil, Alfric, rather does he come to us in aid. Have I not spoken the truth to you, stranger from the wastes?"

Craike broadcast good will as strongly as he could. And they must have been somewhat influenced by that.

"I feel—he *does* have the power!" Alfric burst forth.

"He has power," the Master corrected him. "But has he striven to possess our minds as he could do? We are still our own men. No—this is no renegade Black Hood. Come!"

He beckoned to Craike, and the Esper, the animals still behind him, followed on into the camp, where the rest of the men seized upon the ponies to adjust their packs.

The Master filled a bowl from the contents of a three-legged pot set in the coals of a dying fire. Craike gulped an excellent and filling stew. When he had done, the Master indicated himself.

"I am Kaluf of the Children of Noe, a far trader and trail master. Is it your will, Man of Power, to travel this road with us?"

Craike nodded. This might all be a wild dream. But he was willing to see it to its end. A day with the caravan, the chance to gather more information from the men here, should give him some inkling as to what had happened to him and where he now was.

II

Craike's day with the traders became two and then three. Esper talents were accepted by this company matter-of-factly, even asked in aid. And from the travelers he gained a picture of this world which he could not reconcile with his own.

His first impression of a large continent broken by widely separated holdings of a frontier type remained. In addition there was knowledge of a feudal government, petty lordlings holding title to lands over men of lesser birth.

Kaluf and his men had a mild contempt for their customers. Their own homeland lay to the southeast, where, in some coastal cities, they had built up an overseas trade, retaining its cream for their own consumption, peddling the rest in the barbarous hinterland. Craike, his facility in their click speech growing, asked questions which the Master answered freely enough.

"These inland men know no difference between Saludian silk and the weaving of the looms in our own Kormonian quarter." He shrugged in scorn at such ignorance. "Why should we offer Salud when we can get Salud prices for Kormon lengths and the buyer is satisfied? Maybe—if these lords ever finish their private quarrels and live at peace so that there is more travel and they themselves come to visit in Larud or the other cities of the Children of Noe, then shall we not make a profit on lesser goods"

"Do these Lords never try to raid your caravans?"

Kaluf laughed. "They tried that once or twice. Certainly they saw there was the profit in seizing a train and paying nothing. But we purchased trail rights from the Black Hoods, and there was no more trouble. How is it with you, Ka-rak? Have you lords in your land who dare to stand against the power of the Hooded Ones?''

Craike, taking a chance, nodded. And knew he had been right when some reserve in Kaluf vanished.

"That explains much, perhaps even why such a man of power as you should be adrift in the wilderness. But you need not fear in this country, your brothers hold complete rule—''

A colony of Espers! Craike tensed. Had he, through some weird chance, found here the long-hoped-for refuge of his kind? But where *was* here? His old bewilderment was lost in a shout from the fore of the train.

"The outpost has sighted us and raised the trade banner." Kaluf quickened pace. "Within the hour we'll be at the walls of Sampur. Illif!"

Craike made for the head of the line. Sampur, by the reckoning of the train, was a city of respectable size, the domain of a Lord Ludicar with whom Kaluf had had mutually satisfactory dealings for some time. And the Master anticipated a profitable stay. But the man who had ridden out to greet them was full of news.

Racially he was unlike the traders, taller, longer of arm. His bare chest was a thatch of blond-red hair as thick as a bear's pelt, long braids swung across his shoulders. A leather cap, reinforced with sewn rings of metal, was crammed down over his wealth of hair, and he carried a shield slung from his saddle pad. In addition to sword and knife, he nursed a spear in the crook of his arm, from the point of which trailed a banner strip of blue stuff.

"You come in good time, Master. The Hooded Ones have proclaimed a horning, and all the outbounders have gathered as witnesses. This is a good day for your trading, the Cloudy Ones have indeed favored you. But hurry, the Lord Ludicar is now riding in and soon there will be no good place from which to watch—''

Craike fell back. Punishment? An execution? No, not quite that. He wished he dared ask questions. Certainly the picture which had leaped into Kaluf's mind at the mention of "horning" could not be true!

Caution kept the Esper aloof. Sooner or later his alien origin must be noted, though Kaluf had supplied him with a fur cap, leather jerkin, and boots from the caravan surplus.

The ceremony was to take place just outside the main gate of the stockade, which formed the outer rampart of the town. A group of braided, ring-helmed warriors hemmed in a more imposing figure with a feather plume and a blue cloak, doubtless Lord Ludicar. Thronging at a respectful distance were the townfolk. But they were merely audience; the actors stood apart.

Craike's hands went to his head. The emotion which beat at him from that party brought the metallic taste of fear to his mouth, aroused his own memories. Then he steadied, probed. There was terror there, broadcast from two figures under guard. Just as an impact of Esper power came from the three black-hooded men who walked behind the captives.

He used his own talent carefully, dreading to attract the attention of the men in black. The townsfolk opened an aisle in their ranks, giving free passage to the open moorland and the green stretch of forest not too far away.

Fear—in one of those bound, stumbling prisoners it was abject, the same panic which had hounded Craike into the desert. But, though the other captive had no hope, there was a thick core of defiance, a desperate desire to strike back. And something in Craike arose to answer that.

Other men, wearing black jerkins and no hoods, crowded about the prisoners. When they stepped back Craike saw that the drab clothing of the two had been torn away. Shame, blotting out fear, came from the smaller captive. And there was no mistaking the sex of the curves that white body displayed. A girl, and very young. A violent shake of her head loosened her hair to flow, black and long, clothing her nakedness. Craike drew a deep breath as he had before that plunge into the canyon. Moving quickly he crouched behind a bush.

The Black Hoods went about their business with dispatch, each drawing in turn certain designs and lines in the dust of the road until they had created an intricate pattern about the feet of the prisoners.

A chant began in which the townspeople joined. The fear of the male captive was an almost visible cloud. But the outrage and anger of his feminine companion grew in relation to the chant, and Craike could sense her will battling against that of the assembly.

The watching Esper gasped. He could not be seeing what his eyes reported to his brain! The man was down on all fours, his legs and arms stretched, a mist clung to them, changed to red-brown hide. His head lengthened oddly, horns sprouted. No man, but an antlered stag stood there.

And the girl—?

Her transformation came more slowly. It began and then

faded. The power of the Black Hoods held her, fastening on her the form they visualized. She fought. But in the end a white doe sprang down the path to the forest, the stag leaping before her. They whipped past the bush where Craike had gone to earth, and he was able to see through the illusion. Not a red stag and a white doe, but a man and woman running for their lives, yet already knowing in their hearts there was no hope in their flight.

Craike, hardly knowing why he did it or who he could aid, followed, sure that mind touch would provide him with a guide.

He had reached the murky shadow of the trees when a sound rang from the town. At its summoning he missed a step before he realized it was directed against those he trailed and not himself. A hunting horn! So this world also had its hunted and its hunters. More than ever he determined to aid those who fled.

But it was not enough to just run blindly on the track of stag and doe. He lacked weapons. And his wits had not sufficed to save him in his own world. But there he had been conditioned against turning on his hunters, hampered, cruelly designed from birth to accept the quarry role. That was not true here.

Esper power—Craike licked dry lips. Illusions so well done they had almost enthralled him. Could illusion undo what illusion had done? Again the call of the horn, ominous in its clear tone, rang in his ears, set his pulses to pounding. The fear of those who fled was a cord, drawing him on.

But as he trotted among the trees Craike concentrated on his own illusion. It was not a white doe he pursued but the slim, young figure he had seen when they stripped away the clumsy stuff which had cloaked her, before she had shaken loose her hair veil. No doe, but a woman. She was not racing on four hooved feet, but running free on two, her hair blowing behind her. No doe, but a maid!

And in that moment, as he constructed that picture clearly, he contacted her in thought. It was like being dashed by sea-spray, cool, remote, very clean. And, as spray, the contact vanished in an instant, only to return.

"Who are you?"

"One who follows," he answered, holding to his picture of the running girl.

"Follow no more, you have done what was needful!" There was a burst of joy, so overwhelming a release from terror that it halted him. Then the cord between them broke.

Frantically Craike cast about seeking contact. There was only a dead wall. Lost, he put out a hand to the rough bark of the nearest tree. Wood things lurked here, them only did his mind touch. What did he do now?

His decision was made for him. He picked up a wave of panic again—spreading terror. But this was the fear of feathered and furred things. It came to him as ripples might run on a pool.

Fire! He caught the thought distorted by bird and beast mind. Fire which leaped from tree crown to tree crown, cutting a gash across the forest. Craike started on, taking the way west, away from the menace.

Once he called out as a deer flashed by him, only to know in the same moment that this was no illusion but an animal. Small creatures tunneled through the grass. A dog fox trotted, spared him a measuring gaze from slit eyes. Birds whirred, and behind them was the scent of smoke.

A mountain of flesh, muscle and fur snarled, reared to face him. But Craike had nothing to fear from any animal. He confronted the great red bear until it whined, shuffled its feet and plodded on. More and more creatures crossed his path or ran beside him for a space.

It was their instinct which brought them, and Craike, to a river. Wolves, red deer, bears, great cats, foxes and all the rest came down to the saving water. A cat spat at the flood, but leaped in to swim. Craike lingered on the bank. The smoke was thicker, more animals broke from the wood to take to the water. But the doe—where was she?

He probed, only to meet that blank. Then a spurt of flame ran up a dead sapling, advance scout of the furnace. He yelped as a floating cinder stung his skin and took to the water. But he did not cross, rather did he swim upstream, hoping to pass the flank of the fire and pick up the missing trail again.

III

Smoke cleared as Craike trod water. He was beyond the path of the fire, but not out of danger. For the current against which he had fought his way beat here through an archway of masonry. Flanking that arch were two squat towers. As an erection it was far more ambitious than anything he had seen during his brief glimpse of Sampur. Yet, as he eyed it more closely, he could see it was a ruin. There were gaps in the narrow span across the river, a green bush sprouted from the summit of the far tower.

Craike came ashore, winning his way up the steep bank by handholds of vine and bush no alert castellan would have allowed to grow. As he reached a terrace of cobbles stippled with bunches of coarse grass, a sweetish scent of decay drew him around the base of the tower to look down at a broad ledge extending into the river. Piled on it were small baskets and bowls, some so rotted that only outlines were visible. Others new and all filled with moldering food stuffs. But those who left such offerings must have known that the tower was deserted.

Puzzled, Craike went back to the building. The stone was undressed, yet the huge blocks which formed its base were fitted together with such precision that he suspected he could not force the thin blade of a pocket knife into any crack. There had been no effort at ornamentation, at any lightening of the impression of sullen, brute force.

Wood, split and insect-bored, formed a door. As he put his hand to it Craike discovered the guardian the long-ago owners of the fortress had left in possession. His hands went to his head, the blow he felt might have been physical. Out of the stronghold before him came such a wave of utter terror and dark promise as to force him back. But no farther than the edge of the paved square about the building's foundation.

Grimly he faced that challenge, knowing it for stored emotion and not the weapon of an active will. He had his own defense against such a formless enemy. Breaking a dead branch from a bush, he twisted about it wisps of the sun-bleached grass until he had a torch of sorts. A piece of smoldering tinder blown from the fire gave him a light.

Craike put his shoulder to the powdery remnants of the door, bursting it wide. Light against dark. What lurked there was nourished by dark, fed upon the night fears of his species.

A round room, bare except for some crumbling sticks of wood, a series of steps jutting out from the wall to curl about and vanish above. Craike made no move toward further exploration, holding up the torch, seeking to see the real, not the threat of this place.

Those who had built it possessed Esper talents. And they had used that power for twisted purposes. He read terror and despair trapped here by the castellans' art, horror, an abiding fog of what his race considered evil.

Tentatively Craike began to fight. With the torch he brought light and heat into the dark and cold. Now he struggled to offer peace. Just as he had pictured a girl in flight in place of the doe, so did he now force upon those invisible clouds of stored suffering calm and hope. The gray window slits in the stone were uncurtained to the streaming sunlight.

Those who had set that guardian had not intended it to hold

against an Esper. Once he began the task, Craike found the opposition melting. The terror seeped as if it sank into the floor wave by wave. He stood in a room which smelt of damp and, more faintly, of the rotting food piled below its window slits; but now it was only an empty shell.

Craike was tired, drained by his effort. And he was puzzled. Why had he fought for this? Of what importance to him was the cleansing of a ruined tower?

Though to stay here had certain advantages. It had been erected to control river traffic. Though that did not matter for the present, just now he needed food more—

He went back to the rock of offerings, treading a wary path through the disintegrating stuff. Close to the edge he came upon a clay bowl containing coarsely ground grain and, beside it, a basket of wilted leaves filled with overripe berries. He ate in gulps.

Grass made him a matted bed in the tower, and he kindled a fire. As he squatted before its flames, he sent out a questing thought. A big cat drank from the river. Craike shuddered away from that contact with blood lust. A night-hunting bird provided a trace of awareness. There were small rovers and hunters. But nothing human.

Tired as he was Craike could not sleep. There was the restless sensation of some demand about to be made, some task waiting. From time to time he fed the fire. Towards morning he dozed, to snap awake. A night creature drinking, a screech overhead. He heard the flutter of wings echo hollowly through the tower.

Beyond—darkness—blank, that curious blank which had fallen between him and the girl. Craike got to his feet eagerly. That blank could be traced.

Outside it was raining, and fog hung in murky bands among the river hollows. The blank spot veered. Craike started after it. The tower pavement became a trace of old road he followed, weaving through the fog.

There was the sour smell of old smoke. Charred wood, black muck clung to his feet. But his guide point was now stationary as the ground rose, studded with outcrops of rock. So Craike came to a mesa jutting up into a steel gray sky.

He hitched his way up by way of a long-ago slide. The rain had stopped, but there was no hint of sun. And he was unprepared for the greeting he met as he topped the lip of a small plateau.

A violent blow on the shoulder whirled him halfway around, and only by a finger's width did he escape a fall. A cry echoed his, and the blank broke. She was there.

Moving slowly, using the same technique he knew to sooth frightened animals, Craike raised himself again. The pain in his shoulder was sharp when he tried to put much weight upon his left arm. But now he saw her clearly.

She sat cross-legged, a boulder at her back, her hair a rippling cloud of black through which her hands and arms shown starkly white. She had the thin, three-cornered face of a child who has known much harshness; there was no beauty there—the flesh had been too much worn by spirit. Only her eyes, watchful-wary as those of a feline, considered him bleakly. In spite of his beam of good will, she gave him no welcome. And she tossed another stone from hand to hand with the ease of one who had already scored with such a weapon.

"Who are you?" She spoke aloud.

"He who followed you." Craike fingered the bruise wound on his shoulder, not taking his eyes from hers.

"You are no Black Hood." It was a statement not a question. "But you, also, have been horned." Another statement.

Craike nodded. In his own time and place he had indeed been "horned."

Just as her thrown stone had struck without warning, so came her second attack. There was a hiss. Within striking distance a snake flickered a forked tongue.

Craike did not give ground. The snake head expanded, fur ran over it; there were legs, a plume of tail fluffed. A dog fox yapped once at the girl and vanished. Craike read her recoil, the first faint uncertainty.

"You have the power!"

"I have power," he corrected her.

But her attention was no longer his. She was listening to something he could hear with neither ear nor mind. Then she ran to the edge of the mesa. He followed.

On this side the country was more rolling, and across it now came mounted men moving in and out of mist pools. They rode in silence, and over them was the same blanketing of thought as the girl had used.

Craike glanced about. There were loose stones, and the girl had already proven her marksmanship with such. But they would be no answer to the weapons the others had. Only flight was no solution either.

The girl sobbed once, a broken cry so unlike the iron will she had shown that Craike started. She leaned perilously over the drop, staring down at the horsemen.

Then her hands moved with desperate speed. She tore hairs from her head, twisted and snarled them between her fingers, breathed on them, looped them with a stone for weight, casting the tangled mass out to land before the riders.

The mist curled, took on substance. Where there had been only rock there was now a thicket of thorn, so knotted that no fleshed creature could push through it. The hunters paused, then they rode on again, but now they drove a reeling, naked man, a man kept going by a lashing whip whenever he faltered.

Again the girl sobbed, burying her face in her hands. The wretched captive reached the thorn barrier. Under his touch it melted. He stood there, weaving drunkenly.

A whip sang. He went to his knees under its cut, a trapped animal's wail on the wind. Slowly, with a blind seeking, his hands went out to small stones about him. He gathered them, spread them anew in patterns. The girl had raised her head, watched dry-eyed, but seething with hate and the need to strike back. But she did not move.

Craike dared lay a hand on her narrow shoulder, feeling through her hair the chill of her skin, while the hair itself clung to his fingers as if it had the will to smother and imprison. He tried to pull her away, but he could not move her.

The naked man crouched in the midst of his pattern, and now he chanted, a compelling call the girl could not understand. She wrenched free of Craike's hold. But as she went she spared a thought for the man who had tried to save her. She struck out, her fist landing on the stone bruise. Pain sent him reeling back as she went over the rim of the mesa, her face a mask which no friend nor enemy might read. But there was no resignation in her eyes as she was forced to the meeting below.

IV

By the time Craike reached a vantage point the girl stood in the center of the stone ring. Outside crouched the man, his head on his knees. She looked down at him, no emotion showing on her wan face. Then she dropped her hand on his thatch of wild hair. He jerked under that touch as he had under the whip which had printed the scarlet weals across his back and loins. But he raised his head, and from his throat came a beast's mournful howl. At her gesture he was quiet, edging closer to her as if seeking some easement of his suffering.

The Black Hoods drew in. Craike's probe could make nothing of them. But they could not hide their emotions as well as they concealed their thoughts. And the Esper recoiled from the avid blood lust which lapped at the two by the cliff.

A semicircle of the black-jerkined retainers moved too. And the man who had led them lay on the earth now, moaning softly. But the girl faced them, head unbowed. Craike wanted to aid her. Had he time to climb down the cliff? Clenching his teeth against the pain movement brought to his shoulder, the Esper went back, holding a mind shield as a frail protection.

Directly before him now was one of the guards. His mount caught Craike's scent, stirred uneasily, until the quieting thought of the Esper held it steady. Craike had never been forced into such action as he had these past few days; he had no real plan now, it must depend upon chance and fortune.

As if the force of her enemies' wills had slammed her back against the rock, the girl was braced by the cliff wall, a black-and-white figure.

Mist swirled, took on half substance of a monstrous form, was swept away in an instant. A clump of dried grass broke into flame, sending the ponies stamping and snorting. It was gone, leaving a black smudge on the earth. Illusions, realities—Craike watched. This was so far beyond his own experience that he could hardly comprehend the lightning moves of mind against mind. But he sensed these others could beat down the girl's resistance at any moment they desired, that her last futile struggles were being relished by those who decreed this as part of her punishment.

And Craike, who had believed that he could never hate more than he had when he had been touched by the fawning "hound" of the mob, was filled with a rage tempered into a chill of steel determination.

The girl went to her knees, still clutching her hair about her, facing her tormenters with her still-held defiance. Now the man who had wrought the magic which had drawn her there crawled, all humanity gone out of him, wriggling on his belly back to his captors.

Two of the guards jerked him up. He hung limp in their hands, his mouth open in an idiot's grin. Callously, as he might tread upon a worm, the nearest Black Hood waved a hand. A metal axe flashed, and there came the dull sound of cracking bone. The guards pitched the body from them so that the bloodied head almost touched the girl.

She writhed, a last frenzied attempt to break the force which pinned her. Without haste the guards advanced. One caught at her hair, pulling it tautly from her head.

Craike shivered. The thrill of her agony reached him. This was what she feared most, fought so long to prevent. If ever he must move now. And that part of his brain which had been feverishly seeking a plan went into action.

Ponies pawed, reared, went wild with panic. One of the Black Hoods swung around to face the terrorized animals. But his own mount struck out with teeth and hooves. Guardsmen shouted, and above their cries arose the shrill squeals of the animals.

Craike stood his ground, keeping the ponies in terror-stricken revolt. The guard who held the handful of hair slashed at the tress with his knife, severing it at a palm's distance away from her head. But in that same movement she moved. The knife leaped free from the man's grasp, while the severed hair twined itself about his hands, binding them until the blade buried itself in his throat; and he went down.

One of the Black Hoods was also finished, tramped into a feebly squirming thing by the ponies. Then from the ground burst a sheet of flame which split into balls, drifting through the air or rolling along the earth.

The Esper wet his lips—that was not his doing! He did not have to feed the panic of the animals now; they were truly mad. The girl was on her feet. Before his thought could reach her she was gone, swallowed up in a mist which arose to blanket the fireballs. Once more she cut their contact; there was a blank void where she had been.

Now the fog thickened. Through it came one of the ponies, foam dripping from its blunt muzzle. It bore down on Craike, eyes gleaming red through a tangled forelock. With a scream it reared.

Craike's hand grabbed a handful of mane as he leaped, avoiding teeth and hooves. Then, somehow, he gained the pad saddle, locking his fingers in the coarse hair, striving to hold his seat against the bucking enraged beast. It broke into a run, and the Esper plastered himself to the heaving body. For the moment he made no attempt at mind control.

Behind, the Black Hoods came out of their stunned bewilderment. They were questing feverishly, and he had to concentrate on holding his shield against them. A pony fleeing in terror would not excite them; a pony under control would provide them with a target.

Later he could circle about and try to pick up the trail of the witch girl. Flushed with success, Craike was sure he could provide her with a rear guard no Black Hood could pass.

The fog was thick, and the pace of the pony began to slacken. Once or twice it bucked halfheartedly, giving up when it could not dislodge its rider. Craike drew his fingers in slow, soothing sweeps down the sweating curve of its neck.

There were no more trees about, and the unshod hooves pounded on sand. They were in a dried watercourse, and Craike did not try to turn from that path. Then his luck ran out.

What he had ignorantly supposed to be a rock ahead heaved up seven feet or more. A red mouth opened in a great roar. He had believed the bear he had seen fleeing the fire to be a giant, but this one was a nightmare monster.

The pony screamed with an almost human note of despair and whirled. Craike gripped the mane again and tried to mind-control the bear. But his surprise had lasted seconds too long. A vast clawed paw struck, ripping across pony hide and human thigh. Then Craike could only cling to the running mount.

How long he was able to keep his seat he never knew. Then he slipped; there was a throb of pain as he struck the ground, to be followed by blackness.

It was dusk when he opened his eyes, fighting agony in his head, his leg. But later there was moonlight. And that silver-white spotlighted a waiting shape. Green slits of eyes regarded him remotely. Dizzily he made contact.

A wolf—hungry—yet with a wariness which recognized in the prone man an enemy. Craike fought for control. The wolf whined, then it arose, its prick ears sharp-cut in the moonlight, its nose questing for the scent of other, less disturbing prey, and it was gone.

Craike edged up against a boulder and sorted out sounds. The rush of water. He moved a paper-dry tongue over cracked lips. Water to drink—to wash his wounds—water!

With a groan Craike worked his way to his feet, holding fast to the top of the rock when his torn leg threatened to buckle under him. The same inner drive which had kept him going through the desert brought him down to the river.

By sunrise he was seeking a shelter, wanting to lie up, as might the wolf, in some secret cave until his wounds healed. All chance of finding the witch girl was lost. But as he crawled along the shingle, leaning on a staff he had found in drift wood, he kept alert for any trace of the Black Hoods.

It was midmorning on the second day that his snail's progress brought him to the river towers. And it took another hour for him to reach the terrace. Gaunt and worn, his empty stomach complaining, he wanted nothing more than to sink down in the nest of grass he had gathered and cease to struggle.

Perhaps he might have done so had not a click-clack of sound from the river put him on the defensive, his staff now a club. But these were not Black Hoods. Farmers, local men bound for the market of Sampur with products of their fields. They had paused, were making a choice among the least appetizing of their wares for a tribute to be offered to the tower demon.

Craike hitched stiffly to a point where he could witness that sacrifice. But when he assessed the contents of their dugout, the heaping basket piled between the paddlers, his hunger took command.

Fob off a demon with a handful of meal and a too-ripe melon, would they? With three haunches of cured meat and all that other stuff on board!

Craike voiced a roar which could have done credit to the red bear, a roar which altered into a demand for meat. The paddlers nearly lost control of their crude craft. But one reached for a haunch and threw it blindly on the refuse-covered rock, while his companion added a basket of small cakes into the bargain.

"Enough, little men—" Craike's voice boomed hollowly. "You may pass free."

They needed no urging, they did not look at those threatening towers as their paddles bit into the water, adding impetus to the pull of the current.

Craike watched them well out of sight before he made a slow descent to the rock. The effort he was forced to expend warned him that a second such trip might be impossible, and he inched back to the terrace dragging both meat and cakes.

The cured haunch he worried into strips, using his pocket knife. It was tough, not too pleasant to the taste and unsalted. But he found it more appetizing than the cakes of baked meal. With this supply he could afford to lie up and favor his leg.

About the claw rents the flesh was red and puffed. Craike had no dressing but river water and the leaves he had tied over the tears. Sampur was beyond his power to reach, and to contact men traveling on the river would only bring the Black Hoods.

He lay in his grass nest and tried to sort out the events of the past few days. This was a land in which Esper powers were allowed free range. He had no idea of how he had come here, but it seemed to his feverish mind that he had been granted another chance—one in which the scales of justice were more balanced in his favor. If he could only find the girl, learn from her—

Tentatively, without real hope, he sent out a questing thought. Nothing. He moved impatiently, wrenching his leg, so that his head swam with pain. Throat and mouth were dry. The lap of water sounded in his ears. Water—he was thirsty again. But he could not crawl downslope and up once more. Craike closed his eyes wearily.

V

Craike's memory of the hours which followed thereafter was dim. *Had* he seen a demon in the doorway? A slavering wolf? A red bear?

Then the girl sat there, cross-legged as he had seen her on the mesa, her cloak of hair about her. A hand emerged from the cloak to lay wood on the fire. Illusions?

But would an illusion turn to him, put firm, cool fingers upon his wound, somehow driving out by touch the pain and fire which burned there? Would an illusion raise his head, cradling it against her so that the soft silk of her hair lay against his cheek and throat, urging on him liquid out of a crude bowl? Would an illusion sing softly to herself while she drew a fish-bone comb back and forth through her hair, until the song and the sweep of the comb lulled him into a sleep so deep that no dream walked there?

He awoke, clear-headed. Yet that last illusion lingered. For she came from the sun-drenched world without, a bowl of fruit in her hand. For a long moment she stood gazing at him searchingly. But when he tried mind contact, he met that wall. Not unheeding—but a refusal to answer.

Her hair was now braided. But about her face the lock which the guardsman had shorn made an untidy fringe. While around her thin body was a strip of hide, purposefully arranged to mask all femininity.

"So," Craike spoke rustily, "you are real—"

She did not smile. "I am real. You no longer dream with fever."

"Who are you?" He asked the first of his long hoarded questions.

"I am Takya." She added nothing to that.

"You are Takya, and you are a witch—"

"I am Takya, and I have the power." It was an assertion of fact rather than agreement.

She settled in her favorite cross-legged position, selected a fruit from her bowl and examined it with the interest of a housewife who has shopped for supplies on a limited budget. Then she placed it in his hand before she chose another for herself. He bit into the plumlike globe. If she would only drop her barrier, let him communicate in the way which was fuller and deeper than speech.

"You also have the power—"

Craike decided to be no more communicative than she. He replied to that with a curt nod.

"Yet you have not been horned—"

"Not as you have been. But in my own world, yes."

"Your world?" Her eyes held some of the feral glow of a hunting cat's. "What world, and why were you horned there, man of sand and ash power?"

Without knowing why Craike related the events of the days past. Takya listened, he was certain, with more than ears alone. She picked up a stick from the pile of firewood and drew patterns in the sand and ash, patterns which had something to do with her listening.

"Your power was great enough to break a world wall." She snapped the stick between two fingers, threw it into the flames.

"A world wall?"

"We of the power have long known that different worlds lie together in such a fashion." She held up her hand with the fingers tight lying one to another. "Sometimes there comes a moment when two touch so closely that the power can carry one through if at that moment there is a desperate need for escape. But those places of meeting cannot be readily found, and the moment of their touch can lie only for an instant. Have you in your world no reports of men and women who have vanished almost in sight of their fellows?"

Remembering old tales, he nodded.

"I have seen a summoning from another world," she continued with a shiver, running both hands down the length of her braids as if so she evoked a shield for both mind and body. "To summon so is a great evil, for no man can hold in check the power of something alien. You broke the will of the Black Hoods when I was a beast running from their hunt. When I made

the serpent to warn you off, you changed it into a fox. And when
the Black Hoods would have shorn my power''—she looped the
braids about her wrists, caressing, treasuring them against her
small breasts—''again you broke their hold and set me free for a
second time. But this you could not have done had you been
born into this world, for our power must follow set laws. Yours
lies outside our patterns and can cut across those laws—even as
the knife cut this—'' She touched the rough patch of hair at her
temple.

''Follow patterns? Then it was those patterns in stone which
drew you down from the mesa?''

''Yes. Takyi, my womb-brother, whom they slew there, was
blood of my blood, bone of my bone. When they crushed him,
then they could use him to draw me, and I could not resist. But
in the slaying of his husk they freed me—to their great torment,
as Tousuth shall discover in time.''

''Tell me of this country. Who are the Black Hoods and why
did they horn you? Are you not of their breed since you have the
power?''

But Tayka did not answer at once in words. Nor did she, as he
had hoped, lower her mind barrier.

Her fingers now held one long hair she had pulled from her
head, and this she began to weave in and out, swiftly, intricately,
in a complicated series of loops and crossed strands. After a
moment Craike did not see the white fingers, nor the black hair
they passed in loops from one to another. Rather did he see the
pictures she wrought in her weaving.

A wide land, largely wilderness. The impressions he had
gathered from Kaluf and the traders crystalized into vivid life.
Small holdings here and there, ruled by petty lords, new settle-
ments carved out by a scattered people moving up from the south
in great wheeled wains, bringing flocks and herds, their carefully
treasured seed. Stopping here and there for a season to sow and
reap, until they decided upon a site for their final rooting. Tiny
city-states, protected by the Black Hoods—the Esper born who
purposefully interbred their own gifted stock, keeping their children apart.

Takya and her brother coming, as was sometimes—if rarely—
true, from the common people. Carefully watched by the Black
Hoods. Then discovered to be a new mutation, condemned as
such to be used for experimentation. But for a while protected by
the local lord who wanted Takya.

But he might not take her unwilling. For the power that was

hers as a virgin was wholly rift from her should she be forced. And he had wanted that power, obedient to him, as a check upon the monopoly of the Black Hoods. So with some patience he had set himself to a peaceful wooing. But the Black Hoods had moved first.

Had they accomplished her taking, the end they had intended for her was not as easy as death. And she wove a picture of it, with all its degradation and shame stark and open, for Craike's seeing.

"Then the Hooded Ones are evil?"

"Not wholly." She untwisted the hair and put it with care into the fire. "They do much good, and without them people would suffer. But I, Takya, am different. And after me, when I mate, there will be others also different. How different we are not yet sure. The Hooded Ones want no change, by their thinking that means disaster. So they would use me to their own purposes. Only I, Tayka, shall not be so used!"

"No, you shall not." The vehemence of his own outburst startled him. Craike wanted nothing so much at that moment as to come to grips with the Black Hoods, who had planned this systematic hunt.

"What will you do now?" he asked more calmly, wishing she would share her thoughts with him.

"This is a strong place. Did you cleanse it?"

He nodded impatiently.

"So I thought. That was also a task one born to this world might not have performed. But those who pass are not yet aware of the cleansing. They will not trouble us, but pay tribute."

Craike found her complacency irritating. To lie up here and live on the offerings of river travelers did not appeal to him.

"This stone piling is older work than Sampur and much better," she continued. "It must have been a fortress for some of those forgotten ones who held lands and then vanished long before we came from the south. If it is repaired no lord of this district would have so good a roof."

"Two of us to rebuild it?" he laughed.

"Two of us—working thus."

A block of stone, the size of a brick, which had fallen from the sill of one of the needle-narrow windows, arose slowly in the air, settled into the space from which it had tumbled. Illusion or reality? Craike got to his feet and lurched to the window. His hand fell upon the stone, which moved easily in his grasp. He took it out, weighed it, and then gently returned it to its place. Not illusion.

"But illusion too—if need be." There was, for the first time, a warmth not of amusement in her tone. "Look on your tower, river lord!"

He limped to the door. Outside it was warm, sunny, but it was a site of ruins. Then the picture changed. Brown drifts of grass vanished from the terrace, the fallen stone was all in place. A hard-faced sentry stood wary-eyed on a repaired river arch. Another guardsman led out ponies saddle-padded and ready, other men were about garrison tasks.

Craike grinned. The sentry on the arch lost his helm, his jerkin. He now wore the tight tunic of the Security Police, his spear was a gas rifle. The ponies misted, and in their place a speedster sat on the stone. He heard her laugh.

"*Your* guard, *your* traveling machine. But how grim, ugly. This is better!"

Guards, machine, all were swept away. Craike caught his breath at the sight of delicate winged creatures dancing in the air, displaying a joy of life he had never known. Fawns, little people of the wild, came to mingle with such shapes of beauty and desire that at last he turned his head away.

"Illusion." Her voice was hard, mocking.

But Craike could not believe that what he had seen had been born from hardness and mockery.

"All illusions. We shall be better now with warriors. As for plans, can you suggest any better than to remain here and take what fortune sends—for a space?"

"Those winged dancers—where?"

"Illusions!" she returned harshly. "But such games tire one. I do not think we shall conjure up any garrison before they are needed. Come, do not tear open those wounds of yours anew, for healing is no illusion and drains one even more of the power."

The clawed furrows were healing cleanly, though he would bear their scars for life. He hobbled back to the grass bed and dropped upon it, but regretted the erasure of the sprites she had shown him.

Once he was safely in place, Takya left with the curt explanation she had things to do. But Craike was restless, too much so to remain long inside the tower. He waited until she had gone and then, with the aid of his staff, climbed to the end of the span above the river. From here the twin tower on the other bank looked the same as the one from which he had come. Whether it was also haunted Craike did not know. But, as he looked about, he could see the sense of Tayka's suggestion. A few illusion sentries would discourage any ordinary intrusion.

Takya's housekeeping had changed the rock of offerings. All the rotting debris was gone and none of the odor of decay now offended the nostrils at a change of wind. But at best it was a most uncertain source of supply. There could not be too many farms up river, nor too many travelers taking the water away.

As if to refute that, his Esper sense brought him sudden warning of strangers beyond the upper bend. But, Craike sensed, these were no peasants bound for the market at Sampur. Fear, pain, anger, such emotions heralded their coming. There were three, and one was hurt. But they were not Esper, nor did they serve the Black Hoods. Though they were, or had been, fighting men.

A brutal journey over the mountains where they had lost comrades, the finding of this river, the theft of the dugout they now used so expertly—it was all there for him to read. And beneath that something else, which, when he found it, gave Craike a quick decision in their favor—a deep hatred of the Black Hoods! Outlaws, very close to despair, keeping on a hopeless trail because it was not in them to surrender.

Craike contacted them subtly. They must not think they were heading into an Esper trap! Plant a little hope, a faint suggestion that there was a safe camping place ahead, that was all he could do at present. But so he drew them on.

"No!" A ruthless order cut across his line of contact, striking at the delicate thread with which he was playing the strangers in. But Craike stood firm. "Yes, yes, and yes!"

He was on guard instantly. Takya, mistress of illusion as she had proved herself to be, might act. But surprisingly she did not. The dugout came into view, carried more by the current than the efforts of its crew. One lay full-length in the bottom, while the bow paddler had slumped forward. But the man in the stern was bringing them in. And Craike strengthened his invisible, unheard invitation to urge him on.

VI

But Takya had not yet begun to fight. As the dugout swung in toward the offering ledge one of the Black Hoods' guardsmen appeared there, his drawn sword taking fire from the sun. The fugitive steersman faltered until the current drew his craft on.

Craike caught the full force of the stranger's despair, all the keener for the hope of moments before. The Esper irritation against Takya flared into anger.

He made the illusion reel back, hands clutching at his breast from which protruded the shaft of an arrow. Craike had seen no bows here, but it was a weapon to suit this world. And this should prove to Takya he meant what he had said.

The steersman was hidden as the dugout passed under the arch. There was a scrap of beach, the same to which Craike had swum on his first coming. He urged the man to that, beaming good will.

But the paddler was almost done, and neither of his companions could aid him. He drove the crude craft to the bank, and its bow grated on the rough gravel. Then he crawled over the bodies of the other two and fell rather than jumped ashore, turning to pull up the canoe as best he could.

Craike started down. But he might have known that Takya was not so easily defeated. Though they maintained an alliance of sorts she accepted no order from him.

A brand was teleported from the tower fire, striking spearwise in the dry brush along the slope. Craike's mouth set. He tried no more arguments. They had already tested power against power, and he was willing to so battle again. But this was not the time. However, the fire was no illusion, and he could not fight it, crippled as he was. Or could he?

It was not spreading too fast—though Takya might spur it by the forces at her command. Now—there was just the spot! Craike steadied himself against a mound of fallen masonry and swept out his staff, dislodging a boulder and a shower of gravel. He had guessed right. The stone rolled to crush out the brand, and the gravel he continued to push after it smothered the creeping flames.

Red tongues dashed spitefully high in a sheet of flame, and Craike laughed. *That* was illusion. She was angry. He produced a giant pail in the air, tilted it forward, splashed its contents into the heart of that conflagration. He felt the lash of her rage, standing under it unmoved. So might she bring her own breed to heel, but she would learn he was not of that ilk.

"Holla!" That call was no illusion, it begged help.

Craike picked a careful path downslope until he saw the dugout and the man who had landed it. The Esper waved an invitation, and at his summons the fugitive covered the distance between them.

He was a big man of the same brawny race as those of Sampur, his braids of reddish hair hanging well below his wide shoulders. There was the raw line of a half-healed wound down the angle of his jaw, and his sunken eyes were very tired. For a moment he stood downslope from Craike, his hands on his hips, his head back, measuring the Esper with the shrewdness of a canny officer who had long known how to judge and handle raw levies.

"I am Jorik of the Eagles' Tower." The statement was made with the same confidence as the announcement of rank might have come from one of the petty lords. "Though," he shrugged, "the Eagles' Tower stands no more with one stone upon the other. You have a stout lair here—" He hesitated before he concluded, "—friend."

"I am Craike," the Esper answered as simply, "and I am also one who has run from enemies. This lair is an old one, though still useful."

"Might the enemies from whom you run wear black hoods?" countered Jorik. "It seems to me that things I have just seen here have the stink of that about them."

"You are right. I am no friend to the Black Hoods."

"But you have the power—"

"I have power." Craike tried to make the distinction clear. "You are welcome, Jorik. So all are welcome here who are no friends to Black Hoods."

The big warrior shrugged. "We can no longer run. If the time has come to make a last stand, this is as good a place as any. My men are done." He glanced back at the two in the dugout. "They are good men, but we were pressed when they caught us in the upper pass. Once there were twenty hands of us." He held up his fist and spread the fingers wide for counting. "They drew us out of the tower with their sorcerers' tricks, and then put us to the hunt."

"Why did they wish to make an end to you?"

Jorik laughed shortly. "They dislike those who will not fit into their neat patterns. We are free mountain men, and no Black Hood helped us win the Eagles' Tower; none aided us to hunt. When we took our furs down to the valley they wanted to levy tribute. But what spell of theirs trapped the beasts in our deadfalls, or brought them to our spears? We pay not for what we have not bought. Neither would we have made war on them. Only, when we spoke out and said it so, there were others who were encouraged to do likewise, and the Black Hoods must put an end to us before their rule was broken. So they did."

"But they did not get all of you," Craike pointed out. "Can you bring your men up to the tower? I have been hurt and cannot walk without support or I would lend you a hand."

"We will come." Jorik returned to the dugout. Water was splashed vigorously into the face of the man in the bow, arousing him to crawl ashore. Then the leader of the fugitives swung the third man out of the craft and over his shoulder in a practiced carry.

When Craike had seen the unconscious man established on his own grass bed, he stirred up the fire and set out food while Jorik returned to the dugout to bring in their gear.

Neither of the other men was of the same size as their leader. The one who lay limp, his breath fluttering between his slack lips, was young, hardly out of boyhood, his thin frame showing bones rather than muscled flesh under the rags of clothing. The other was short, dark-skinned, akin by race to Kaluf's men, his jaw sprouting a curly beard. He measured Craike with suspicious glances from beneath lowered red lids, turning that study to the walls about him and the unknown reaches at the head of the stair.

Craike did not try mind touch. These men were rightly suspicious of Esper arts. But he did attempt to reach Takya, only to meet that nothingness with which she cloaked her actions. Craike was disturbed. Surely now that she was convinced he was determined to give the harborage to the fugitives, she would not oppose him. They had nothing to fear from Jorik and his men, but rather would gain by joining forces.

Until his wounds were entirely healed he could not go far. And without weapons they would have to rely solely upon Esper powers for defense. Having witnessed the efficiency of the Hooded Ones' attack, Craike doubted a victory in any engagement to which those masters came fully prepared. He had managed to upset their spells merely because they had not known of his existence. But the next time he would have no such advantage.

On the other hand the tower could be defended by force of arms. With bows—Craike savored the idea of archers giving a Hooded force a devastating surprise. The traders had had no such arm, as sophisticated as they were. And he had seen none among the warriors of Sampur. He'd have to ask Jorik if such were known.

In the meantime he sat among his guests, watching Jorik feed the semiconscious boy with soft fruit pulp and the other man wolf down dried meat. When the latter had done, he hitched himself closer to the fire and jerked a thumb at his chest.

"Zackuth," he identified himself.

"From Larud?" Craike named the only city of Kaluf's people he could remember.

The dark man's momentary surprise had no element of suspicion. 'What do you know of the Children of Noe, stranger?"

"I journeyed the plains with one called Kaluf, a Master Trader of Larud."

"A fat man who laughs much and wears a falcon plume in his cap?"

"Not so." Craike allowed a measure of chill to ice his reply. "The Kaluf who led this caravan was a lean man who knew the edge of a good blade from its hilt. As for cap ornaments—he had a red stone to the fore of his. Also he swore by the Eyes of the Lady Lor."

Zackuth gave a great bray of laughter. "You are no stream fish to be easily hooked, are you, tower dweller? I am not of Larud, but I know Kaluf, and those who travel in his company do not wear one badge one day and another the next. But, by the looks of you, you have fared little better than we lately. Has Kaluf also fallen upon evil luck?"

"I traveled safely with his caravan to the gates of Sampur. How it fared with him thereafter I cannot tell you."

Jorik grinned and settled his patient back on the bed. "I believe you must have parted company in haste, Lord Ka-rak?"

Craike answered that with the truth. "There were two who were horned. I followed them to give what aid I could."

Jorik scowled, and Zackuth spat into the fire.

"We were not horned; we have no power," the latter remarked. "But they have other tricks to play. So you came here?"

"I was clawed by a bear," Craike supplied a meager portion of his adventures, "and came here to lie up until I can heal me of that hurt."

"This is a snug hole." Jorik was appreciative. "But how got you such eating?" He popped half a fruit into his mouth and licked his juicy fingers. "This is no wilderness feeding."

"The tower is thought to be demon-haunted. Those taking passage downstream leave tribute."

Zackuth slapped his knee. "The Gods of the Waves are good to you, Lord Ka-rak, that you should stumble into such fortune. There is more than one kind of demon for the haunting towers. How say you, Lord Jorik?"

"That we have also come into luck at last, since Lord Ka-rak has made us free of this hold. But perhaps you have some other thought in your head?" He spoke to the Esper.

Craike shrugged. "What the clouds decree shall fall as rain or snow," he quoted a saying of the caravan men.

It was close to sunset, and he was worried about Takya. He could not believe that she had gone permanently. And yet, if she returned, what would happen? He had been careful not to use Esper powers. Takya would have no such compunctions.

He could not analyze his feelings about her. She disturbed him, awoke emotions he refused to face. There was a certain way she had of looking sidewise— But her calm assumption of superiority pricked beneath his surface armor. And the antagonism fretted against the feeling which had drawn him after her from the gates of Sampur. Once again he sent out a quest-thought and, to his surprise, was answered.

"They must go!"

"They are outlaws, even as we. One is ill, the others worn with long running. But they stood against the Black Hoods. As such they have a claim on roof, fire and food from us."

"They are not as we!" Again arrogance. "Send them or I shall drive them. I have the power—"

"Perhaps you have the power, but so do I!" He put all the assurance he could muster into that. "I tell you, no better thing could happen than for us to give these men aid. They are proven fighters—"

"Swords cannot stand against the power!"

Craike smiled. His plans were beginning to move even as he carried on this voiceless argument. "Not swords, no, Takya. But all fighting is not done with swords nor spears. Nor with the power either. Can a Black Hood think death to his enemy when he himself is dead, killed from a distance, and not by mind power his fellows could trace and be armored against?"

He had caught her attention. She was acute enough to know that he was not playing with words, that he knew of what he spoke. Quickly he built upon that spark of interest. "Remember how your illusion guard died upon the offering rock when you would warn off these men?"

"By a small spear." She was contemptuous again.

"Not so." He shaped a picture of an arrow and then of an archer releasing it from the bow cord, of its speeding true across the river to strike deep into the throat of an unsuspecting Black Hood.

"You have the secret of this weapon?"

"I do. And five such arms are better than two, is that not the truth?"

She yielded a fraction. "I will return. But they will not like that."

"If you return, they will welcome you. These are no hunters of witch maidens—" he began, only to be disconcerted by her obvious amusement. Somehow he had lost his short advantage over her. Yet she did not break contact.

"Ka-rak, you are very foolish. No, these will not try to mate with me, not even if I willed it so. As you will see. Does the eagle mate with the hunting cat? But they will be slow to trust me, I think. However, your plan has possibilities, and we shall see."

VII

Takya had been right about her reception by the fugitives. They knew her for what she was, and only Craike's acceptance of her kept them in the tower. That and the fact, which Jorik did not try to disguise, that they could not hope to go much farther on their own. But their fears were partly allayed when she took over the nursing of the sick youngster, using on him the same healing power she had produced for Craike's wound. By the new day she was feeding him broth and demanding service from the others as if they had been her liegemen from birth.

The sun was well up when Jorik came in whistling from a dip in the river.

"This is a stout stronghold, Lord Ka-rak. And with the power aiding us to hold it, we are not likely to be shaken out in a hurry. Doubly is that true if the Lady aids us."

Takya laughed. She sat in the shaft of light from one of the narrow windows, combing her hair. Now she looked over her shoulder at them with something approaching a pert archness. In that moment she was more akin to the women Craike had known in his own world.

"Let us first see how the Lord Ka-rak proposes to defend us." There was mockery in that, enough to sting, as well as a demand that he make good his promise of the night before.

But Craike was prepared. He discarded his staff for a hold on Jorik's shoulder, while Zackuth slogged behind. They climbed into the forest. Craike had never fashioned a bow, and he did not doubt that his first attempts might be failures. But, as the three made their slow progress, he explained what they must look for and the kind of weapon he wanted to produce. They returned within the hour with an assortment of wood lengths with which to experiment.

After noon Zackuth grew restless and went off, to come back with a deer, visibly proud of his hunting skill. Craike saw bowstrings where the others saw meat and hide for the refashioning of foot wear. For the rest of the day they worked with a will. It was Takya who had the skill necessary for the feathering of the arrows after Zackuth netted two black river birds.

Four days later the tower community had taken on the aspect of a real stronghold. Many of the fallen stones were back in the walls. The two upper rooms of the tower had been explored, and a vast collection of ancient nests had been swept out. Takya chose the topmost one for her own abode and, aided by her convalescing charge, the boy Nickus, had carried armloads of sweat scented grass up for both carpeting and bedding. She did not appear to be inconvenienced by the bats that still entered at dawn to chitter out again at dusk. And she crooned a welcome to the snowy owl that refused to be dislodged from a favorite roost in the very darkest corner of the roof.

River travel had ceased. There were no new offerings on the rock. But Jorik and Zackuth hunted. And Craike tended the smoking fires which cured the extra meat against coming need, while he worked on the bows. Shortly they had three finished and practiced along the terrace, using blunt arrows.

Jorik had a true marksman's eye and took to the new weapon quickly, as did Nickus. But Zackuth was more clumsy, and Craike's stiff leg bothered him. Takya was easily the best shot when she would consent to try. But while agreeing it was an excellent weapon, she preferred her own type of warfare and would sit on the wall, braiding and rebraiding her hair with flying fingers, to watch their shooting at marks and applaud or jeer lightly at the results.

However, their respite was short. Craike had the first warning of trouble. He awoke from a dream in which he had been back in the desert panting ahead of the mob. Awoke, only to discover that some malign influence filled the tower. There was a compulsion on him to get out, to flee into the forest.

He tested the silences about him tentatively. The oppression which had been in the ancient fort at his first coming had not returned, that was not it. But what?

Someone moved restlessly in the dark.

"Lord Ka-rak?" Nickus' voice was low and hoarse, as if he struggled to keep it under control.

"What is it?"

"There is trouble—"

A bulk which could only belong to Jorik heaved up black against the faint light of the doorway.

"The hunt is up," he observed. "They move to shake us out of here like rats out of a nest."

"They did this before with you?" asked the Esper.

Jorik snorted. "Yes. It is their favorite move to battle. They would give us such a horror of our tower that we will burst forth and scatter. Then they can cut us down as they wish."

But Craike could not isolate any thought beam carrying that night terror. It seeped from the walls about them. He sent probes unsuccessfully. There was the pad of feet on the stairs, and then he heard Takya call:

"Build up the fire, foolish ones. They may discover that they do not deal with those who know nothing of them."

Flame blossomed from the coals to light a circle of sober faces. Zackuth caressed the spear lying across his knees, but Nickus and Jorik had eyes only for the witch maid as she knelt by the fire, laying out some bundles of dried leaf and fern. Her thoughts reached Craike.

"We must move or these undefended ones will be drawn out from here as nut meats are picked free from the shell. Give me of your power—in this matter I must be the leader."

Though he resented anew her calm assumption of authority, Craike also recognized in it truth. But he shrank from the task she demanded of him. To have no control over his own Esper arts, to allow her to use them to feed hers—it was a violation of a kind, the very thing he had so feared in his own world that he had been willing to kill himself to escape it. Yet now she asked it of him as one who had the right!

"Forced surrender is truly evil—but given freely in our defense this is different." Her thoughts swiftly answered his wave of repulsion.

The command to flee the tower was growing stronger. Nickus got to his feet as if dragged up. Suddenly Zackuth made for the door, only to have Jorik reach forth a long arm to trip him.

"You see," Takya urged, "they are already half under the spell. Soon we shall not be able to hold them, either by mind or body. And then they shall be wholly lost—for ranked against us now is the high power of the Black Hoods."

Craike watched the scuffle on the floor and then, still reluctant and inwardly shrinking, he limped around the fire to her side, lying down at her gesture. She threw on the fire two of her bundles of fern, and a thick, sweet smoke curled out to engulf them. Nickus coughed, put his hands uncertainly to his head and slumped, curling up as a tired child in deep slumber. And the struggle between Jorik and his man subsided as the fumes reached them.

Takya's hand was cool as it slipped beneath Craike's jerkin, resting over his heart. She was crooning some queer chant, and, though he fought to hold mind contact, there was a veil between them as tangible to his inner senses as the fern smoke was to his outer ones. For one wild second or two he seemed to see the tower room through her eyes instead of his own, and then the room was gone. He sped bodiless across the night world, casting forth as a hound on the trail.

All that had been solid in his normal sight was now without meaning. But he was able to see the dark cloud of pressure closing in on the tower and trace that back to its source, racing along the slender thread of its spinners.

There was another fire, and about it four of the Black Hoods. Here, too, was scented smoke to free minds from bodies. The essence which was Craike prowled about that fire, counting guardsmen who lay in slumber.

With an effort of will which drew heavily upon his strength, he concentrated on the staff which lay before the leader of the company, setting upon it his own commands.

It flipped up into the air, even as its master roused and clutched at it, falling into the fire. There was a flash of blue light, a sound which Craike felt rather than heard. The Hooded Ones were on their feet as their master stared straight across the flames to Craike's disembodied self. His was not an evil face, rather did it hold elements of nobility. But the eyes were pitiless, and Craike knew that now it was not only war to the death between them, but war beyond death itself. The Esper sensed that this was the first time that other had known of his existence, had been able to consider him as a factor in the tangled game.

There was a flash of lightning knowledge of each other, and then Craike was again in the dark. He heard once more Takya's crooning, was conscious of her touch resting above the slow, pulsating beat of his heart.

"That was well done," her thought welcomed him. "Now they must meet us face to face in battle."

"They will come." He accepted the dire promise that Black Hood had made.

"They will come, but now we are more equal. And there is not the Rod of Power to fear."

Craike tried to sit up and discovered that the weakness born of his wounds was nothing to that which now held him.

Takya laughed with some of her old mockery. "Do you think you can make the Long Journey and then romp about as a fawn, Ka-rak? Not three days on the field of battle can equal this. Sleep now and gather again the inner power. The end of this venture is still far from us."

He could no longer see her face, the glimmer of her hair veiled it, and then that shimmer reached his mind and shook him away from consciousness; and he slept.

It might have been early morning when he had made that strange visit to the camp of the Black Hoods. By the measure of the sun across the floor it was late afternoon when he lifted heavy eyelids again. Takya gazed down upon him. Her summons had brought him back, just as her urging had sent him to sleep. He sat up with a smile, but she did not return it.

"All is right?"

"We have time to make ready before we are put to the test. Your mountain captain is not new to this game. Matters of open warfare he understands well, and he and his men have prepared a rude welcome for those who come. And," her faint smile deepened, "I, too, have done my poor best. come and see."

He limped out on the terrace and for a moment was startled. Illusion, yes, but some of it was real.

Jorik laughed at the expression on Craike's face, inviting the Esper with a wave of the hand to inspect the force he captained. For there were bowmen in plenty, standing sentinel on the upper walls, arch, and tower, walking beats on the twin buildings across the river. And it took Craike a few seconds to sort out the ones he knew from those who served Takya's purposes. But the real had been as well posted as their illusionary companions. Nickus, for his superior accuracy with the new weapon, held a vantage point on the wall, and Zackuth was on the river arch where his arrows needed only a short range to be effective.

"Look below," Jorik ugred, "and see what shall trip them up until we can pin them."

Again Craike blinked. The illusion was one he had seen before, but that had been a hurried erection on the part of a desperate girl; this was better contrived. For all the ways leading to the river towers were cloaked with a tangled mass of thorn trees, the spiked branches interlocking into a wall no sword, no spear could hope to pierce. It might be an illusion, but it would require a weighty counterspell on the part of the Hooded Ones to clear it.

"She takes some twigs Nickus finds, and a hair, and winds them together, then buried all under a stone. After she sings over it—and we have this!" Jorik babbled. "She is worth twenty hands—no, twice twenty hands, or fighting men, is the Lady Takya! Lord Ka-rak, I say that there is a new day coming for this land when such as you two stand up against the Hooded Ones."

"Aaaay—" the warning was soft but clear, half whistle, half call, issuing from Nickus' lofty post. "They come!"

"So do they!" That was a sharp echo from Zackuth, "and down river as well."

"For which we have an answer," Jorik was undisturbed.

Those in the tower held their fire. To the confident attackers it was as such warfare had always been for them. If half their company was temporarily halted by the spiny maze, the river party had only to land on the offering rock and fight their way in, their efforts reinforced by the arts of their Masters.

But, as their dugout nosed in, bow cords sang. There was a voiceless scream which tore through Craike's head as the hooded man in its bow clutched at the shaft protruding from his throat and fell forward into the river. Two more of the crew followed him, and the rest stopped paddling, dismayed. The current pulled them on under the arch, and Zackuth dropped a rock to good purpose. It carried one of the guardsmen down with it as it hit the craft squarely. The dugout turned over, spilling all the rest into the water.

Zackuth laughed; Jorik roared.

"Now they learn what manner of bloodletting lies before them!" he cried so that his words must have reached the ears of the besiegers. "Let us see how eagerly they come to such feasting."

VIII

It was plain that the Black Hoods held their rulership by more practical virtues than just courage. Having witnessed the smashing disaster of the river attack, they made no further move. Night was coming, and Craike watched them withdraw downstream with no elation. Nor did Jorik retain his cheerfulness.

"Now they will try something else. And since we did not fall easily into their jaws, it will be harder to face. I do not like it that we must so face it during the hours of dark.''

"There will be no dark," Takya countered. One slim finger pointed at a corner of the terrace, and up into the gathering dusk leaped a pencil of clear light. Slowly she turned and brought to life other torches on the roof of the tower over river, on the arch spanning the water, on the parapet—and in that radiance nothing could move unseen.

"So!" Her fingers snapped, and the beacons vanished. "When they are needed, we shall have them."

Jorik blinked. "Well enough, Lady. But honest fire is also good, and it provides warmth for a man's heart as well as light for his eyes."

She smiled as a mother might smile at a child. "Build your fire, Captain of Swords. But we shall have ample warning when the enemy comes." She called. A silent winged thing floated down and alighted on the arm she held out to invite it. The white owl, its eyes seeming to observe them all with intelligence, snapped its wicked beak as Takya stared back at it. Then with a flap of wings, it went.

"From us they may hide their thoughts and movements. But they cannot close the sky to those things whose natural home it is. Be sure we shall know, and speedily, when they move against us."

They did not leave their posts, however. And Zackuth readied for action by laying up pieces of rubble which might serve as well as his first lucky shot.

It was a long night, wearing on the tempers of all but Takya. Time and time again Craike tried to probe the dark. But a blank wall was all he met. Whatever moves the Black Hoods considered, they were protected by an able barrier.

Jorik took to pacing back and forth on the terrace, five strides one way, six the other, and he brought down his bow with a little click on the time-worn stones each time he turned.

"They are as busy hatching trouble as a forest owl is in hatching an egg! But what kind of trouble?"

Craike had schooled himself into an outward patience. "For the learning of that we shall have to wait. But why do they delay—?"

Why did they? The more on edge he and his handful of defenders became, the easier meat they were. And he had no doubt that the Black Hoods were fertile in surprise. Though, judging by what Takya and Jorik reported, they were not accustomed to such determined and resourceful opposition to their wills. Such opposition would only firm their desire to wipe out the rebels.

"They move," Takya's witch fires leaped from every point she had earlier indicated. In that light she sped across the terrace to stand close to Jorik and Craike, close to the parapet wall. "This is the lowest hour of the night when the blood runs slow and resistance is at its depth. So they choose to move—"

Jorik snapped his bow cord, and the thin twang was a harp's note in the silence. But Takya shook her head.

"Only the Hooded Ones come, and they are well armored. See!" She jumped to the parapet and clapped her hands.

The witch light shone down on four standing within the thorn barrier, staring up from under the shadow of their hoods. An arrow sang, but it never reached its mark. Still feet away from the leader's breast it fell to earth.

But Jorik refused to accept defeat. With all the force of his arm he sent a second shaft after the first. And it, too, landed at the feet of the silent four. Craike grasped at Takya, but she eluded him, moving to call down to the Hooded Ones:

"What would you, men of power—a truce?"

"Daughter of evil, you are not alone. Let us speak with your lord."

She laughed, shaking out her unbound hair, rippling it through her fingers, gloatingly. "Does this show that I have taken a lord, men of power? Takya is herself, without division, still. Let that hope die from your hearts. I ask you again, what is it you wish—a truce?"

"Set forth your lord, and with him we will bargain."

She smoothed back her hair impatiently. "I have no lord, I and my power are intact. Try me and see, Tousuth. Yes, I know you, Tousuth, the Master, and Salsbal, Bulan, Yily—" she told them off with a pointed forefinger, a child counting out in some game.

Jorik stirred and drew in a sharp breath, and the men below shifted position. Craike caught thoughts—to use a man's name in the presence of hostile powers, that was magic indeed.

"Takya!" It was a reptile's hiss.

Again she laughed. "Ah, but the first naming was mine, Tousuth. Did you believe me so poor and power lost that I would obey you tamely? I did not at the horning, why should I now when I stand free of you? Before you had to use Takyi to capture me. But Takyi is gone into the far darkness, and over me now you can lay no such net! Also I have summoned one beside me—'' Her hand closed on Craike's arm, drawing him forward.

He faced the impact of those eyes meeting them squarely. Raising his hand he told them off as the girl had done:

"Tousuth, Master of women baiters, Salsbal, Bulan, Yily, the wolves who slink behind him. I am here, what would you have of me?"

But they were silent, and he could feel them searching him out, making thrusts against his mind shield, learning in their turn that he was of their kind; he was Esper born.

"What would you have?" he repeated more loudly. "If you do not wish to treat—then leave the night undisturbed for honest men's sleep."

"Changling!" It was Tousuth who spat that. It was his turn to point a finger and chant a sentence or two, his men watching him with confidence.

But Craike, remembering that other scene before Sampur, was trying a wild experiment of his own. He concentrated upon the man Takya had named Yily. Black cloak, black hood making a vulture's shadow against the rock. Vulture—vulture!

He did not know that he had pointed to his chosen victim, nor that he was repeating that word aloud in the same intonation as Tousuth's chant. "Vulture!"

Cool hand closed about his other wrist, and from that contact power flowed to join his. It was pointed, launched—

"Vulture!"

A black bird flapped and screamed, arose on beating wings to fly at him, raw red head outstretched, beak agap. There was the twang of a bow cord. A scream of agony and despair and a black-cloaked man writhed out his life on the slope by the thorn thicket.

"Good!" Takya cried. "That was well done, Ka-rak, very well done! But you cannot use that weapon a second time."

Craike was filled with a wild elation, and he did not listen to her. His finger already indicated Bulan and he was chanting: "Dog—"

But to no purpose. The Black Hood did not drop to all fours, he remained human; and Craike's voice faded. Takya spoke in swift whisper:

"They are warned, you can never march against them twice by the same path. Only because they were unprepared did you succeed. Ho, Tousuth," she called, "do you now believe that we are well armed? Speak with a true tongue and say what you want of us."

"Yes," Jorik boomed, "you cannot take us, Master of power. Go your way, and we shall go ours—"

"There cannot be two powers in any land, as you should know, Jorik of the Eagles' towers, who tried once before to prove that and suffered thereby. There must be a victor here—and to the vanquished—naught!"

Craike could see the logic in that. But the Master was continuing: "As to what we want here—it is a decision. Match your power against ours, changeling. And since you have not taken the witch, use her also if you wish. In the end it will come to the same thing, for both of you must be rendered helpless."

"Here and now?" asked Craike.

"Dawn comes, it will soon be another day. By sun or shadow, we care not in such a battle."

The elation of his quick success in that first try was gone. Craike fingered the bow he had not yet used. He shrank inwardly from the contest the other proposed, he was too uncertain of his powers. One victory had come from too little knowledge. Takya's hand curled about his stiff fingers once again. The impish mockery was back in her voice, ruffling his temper, irritating him into defiance.

"Show them what you can do, Lord Ka-rak, you who can master illusions."

He glanced down at her, and the sight of that cropped lock of hair at her temple gave him an odd confidence. Neither was Takya as all-powerful as she would have him believe.

"I accept your challenge," he called "Let it be here and now."

"*We* accept your challenge!" Takya's flash of annoyance, her quick correction, pleased him. Before the echo of her words died away she hurled her first attack.

Witchfire leaped downslope to ring in the three men, playing briefly along the body of the dead Yily. It flickered up and down about their feet and legs so they stood washed in pallid flame, while about their heads darted winged shapes which might have been owls or other night hunters.

There was a malignant hissing, and the slope sprouted reptiles, moving in a wave. Illusions? All—or some. But designed, Craike understood, to divert the enemy's minds. He added a few of his own—a wolfish shape crouching in the shadow—leaping—to vanish as its paws cut the witchfire.

Swift as had been Takya's attack, so did those below parry.

An oppressive weight, so tangible that Craike looked up to see if some mountain threatened them from overhead, began to close down upon the parapet. He heard a cry of alarm. There *was* a black cloud to be seen now, a giant press closing upon them.

Balls of witchfire flashed out of the light pillars, darted at those on the parapet. One flew straight at Craike's face, its burning breath singeing his skin.

"Fool!" Takya's thought was a whip lash, "Illusions are only real for the believer."

He steadied, and the witch ball vanished. But he was badly shaken. This was outside any Esper training he had had, it was the very thing he had been conditioned against. He felt slow, clumsy, and he was ashamed that upon Takya must the burden of their defense now rest.

Upon her—Craike's eyes narrowed. He loosened her hold on .1im, did not try to contact her. There was too much chance of self-betrayal in that. His plan was utterly wild, but it had been well demonstrated that the Black Hoods could only be caught by the unexpected.

Another witch ball hurtled at him, and he leaped to the terrace, landing with a force which sent a lance of pain up his healing leg. But on the parapet a Craike still stood, shoulder to shoulder with Takya. To maintain that illusion was a task which made him sweat as he crept silently away from the tower.

He had made a security guard to astonish Takya, the wolf, all the other illusions. But they had been only wisps, things alive for the moment with no need for elaboration. To hold this semblance of himself was in some ways easier, some ways harder. It was easier to make, for the image was produced of self-knowledge, and it was harder, for it was meant to deceive masters of illusion.

Craike reached the steps to the rock of the offerings. The glow of the witch lights here was pale, and the ledge below dark. He crept down, one arrow held firmly in his hand.

Here the sense of oppression was a hundredfold worse, and he moved as one wading through a flood which entrapped limbs and brain. Blind, he went to all fours, feeling his way to the river.

He set the arrow between his teeth in a bite which indented its shaft. A knife would have been far better, but he had no time to beg Jorik's. He slipped over, shivering as the chill water took him. Then he swam under the arch.

It was comparatively easy to reach the shingle where the dugout of the Black Hoods had turned over. As he made his way to the shore he brushed against water-soaked cloth and realized he shared this scrap of gravel with the dead. Then, arrow still between his teeth, Craike climbed up behind the Black Hoods' position.

IX

The thorn hedge cloaked the rise above him. But he concentrated on the breaking of that illusion, wading on through a mass of thorns, intact to his eyes, thin air at his passing. Then he was behind the Black Hoods. Takya stood, a black-and-white figure on the wall above, beside the illusion Craike.

Now!

The illusion Craike swelled a little more than life size, while his creator gathered his feet under him, preparatory to attack. The Craike on the wall altered—anything to hold the attention of Tousuth for a crucial second or two. Monster grew from man, wings, horns, curved tusks, all embellishments Craike's imagination could add. He heard shouts from the tower.

But with the arrow as a dagger in his hand, he sprang, allowing himself in that moment to see only, to think only of a point on Tousuth's back.

The head drove in and in, and Tousuth went down on his knees, clutching at his chest, coughing. While Craike, with a savagery he had not known he possessed, leaned on the shaft to drive it deeper.

Fingers hooked about Craike's throat, cutting off air, dragging him back. He was pulled from Tousuth, loosing his hold on the arrow shaft to tear at the hands denying him breath. There was a red fog which even the witch lights could not pierce and the roaring in his head was far louder than the shouts from the tower.

Then he was flat on the ground, still moving feebly. But the hands were gone from his throat, and he gasped in air. Around him circled balls of fire, dripping, twirling, he closed his eyes against their glare.

"Lord—Lord!"

The hail reached him only faintly. Hands pulled at him, and he tried to resist. But when he opened his eyes it was to see Jorik's brown face. Jorik was at the tower—how had Craike returned there? Surely he *had* attacked Tousuth? Or was it all illusion?

"He is not dead."

Whether or not that was said to him, Craike did not know. But his fingers were at his throat and he winced from his own touch. Then an arm came under his shoulders, lifting him, and he had a dizzy moment until earth and gray sky settled into their proper places.

Takya was there, with Nickus and Zackuth hovering in the background of black-jerkined guardsmen who stared back at her sullenly over the bodies of the dead. For they were all dead—the Hooded Ones. There was Tousuth, his head in the sand. And his fellows crumpled beside him.

The witch girl chanted, and in her hands was a cat's cradle of black strands. The men who followed Tousuth cringed, and their fear was a cloud Craike could see. He grabbed at Jorik, won to his feet, and tried to hail Takya. But not even a croak came from his tortured throat. So he flung himself at her, one hand out like a sword blade to slash. It fell across that wicked net of hair, breaking it, and went to close upon Takya's wrist in a crushing grip.

"Enough!" He could get out that command mind to mind.

She drew in upon herself as a cat crouches for a spring, and spat, her eyes green with feral lusting fire. But he had an answer to that, read it in her own spark of fear at his touch. His hands twined in her hair.

"They are men," he pulled those black strands to emphasize his words, "they only obeyed orders. We have a quarrel with their masters, but not with them!"

"They hunted, and now they shall be hunted!"

"I have been hunted, as have you, witch woman. And while I live there shall be no more such hunts—whether I am hound or quarry."

"While you live—" Her menace was ready.

Suddenly Craike forced out a hoarse croak meant for laughter. "You, yourself, Takya, have put the arrow to this bow cord!"

He kept one hand tangled in her hair. But with the other he snatched from her belt the knife she had borrowed from Nickus and not returned. She screamed, beat against him with her fists, tried to bite. He mastered her roughly, not loosing his grip on that black silk. And then in sweeps of that well-whetted blade he did what the Black Hoods had failed in doing, he sawed through those lengths.

"I am leaving you no weapons, Takya. You shall not rule here as you have thought to do—" The exultation he had known when he had won his first victory against the Black Hoods was returning a hundredfold. "For a while I shall pull those pretty claws of yours!" He wondered briefly how long it would take her hair to regrow. At least they would have a breathing spell before her powers returned.

Then, his arm still prisoning her shoulders, the mass of her hair streaming free from his left hand, he turned to face the guardsmen.

"Tell them to go," he thought, "taking their dead with them."

"You will go, taking these with you," she repeated aloud, stony calm.

One of the men dropped to his knees by Tousuth's body, then abased himself before Craike.

"We are your hounds, Master."

Craike found his voice at last. "You are no man's hound—for you are a man. Get you gone to Sampur and tell them that the power is no longer to make hind nor hound. If there are those who wish to share the fate of Tousuth, perhaps when they look upon him as dead they will think more of it."

"Lord, do you come also to Sampur to rule?" the other asked timidly.

Craike laughed. "Not until I have established my lordship elsewhere. Get you back to Sampur and trouble us no more."

He turned his back on the guardsmen and, drawing the silent Takya, still within the circle of his arm, with him, started back to the tower. The bowmen remained behind, and Craike and the girl were alone as they reached the upper level. He paused then and looked down into her set, expressionless face.

"What shall I do with you?"

"You have shamed me and taken my power from me. What does a warrior do with a female slave?" She formed a stark mind picture, hurling it at him as she had hurled the stone on the mesa.

With his left hand he whipped her hair across her face, smarting under that taunt.

"I have taken no slave, nor any woman in that fashion, nor shall I. Go your way, Takya, and fight me again if you wish when your hair has grown."

She studied him, and her astonishment was plain. Then she laughed and clutched at the hair, tearing it free from his grasp, bundling it into the front of her single garment.

"So be it, Ka-rak. It is war between us. But I am not departing hence yet a while." She broke away, and he could hear the scuff of her feet on the steps as she climbed to her own chamber in the tower.

"They are on their way, Lord, and they will keep to it." Jorik came up. He stretched. "It was a battle not altogether to my liking. For the honest giving of blows from one's hand is better than all this magic, potent as it is."

Craike sat down beside the fire. He could not have agreed more heartily with any suggestion. Now that it was over he felt drained of energy.

"I do not believe they will return," he wheezed hoarsely, very conscious of his bruised throat.

Nickus chuckled, and Zackuth barked his own laughter.

"Seeing how you handled the Lady, Lord, they want nothing more than to be out of your grasp and that as speedily as possible. Nor, when those of Sampur see what they bring with them, do I think we shall be sought out by others bearing drawn swords. Now," Jorik slapped his fat middle, "I could do with meat in my belly. And you, Lord, have taken such handling as needs good food to counter."

There was no mention of Takya, nor did any go to summon her when the meat was roasted. And Craike was content to have it so. He was too tired for any more heroics.

Nickus hummed a soft tune as he rubbed down his unstrung bow before wrapping it away from the river damp. And Craike was aware that the younger man glanced at him slyly when he thought the Esper's attention elsewhere. Jorik, too, appeared highly amused at some private thoughts, and he had fallen to beating time with one finger to Nickus' tune. Craike shifted uncomfortably. He was an actor who had forgotten his lines, a novice required to make a ritual move he did not understand. What they wanted of him he could not guess, for he was too tired to mind-touch. He only wanted sleep, and that he sought as soon as he painfully swallowed his last bite. But he heard through semistupor a surprised exclamation from Nickus.

"He goes not to seek her—to take her!"

Jorik's answer held something of approval in it. "To master such as the Lady Takya he will need full strength of power and limb. His is the wisest way, not to gulp the fruits of battle before the dust of the last charge is laid. She is his by shearing, but she is no meek ewe to come readily under any man's hand."

Takya did not appear the next day, nor the next. And Craike made no move to climb to her. His companions elaborately did not notice her absence as they worked together, setting in place fallen stones, bringing the tower into a better state of repair, or killing deer to smoke the meat. For as Jorik pointed out:

"Soon comes the season of cold. We must build us a snug place and have food under our hands before then." He broke off and gazed thoughtfully down stream. "This is also the fair time when countrymen bring their wares to market. There are traders in Sampur. We could offer our hides, even though they be newly fleshed, for salt and grain. And a bow—this Kaluf of whom you have spoken, would he not give a good price for a bow?"

Craike raised an eyebrow. "Sampur? But they have little cause to welcome us in Sampur."

"You and the Lady Takya, Lord, they might take arms against in fear. But if Zackuth and I went in the guise of wandering hunters—and Zackuth is of the Children of Noe, he could trade privately with his kin. We must have supplies, Lord, before the coming of the cold, and this is too fine a fortress to abandon."

So it was decided that Jorik and Zackuth were to try their luck with the traders. Nickus went to hunt, wrecking havoc among the flocks of migrating fowl, and Craike held the tower alone.

As he turned from seeing them away, he sighted the owl wheel out from the window slit of the upper chamber, its mournful cry sounding loud. On sudden impulse he went inside to climb the stair. There had been enough of her sulking. He sent that thought before him as an order. She did not reply. Craike's heart beat faster. Was—had she gone? The rough outer wall was it possible to climb down that?

He flung himself up the last few steps and burst into the room. She was standing there, her shorn head high as if she and not he had been the victor. When he saw her Craike stopped. Then he moved again, faster than he had climbed those stairs. For in that moment the customs of this world were clear, he knew what he must do, what he wanted to do. If this revelation was some spell of Takya's he did not care.

Later he was aroused by the caress of silk on his body, felt her cool fingers as he had felt them drawing the poison from his wounds. It was a black belt, and she was making fast about him, murmuring words softly as she interwove strand with strand about his waist until there was no beginning nor end to be detected.

"My chain on you, man of power." Her eyes slanted down at him.

He buried both his hands in the ragged crop of hair from which those threads had been severed and so held her quiet for his kiss.

"My seal upon you, witch."

"What Tousuth would have done, you have accomplished for him," she observed pensively when he had given her a measure of freedom once again. "Only through you may I now use my power."

"Which is perhaps well for this land and those who dwell in it," he laughed. "We are now tied to a common destiny, my lady of river towers."

She sat up running her hands through her hair with some of her old caress.

"It will grow again," he consoled.

"To no purpose, except to pleasure my vanity. Yes, we are tied together. But you do not regret it, Ka-rak—"

"Neither do you, witch." There was no longer any barrier between their minds, as there was none between their bodies. "What destiny will you now spin for the two of us?"

"A great one. Tousuth knew my power-to-come. I would now realize it." Her chin went up. "And you with me, Ka-rak. By this," her hand rested lightly on the belt.

"Doubtless you will set us up as rulers over Sampur?" he said lazily.

"Sampur!" she sniffed. "This world is wide—" Her arms went out as if to encircle all which lay beyond the tower walls.

Craike drew her back to him jealously. "For that there is more than time enough. This is an hour for something else, even in a warlock's world."

Sweets to the Sweet
by Robert Bloch

*Robert Bloch has been scaring the daylights out of
people for more than forty years. He got his start as a
member of the famous "Lovecraft Circle" of correspon-
dents and soon moved on to the pulp magazines, where
he specialized in both supernatural and psychological
horror. His book* Psycho *(1959) was made into an
immortal film by Alfred Hitchcock; more recently, he
has given us* Psycho II *(1983). In many ways he still
remains an underrated writer, although he has been
honored by his readers and his peers with a Hugo
Award and an Edgar Allan Poe Award.* The Best of
Robert Bloch *contains some of his most outstanding
work, but it would take several volumes to accommo-
date all his most worthy stories.*

Irma didn't look like a witch.

She had small, regular features, a peaches-and-cream complex-
ion, blue eyes, and fair, almost ash-blond hair. Besides, she was
only eight years old.

"Why does he tease her so?" sobbed Miss Pall. "That's
where she got the idea in the first place—because he always
insists on calling her a little witch."

Sam Steever bulked his paunch back into the squeaky swivel
chair and folded his heavy hands in his lap.

His fat lawyer's mask was immobile, but he was really quite
distressed.

Women like Miss Pall should never sob. Their glasses wiggle,
their thin noses twitch, their creasy eyelids redden, and their
stringy hair becomes disarrayed.

"Please, control yourself," coaxed Sam Steever. "Perhaps if
we could just talk this whole thing over sensibly—"

"I don't care!" Miss Pall sniffled. "I'm not going back there
again. I can't stand it. There's nothing I can do, anyway. The

man is your brother, and she's your brother's child. It's not my responsibility. I've tried—''

"Of course you've tried." Sam Steever smiled benignly, as if Miss Pall were foreman of a jury. "I quite understand. But I still don't see why you are so upset, dear lady."

Miss Pall removed her spectacles and dabbed at her eyes with a floral-print handkerchief. Then she deposited the soggy ball in her purse, snapped the catch, replaced her spectacles, and sat up straight.

"Very well, Mr. Steever," she said. "I shall do my best to acquaint you with my reasons for quitting your brother's employ."

She suppressed a tardy sniff.

"I came to John Steever two years ago in response to an advertisement for a housekeeper, as you know. When I found that I was to be governess to a motherless six-year-old child, I was at first distressed. I knew nothing of the care of children."

"John had a nurse the first six years." Sam Steever nodded. "You know Irma's mother died in childbirth."

"I am aware of that," said Miss Pall primly. "Naturally, one's heart goes out to a lonely, neglected little girl. And she was so terribly lonely, Mr. Steever—if you could have seen her, moping around in the corners of that big, ugly old house—''

"I have seen her," said Sam Steever hastily, hoping to forestall another outburst. "And I know what you've done for Irma. My brother is inclined to be thoughtless, even a bit selfish, at times. He doesn't understand."

"He's cruel!" declared Miss Pall, suddenly vehement. "Cruel and wicked. Even if he is your brother, I say he's no fit father for any child. When I came there, her little arms were black-and-blue from beatings. He used to take a belt—''

"I know. Sometimes I think John never recovered from the shock of Mrs. Steever's death. That's why I was so pleased when you came, dear lady. I thought you might help improve the situation."

"I tried," Miss Pall whimpered. "You know I tried. I never raised a hand to that child in two years, though many's the time your brother told me to punish her. 'Give the little witch a beating,' he used to say. 'That's all she needs—a good thrashing.' And then she'd hide behind my back and whisper to me to protect her. But she wouldn't cry, Mr. Steever. Do you know, I've never seen her cry."

Sam Steever felt vaguely irritated and a bit bored. He wished the old hen would get on with it. So he smiled and oozed treacle.

"But just what exactly is your problem, dear lady?"

"Everything was all right when I came there. We got along just splendidly. I started to teach Irma to read—and was surprised to find that she had already mastered reading. Your brother disclaimed having taught her, but she spent hours curled up on the sofa with a book. 'Just like her,' he used to say. 'Unnatural little witch. Doesn't play with the other children. Little witch.'

"That's just the way he kept talking, Mr. Steever. As if she were some sort of . . . I don't know what. And she so sweet and quiet and pretty!

"Is it any wonder she read? I used to be that way myself when I was a girl, because— But never mind.

"Still, it was a shock that day I found her looking through the *Encyclopaedia Britannica*. 'What are you reading, Irma?' I asked her. And she showed me. It was the article on witchcraft.

"You see what morbid thoughts your brother has inculcated in her poor little head?

"I did my best. I went out and bought her some toys—she had absolutely nothing, you know, not even a doll. She didn't even know how to *play!* I tried to get her interested in some of the other little girls in the neighborhood, but it was no use. They didn't understand her, and she didn't understand them. There were scenes. Children can be cruel, thoughtless. And her father wouldn't let her go to public school. I was to teach her.

"Then I brought her the modeling clay. She liked that. She would spend hours just making faces with clay. For a child of six, Irma displayed real talent.

"We made little dolls together, and I sewed clothes for them. That first year was a happy one, Mr. Steever. Particularly during those months when your brother was away in South America. But this year, when he came back—oh, I can't bear to talk about it!"

"Please," said Sam Steever. "You must understand. John is not a happy man. The loss of his wife, the decline of his import trade, and his drinking—but you know all that."

"All I know is that he hates Irma," snapped Miss Pall suddenly. "He hates her. He wants her to be bad, so he can whip her. 'If you don't discipline the little witch, I shall,' he always says. And then he takes her upstairs and thrashes her with his belt. You must do something, Mr. Steever, you must—or I'll go to the authorities myself."

The crazy old biddy would, at that, Sam Steever thought. Remedy—more treacle. "But about Irma," he persisted.

"She's changed, too. Ever since her father returned this year. She won't play with me anymore. Hardly looks at me. It's as though I failed her, Mr. Steever, in not protecting her from that man. Besides—she thinks she's a witch."

Crazy. Stark, staring crazy. Sam Steever creaked upright in his chair.

"Oh, you needn't look at me like that, Mr. Steever. She'd tell you so herself—if you ever visited the house!"

He caught the reproach in her voice and assuaged it with a deprecating nod.

"She told me, all right: If her father wants her to be a witch, she'll be a witch. And she won't play with me or anyone else, because witches don't play. Last Halloween she wanted me to give her a broomstick. Oh, it would be funny if it weren't so tragic.

"Just a few weeks ago, I thought she'd changed. That's when she asked me to take her to church one Sunday. 'I want to see the baptism,' she said. Imagine that—an eight-year-old interested in baptism! Reading too much, that's what does it.

"Well, we went to church, and she was as sweet as can be, wearing her new blue dress and holding my hand. I was proud of her, Mr. Steever, really proud.

"But after that, she went right back into her shell. Reading around the house, running through the yard at twilight, talking to herself.

"Perhaps it's because your brother wouldn't bring her a kitten. She was pestering him for a black cat, and he asked why, and she said, 'Because witches always have black cats.' Then he took her upstairs.

"I can't stop him, you know. He beat her again the night the power failed and we couldn't find the candles. He said she'd stolen them. Imagine that—accusing an eight-year-old child of stealing candles!

"That was the beginning of the end. Then today, when he found his hairbrush missing—"

"You say he beat her with his hairbrush?"

"Yes. She admitted having stolen it. Said she wanted it for her doll."

"But didn't you say she has no dolls?"

"She made one. At least, I think she did. I've never seen it. She won't show us anything anymore; won't talk to us at table. It's just impossible to handle her.

"But this doll she made—it's a small one, I know, because at times she carries it tucked under her arm. She talks to it and pets it, but she won't show it to me or to him. He asked her about the hairbrush, and she said she took it for the doll.

"Your brother flew into a terrible rage—he'd been drinking in his room again all morning; don't think I don't know it!—and she just smiled and said he could have it now. She went over to her bureau and handed it to him. She hadn't harmed it in the least; his hair was still in it, I noticed.

"But he snatched it up, and then he started to strike her about the shoulders with it, and he twisted her arm, and then he—"

Miss Pall huddled in her chair and summoned great racking sobs from her thin chest.

Sam Steever patted her shoulder, fussing about her like an elephant over a wounded canary.

"That's all, Mr. Steever. I came right to you. I'm not even going back to that house to get my things. I can't stand any more—the way he beat her—and the way she didn't cry, but just giggled and giggled and giggled. Sometimes I think she *is* a witch—that he made her into a witch. . . ."

Sam Steever picked up the phone. The ringing had broken the relief of silence after Miss Pall's hasty and not unwelcome departure.

"Hello—that you, Sam?"

He recognized his brother's voice, somewhat the worse for drink.

"Yes, John."

"I suppose the old bat came running straight to you to shoot her mouth off."

"If you mean Miss Pall, I've seen her, yes."

"Pay no attention to her. I can explain everything."

"Do you want me to stop in? I haven't paid you a visit in months."

"Well—not right now. Got an appointment with the doctor this evening."

"Something wrong?"

"Pain in my arm. Rheumatism or something. Getting a little diathermy. But I'll call you tomorrow, and we'll straighten this whole mess out."

"Right."

But John Steever did not call his brother the next day. Along about suppertime, Sam called him.

Surprisingly enough, Irma answered the phone.

Her thin, squeaky little voice sounded faintly in Sam's ear.

"Daddy's upstairs sleeping," she said. "He's been sick."

"Well, don't disturb him. What is it—his arm?"

"His back, now. He has to go to the doctor again in a little while."

"Tell him I'll call tomorrow, then. Uh—everything all right, Irma? I mean, don't you miss Miss Pall?"

"No. I'm glad she went away. She's stupid."

"Oh. Yes. I see. But you phone me if you want anything. And I hope your daddy's better."

"Yes. So do I," said Irma. Then she began to giggle, and then she hung up.

There was no giggling the following afternoon when John Steever called Sam at the office. His voice was sober—with the sharp sobriety of pain.

"Sam—for the love of heaven, get over here. Something's happening to me!"

"What's the trouble?"

"The pain—it's killing me! I've got to see you. Quickly!"

"There's a client in the office, but I'll get rid of him. Say, wait a minute. Why don't you call the doctor?"

"That quack can't help me. He gave me diathermy for my arm, and yesterday he did the same thing for my back."

"Didn't it help?"

"The pain went away, yes. But it's back now. I feel . . . as if I'm being crushed. Squeezed, here in the chest. I can't breathe."

"Sounds like pleurisy. Why don't you call him?"

"It isn't pleurisy. He examined me. Said I was sound as a dollar. No, there's nothing organically wrong. And I couldn't tell him the real cause."

"Real cause?"

"Yes. The pins. The pins that little fiend is sticking into the doll she made. Into the arm, the back. And now heaven only knows how she's causing *this*."

"John, you mustn't—"

"Oh, what's the use of talking? I can't move off the bed here. She has me now. I can't go down and stop her, get hold of the doll. And nobody else would believe it. But it's the doll, all right, the one she made with the candle wax and the hair from my brush. Oh—it hurts to talk—that cursed little witch! Hurry, Sam. Promise me you'll do something—anything to get that doll from her—get that doll—"

      *   *   *

Half an hour later, at four-thirty, Sam Steever entered his brother's house.

Irma opened the door.

It gave Sam a shock to see her standing there, smiling and unperturbed, pale blond hair brushed immaculately back from the rosy oval of her face. She looked just like a little doll. A little doll—

"Hello, Uncle Sam."

"Hello, Irma. Your daddy called me; did he tell you? He said he wasn't feeling well—"

"Yes, I know. But he's all right now. He's sleeping."

Something happened to Sam Steever; a drop of icewater trickled down his spine.

"Sleeping?" he croaked. "Upstairs?"

Before she opened her mouth to answer, he was bounding up the steps to the second floor and striding down the hall to his brother John's bedroom.

John lay on the bed. He was asleep—only alseep. Sam Steever noted the regular rise and fall of his chest as he breathed. His face was calm, relaxed.

Then the drop of icewater evaporated, and Sam could afford to smile—and even to murmur, "Nonsense!" under his breath as he turned away.

As he went downstairs, he hastily improvised plans. A six-month vacation for his brother; avoid calling it a "cure." An orphanage for Irma; give her a chance to get away from this morbid old house, all those books. . . .

He paused halfway down the stairs. Peering over the banister through the twilight, he saw Irma on the sofa, cuddled up like a little white ball. She was talking to something she cradled in her arms, rocking it to and fro.

Then there was a doll, after all.

Sam Steever tiptoed very quietly down the stairs and walked over to Irma.

"Hello," he said.

She jumped. Both arms rose to cover completely whatever it was she had been fondling. She squeezed it tightly.

Sam Steever thought of a doll being squeezed across the chest. . . .

Irma stared up at him, her face a mask of innocence. In the half-light her face did resemble a mask. The mask of a little girl, covering—what?

"Daddy's better now, isn't he?" lisped Irma.

"Yes, much better."

"I knew he would be."

"But I'm afraid he's going to have to go away for a rest—a long rest."

A smile filtered through the mask. "Good," said Irma.

"Of course," Sam went on, "you couldn't stay here all alone. I was wondering—maybe we could send you off to school or to some kind of home—"

Irma giggled. "Oh, you needn't worry about me," she said. She shifted about on the sofa as Sam sat down, then sprang up quickly as he came close to her.

Her arms shifted with the movement, and Sam Steever saw a pair of tiny legs dangling below her elbow. There were trousers on the legs, and little bits of leather for shoes.

"What's that you have, Irma?" he asked. "Is it a doll?"

Slowly he extended his pudgy hand.

She pulled back.

"You can't see it," she said.

"But I want to. Miss Pall said you made such lovely ones."

"Miss Pall is stupid. So are you," Irma said. "Go away."

"Please, Irma. Let me see it."

But even as he spoke, Sam Steever was staring at the top of the doll, momentarily revealed when she backed away. It was a head, all right, with wisps of hair over a white face. Dusk dimmed the features, but Sam recognized the eyes, the nose, the chin.

He could keep up the pretense no longer.

"Give me that doll, Irma!" he snapped. "I know what it is. I know *who* it is—"

For an instant, the mask slipped from Irma's face, and Sam Steever stared into naked fear.

She knew. She knew he knew.

Then, just as quickly, the mask was replaced.

Irma was only a sweet, spoiled, stubborn little girl as she shook her head merrily and smiled with impish mischief in her eyes.

"Oh, Uncle Sam," she giggled, "you're so silly! Why, this isn't a *real* doll."

"What is it, then?" he muttered.

Irma giggled once more, raising the figure as she spoke. "Why, it's only—candy!" she said.

"Candy?"

Irma nodded. Then, very swiftly, she slipped the tiny head of the image into her mouth.

And bit it off.

There was a single piercing scream from upstairs.

As Sam Steever turned and ran up the steps, little Irma, still gravely munching, skipped out of the front door and into the night beyond.

Poor Little Saturday

by Madeleine L'Engle

Madeleine L'Engle is one of the most popular contemporary children's writers. Her most famous books for young people are both fantasies: A Wrinkle in Time *(1963), which won the Newbery Medal as the outstanding children's book of that year; and* A Swiftly Tilting Planet, *winner of the National Book Award for Children's Literature in 1980. Both of these are part of her "Time" trilogy, the middle book being* A Wind in the Door *(1973). Another fantasy for younger readers is* A Ring of Endless Light *(1980). "Poor Little Saturday" appeared in the October 1956 issue of the late and lamented* Fantastic Universe, *and is her only known publication in the genre magazines.*

The witch woman lived in a deserted, boarded-up plantation house, and nobody knew about her but me. Nobody in the nosy little town in south Georgia where I lived when I was a boy knew that if you walked down the dusty main street to where the post office ended it, and then turned left and followed that road a piece until you got to the rusty iron gates of the drive to the plantation house, you could find goings-on would make your eyes pop out. It was just luck that I found out. Or maybe it wasn't luck at all. Maybe the witch woman wanted me to find out because of Alexandra. But now I wish I hadn't because the witch woman and Alexandra are gone forever and it's much worse than if I'd never known them.

Nobody'd lived in the plantation house since the Civil war when Colonel Londermaine was killed and Alexandra Londermaine, his beautiful young wife, hung herself on the chandelier in the ballroom. A while before I was born some northerners bought it but after a few years they stopped coming and people said it was because the house was haunted. Every few years a gang of boys or men would set out to explore the house but

nobody ever found anything, and it was so well boarded up it
was hard to force an entrance, so by and by the town lost interest
in it. No one climbed the wall and wandered around the grounds
except me.

I used to go there often during the summer because I had bad
spells of malaria when sometimes I couldn't bear to lie on the
iron bedstead in my room with the flies buzzing around my face,
or out on the hammock on the porch with the screams and
laughter of the other kids as they played torturing my ears. My
aching head made it impossible for me to read, and I would drag
myself down the road, scuffling my bare sunburned toes in the
dust, wearing the tattered straw hat that was supposed to protect
me from the heat of the sun, shivering and sweating by turns.
Sometimes it would seem hours before I got to the iron gates
near which the brick wall was lowest. Often I would have to lie
panting on the tall prickly grass for minutes until I gathered
strength to scale the wall and drop down on the other side.

But once inside the grounds it seemed cooler. One funny thing
about my chills was that I didn't seem to shiver nearly as much
when I could keep cool as I did at home where even the walls
and the floors, if you touched them, were hot. The grounds were
filled with live oaks that had grown up unchecked everywhere
and afforded an almost continuous green shade. The ground was
covered with ferns which were soft and cool to lie on, and when
I flung myself down on my back and looked up, the roof of
leaves was so thick that sometimes I couldn't see the sky at all.
The sun that managed to filter through lost its bright pitiless
glare and came in soft yellow shafts that didn't burn you when
they touched you.

One afternoon, a scorcher early in September, which is usually our hottest month (and by then you're fagged out by the heat
anyhow), I set out for the plantation. The heat lay coiled and
shimmering on the road. When you looked at anything through
it, it was like looking through a defective pane of glass. The dirt
road was so hot that it burned even through my calloused feet
and as I walked clouds of dust rose in front of me and mixed
with the shimmying of the heat. I thought I'd never make the
plantation. Sweat was running into my eyes, but it was cold
sweat, and I was shivering so that my teeth chattered as I
walked. When I managed finally to fling myself down on my
soft green bed of ferns inside the grounds I was seized with one
of the worst chills I'd ever had in spite of the fact that my mother
had given me an extra dose of quinine that morning and some

666 malaria medicine to boot. I shut my eyes tight and clutched the ferns with my hands and teeth to wait until the chill had passed, when I heard a soft voice call:

"Boy."

I thought at first I was delirious, because sometimes I got light-headed when my bad attacks came on; only then I remembered that when I was delirious I didn't know it; all the strange things I saw and heard seemed perfectly natural. So when the voice said, "Boy," again, as soft and clear as the mockingbird at sunrise, I opened my eyes.

Kneeling near me on the ferns was a girl. She must have been about a year younger than I. I was almost sixteen so I guess she was fourteen or fifteen. She was dressed in a blue-and-white gingham dress; her face was very pale, but the kind of paleness that's supposed to be, not the sickly pale kind that was like mine showing even under the tan. Her eyes were big and very blue. Her hair was dark brown and she wore it parted in the middle in two heavy braids that were swinging in front of her shoulders as she peered into my face.

"You don't feel well, do you?" she asked. There was no trace of concern or worry in her voice. Just scientific interest.

I shook my head. "No," I whispered, almost afraid that if I talked she would vanish, because I had never seen anyone here before, and I thought that maybe I was dying because I felt so awful, and I thought maybe that gave me the power to see the ghost. But the girl in blue-and-white-checked gingham seemed as I watched her to be good flesh and blood.

"You'd better come with me," she said. "She'll make you all right."

"Who's she?"

"Oh—just Her," she said.

My chill had begun to recede by now, so when she got up off her knees, I scrambled up, too. When she stood up her dress showed a white ruffled petticoat underneath it, and bits of green moss had left patterns on her knees and I didn't think that would happen to the knees of a ghost, so I followed her as she led the way towards the house. She did not go up the sagging, half-rotted steps which led to the veranda about whose white pillars wisteria vines climbed in wild profusion, but went around to the side of the house where there were slanting doors to a cellar. The sun and rain had long since blistered and washed off the paint, but the doors looked clean and were free of the bits of bark from the eucalyptus tree which leaned nearby and which had dropped its bits of dusty peel on either side; so I knew that these cellar stairs must frequently be used.

The girl opened the cellar doors. "You go down first," she said. I went down the cellar steps, which were stone, and cool against my bare feet. As she followed me she closed the cellar doors after her and as I reached the bottom of the stairs we were in pitch darkness. I began to be very frightened until her soft voice came out of the black.

"Boy, where are you?"

"Right here."

"You'd better take my hand. You might stumble."

We reached out and found each other's hands in the darkness. Her fingers were long and cool and they closed firmly around mine. She moved with authority as though she knew her way with the familiarity born of custom.

"Poor Sat's all in the dark," she said, "but he likes it that way. He likes to sleep for weeks at a time. Sometimes he snores awfully. Sat, darling!" she called gently. A soft, bubbly, blowing sound came in answer, and she laughed happily. "Oh, Sat, you are sweet!" she said, and the bubbly sound came again. Then the girl pulled at my hand and we came out into a huge and dusty kitchen. Iron skillets, pots and pans were still hanging on either side of the huge stove, and there was a rolling pin and a bowl of flour on the marble-topped table in the middle of the room. The girl took a lighted candle off the shelf.

"I'm going to make cookies," she said as she saw me looking at the flour and the rolling pin. She slipped her hand out of mine. "Come along." She began to walk more rapidly. We left the kitchen, crossed the hall, went through the dining room, its old mahogany table thick with dust although sheets covered the pictures on the walls. Then we went into the ballroom. The mirrors lining the walls were spotted and discolored; against one wall was a single delicate gold chair, its seat cushioned with pale rose and silver-woven silk; it seemed extraordinarily well preserved. From the ceiling hung the huge chandelier from which Alexandra Londermaine had hung herself, its prisms catching and breaking up into a hundred colors the flickering of the candle and the few shafts of light that managed to slide in through the boarded-up windows. As we crossed the ballroom the girl began to dance by herself, gracefully, lightly, so that her full blue-and-white-checked gingham skirts flew out around her. She looked at herself with pleasure in the old mirrors as she danced, the candle flaring and guttering in her right hand.

"You've stopped shaking. Now what will I tell Her?" she

said as we started to climb the broad mahogany staircase. It was
very dark, so she took my hand again, and before we had
reached the top of the stairs I obliged her by being seized by
another chill. She felt my trembling fingers with satisfaction.
"Oh, you've started again. That's good." She slid open one of
the huge double doors at the head of the stairs.

As I looked into what once must have been Colonel Londermaine's study I thought that surely what I saw was a scene in a
dream or a vision in delirium. Seated at the huge table in the
center of the room was the most extraordinary woman I had ever
seen. I felt that she must be very beautiful, although she would
never have fulfilled any of the standards of beauty set by our
town. Even though she was seated I felt that she must be
immensely tall. Piled up on the table in front of her were several
huge volumes, and her finger was marking the place in the open
one in front of her, but she was not reading. She was leaning
back in the carved chair, her head resting against a piece of
blue-and-gold-embroidered silk that was flung across the chair
back, one hand gently stroking a faun that lay sleeping in her
lap. Her eyes were closed and somehow I couldn't imagine what
color they would be. It wouldn't have surprised me if they had
been shining amber or the deep purple of her velvet robe. She
had a great quantity of hair, the color of mahogany in firelight,
which was cut quite short and seemed to be blown wildly about
her head like flame. Under her closed eyes were deep shadows,
and lines of pain about her mouth. Otherwise there were no
marks of age on her face, but I would not have been surprised to
learn that she was any age in the world—a hundred, or twenty-
five. Her mouth was large and mobile and she was singing
something in a deep, rich voice. Two cats, one black, one white,
were coiled up, each on a book, and as we opened the doors a
leopard stood up quietly beside her, but did not snarl or move. It
simply stood there and waited, watching us.

The girl nudged me and held her finger to her lips to warn
me to be quiet, but I would not have spoken—could not,
anyhow, my teeth were chattering so from my chill which I
had completely forgotten, so fascinated was I by this woman
sitting back with her head against the embroidered silk, soft
deep sounds coming out of her throat. At last these sounds
resolved themselves into words, and we listened to her as
she sang. The cats slept indifferently, but the leopard listened,
too:

"I sit high in my ivory tower,
    The heavy curtains drawn.
I've many a strange and lustrous flower,
    A leopard and a fawn

Together sleeping by my chair
    And strange birds softly winging,
And ever pleasant to my ear
    Twelve maidens' voices singing.

Here is my magic maps' array,
    My mystic circle's flame.
With symbol's art He lets me play,
    The unknown my domain,

And as I sit here in my dream
    I see myself awake,
Hearing a torn and bloody scream,
    Feeling my castle shake . . ."

Her song wasn't finished but she opened her eyes and looked at us. Now that his mistress knew we were here the leopard seemed ready to spring and devour me at one gulp, but she put her hand on his sapphire-studded collar to restrain him.

"Well, Alexandra," she said, "Who have we here?"

The girl, who still held my hand in her long, cool fingers, answered, "It's a boy."

"So I see. Where did you find him?"

The voice sent shivers up and down my spine.

"In the fern bed. He was shaking. See? He's shaking now. Is he having a fit?" Alexandra's voice was filled with pleased interest.

"Come here, boy," the woman said.

As I didn't move, Alexandra gave me a push, and I advanced slowly. As I came near, the woman pulled one of the leopard's ears gently, saying, "Lie down, Thammuz." The beast obeyed, flinging itself at her feet. She held her hand out to me as I approached the table. If Alexandra's fingers felt firm and cool, hers had the strength of the ocean and the coolness of jade. She looked at me for a long time and I saw that her eyes were deep blue, much bluer than Alexandra's, so dark as to be almost black. When she spoke again her voice was warm and tender: "You're burning up with fever. One of the malaria bugs?" I nodded. "Well, we'll fix that for you."

When she stood and put the sleeping faun down by the leopard, she was not as tall as I had expected her to be; nevertheless she gave an impression of great height. Several of the book-shelves in one corner were emptied of books and filled with various-shaped bottles and retorts. Nearby was a large skeleton. There was an acid-stained washbasin, too; that whole section of the room looked like part of a chemist's or physicist's laboratory. She selected from among the bottles a small amber-colored one, and poured a drop of the liquid it contained into a glass of water. As the drop hit the water there was a loud hiss and clouds of dense smoke arose. When it had drifted away she handed the glass to me and said, "Drink. Drink, my boy!"

My hand was trembling so that I could scarcely hold the glass. Seeing this, she took it from me and held it to my lips.

"What is it?" I asked.

"Drink it," she said, pressing the rim of the glass against my teeth. On the first swallow I started to choke and would have pushed the stuff away, but she forced the rest of the burning liquid down my throat. My whole body felt on fire. I felt flame flickering in every vein, and the room and everything in it swirled around. When I had regained my equilibrium to a certain extent I managed to gasp out again, "What is it?"

She smiled and answered,

"Nine peacocks' hearts, four bats' tongues,
A pinch of moondust and a hummingbird's lungs."

Then I asked a question I would never have dared ask if it hadn't been that I was still half drunk from the potion I had swallowed, "Are you a witch?"

She smiled again, and answered, "I make it my profession."

Since she hadn't struck me down with a flash of lightning, I went on. "Do you ride a broomstick?"

This time she laughed. "I can when I like."

"Is it—is it very hard?"

"Rather like a bucking bronco at first, but I've always been a good horsewoman, and now I can manage very nicely. I've finally progressed to sidesaddle, though I still feel safer astride. I always rode my horse astride. Still, the best witches ride sidesaddle, so . . . Now run along home. Alexandra has lessons to study and I must work. Can you hold your tongue or must I make you forget?"

"I can hold my tongue."

She looked at me and her eyes burnt into me like the potion she had given me to drink. "Yes, I think you can," she said.

"Come back tomorrow if you like. Thammuz will show you out."

The leopard rose and led the way to the door. As I hesitated, unwilling to tear myself away, it came back and pulled gently but firmly on my trouser leg.

"Good-bye, boy," the witch woman said. "And you won't have any more chills and fever."

"Good-bye," I answered. I didn't say thank you. I didn't say good-bye to Alexandra. I followed the leopard out.

She let me come every day. I think she must have been lonely. After all, I was the only thing there with a life apart from hers. And in the long run the only reason I have had a life on my own is because of her. I am as much a creation of the witch woman's as Thammuz the leopard was, or the two cats, Ashtaroth and Orus (it wasn't until many years after the last day I saw the witch woman that I learned that those were the names of the fallen angels).

She did cure my malaria, too. My parents and the townspeople thought that I had outgrown it. I grew angry when they talked about it so lightly and wanted to tell them that it was the witch woman, but I knew that if ever I breathed a word about her I would be eternally damned. Mamma thought we should write a testimonial letter to the 666 Malaria Medicine people, and maybe they'd send us a couple of dollars.

Alexandra and I became very good friends. She was a strange, aloof creature. She liked me to watch her while she danced alone in the ballroom or played on an imaginary harp—though sometimes I fancied I could hear the music. One day she took me into the drawing room and uncovered a portrait that was hung between two of the long boarded up windows. Then she stepped back and held her candle high so as to throw the best light on the picture. It might have been a picture of Alexandra herself, or Alexandra as she might be in five years.

"That's my mother," she said. "Alexandra Londermaine."

As far as I knew from the tales that went about town, Alexandra Londermaine had given birth to only one child, and that stillborn, before she had hung herself on the chandelier in the ball room—and anyhow, any child of hers would have been Alexandra's mother or grandmother. But I didn't say anything because when Alexandra got angry she became ferocious like one of the cats, and was given to leaping on me, scratching and biting. I looked at the portrait long and silently.

"You see, she has on a ring like mine," Alexandra said, holding out her left hand, on the fourth finger of which was the most beautiful sapphire-and-diamond ring I had ever seen, or rather, that I could ever have imagined, for it was a ring apart from any owned by even the most wealthy of the townsfolk. Then I realized that Alexandra had brought me in here and unveiled the portrait simply that she might show me the ring to better advantage, for she had never worn a ring before.

"Where did you get it?"

"Oh, she got it for me last night."

"Alexandra," I asked suddenly, "how long have you been here?"

"Oh, a while."

"But how long?"

"Oh, I don't remember."

"But you must remember."

"I don't. I just came—like Poor Sat."

"Who's Poor Sat?" I asked, thinking for the first time of whoever it was that had made the gentle bubbly noises at Alexandra the day she found me in the fern bed.

"Why, we've never shown you Sat, have we!" she exclaimed. "I'm sure it's all right, but we'd better ask her first."

So we went to the witch woman's room and knocked. Thammuz pulled the door open with his strong teeth and the witch woman looked up from some sort of experiment she was making with test tubes and retorts. The fawn, as usual, lay sleeping near her feet. "Well?" she said.

"Is it all right if I take him to see Poor Little Saturday?" Alexandra asked her.

"Yes, I suppose so," she answered. "But no teasing," and turned her back to us and bent again over her test tubes as Thammuz nosed us out of the room.

We went down to the cellar. Alexandra lit a lamp and took me back to the corner furthest from the doors, where there was a stall. In the stall was a two-humped camel. I couldn't help laughing as I looked at him because he grinned at Alexandra so foolishly, displaying all his huge buck teeth and blowing bubbles through them.

"She said we weren't to tease him," Alexandra said severely, rubbing her cheek against the preposterous splotchy hair that seemed to be coming out, leaving bald pink spots of skin on his long nose.

"But what—" I started.

"She rides him sometimes." Alexandra held out her hand while he nuzzled against it, scratching his rubbery lips against the diamond and sapphire of her ring. "Mostly She talks to him.

She says he is very wise. He goes up to Her room sometimes and they talk and talk. I can't understand a word they say. She says it's Hindustani and Arabic. Sometimes I can remember little bits of it, like: *iderow, sorcabatcha,* and *anna bihed bech.* She says I can learn to speak with them when I finish learning French and Greek.''

Poor Little Saturday was rolling his eyes in delight as Alexandra scratched behind his ears. "Why is he called Poor Little Saturday?" I asked.

Alexandra spoke with a ring of pride in her voice. "I named him. She let me."

"But why did you name him that?"

"Because he came last winter on the Saturday that was the shortest day of the year, and it rained all day so it got light later and dark earlier than it would have if it had been nice, and so it really didn't have as much of itself as it should, and I felt so sorry for it I thought maybe it would feel better if we named him after it . . . She thought it was a nice name!" she turned on me suddenly.

"Oh, it is! It's a fine name!" I said quickly, smiling to myself as I realized how much greater was this compassion of Alexandra's for a day than any she might have for a human being. "How did She get him?" I asked.

"Oh, he just came."

"What do you mean?"

"She wanted him so he came. From the desert."

"He *walked!*"

"Yes. And swam part of the way. She met him at the beach and flew him here on the broom stick. You should have seen him. She was still all wet and looked so funny. She gave him hot coffee with things in it."

"What things?"

"Oh, just things."

Then the witch woman's voice came from behind us. "Well, children?"

It was the first time I had seen her out of her room. Thammuz was at her right heel, the fawn at her left. The cats, Ashtaroth and Orus, had evidently stayed upstairs. "Would you like to ride Saturday?" she asked me.

Speechless, I nodded. She put her hand against the wall and a portion of it slid down into the earth so that Poor Little Saturday was free to go out. "She's sweet, isn't she?" the witch woman asked me, looking affectionately at the strange, bumpy-kneed, splay-footed creature. "Her grandmother was very good to me in Egypt once. Besides, I love camel's milk."

"But Alexandra said she was a he!" I exclaimed.

"Alexandra's the kind of woman to whom all animals are he except cats, and all cats are she. As a matter of fact, Ashtaroth and Orus are she, but it wouldn't make any difference to Alexandra if they weren't. Go on out, Saturday. Come on!"

Saturday backed out, bumping her bulging knees and ankles against her stall, and stood under a live oak tree. "Down," the witch woman said. Saturday leered at me and didn't move. "Down, sorcabatcha!" the witch woman commanded, and Saturday obediently got down on her knees. I clambered up onto her, and before I had managed to get at all settled she rose with such a jerky motion that I knocked my chin against her front hump and nearly bit my tongue off. Round and round Saturday danced while I clung wildly to her front hump and the witch woman and Alexandra rolled on the ground with laughter. I felt as though I were on a very unseaworthy vessel on the high seas, and it wasn't long before I felt violently seasick as Saturday pranced among the live oak trees, sneezing delicately.

At last the witch woman called out, "Enough!" and Saturday stopped in her traces, nearly throwing me, and kneeling laboriously. "It was mean to tease you," the witch woman said, pulling my nose gently. "You may come sit in my room with me for a while if you like."

There was nothing I liked better than to sit in the witch woman's room and to watch her while she studied from her books, worked out strange-looking mathematical problems, argued with the zodiac, or conducted complicated experiments with her test tubes and retorts, sometimes filling the room with sulphurous odors or flooding it with red or blue light. Only once was I afraid of her, and that was when she danced with the skeleton in the corner. She had the room flooded with a strange red glow and I almost thought I could see the flesh covering the bones of the skeleton as they danced together like lovers. I think she had forgotten that I was sitting there, half hidden in the wing chair, because when they had finished dancing and the skeleton stood in the corner again, his bones shining and polished, devoid of any living trappings, she stood with her forehead against one of the deep red velvet curtains that covered the boarded-up windows and tears streamed down her cheeks. Then she went back to her test tubes and worked feverishly. She never alluded to the incident and neither did I.

As winter drew on she let me spend more and more time in the room. Once I gathered up courage enough to ask her about herself, but I got precious little satisfaction.

"Well, then, are you maybe one of the northerners who bought the place?"

"Let's leave it at that, boy. We'll say that's who I am. Did you know that my skeleton was old Colonel Londermaine? Not so old, as a matter of fact; he was only thirty-seven when he was killed at the battle of Bunker Hill—or am I getting him confused with his great-grandfather, Rudolph Londermaine? Anyhow he was only thirty-seven, and a fine figure of a man, and Alexandra only thirty when she hung herself for love of him on the chandelier in the ballroom. Did you know that the fat man with the red mustaches has been trying to cheat your father? His cow will give sour milk for seven days. Run along now and talk to Alexandra. She's lonely."

When the winter had turned to spring and the camellias and azaleas and Cape jessamine had given way to the more lush blooms of early May, I kissed Alexandra for the first time, very clumsily. The next evening when I managed to get away from the chores at home and hurried out to the plantation, she gave me her sapphire-and-diamond ring, which she had swung for me on a narrow bit of turquoise satin. "It will keep us both safe," she said, "if you wear it always. And then when we're older we can get married and you can give it back to me. Only you mustn't let anyone see it, ever, ever, or She'd be very angry."

I was afraid to take the ring but when I demurred Alexandra grew furious and started kicking and biting and I had to give in.

Summer was almost over before my father discovered the ring hanging about my neck. I fought like a witch boy to keep him from pulling out the narrow ribbon and seeing the ring, and indeed the ring seemed to give me added strength and I had grown, in any case, much stronger during the winter than I had ever been in my life. But my father was still stronger than I, and he pulled it out. He looked at it in dead silence for a moment and then the storm broke. That was the famous Londermaine ring that had disappeared the night Alexandra Londermaine hung herself. That ring was worth a fortune. Where had I got it?

No one believed me when I said I had found it in the grounds near the house—I chose the grounds because I didn't want anybody to think I had been in the house or indeed that I was able to get in. I don't know why they didn't believe me; it still seems quite logical to me that I might have found it buried among the ferns.

It had been a long, dull year, and the men of the town were all bored. They took me and forced me to swallow quantities of corn liquor until I didn't know what I was saying or doing. When they had finished with me I didn't even manage to reach home before I was violently sick and then I was in my mother's arms and she was weeping over me. It was morning before I was able to slip away to the plantation house. I ran pounding up the mahogany stairs to the witch woman's room and opened the heavy sliding doors without knocking. She stood in the center of the room in her purple robe, her arms around Alexandra, who was weeping bitterly. Overnight the room had completely changed. The skeleton of Colonel Londermaine was gone, and books filled the shelves in the corner of the room that had been her laboratory. Cobwebs were everywhere, and broken glass lay on the floor; dust was inches thick on her work table. There was no sign of Thammuz, Ashtaroth or Orus, or the fawn, but four birds were flying about her, beating their wings against her hair.

She did not look at me or in any way acknowledge my presence. Her arm about Alexandra, she led her out of the room and to the drawing room where the portrait hung. The birds followed, flying around and around them. Alexandra had stopped weeping now. Her face was very proud and pale and if she saw me miserably trailing behind them she gave no notice. When the witch woman stood in front of the portrait the sheet fell from it. She raised her arm; there was a great cloud of smoke; the smell of sulphur filled my nostrils, and when the smoke was gone, Alexandra was gone, too. Only the portrait was there, the fourth finger of the left hand now bearing no ring. The witch woman raised her hand again and the sheet lifted itself up and covered the portrait. Then she went, with the birds, slowly back to what had once been her room, and still I tailed after, frightened as I had never been before in my life, or have been since.

She stood without moving in the center of the room for a long time. At last she turned and spoke to me.

"Well, boy, where is the ring?"

"They have it."

"They made you drunk, didn't they?"

"Yes."

"I was afraid something like this would happen when I gave Alexandra the ring. But it doesn't matter . . . I'm tired . . ." She drew her hand wearily across her forehead.

"Did I—did I tell them everything?"

"You did."

"I—I didn't know."

"I know you didn't know, boy."

"Do you hate me now?"

"No, boy, I don't hate you."

"Do you have to go away?"

"Yes."

I bowed my head. "I'm so sorry . . ."

She smiled slightly. "The sands of time . . . Cities crumble and rise and will crumble again and breath dies down and blows once more . . ."

The birds flew madly about her head, pulling at her hair, calling into her ears. Downstairs we could hear a loud pounding, and then the crack of boards being pulled away from a window.

"Go, boy," she said to me. I stood rooted, motionless, unable to move. "*Go!*" she commanded, giving me a mighty push so that I stumbled out of the room. They were waiting for me by the cellar doors and caught me as I climbed out. I had to stand there and watch when they came out with her. But it wasn't the witch woman, my witch woman. It was *their* idea of a witch woman, someone thousands of years old, a disheveled old creature in rusty black, with long wisps of gray hair, a hooked nose, and four wiry black hairs springing out of the mole on her chin. Behind her flew the four birds and suddenly they went up, up, into the sky, directly in the path of the sun until they were lost in its burning glare.

Two of the men stood holding her tightly, although she wasn't struggling, but standing there, very quiet, while the others searched the house, searched it in vain. Then as a group of them went down into the cellar I remembered, and by a flicker of the old light in the witch woman's eyes I could see that she remembered, too. Poor Little Saturday had been forgotten. Out she came, prancing absurdly up the cellar steps, her rubbery lips stretched back over her gigantic teeth, her eyes bulging with terror. When she saw the witch woman, her lord and master, held captive by two dirty, insensitive men, she let out a shriek and began to kick and lunge wildly, biting, screaming with the blood-curdling, heart-rending screams that only a camel can make. One of the men fell to the ground, holding a leg in which the bone had snapped from one of Saturday's kicks. The others scattered in terror, leaving the witch woman standing on the veranda supporting herself by clinging to one of the huge wistaria vines that curled around the columns. Saturday clambered up onto the veranda, and knelt while she flung herself between the two humps. Then off they ran, Saturday still screaming, her knees knocking together, the ground shaking as she pounded along.

Down from the sun plummeted the four birds and flew after them.

Up and down I danced, waving my arms, shouting wildly until Saturday and the witch woman and the birds were lost in a cloud of dust, while the man with the broken leg lay moaning on the ground beside me.

Squeakie's First Case

by Margaret Manners

The late Margaret Manners was a fine mystery and suspense writer who wrote for such markets as Street & Smith's Detective Story Magazine, Alfred Hitchcock's Mystery Magazine, and Ellery Queen's Mystery Magazine. She published more than forty stories, including "Death Is My Legacy," "Trial by Fire," and "An Instrument of Justice." A collection of her best work would make an excellent book. "Squeakie's First Case," one of her rare ventures into fantasy, is from EQMM, May 1943.

I'll never forget that night, not if I live to be as old as Methuselah and have as many wives as Solomon, God forbid!

Squeakie was brushing her hair and counting. She's been doing a hundred strokes lately. I usually put pink-wax stopples in my ears, but that night I was too busy trying to lay down the law to her. A husband has some rights and one of them ought to be a power of veto, especially if his wife goes in for learned courses in anything from Shakespeare to hobgoblins. The last time it was psychology and she was "handling" me.

Squeakie (her real name is Desdemona, her father was mad . . . about Shakespeare, so is she) is difficult to approach in these matters; the effect is about the same as if you walk on a step that isn't there.

Squeakie's voice went on. "Twenty-two, twenty-three . . ."

"But look, Squeakie," I said, "I don't want you to ride a broomstick."

"Twenty-eight, twenty-nine. Don't be silly, David."

"I don't know why you of all people should want me not to be silly," I said.

She peeped at me between the strands of hovering hairs that were trying to follow the brush that attracted them. She made a good-looking witch.

"I don't intend to ride any broomstick. I've told you over and over. The idea is to get a complete historic view of the insides of people. Thirty-four, thirty-five."

I stared at her. Where had thirty to thirty-three gone? Had she been counting by remote control? "Insides of people" suggested lots of things.

She said, "I wish you wouldn't wear those purple pajamas. I always have nightmares when you do. Thirty-nine, forty."

I said sternly, "They're not purple, they're mauve. Anyway, you bought them." Then I came down as I thought to brass tacks.

"I won't have any more of this foolishness; you've got to give it up."

She turned away from the mirror and shook her curly brown mop at me. "Brushing is doing wonders. Can't you see the life in it?" she said seriously.

I was caught off guard. I said, "Yes," and began to look for the life in it. Then I ground my teeth and sprang off the bed. "Squeakie! I don't mean the hair. You know what I'm talking about. I mean that so-called esoteric study—"

She smiled and interrupted me. "Oh, that. I've been trying to tell you. It helps me to understand people. You can't understand people's minds in the tenth century or in any other century unless you can share their thoughts. You know—what they believed, their superstitions, their crimes. It's a kind of mythology. Every age has one. As a reporter that should be clear to you. For example, everyone today believes in microbes and germs. Causing disease, you know."

"But Squeakie," I gasped, "that's not a superstition. Bacteria do cause disease."

Her sweet little face became darkly prophetic under the halo of electrified hair. "Ha!" she said triumphantly. "Living today, that's what you think. But what will people think two hundred years from now?"

I bit the cuff of the mauve pajamas and gave up.

She looked at the clock and began counting again. "Sixty-one, sixty-two."

I couldn't stand it any longer. "Squeakie," I said gently.

"Mmmmm? Sixty-four, sixty-five . . ."

"How do you know it's sixty-one? You stopped counting strokes at forty. How do you know?"

She pointed to the leather-framed clock.

"The clock? Squeakie!"

"Oh, David, don't you see? I look at the second hand when I stop counting. I allow one second per stroke. It's easy."

There was something wrong somewhere. "But," I said, "you can't add, darling!"

"David, don't be silly. Of course I can add. I just don't do it your way. I subtract. Eighty-two . . ."

"Kiss me goodnight, darling," I said, "I want to go to sleep."

She's wonderful. But sometimes I get a little confused.

The last thing I remembered was Squeakie saying "ninety-two." I was listening to her chest with a huge stethoscope, begging her to say ninety-nine. But she wouldn't. Then I tried to pull the stethoscope out of my ears. There was a terrible noise in my head, like a siren shrieking, but the ear pieces wouldn't come out. I shook them and shook them and . . .

I opened my eyes and felt as if the top of my head were coming off.

Squeakie was shaking me. "David! David! Wake up!"

I spoke through the layers of fur in my mouth. "Huh? What is it?"

She was scared; her nails were digging into my arms. I pushed her away and sat up.

"David, a woman in the next house screamed. It was terrible!"

I was awake now, enough to be sore. "What do you want me to do, scream back?"

But she was trembling, so I put my arms around her. "What's the matter, darling?"

"David, she was being killed, I know it."

I took my arms away again, quick. That's just like Squeakie. Give her an inch . . . Before I could recover she took more territory and I hardly had room to stand up in. I was lying in bed, of course, but you see what I mean.

She said, "David, call Gregory!"

I'd better stop here for a minute. Gregory Sawyer is a good friend of ours and in addition he's a police lieutenant on New York's Homicide Squad. He likes Squeakie too.

I glanced at the clock. "Darling," I said. My voice was full of what I hoped was convincing authority and disapproval. "If you hear a scream in New York at twelve midnight, even in a nice early-to-bed neighborhood like this, you don't call a lieutenant of the Homicide Squad. At the most you call the local precinct and report it. Get into bed, you'll catch cold."

Not Squeakie. She couldn't do anything that simple. She

shook all over until her teeth chattered. "It's raining," she moaned. "Listen!"

I listened obligingly. After all, that was easy. It was pouring outside, nasty chill March rain. You could hear it splashing and plopping in the courtyard between the two houses. The soft swish of wheels in the wet street made bed seem a good place to be in.

We live in a very quiet street in that part of Manhattan which just stops being the Village and starts to be Chelsea. Contrary to all you've read and heard, we're quiet, nice, working people. The long-haired Bohemian is a vanishing race. They paint camouflage these days, I suppose, and get paid for it.

I sat up higher in bed and tried to see 313, the house across the court, but the angle was wrong, and anyway it was pitch-black outside.

We live in 315, its companion house, and the court runs in from the street, giving us light, air and street noises. However, the kids can't get in and play there, thank the lord. We have a high board fence, nicely painted battleship-gray, spanning the space between the two houses and shielding us from the public eye when we take our sunbaths in summer.

The door in the fence can't be entered from the outside, but you can always get out from the inside—a sort of latch arrangement. Small shrubs and fancy fire escapes, New Orleans wrought-iron style, leading down to our glorified playpen, take the curse off concrete and raise the rent. But iron balustrades are too stagy for us; we use the basement door to enter the court.

Do you follow me? For the sake of the story I had to make it clear about the houses.

Now back to Squeakie. She fidgeted while I listened to the rain. Then she went to the window.

"The second floor across the court has a light on," she said. "Oh, it's gone out. David, it was a horrible scream. Please call Gregory."

I stalled for time. "He's probably asleep. Squeakie, I don't want to wake a hardworking police officer."

"It's not late. Besides, he never goes to bed early. He's probably not at home anyway. You don't need to be scared."

I'd been caught that way before. "If you are worried," I pointed out, "why don't *you* call the police station? You're a citizen too."

To make a long story short I found myself dialing Gregory's number. His phone rang twice. "There," I said, "he's not in. I'll just . . ."

Before I could slam down the receiver Squeakie stayed my hand. "Give him time," she said, a cold glitter in her eye.

I gave him time.

"Hullo, what is it?" he said.

Just my luck! This had to be the night he went to bed early. He sounded fuzzy, and I felt like a fool.

"Squeakie wanted me to call you," I said weakly.

I waited for the sound and fury at his end, but he just said, "Oh, it's you." Very unencouraging.

I tried again. "Squeakie heard a scream."

"Really?"

"Oh, hell!" I said. "You don't think I wanted to call you, do you?"

"I wouldn't know."

Squeakie glared at me and snatched the phone. She had intended to do the talking all along, and we both knew it.

I was glad to see she wasn't doing any too well. The horrendous tale failed to impress. She hung up sadly. "He told me to go back to bed."

"Good," I said. "That's fine. Let's get some sleep."

"No," she said, tight-lipped. "I'm going to get dressed and make some coffee. We'll probably need it tonight."

"Squeakie, darling!" I wailed. "There's no murder. There's no fire. No tired minions of the law will troop in here for refreshment. Why do you want to make coffee?"

"Don't scream at me, David. How do you know?"

"How do I know what?"

"That there hasn't been a murder?"

She had donned her air-raid-warden slacks and and a sweater. She's prepared, all right.

"How do you know there has?" I asked.

She looked at me somberly. "By the prickling of my thumb."

I thought she was swearing. "By the what?"

"By the prickling of my thumb. That's how I know. It's from *Macbeth*. The witch says it. Well, are you getting up?"

"I am not."

She marched out to the kitchen. I could hear the rattle of pots as she went about making coffee.

The phone rang.

I picked up the receiver with fear in my heart. It was Gregory.

"Apologize to your wife."

"My God, no!"

"Yes. Two of your neighbors heard the scream and phoned the police. A man went over and broke down a door. Found a woman murdered. I'm coming right down. Looks like an all-night job. Tell Squeakie to put the coffee on, will you?''

I said dully, ''She has,'' and hung up.

Squeakie came in self-consciously trying not to look smug. ''There, I was right, wasn't I? Oh, darling, isn't it dreadful?'' She suddenly looked frightened and pitifully incapable of dealing with this harsh world. But you can't fool one of the people all of the time. I just looked at her little pink thumb. Then I said, ''You ought to keep that out of other people's business.''

Even that was too much. She gave me a lecture on my moral duties as a citizen.

I was very meek while we waited for Gregory. There was something I wanted to do, but I wanted to do it alone. Squeakie was sitting over the coffeepot, looking like a superefficient ''Angel of Mercy.''

''How was she killed, David?''

''I don't know. Gregory didn't say.''

''Well, anyway, she wasn't shot.''

I stared at her. ''Did your thumb tell you that?''

''O David, you don't think!'' (*I* don't think!) ''If I heard the scream I'd have heard the shot, wouldn't I?''

I flattered her by looking wonder and admiration—hard. Then I put on my act.

''Good Lord!'' I exclaim. ''I'd almost forgotten that I'm a newspaperman. I think I'll just step over and find out who it is, etc., so that I can phone the paper. I'll be back in a few minutes.''

Squeakie pours a cup of coffee and hands it to me. ''Good idea, I think I'll come along.''

''Swell,'' I say heartily, ''put on your raincoat.'' But I don't let her get that far. ''Darn it!'' I add, pulling a long face. ''We're forgetting, Squeakie. You can't leave the apartment.'' I imply that she shoulders a great responsibility. ''Gregory will be here any minute.''

Believe it or not, she really thinks Gregory will fly to her before he even peeps at the corpse. To consult the oracle of her thumb, I have no doubt. After that she folds up, forlorn as a wet umbrella, and I am free to do a little quiet snooping.

There were cars parked outside 313. Doc Evans and his little black bag were upstairs, and so was Haley with a couple of the boys. Gregory was probably still on his way.

I studied the names and the apartment numbers displayed in the mail boxes. This was the arrangement:

First floor:	1A VERA GRAY
	1B LEONARD S. COBALT
Second floor:	2A JONATHAN WEST
	2B MARY ELLEN MEREDITH
Third floor:	3A Vacant
	3B JUDYTHA PERRY
Fourth floor:	4A ARISTODEMUS KORDIS
	4B JOHN SLATER

Then I peeked into the hallway through the thinly curtained glass panel of the door.

Standing near the open door of apartment 1B was a middle-aged couple. They looked worried and at the isn't-it-dreadful-you-never-know stage. I tapped on the glass and showed my police card. Reluctantly Papa Cobalt opened the door.

"It's all right," I told him. "I live next door. David Meadow. I'm a reporter. *Herald*. My wife heard the scream. What happened?"

Mrs. Cobalt answered for him. Now that I come to think of it, I never did hear her husband's voice, but then there are women like that. "She's been murdered. Miss Perry's been murdered!" She whispered the word.

"Miss Perry?" I said. "Oh, you mean the one in apartment 3B. Did you know her? What did she do?"

Mrs. Cobalt shook her head. "I don't know, but she was a friend of Miss Gray across the hall and you know who *she* is."

I disclaimed all knowledge.

Mrs. Cobalt warmed to the task. "She's an actress. In that new hit play at the Village Little Theater. You know the one about ghosts; been in the papers such a lot lately. *Dark World*. Miss Gray plays the dead wife."

"But look here," I protested. "Vivian Gaylord plays that zombie."

Mrs. Cobalt smiled. "That's her stage name. She's really Vera Gray. Lucky girl!" She glanced with benevolent interest at the door marked 1A.

Lucky girl was right. The Little Theater had struggled on tiny subsidies for years and then out of a clear sky some striving Villager had written a hit for them. Vivian Gaylord! No one had ever heard of her till she was discovered in one of its eerie roles, not the lead but still . . .

I moved over to 1A.

"She's not there," Mrs. Cobalt offered. "She's telling the policeman what happened."

Someone was coming down the stairs. I looked up and saw a slender young woman with a white, set face looking down and through us. She was wearing one of those new hats that have a brim and then yards of stuff hanging around the face and swathing the chin.

"Miss Gaylord," I said. But Mama Cobalt was too quick for me.

"Poor child," she said, and advanced to take the actress to her bosom.

Gray, alias Gaylord, was not tall, but she looked really tiny sobbing on the Cobalt bust.

Again there was a step on the stairs, and this time a heavy one. Sergeant Haley lumbered down to us. He offered me his hand and spoke to Mrs. Cobalt.

"She's had a nasty shock," he said, glancing at the draped head under Mrs. Cobalt's chin. "Take her in and give her a cup of tea. Don't let her go to bed yet; the lieutenant will want to talk to her again."

The Cobalts, looking heavily co-operative, withdrew into 1B and closed the door.

Tim Haley, otherwise known as "The Comet," gave me the eye. "You reporters waste more good time," he said, gently reproving me. "Whyn't you come up and ask me?"

I agreed with him and tried to follow his suggestion.

He shook his head. "Wait'll the lieutenant gets here. I don't wanna tell it twice."

"Well, tell me how she was killed," I said as we were going upstairs.

"She was lying in bed. Her skull was beaten in with a base of a marble statue. Diana the Huntress."

"Diana the Huntress?"

"Sure. Don't you know your mythology? The lady with the bow. It's a copy of the one in the Metropolitan."

Haley is occasionally quite surprising. Now when and why would he have ever been in a museum? But we were at the door of 3B. He remarked that Doc Evans was inside.

"Well," said I, "it can't have been premeditated."

His hand on the doorknob, Haley looked at me.

"Because of the weapon," I added.

"That doesn't always follow," he said, and opened the door.

The layout of the apartment was like ours, but in reverse. We crossed the hall to the large bedroom, the one with windows on the court fire escape. But before we went in, the hall door opened behind us and there was Gregory. Squeakie says with emphasis that he's "very attractive." He's the rugged but well-washed-behind-the-ears type. The boys under him think he's swell. I do and I don't. I mean you can appreciate a guy and still not be blind to his faults.

Haley was just drawing himself up and getting ready to make his report when there was a loud thump at the door. I had dire forebodings, and alas, my instincts were right.

When Gregory opened the door there stood Squeakie. From somewhere about her person, which was well hung with flashlights, first-aid kits, spare parts and divers other things to help us beat the enemy, she produced a stenographer's notebook and pencil.

"I thought you might like nice transcribed reports of your investigation," she chirped at him.

Haley looked pleased: he hates to take down anything. But Gregory played hard to get.

"Now, Squeakie, you can't fool around with this. It's a murder case."

She opened her big blue eyes very wide and registered shocked surprise. "Why, Gregory! You know how serious I am about things like this. You'll have to question people. Can't I be your secretary? I won't say a word."

I flagged him behind her back and shook my head till it rattled. But in a few seconds she had him neatly tied up. No rescue was possible.

"I'm going to phone the paper," I said, and left.

When I returned Squeakie was sitting in the apartment hallway on a kitchen chair. The door to the bedroom was closed.

"Where are Gregory and The Comet?" I asked.

She shivered. "In there with the . . ."

"Corpse?" I said. "Squeakie, you are a sweet little ghoul." Which struck home. For the next five minutes she stared past me at a spot on the wall behind my left ear.

Gregory came out of the bedroom. "Go sit in the living room, Squeakie." He pointed to the front of the house. "We're going to bring out the body." She fled down the hall.

Doc Evans came out and said hello, and I went in. I saw the face before it was covered up. The head was badly battered. The face I had seen before, casually now and then, on the street. It was long and very white, but the mouth which on the street was usually a hard crimson gash was now revealed thin, tight and bloodless. The eyes were long and oval with pale lashes which hardly showed without the mascara. The hair was a greenish-bronze and spilled out in a kind of tangled bloodstained mass on the pillow. It was a strong handsome face, but it was not a kind face. I looked around the bedroom as they carried her out.

It was identical with ours in size and shape but was very pretentiously decorated. There was a lot of green around mingled with hot blues and reds. It was well done yet definitely theatrical, a setting.

The fire-escape window was open and the curtain blew hard. The rain was slanting into the room and the rug was wet.

I noted the ornate desk and dressing table and a heavy walnut Spanish-type chest. A straight two-edged sword, shining and unsheathed, hung from a crimson cord on the wall above the chest. I tried the lid. It was open. Inside were packets of letters. Each marked with a name which was followed by a series of figures. What the fair Perry had done was no longer a mystery. The packets were tumbled about a bit as if somebody had looked for something hurriedly. I let the lid fall.

Haley pointed to something lying beside the bed. "Exhibit A," he said.

It was a heavy-based marble statue of Diana. There was an irregular purplish stain on one corner of the pedestal.

It was pretty clear to the three of us that Judytha Perry was a clever girl. The apartment furnishings had cost her plenty. She had done well for herself, she and her little collection of letters.

Haley showed us that somebody had left the apartment via the fire escape. Though the "fresh scrapings" he pointed out did not impress me as conclusive evidence, they seemed to satisfy Gregory. Especially after he had discovered that those marks in the damp rug were footprints—large and masculine.

Squeakie burst in on us.

"Look, David, she had a copy of the book I'm studying." She waved a too, too familiar volume under my nose, *Medieval Witchcraft in Modern Practice*. "I found it in her bookcase; she has a wonderful collection . . . !"

"Squeakie!" I thundered. She subsided with a contrite little "Oh."

Haley made his report then. He'd been trying to ever since Gregory arrived. Squeakie wandered about the bedroom poking in drawers and looking in closets while he talked.

I sum up Haley's report: People in the two houses on the court had been startled or awakened, as the case may be, by a scream at a few minutes after midnight. Calls from the Cobalts, who had been playing gin rummy, and from Greerson, on the top floor of our house, had started the investigation. Miss Gray had been returning from the theater and was about to open her apartment door when she heard the scream. She thought she recognized her friend's voice and ran up the stairs. But there was no answer and she couldn't get into the apartment. She started upstairs for Mr. Slater, remembered he was working nights in defense and went downstairs to get help. She met the Cobalts coming up.

Miss Meredith on the second floor stuck her head out the door as they passed. She said she had been awakened by what she thought was a scream. She had not connected it with the apartment above her because as she raised her head from the pillow she had been attracted by a movement on the second-floor fire escape of the house across the court (our house, 315). Her fears had been dissipated (the phraseology is Haley's) when she saw that it was only the curtain of the open window blowing out in the rain. She would have gone back to sleep but the sound of running feet (the Cobalts and Miss Gray) aroused her curiosity. She was sitting below in her apartment and would be glad to answer any questions, but she didn't know what she could possibly add.

Suddenly we all looked up startled. Squeakie was speaking.

"I wonder where her cold cream is." She was tapping her lips and staring at an array of vermilion-capped bottles and jars on the dressing table. "Look, she had everything—astringent, mask, grits, lotion, foundation cream—but no cleansing cream and no cold cream. She must have had a jar."

Haley stared at me and I stared at Haley. But Gregory went over and with infinite patience . . .

"Of course she had some, Squeakie. She just used it more often than the other things, and she used it all up." He turned back to us. But he didn't know Squeakie like I know Squeakie.

"Well," said she, "if she used it up where's the jar? The government says we ought to keep them for refills. Conservation, you know."

I raised my eyebrows and shrugged my shoulders trying vainly to indicate that I was in no way responsible for the behavior of my wife. She went on rooting around in things. The sword seemed to fascinate her.

"It has a copper hilt!" she announced as if confiding to us something of great significance.

Haley went over to her. Deliberately ignoring the dramatic wall decoration he stared down at Squeakie. She fluttered a bit and was still.

As she turned away from him she stumbled awkwardly. Then she stooped and picked something from the floor. "Look!" She held it up. "A little doll!"

"Doll me eye," Haley growled. He snatched it out of her hand. "It's not a doll, Mrs. Meadow. It's a pin cushion."

He held the miniature female figure out and we all saw the pins sticking in the head. Squeakie gasped as he placed it with a careful eye for position on the dressing table.

"It's a real cute one, too. They think up all sorts of crazy things like that to sell for ladies' boudoirs," he instructed her.

"Cute! I think it's ugly," Squeakie said.

"Well, I'll be . . . !" Gregory jumped on Haley. "Are we playing house here, Sergeant?"

The Comet answered stolidly, "No, sir."

"All right, let's go down and interview Miss Gray. I suppose we'd better say Miss Gaylord. Squeakie, if you can't be seen and not heard, please don't come."

We called at the Cobalts' and found Miss Gaylord waiting for us. She led us across the hall to her apartment and Gregory questioned her. As she took off her hat with its draped blinkers I noticed she looked pale and washed-out. She sat, her head propped on her hand, her elbow resting on the table. She seemed to be answering automatically, not thinking about what she was saying at all.

Squeakie was very attentive and conspicuously quiet, which was very nice for all of us.

Gaylord's story only repeated in detail what she had told Haley. I select the important points. The play was an unusually long one, but Gaylord did not appear in the last act. However, she rarely left the theater immediately. One had to remove one's makeup. She smiled apologetically for mentioning it. I remembered then, and Squeakie, who had seen the play, was obviously on pins and needles to say so, that Gaylord as the dead wife wore a striking phosphorescent makeup that glowed like ectoplasm on a dimmed stage. She explained that it took only a few seconds to remove it, but that she loafed around in her dressing room. It was her habit to leave the theater at about eleven-forty and walk home. She arrived as she had done tonight, around midnight. She doubted whether anyone at the theater had seen her leave; they were all on stage at the time.

Doorman? We evidently had no idea of the size of the Little Theater. They didn't have a doorman. Of course if this run kept up they'd move to a larger house; you never could tell.

Gregory nodded and Squeakie's fingers flew. That she's as fast as a court stenographer has always amazed me.

Then Gregory hit something.

He asked the routine questions about knowing anyone who knew the victim and if she could help them in any way.

She hesitated and seemed ill at ease. "Why, no," she said, "I guess not." Then, "Oh, I don't know." She twisted her fingers and peered at us in an agony of uncertainty.

Gregory said, "Miss Gaylord, there is no compulsion on you to speak at this moment. But I do advise you that nothing is too slight to tell us, especially if you are in doubt." He leaned forward and spoke earnestly. "I don't need to remind you that your friend has been murdered. Murder rules out all minor considerations. Nothing you can say will harm anyone who is innocent."

She answered him reluctantly and in a whisper. "I knew someone who knew her well a few years ago, still knows her, I suppose . . . but . . ."

Gregory waited.

Her voice grew firmer and she went on. "His name is Bob Morgan. He used to be quite fond of Judy. I think a few years ago they were—well—they went around together a lot." She hesitated again. "I wish you'd talk to him. I don't like to say anything further, especially as I'm not very sure."

"Do you know where he lives?"

She raised her head and looked straight at Gregory, yet I had the impression that she was looking beyond him. It was a concentrated vagueness that I couldn't explain.

"Yes, I know. He lives next door in 315."

We all stiffened like hounds on a live scent. It was too much for Squeakie. She forgot all about not being heard.

"You don't mean that nice-looking young man who has the apartment below us!" she exclaimed.

Haley coughed warningly. Miss Gaylord ignored her. Only Gregory spoke.

He said, "Under you, Squeakie?" He glanced at Haley, who nodded.

"That's right, Lieutenant. That's the apartment Miss Meredith saw, with the fire-escape window open."

"Is there anything else, Miss Gaylord? Anything you think would be of use to us?" He rose and Gaylord looked up at him.

"No," she said quickly. "I really have a dreadful headache. I'd like to lie down if I may."

"Do," he said. Then he spoke rather diffidently. I could see what Squeakie meant when she said he has charm. "I had intended to ask you more about Miss Perry, her past life, and the usual things that policemen have to ask, but I think I'll try Mr.

Morgan who seems to have been an old friend too. If I don't get what I want, I wonder—I know it's an imposition at this hour— but may I call back to see you again?''

She smiled wanly, but nodded her head as if she didn't much care.

"Oh, just one thing more, Miss Gaylord." He stopped half- way to the door. "How does it happen that Miss Perry and Mr. Morgan lived so close to one another? It wasn't chance, I take it."

Her face was haggard under the pale-gold hair. "No," she said very softly, "it wasn't chance. Judytha and I shared an apartment when we moved here. She insisted that we move. She said she wanted to keep an eye on Bob. I took a separate apartment later when the show did so well. Judytha was nervous and wanted to be alone."

She spoke in such a frightened tone that I was sure she was holding something back.

At the apartment door Squeakie turned and said gently, "You suffer with headaches, Miss Gaylord?"

Gaylord narrowed her eyes as if making an effort to see Squeakie. "Yes," she said. "Well, not really, just sometimes."

"It's your eyes," said Squeakie, paying no attention to Gregory, who was waiting impatiently at the door.

Gaylord gave a scared bleat. "No, it isn't. It can't be my eyes!" Her hands were shaking.

Squeakie went on. "I don't think it's serious. But you are frightfully nearsighted. You'll have to wear glasses someday. You'd relieve yourself if you'd do it now."

Gaylord went white. She turned on Gregory. "Take her out of here," she said huskily. "She gets on my nerves." Then to Squeakie, "For God's sake leave me alone. Is the police depart- ment short manpower?"

Outside, Gregory gave Squakie a piece of his mind. She took it without a murmur. "Squeakie, you tactless, scatter-brained little . . ."

When he had finished, Squeakie said, "Well, it's silly to suffer like that because you're too vain to wear glasses."

I butted in. "Look, darling, lots of actresses should and don't wear glasses. It's more than vanity; they're afraid."

The rain was letting up and the air was fresh and somehow one smelled spring in the air. Squeakie tucked her arm through mine and we followed Haley, who was following Gregory into 315.

"We can have coffee in our place," I said, "whenever you like," and Gregory nodded absently.

We rang Bob Morgan's bell a few times and Gregory made Haley thump on the door. At last we heard a door open somewhere inside and a lot of uncertain shuffling and groping.

When he opened the door and stood teetering, staring out vaguely, we all recoiled as if slapped. The odor of whisky filled the place and overflowed into the hall.

"Whar is it?" He spoke thickly and truculently.

"How long have you been at home?" asked Gregory.

The drunk looked helpless, and then he asked, "What time is it now?"

"About two o'clock," Haley told him, looking at his watch.

Morgan counted on wavering fingers, "Twelve o'clock, one o'clock, two o'clock. Been here two hours." Then he added slyly: "Came home drunk, sleeping it off now." He held his fingers to his lips and winked solemnly.

Gregory said, "May we come in? We want to talk to you."

"Sure." He swung away from the door and I noticed that though he was fully dressed he was in his stocking feet. Then he turned back and growled at us. "Say, who are you? What do you want?"

"We are the police," Gregory told him a trifle inaccurately. "Did you hear a scream when you came home tonight?"

"Nope. What do you police want with me? Is she a police?" He pointed at Squeakie in her air-raid-warden costume.

"She's a stenographer." Gregory was annoyed, but it was his own fault. "Did you know a Miss Perry living next door in apartment 3B?"

I thought the eyes in the doorway grew a little wary. "Sure, I know Judytha. What of it?"

Gregory pushed him inside as he spoke. "She's been murdered," he said quietly. "Would you know anything about that?"

"Oh, my God!" He jerked back as if he had been struck. He shivered and leaned against the wall; for a minute I thought he would be sick. Then his whole manner changed. "Come in," he said soberly and he led us across the hall into his bedroom.

The room was warm and in disorder. The tightly closed window kept the air foul with the smell of liquor. A depression showed in the rumpled bedspread where someone had been lying. A pair of hastily discarded shoes, laces not untied, lay in the middle of the rug.

"Just a minute," he said thickly. He vanished into the bathroom and I could hear him snorting under the cold water. He came out slicking his wet hair back from his face. He was a good-looking kid in a rather worn sort of way.

He apologized sheepishly and asked us to go into the living room. But Gregory preferred the bedroom and I could see why.

Morgan threw the windows wide open. "Sorry, but I came home pickled. I didn't open the window. Must have been in a state. I guess I passed out."

This was going to be pretty easy, I thought. He wasn't acting any too smart.

Haley saw it, too. The curtains of the window that hadn't been opened were wet! He went round the room making a perfunctory tour of inspection, then he peered out of the window and waited.

Still Gregory didn't speak, and after an awkward silence Morgan said, "How was she killed? When?" His voice was dry. He was dead sober now.

"She was lying in bed with her head bashed in. She screamed at midnight, was found a short time after. Where were you at that time, Mr. Morgan?"

"Still on the street drunk, I guess."

"Ah, well." Gregory dismissed it with a shrug. "How well did you know Miss Perry?"

He answered frankly enough. "Very well indeed, at one time—not lately."

"When did you last see her?"

"Two weeks ago."

Gregory leaned forward. "You don't seem sorry she's dead."

He considered that. "I'm shocked," he said, "naturally. I don't think I'm very sorry; she was such a malicious little . . ." He stopped short.

"Really? You resented her treatment of you, then?"

"I?" He raised his head. "No, I was thinking of Vera. Judytha was jealous of her work in the Theater. You see, Judytha had stage ambitions too. They met each other through theater work. She used to hound poor Vera."

"What did Miss Perry mean when she said she moved next door to keep an eye on you?"

I thought that had him, but he recovered and hurdled it easily enough. "Did she say that? Well, she may have been a bit jealous of me, but frankly I can't see her moving for that. She probably moved because she liked the apartment and then she said that to be mysterious. Mystery was her forte." He seemed to be puzzled. "I can't understand . . ."

"What?"

"Oh? The murder." But it was something else I thought that he couldn't understand.

Gregory's eyes roved around the room.

And then Squeakie spoke. She said, and I jumped at the familiarity, "Bob, tell them the truth. You're making it worse for yourself."

I thought Haley would put her out the door. He made a move but Gregory held him back. I couldn't understand that.

"The curtains," Squeakie said. "They were seen blowing. They know your window wasn't closed. They want to trap you. Look!" She pointed to the window. "They're wet!"

Bob Morgan stared at Squeakie as if he couldn't believe what she was saying to him. It was as if they were alone in the room. I could have throttled her. Even in the light of subsequent events it gives me the creeps to think of it. Just shows you what some people will risk when they have complete confidence in their own rightness.

"The whisky," Squeakie went on. "It was too fresh; you just spilled it around. And besides your eyes were too clear. The lieutenant wasn't fooled." She looked at a photograph on the dresser. "Is that the girl you want to marry? She looks sweet."

Gregory saw that Squeakie was off on a tangent again. He took over.

"Well?" he said.

Morgan straightened his shoulders and faced us boldly, but there was a slight tremulous twitch in his lips that he couldn't control. "All right," he said flatly. "I was there. But I left before she screamed. I know you won't believe me, and I can't prove it. I'll tell you what I did, just as I did it."

He sat and stared at the wall and talked a noose around his neck.

"Judy and I had a love affair a long time ago. After it was over she found out that I wanted to marry someone else. She made me pay for some letters that would have wrecked my life. She had something on me and she'd been smart enough to get letters from me referring to it." A bitter smile twisted his mouth. "I was innocent but I couldn't have proved it. I suppose it's an old story to you. Do I have to say what it was?" He held his head proudly as he pleaded not to be humiliated.

Gregory shook his head. "You don't have to say anything unless you want to," he said. "Let it go. Time for details when you make an official statement."

I don't think Morgan realized what a sinister forbearance this was.

"Thanks," he said and went on. "It kept me poor paying for the letters and I couldn't get married. This last year I went through hell. I tried to run from her; I didn't care what happened. But she followed me. Moved next door. That's what she meant. I'd have committed suicide to get away from her, but I thought I'd make one more try."

Haley said softly, "Murder?"

The young man blanched. "No," he said, "not murder. I'd managed to get a key to the chest where I thought she kept the letters. I went over there tonight, down the fire escape and up on her side. I went in the window. She was lying in bed asleep."

He reflected bitterly: "The only normal thing about Judytha was that she went to bed early; she thought it kept her young.

"I opened the chest and used a tiny blackout flashlight to get the letters. There were plenty of others I hadn't heard about there. I heard a key turning in the apartment door. I grabbed the key to the chest but didn't have time to lock it. Oh, I wore gloves—naturally. I went out the fire-escape window, and I didn't wait to see who came into the apartment either. I wasn't particularly surprised that there should have been someone. After all . . . !" He shrugged and went on.

"I didn't think she'd go to the police, considering the circumstances, yet I couldn't be sure of anything. She was a poisonous person to cross. I went down the fire escape cautiously. When I was in the middle of the courtyard I heard the scream. I didn't know what trick she'd pull. I couldn't go back up my fire escape for fear of being seen. I didn't like to go through the basement and risk meeting the superintendent. So I went out into the street through the little door in the fence and came in through the front door of the house. I acted drunk in case I met anyone. Then I came in here and set the stage just in case she tried to frame me for something. I burnt the letters in the living-room fireplace."

Gregory shook his head slowly. "Clever," he said, "clever of you to keep it close to the truth. But it won't do. She woke up and you killed her, didn't you?"

The misery and terror in his eyes made me feel sick.

"No," he said over and over again, "I didn't. I didn't kill her, I tell you I didn't."

In a casual tone Gregory asked, "How did you get the key to the chest?"

Bob Morgan shook his head.

"Miss Gaylord took an impression for you, didn't she? You told her about the letters. She pitied you, and when the opportunity presented itself she took an impression of the key for you. That's why she was so frightened tonight. She thought you had gone letter hunting and killed Judytha Perry. I'm going to arrest you for that murder, Mr. Morgan."

"Gregory, you can't!" It was Squeakie again.

I said, "Squeakie, shut up!"

But Gregory said, "Why can't I, Squeakie?"

"He didn't do it."

Gregory came over and looked at her closely. I believe he thinks she's psychic. "Can you prove that?" he asked.

She almost cried with vexation. "You know I can't, Gregory—but I can prove who did."

Gregory said, "Can you, Squeakie?"

She backed down. "Not yet, Gregory, but let me try. He won't run away." I was afraid she'd think she was Portia and that at any moment she'd break into "The quality of mercy," but I underestimated her.

She stopped dead and said, "Let's all have a cup of coffee." That is what is called a strategic retreat. We, including Bob Morgan, prisoner, went up to the apartment and drank Squeakie's coffee.

"You know," she said, sitting cross-legged on the floor (she always lives up to slacks), "for an actress, Miss Gaylord hasn't much taste."

We all opened our eyes. "That home-made wimple," she went on. "Her face is all wrong for it; she shouldn't wear one. Besides, she's too short."

"Home-made wimple! My God!" said Gregory. "I didn't see anything like that; she looked all right to me."

"I mean the hat," Squeakie told him scornfully. "She draped it herself."

"Look," I said, "leave her wimple alone. She probably had her reasons."

Squeakie set down her cup so hard that I thought it would split. She stared at me for a long time. I began to feel uncomfortable.

Suddenly she moaned and jumped up. "Oh, Gregory, oh, Gregory!" She said it in a way that made my flesh creep. "I've got to go," she said. "Wait for me, I'll be back."

"Well . . ." I began.

Gregory said, "Shut up. I'll stay here with Morgan and Haley. Go after her. See what she's up to."

I caught up with her on the stairs of 313. She went up to the third floor. But she didn't go into 3B; she went into the vacant apartment across the hall.

I followed her into the kitchen of the empty apartment. She opened the cupboards, looked on the shelves, sighed and went out. In every room she looked in the empty closets.

"Darling, what are you looking for?" I inquired as sweetly as I could.

"Cold cream, David."

What could I do? I looked, too.

We found Judytha Perry's cold cream in the bathroom medicine chest. Squeakie unscrewed the vermilion lid of the jar. She turned out the light and I heard her say with definite satisfaction, "There, I knew he didn't do it!"

"Good Lord," I said.

"Here!" She pushed the jar into my hands. "Take this to Gregory. Tell him to look at it under the bed, way under. And don't gape at me, David. Do it right away. It's important."

I did it. What the hell! I couldn't read her mind. I didn't know.

Gregory raised one eyebrow when I told him. There's one thing I'll always resent. He went into the guest room and shut the door behind him. I never did know whether he crawled under the bed to look at a jar of cold cream. But I heard the light switch go on and off.

His face was rigid when he came out. "Come on," he said. "Quick! Why didn't you stay with her, you chump?"

When we got there Vera Gray alias Vivian Gaylord was having hysterics and Squeakie was throwing cold water on her. When we had her calmed down Gregory arrested her for the murder of Judytha Perry. Squeakie spent some time telling him how it was really self-defense because the poor girl believed she was being made blind.

I got it all out of Squeakie the hard way later.

It was just getting light outside and we were in bed again.

"Squeakie?"

"Hmmmm?"

"Darling, how did you know?"

"Special knowledge, plus psychology."

I determined to be patient. "Yes, go on."

"Well, first of all, he hadn't, so she must have."

I gathered she meant, must have committed the murder.

"Then there was Vera's psychology. Something like *Macbeth:* 'And that which rather thou dost fear to do than wishest should be undone.' "

"Oh, my God," I said prayerfully.

"Silly, that only means she had the murder all thought out without ever admitting to herself that she was really going to do it. Even when the murder plan was in operation she told herself up to the last minute that all she was going to do was frighten Judytha into releasing her from the spell. Visiting Judytha in her glowing makeup and staging a mystic scene or something was her way of justifying herself. She was giving Judytha her chance to raise the spell she had put on her."

"Spell?"

"Yes. It wasn't a pin cushion, you know. It was a doll which represented Vera. The pins were sticking in the eyes. Vera believed she was making her blind."

I said, "People don't believe that stuff."

"Oh, yes they do. And if they believe it hard enough it sometimes happens. Ask a doctor. Of course, she needed glasses anyway. That made it easier for Judytha; she was exploiting a fear that was already there."

She went on enlightening me. "You see, there was the book, and the copper-handled sword which is an attribute of the magician. Judytha began her reign of terror for a lark, out of boredom. But when she saw how easy it was—Vera was a good subject—she went further. She was jealous of Vera's success and enjoyed making her suffer. It gave her a sense of power. She had no real understanding of the primitive fear she had aroused in Vera, nor how dangerous it was."

I said, "Tell me about the crime."

"Well, Vera thought of it first because of the opportunity she had of leaving the theater unnoticed. Last night she started home earlier than she said, and she did not remove her makeup at the theater. The wimple was draped to hide it, and remember she walked home in the rain through empty streets.

"It was her key that Bob heard. Judytha awakened just as she opened the door. They had a scene. Vera found the doll and begged her to do something about it. Judytha said some awful things to her. Vera wasn't very clear when she told me this part, but I think the plan in her mind was like a will that she had to obey. She killed her with the statue which she had seen as the weapon in her mind's eye. Diane isn't only the Huntress, you know, she's the Moon Goddess. People used to think there was such a thing as moon blindness. Perhaps Vera thought her a suitable goddess to administer justice.

"After she killed Judytha she went across the hall into the empty apartment and removed the makeup. If anyone had come through the halls she would have stayed there or gone down the back fire escape on the side of the house. But no one came, so she walked down, met the Cobalts and told her story of hearing the scream and trying to get into the apartment.''

I said, ''Why did you want Gregory to look at the cold cream under the bed? Why didn't you tell him to look at it in the dark if you wanted him to see the traces of phosphorescent makeup in it?''

She blushed. ''Well, it is dark under a bed,'' she said weakly. And then, ''Oh, David, did he really do it?''

I had to confess I didn't know.

''What do you think of it all?'' she asked me.

I chose my words carefully. ''Well,'' I said, ''I really think a little knowledge is a dangerous thing, darling.''

''Oh, David, I'm so glad that you realize your limitations. That's the most important step.'' Her face was radiant. ''Now if you want to enroll for some of my courses, I'll . . . Oh, darling, this is grand!''

She kissed me. Now really! Could I bring it up again? Could I say that I wanted her to abandon the fascinating study of medieval witchcraft? Could I? I kissed her little pink thumb and let it go at that.

The Ipswich Phial

by Randall Garrett

In an incredibly prolific career that began (except for one story) in the early 1950s, Randall Garrett published several hundred science fiction stories. He was also Walter Bupp, David Gordon, Darrel T. Langart, and one half of Mark Phillips and Robert Randall, to mention only a few of his many pseudonyms. During one stretch in the 1960s he had more stories in Astounding/Analog *than any other writer. Unfortunately, very few of these stories have been collected, although* The Best of Randall Garrett *(1982) is an almost definitive volume. He is best known for his "Lord Darcy" series about a detective in an alternate world where England is still ruled by the Plantagenets and magic has become a science. Perhaps his most popular book,* Too Many Magicians *(1967), is part of the series, as is the present selection.*

The pair-drawn brougham moved briskly along the Old Shore Road, moving westward a few miles from the little village of St.-Matthew's-Church, in the direction of Cherbourg.

The driver, a stocky man with a sleepy smile on his broad face, was well bundled up in a gray driving cloak, and the hood of his cowl was pulled up over his head and covered with a wide-brimmed slouch hat. Even in early June, on a sunshiny day, the Normandy coast can be chilly in the early morning, especially with a stiff wind blowing.

"Stop here, Danglars," said a voice behind him. "This looks like a good place for a walk along the beach."

"Yus, mistress." He reined in the horses, bringing the brougham to an easy stop. "You sure it's safe down there, Mistress Jizelle?" he asked, looking to his right, where the Channel stretched across to the north, toward England.

"The tide is out, is it not?" she asked briskly.

Danglars looked at his wristwatch. "Yus. Just at the ebb now."

"Very well. Wait for me here. I may return here, or I may walk on. If I go far, I will signal you from down the road."

"Yus, mistress."

She nodded once, sharply, then strode off toward the beach.

She was a tall, not unhandsome woman, who appeared to be in late middle age. Her gray-silver hair was cut rather shorter than the usual, but was beautifully arranged. Her costume was that of an upper-middle-class Anglo-French woman on a walking tour, but it was more in the British style than the Norman: well-burnished knee-high boots; a Scottish woolen skirt, the hem of which just brushed the boot-tops; a matching jacket; and a soft sweater of white wool that covered her from waist to chin. She wore no hat. She carried herself with the brisk, no-nonsense air of a woman who knows what she is and who she is, and will brook no argument from anyone about it.

Mistress Jizelle de Ville found a pathway down to the beach. There was a low cliff, varying from fifteen to twenty feet high, which separated the upper downs from the beach itself, but there were slopes and washes here and there which could be maneuvered. The cliff itself was the ultimate high-tide mark, but only during great storms did the sea ever come up that high; the normal high tide never came within fifteen yards of the base of the cliff, and the intervening space was covered with soft, dry sand which was difficult to walk in. Mistress Jizelle crossed the dry sand to the damper, more solidly packed area, and began walking westward.

It was a beautiful morning, in spite of the slight chill; just the sort of morning one would choose for a brisk, healthful walk along a pleasant beach. Mistress Jizelle was a woman who liked exercise and long walks, and she was a great admirer of scenic beauty. To her right, the rushing wind made scudding whitecaps of the ebbing tide and brought the "smell of the sea"—an odor never found on the open expanse of the sea itself, for it is composed of the aroma of the sea things which dwell in the tidal basins and the shallow coastal waters and the faint smell of the decomposition of dead and dying things beached by the rhythmic ebb and flow of tide and wave.

Overhead, the floating gulls gave their plaintive, almost cat-like cries as they soared in search of the rich sustenance that the sea and shore gave them.

Not until she had walked nearly a hundred yards along the beach did Mistress Jizelle see anything out of the ordinary. When she did, she stopped and looked at it carefully. Ahead and to her left, some eight or nine yards from the base of the cliff, a man lay sprawled in the dry sand, twenty feet or so above the high-tide line.

After a moment, she walked toward the man, carefully and cautiously. He was certainly not dressed for bathing; he was wearing the evening dress of a gentleman. She walked up to the edge of the damp sand and stopped again, looking at the man carefully.

Then she saw something that made the hairs on the back of her neck rise.

Danglars was sitting placidly in the driver's seat of the brougham, smoking his clay pipe, when he saw the approaching trio. He eyed them carefully as they came toward the carriage. Two young men and an older one, all dressed in the work clothes typical of a Norman farmer. The eldest waved a hand and said something Danglars couldn't hear over the sound of the waves and the wind. Then they came close enough to be audible, and the eldest said: "Allo! Got dee any trouble here?"

Danglars shook his head. "Nup."

The farmer ignored that. "Me an' m'boys saw dee stop up here, an' thought mayap we could help. Name's Champtier. Samel Champtier. Dese two a my tads, Evrit an' Lorin. If dou hass need a aid, we do what we can."

Danglars nodded slowly, then took his pipe from his mouth. "Good o' ya, Goodman Samel. Grace to ya. But I got no problem. Mistress wanted to walk along the beach. Likes that sort of thing. We head on pretty soon."

Samel cleared his throat. "Hass dou broke dy fast, dou an' d' miss-lady? Wife fixin' breakfast now. Mayap we bring du somewhat?"

Danglars took another puff and sighed. Norman farmers were good, kindly folk, but sometimes they overdid it. "Broke fast, Goodman Samel. Grace to ya. Mistress comes back, we got to be gettin' on. Again, grace to ya."

"Caffe, then," Samel said decisively. He turned to the elder son. "Evrit! Go tell dy mama for a pot a caffe an' two mugs! Run it, now!"

Evrit took off like a turpentined ostrich.

Danglars cast his eyes toward heaven.

Mistress Jizelle swallowed and again looked closely at the dead man. There was a pistol in his right hand and an ugly hole in his right temple. There was blood all over the sand around his head. And there was no question about his being dead.

She looked up and down the beach while she rather dazedly brushed at her skirt with the palms of her hands. Then, bracing her shoulders, Mistress Jizelle turned herself about and walked back the way she had come, paralleling her own footprints. There were no others on the beach.

Three men were talking to Danglars, and Danglars did not seem to be agitated about it. Determinedly, she strode onward.

Not until she was within fifteen feet of the brougham did Danglars deign to notice her. Then he tugged his forelock and smiled his sleepy smile. "Greeting, mistress. Have a nice walk?" He had a mug of caffe in one hand. He gestured with the other. "Goodman Samel and his boys, mistress, from the near farm. Brought a pot o' caffe."

The three farmers were tugging at their forelocks, too.

"I appreciate that," she said. "Very much. But I fear we have an emergency to attend to. Come with me, all of you."

Danglars widened his eyes. "Emergency, mistress?"

"That's what I said, wasn't it? Now, all of you follow me, and I shall show you what I mean."

"But, mistress—" Danglars began.

"Follow me," she said imperatively.

Danglars got down from the brougham. He had no choice but to follow with the others.

Mistress Jizelle led them across the sparse grass to the edge of the cliff that overlooked the place where the dead man lay.

"Now look down there. There is a dead man down there. He has, I think, been shot to death. I am not much acquainted with such things, but that is what it looks like to me."

The four knelt and looked at the body below. There was silence for a moment, then Samel said, rather formally: "Dou be right, mistress. Dead he be."

"Who is he, goodman?" she asked.

Samel stood up slowly and brushed his trousers with calloused hands. "Don't rightly know, mistress." He looked at his two sons, who were still staring down with fascination. "Who be he, tads?"

They stood up, brushing their trousers as their father had. Evrit, the elder, spoke. "Don't know, papa. Ee not from hereabout." He nudged his younger brother with an elbow. "Lorin?"

Lorin shook his head, looking at his father.

"Well, that does not matter for the moment," Mistress Jizelle said firmly. "There is Imperial Law to follow in such cases as this, and we must do so. Danglars, get in the brougham and return to—"

"But, Mistress Jizelle," Danglars cut in, "I can't—"

"You must do exactly as I tell you, Danglars," she said forcefully. "It is most important. Go back to St.-Matthew's-Church and notify the Rector. Then go on to Caen and notify the Armsmen. Goodman Samel and his boys will wait here with me and make sure nobody disturbs anything. Do you understand?"

"Yus, mistress. Perfec'ly." And off he went.

She turned to Samel. "Goodman, can you spare some time? I am sure you have work to do, but I shouldn't like to be left here alone."

Samel smiled. "Mornin' chores all done, mistress. Eldest tad, Orval, can take care of all for a couple hours. Don't fret." He looked at the younger boy. "Lorin, go dou an tell dy mama an' dy brother what happen, but nobody else. An' say dey tell nobody. Hear?"

Lorin nodded and ran.

"And bring dou back somewat ta eat!" Evrit yelled after him.

Samel looked worried. "Mistress?"

"Yes, Goodman Samel?"

"Hass dou noticed somewat funny about d' man dere?"

"Funny?" She raised an eyebrow.

"Yea, mistress." He pointed down. "All around him, sand. Smooth. No footprints but dine own, an' dey come nowhere near him. Fresh dead, but—how he get dere?"

Five days later, Sir James le Lien, Special Agent of His Majesty's Secret Service, was seated in a comfortable chair in the studylike office of Lord Darcy, Chief Investigator for His Royal Highness, Richard, Duke of Normandy.

"And I still don't know where the Ipswich Phial is, Darcy," he was saying with some exasperation. "And neither do they."

Outside the open window, sounds of street traffic—the susurration of rubber-tired wheels on pavement, the clopping of horses' hooves, the footsteps and voices of a thousand people, and the myriad of other small noises that make up the song of a city—where wafted up from six floors below.

Lord Darcy leaned back in the chair behind his broad desk and held up a hand.

"Hold it, Sir James. You're leaping far ahead of yourself. I presume that by 'they' you mean the *Serka*—the Polish Secret Service. But what is this Phial, anyway?''

"I can't tell you for two reasons. First, you have no need to know. Second, neither do I, so I couldn't tell you if I wanted. Physically, it's a golden cylinder the size of your thumb, stoppered at one end with a golden stopper, which is sealed over with soft gold. Other than that, I know nothing but the code name: The Ipswich Phial.''

Sean O Lochlainn, Master Sorcerer, who had been sitting quietly in another chair with his hands folded over his stomach, his eyes half closed, and his ears wide open, said: "I'd give a pretty to know who assigned that code name; sure and I'd have him sacked for incompetence.''

"Oh?'' said Sir James. "Why?''

Master Sean opened his eyes fully. "If the Poles don't know that the Ipswich Laboratories in Suffolk, under Master Sir Greer Davidson, is devoted to secret research in magic, then they are so incredibly stupid that we need not worry about them at all. With a name like 'Ipswich Phial' on it, the *Serka* would *have* to investigate, if they heard about it.''

"Maybe it's just a red herring designed to attract their attention while something else is going on,'' said Lord Darcy.

"Maybe,'' Master Sean admitted, "but if so, me lord, it's rather dear. What Sir James has just described is an auric-stabilized psychic shield. What would you put in such a container? Some Khemic concoction, like an explosive or a poison? Or a secret message? That'd be incompetence compounded, like writing your grocery list on vellum in gold. Conspicuous consumption.''

"I see,'' said Lord Darcy. He looked at Sir James. "What makes you think the *Serka* hasn't got it already?''

"If they had it,'' Sir James said, "they'd have cut and run. And they haven't; they're still swarming all over the place. There must be a dozen agents there.''

"I presume that your own men are all over the place, too?''

"We're trying to keep them covered,'' Sir James said.

"Then they know you don't have the Phial, either.''

"Probably.''

Lord Darcy sighed and began filling his silver-chased porcelain pipe. "You say the dead man is Noel Standish.'' He tapped a sheaf of papers with his pipestem. "These say he was identified as a man named Bourke. You say it was murder. These say that the court of His Majesty's Coroner was ready to call it suicide until you put pressure on to keep the decision open. I have the vague feeling, James, that I am being used. I should like to point out that I am Chief Criminal Investigator for the Duke of Normandy, not—repeat: *not*—an agent of His Majesty's Secret Service.''

"A crime has been committed," Sir James pointed out. "It is your duty to investigate it."

Lord Darcy calmly puffed his pipe alight. "James, James." His lean, handsome face was utterly impassive as he blew out a long plume of smoke. "You know perfectly well I am not obliged to investigate every homicide in the Duchy. Neither Standish nor Bourke was a member of the aristocracy. I don't *have* to investigate this mess unless and until I get a direct order from either His Highness the Duke or His Majesty the King. Come on, James—convince me."

Master Sean did not smile, although it was somewhat of a strain to keep his face straight. The stout little Irish sorcerer knew perfectly well that his lordship was bluffing. Lord Darcy could no more resist a case like this than a bee can resist clover blossoms. But Sir James did not know that. He did know that by bringing the case before his superiors, he could eventually get an order from the King, but by then the whole thing would likely be over.

"What do you want, Darcy?" the King's agent asked.

"Information," his lordship said flatly. "You want me to go down to St.-Matthew's-Church and create a diversion while you and your men do your work. Fine. But I will not play the part of a dupe. I damn well want to know what's going on. I want the whole story."

Sir James thought it over for ten or fifteen seconds, then said: "All right, my lord. I'll give it to you straight."

For centuries, the Kings of Poland had been expanding, in an ebb-and-flow fashion, the borders of their territories, primarily toward the east and south. In the south, they had been stopped by the Osmanlis. In the east, the last bite had been taken in the early 1930s, when the Ukraine was swallowed. King Casimir IX came to the throne in 1937 at the age of twenty, and two years later had plunged his country into a highly unsuccessful war with the Empire and her Scandinavian allies, and any further thought of expansion to the east was stopped by the threat of the unification of the Russian States.

Poland was now, quite literally, surrounded by enemies who hated her and neighbors who feared her. Casimir should have taken a few years to consolidate and conciliate, but it was apparent that the memory of his father and his own self-image as a conqueror were too strong for him. Knowing that any attempt to march his armies into the German buffer states that lay between his own western border and the eastern border of the Empire would be suicidal as things stood, Casimir decided to use his strongest nonmilitary weapon: the *Serka*.

The nickname comes from a phrase meaning roughly: "The king's Right Arm." For financial purposes, it is listed in the books as the Ministry of Security Control, making it sound as if it were a division of the King's Government. It is not; none of his Slavonic Majesty's ministers or advisors know anything about, or have any control over, its operation. It is composed of fanatically loyal men and women who have taken a solemn vow of obedience to the King himself, *not* to the Government. The *Serka* is responsible to no one but the King's Person.

It is composed of two main branches: The Secret Police (domestic), and the Secret Service (foreign). This separation, however, is far from rigid. An agent of one branch may at any time be assigned to the other.

The *Serka* is probably the most powerful, most ruthless instrument of government on the face of the Earth today. Its agents, many of them Talented sorcerers, infest every country in Europe, most especially the Anglo-French Empire.

Now, it is a historical fact that Plantagenet Kings do not take kindly to invasion of their domain by foreign sovereigns; for eight centuries they have successfully resisted such intrusive impudence.

There is a saying in Europe: "He who borrows from a Plantagenet may repay without interest; he who steals from a Plantagenet will repay at ruinous rates."

His present Majesty, John IV—by the Grace of God, King of England, Ireland, Scotland, and France; Emperor of the Romans and Germans; Premier Chief of the Moqtessumid Clan; Son of the Sun; Count of Anjou and Maine; Prince Donator of the Sovereign Order of St. John of Jerusalem; Sovereign of the Most Ancient Order of the Round Table, of the Order of the Leopard, of the Order of the Lily, of the Order of the Three Crowns, and of the Order of St. Andrew; Lord and Protector of the Western Continents of New England and New France; Defender of the Faith—was no exception to that rule.

Unlike his medieval predecessors, however, King John had no desire to increase Imperial holdings in Europe. The last Plantagenet to add to the Imperial domain in Europe was Harold I, who signed the original Treaty of København in 1420. The Empire was essentially frozen within its boundaries for more than a century until, during the reign of John III, the discovery of the continents of the Western Hemisphere opened a whole new world for Anglo-French explorers.

John IV no longer thought of European expansion, but he deeply resented the invasion of his realm by Polish *Serka* agents. Therefore, the theft of a small golden phial from the Ipswich Laboratories had provoked instant reaction from the King and from His Majesty's Secret Service.

"The man who actually stole it," Sir James explained, "is irrelevant. He was merely a shrewd biscuit who accidentally had a chance to get his hands on the Phial. Just how is immaterial, but rest assured that that hole has been plugged. The man saw an opportunity and grabbed it. He wasn't a Polish agent, but he knew how to get hold of one, and a deal was made."

"How much time did it take him to deal, after the Phial was stolen?" Lord Darcy asked.

"Three days, my lord. Sir Greer found it was missing within two hours of its being stolen, and notified us straight away. It was patently obvious who had taken it, but it took us three days to trace him down. As I said, he was a shrewd biscuit.

"By the time we'd found him, he'd made his deal and had the money. We were less than half an hour too late. A *Serka* agent already had the Phial and was gone.

"Fortunately, the thief was just that—a thief, not a real *Serka* agent. When he'd been caught, he freely told us everything he knew. That, plus other information received, convinced us our quarry was on a train for Portsmouth. We got hold of Noel Standish at the Portsmouth office by teleson, but . . ."

The plans of men do not necessarily coincide with those of the Universe. A three-minute delay in a traffic jam had ended with Noel Standish at the slip, watching the Cherbourg boat sliding out toward the Channel, with forty feet between himself and the vessel.

Two hours later, he was standing at the bow of H.I.M.S *Dart*, staring southward into the darkness, listening to the rushing of the Channel waters against the hull of the fast cutter. Standish was not in a good mood.

In the first place, the teleson message had caught him just as he was about to go out to dine with friends at the Bellefontaine, and he had had no chance to change; he felt silly as hell standing on the deck of a Navy cutter in full evening dress. Further, it had taken better than an hour to convince the Commanding Admiral at the Portsmouth Naval Docks that the use of a cutter was imperative—and then only at the cost of a teleson connection to London.

There was but one gem in these otherwise bleak surroundings: Standish had a firm psychic lock on his quarry.

He had already had a verbal description from London. *Young man, early to middle twenties. Five feet nine. Slender, but well-muscled. Thick, dark brown hair. Smooth shaven. Brown eyes. Well formed brows. Face handsome, almost pretty. Well-dressed. Conservative dark green coat, puce waistcoat, gold-brown trousers. Carrying a dark olive attaché case.*

And he had clearly seen the quarry standing on the deck of the cross-Channel boat as it had pulled out of Portsmouth, heading for Cherbourg.

Standish had a touch of the Talent. His own name for a rather specialized ability was "the Game of Hide and Seek," wherein Standish did both the hiding and the seeking. Once he got a lock on someone he could follow him anywhere. Further, Standish became psychically invisible to his quarry; even a Master Sorcerer would never notice him as long as Standish took care not to be located visually. Detection range, however, was only a matter of miles, and the man in the puce waistcoat, Standish know, was at the limit of that range.

Someone tapped Standish on the shoulder. "Excuse me, sir—"

Standish jerked round nervously. "*What? What?*"

The young officer lifted his eyebrows, taken aback by the sudden reaction. This Standish fellow seemed to have every nerve on edge. "Begging your pardon, sir, but the Captain would have a word with you. Follow me, please."

Senior Lieutenant Malloix, commanding H.I.M.S. *Dart*, wearing his royal blue uniform, was waiting in his cabin with a glass of brandy in each hand. He gave one to Standish while the junior officer quietly disappeared. "Come in, Standish. Sit and relax. You've been staring off the starboard bow ever since we cast off, and that's no good. Won't get us there any the faster, you know."

Standish took the glass and forced a smile. "I know, Captain. Thanks." He sipped. "Still, do you think we'll make it?"

The captain frowned, sat down, and waved Standish to a chair while he said: "Hard to say, frankly. We're using all the power we have, but the sea and the wind don't always do what we'd like 'em to. There's not a damn thing we can do about it, so breathe deep and see what comes, eh?"

"Right you are, Captain." He took another swallow of brandy. "How good a bearing do we have on her?"

S/Lt Malloix patted the air with a hand. "Not to worry. Lieutenant Seamus Mac Lean, our navigator, has a Journeyman's rating in the Sorcerer's Guild, and this sort of thing is his speciality. The packet boat is two degrees off to starboard and, at our present speed, forty-one minutes ahead of us. That's the good news."

"And the bad news?"

Malloix shrugged. 'Wind variation. We haven't gained on her in fifteen minutes. Cheer up. Pour yourself another brandy."

Standish cheered up and drank more brandy, but it availed him nothing. The *Dart* pulled into the dock at Cherbourg one minute late, in spite of all she could do.

Nevertheless, Goodman Puce-Weskit was less than a hundred yards away as Standish ran down the gangplank of the *Dart*, and the distance rapidly closed as he walked briskly toward his quarry, following his psychic compass that pointed unerringly toward Puce-Weskit.

He was hoping that Puce-Weskit was still carrying the Phial; if he wasn't, if he had passed it on to some unknown person aboard the packet, the whole thing was blown. The thing would be in Krakowa before the month was out.

He tried not to think about that.

The only thing to do was follow his quarry until there came a chance to waylay and search him.

He had already given a letter to the captain of the *Dart*, to be delivered as soon as possible to a certain address on the Rue Queen Brigid, explaining to the agent in charge of the Cherbourg office what was going on. The trouble was, Standish was not carrying a tracer attuned to the Cherbourg office; there was no way to get in touch with them, and he didn't dare leave Puce-Weskit. He couldn't even set up a rendezvous, since he had no idea where Puce-Weskit would lead him.

And, naturally, when one needed an Armsman, there wasn't one in sight.

Twenty minutes later, Puce-Weskit turned on to the Rue Queen Brigid.

Don't tell me he's headed for the Service office, Standish thought. *My dear Puce-Weskit, surely you jest.*

No fear. A dozen squares from the Secret Service office, Goodman Puce-Weskit turned and went into a caffe-house called the Aden. There, he stopped.

Standish had been following on the opposite side of the street, so there was less chance of his being spotted. Dodging the early morning traffic, narrowly avoiding the lead horse of a beer lorry, he crossed the Rue Queen Brigid to the Aden.

Puce-Weskit was some forty feet away, toward the rear of the caffehouse. Could he be passing the Phial on to some confederate?

Standish was considering what to do next when the decision was made for him. He straightened up with a snap as his quarry suddenly began to move southward at a relatively high rate of speed.

He ran into the Aden. And saw his mistake.

The rear wall was only thirty feet away. Puce-Weskit had gone through the rear door, and had been standing *behind* the Aden.

He went right on through the large room, out the back door. There was a small alleyway there, but the man standing a few feet away was most certainly not his quarry.

"Quick!" Standish said breathlessly. "The man in the puce waistcoat! Where did he go?"

The man looked a little flustered. "Why—uh—I don't know, sir. As soon as his horse was brought—"

"Horse? Where did he get a horse?"

"Why, he left it in the proprietor's charge three or four days ago. Four days ago. Paid in advance for the keeping of it. He asked it to be fetched, and then he went. I don't know where."

"Where can I rent a horse?" Standish snapped.

"The proprietor—"

"Take me to him immediately!"

"And that," said Sir James le Lien, "is the last trace we were able to uncover until he reported in at Caen two days later. We wouldn't even know that much if one of our men hadn't been having breakfast at the Aden. He recognized Standish, of course, but didn't say anything to him, for obvious reasons."

Lord Darcy nodded. "And he turns up dead the following morning near St.-Matthew's-Church. Any conjecture on what he may have been doing during those two days?"

"It seems fairly clear. The proprietor of the Aden told us that our quarry—call him Bourke—had his saddlebags packed with food packets in protective-spell wrappers, enough for a three, maybe four-day trip. You know the Old Shore Road that runs southeast from Cherbourg to the Vire, crosses the river, then goes westward, over the Orne, and loops around to Harfleur?"

"Of course," Lord Darcy said.

"Well, then, you know it's mostly farming country, with only a few scattered villages, and no teleson connections. We think Bourke took that road, and that Standish followed him. We think Bourke was headed for Caen.''

Master Sean lifted an eyebrow. "Then why not take the train? 'Twould be a great deal easier and faster, Sir James.''

Sir James smiled. "It would be. But not safer. The trouble with public transportation is that you're essentially trapped on it. When you're fleeing, you want as much freedom of choice as possible. Once you're aboard a public conveyance, you're pretty much constrained to stay on it until it stops, and that isn't under your control.''

"Aye, that's clear," said Master Sean. He looked thoughtful. "This psychic lock-on you mentioned—you're sure Standish used it on Bourke?''

"Not absolutely certain, of course," Sir James admitted. "But he certainly had that Talent; he was tested by a board of Masters from your own Guild. Whether he used it or not at that particular time, I can only conjecture, but I think it's a pretty solid assumption.''

Lord Darcy carefully watched a column of pipesmoke rise toward the ceiling and said nothing.

"I'll agree with you," Master Sean said. "There's no doubt in me mind he did just that, and I'll not say he was wrong to do so. *De mortuis non disputandum est.* I just wonder if he knew how to handle it.''

"How do you mean?" Sir James asked.

"Well, let's suppose a man could make himself perfectly transparent—'invisible,' in other words. The poor lad would have to be very careful, eh? In soft ground or in snow, he'll leave footprints; in a crowd, he may brush up against someone. Can you imagine what it would be like if you grabbed such a man? There you've got an armful of air that feels fleshy, smells sweaty, sounds excited, and would taste salty if you cared to try the experiment. You'll admit that such an object would be suspect?''

"Well, yes," Sir James admitted, "but—"

"Sir James," Master Sean continued, "you have no idea how conspicuous a psychically invisible person can be in the wrong circumstances. There he stands, visible to the eye, sensible to the touch, audible to the ear, and all the rest—*but there's nobody home!*

"The point I'm making, Sir James, is this: How competent was Noel Standish at handling his ability?''

Sir James opened his mouth, shut it, and frowned. After a

second, he said: "When you put it that way, Master Sean, I must admit I don't know. But he handled it successfully for twelve years."

"And failed once," said Master Sean. "Fatally."

"Now hold, my dear Sean," Lord Darcy said suddenly. "We have no evidence that he failed in that way. That he allowed himself to be killed is a matter of cold fact; that he did so in that way is pure conjecture. Let's not leap to totally unwarranted conclusions."

"Aye, me lord. Sorry."

Lord Darcy focused his gray eyes on Sir James. "Then I have not been called in merely to create a diversion, eh?"

Sir James blinked. "I beg your pardon, my lord?"

"I mean," said his lordship patiently, "that you actually want me to solve the problem of 'who killed Noel Standish?' "

"Of course! Didn't I make that clear?"

"Not very," Lord Darcy picked up the papers again. "Now let's get a few things straight. How did the body come to be identified as Bourke, and where is the real Bourke? Or whoever he was."

"The man Standish was following checked into the Green Seagull Inn under that name." Sir James said. "He'd used the same name in England. He was a great deal like Standish in height, weight, and coloring. He disappeared that night, and we've found no trace of him since."

Lord Darcy nodded thoughtfully. "It figures. Young gentleman arrives at village inn. Body of young gentleman found next morning. Since there is only one young gentleman in plain sight, they are the same young gentleman. Identifying a total stranger is a chancy thing at best."

"Exactly. That's why I held up my own identification."

"I understand. Now, exactly how did you happen to be in St.-Matthew's-Church that night?" Lord Darcy asked.

"Well, as soon as Standish was fairly certain that his quarry had settled down at the Green Seagull, he rode for Caen and sent a message to my office, here in Rouen. I took the first train, but by the time I got there, they were both missing."

"Yes," Lord Darcy sighed. "Well, I suppose we'd best be getting down there. I'll have to ask His Royal Highness to order me to, so you may as well come along with me and explain the whole thing all over again to Duke Richard."

Sir James looked pained. "I suppose so. We want to get there as soon as possible, or the whole situation will become impossible.

Their silly Midsummer Fair starts the day after tomorrow, and there are strangers showing up already.''

Lord Darcy closed his eyes. "That's all we need. Complications.''

Master Sean went to the door of the office. "I'll have Ciardi pack our bags, me lord. Looks like a long stay.''

The little village of St.-Matthew's-Church was transforming itself. The Fair proper was to be held in a huge field outside of town, and the tents were already collecting on the meadow. There was, of course, no room in the village itself for people to stay; certainly the little Green Seagull couldn't hold a hundredth of them. But a respectable tent-city had been erected in another big field, and there was plenty of parking space for horse-wagons and the like.

In the village, the storefronts were draped with bright bunting, and the shopkeepers were busy marking up all the prices. Both pubs had been stocking up on extra potables for weeks. For nine days, the village would be full of strangers going about their hectic business, disrupting the peace of the local inhabitants, bringing with them a strange sort of excitement. Then they would go, leaving behind acres of ugly rubbish and bushels of beautiful cash.

In the meanwhile, a glorious time would be had by all.

Lord Darcy cantered his horse along the River Road up from Caen and entered St.-Matthew's-Church at noon on that bright sunshiny day, dressed in the sort of riding clothes a well-to-do merchant might wear. He wasn't exactly incognito, but he didn't want to attract attention, either. Casually, he made his way through the already gathering throngs toward the huge old church dedicated to St. Matthew, which had given the village its name. He guided his mount over to the local muffin square, where the array of hitching posts stood, tethered his horse, and walked over to the church.

The Reverend Father Arthur Lyon, Rector of the Church of St.-Matthew, and *ipso facto*, Rector of St.-Matthew's-Church, was a broad-shouldered man in his fifties who stood a good two inches taller than six feet. His bald head was fringed with silvery hair, and his authoritative, pleasant face was usually smiling. He was sitting behind his desk in his office.

There came a rap at his office door. A middle-aged woman came in quickly and said: "Sorry to bodder dee, Fahder, but dere's a Lord Darcy to see dee.''

"Show him in, Goodwife Anna."

Lord Darcy entered Father Art's office to find the priest waiting with outstretched hand. "It's been some time, my lord," he said with a broad smile. "Good to see you again."

"I may say the same. How have you been, old friend?"

"Not bad. Pray, sit down. May I offer you a drink?"

"Not just now, Father." He took the proffered seat. "I understand you have a bit of a problem here."

Father Art leaned back in his chair and folded his hands behind his head. "Ahh, yes. The so-called suicide. Bourke." He chuckled. "I thought higher authority would be in on that, sooner or later."

"Why do you say 'so-called suicide,' Father?"

"Because I know people, my lord. If a man's going to shoot himself, he doesn't go out to a lonely beach for it. If he goes to a beach, it's to drown himself. A walk into the sea. I don't say a man has never shot himself by the seaside, but it's so rare that when it happens I get suspicious."

"I agree," Lord Darcy said. He had known Arthur Lyon for some years, and knew that the man was an absolutely dedicated servant of his God and his King. His career had been unusual. During the '39 war, he had risen to the rank of Sergeant-Major in the Eighteenth Infantry. Afterwards, he had become an Officer of the King's Peace, and had returned as a Chief Master-at-Arms before taking up his vocation as a priest. He had shown himself to be not only a top-grade priest, but also a man with the Talent as a brilliant Healer, and had been admitted, with honors, to the Order of St. Luke.

"Old friend," Lord Darcy said, "I need your help. What I am about to tell you is most confidential; I will have to ask you to disclose none of it without official permission."

Father Art took his hands from behind his head and leaned forward with a gleam in his eyes. "As if it were under the Seal of the Confessional, my lord. Go ahead."

It took better than half an hour for Lord Darcy to give the good father the whole story as he knew it. Father Art had leaned back in his chair again with his hands locked behind his head, smiling seraphically at the ceiling. "Ah, yes, my lord. Utterly fascinating. I remember Friday, sixth June, very well. Yes, very well indeed." He continued to smile at the ceiling.

Lord Darcy closed his right eye and cocked his left eyebrow. "I trust you intend to tell me what incident stamped that day so indelibly on your mind."

"Certainly, my lord. I was just reveling in having made a deduction. When I tell my story, I dare say you'll make the same deduction." He brought his gaze down from the ceiling and his hands from behind his head. "You might say it began late Thursday night. Because of a sick call which had kept me up most of the previous night, I went to bed quite early Thursday evening. And, naturally, I woke up a little before midnight and couldn't get back to sleep. I decided I might as well make use of the time, so I did some paper work for a while and then went into the church to say the morning office before the altar. Then I decided to take a walk in the churchyard. I often do that; it's a pleasant place to meditate.

"There was no moon that night," the priest continued, "but the sky was cloudless and clear. It was about two hours before dawn. It was quite dark, naturally, but I know my way about those tombstones pretty well by now. I'd been out there perhaps a quarter of an hour when the stars went out."

Lord Darcy seemed to freeze for a full second. "When the *what?*"

"When the stars went out," Father Art repeated. "One moment, there they were, in their accustomed constellations—I was looking at Cygnus in particular—and the next moment the sky was black all over. Everywhere. All at once."

"I see," said Lord Darcy.

"Well, *I* couldn't," the priest said, flashing a smile. "It was black as the Pit. For a second or two, I confess, I was almost panicky. It's a weird feeling when the stars go out."

"I dare say," Lord Darcy murmured.

"But," the Father continued, "as a Sensitive, I knew that there was no threat close by, and, after a minute, I got my bearings again. I could have come back to the church, but I decided to wait for a while, just to find out what would happen next. I don't know how long I stood there. It seemed like an hour, but it was probably less than fifteen minutes. Then the stars came back on the same way they'd gone out—all at once, all over the sky."

"No dimming out?" Lord Darcy asked. "No slow brightening back on?"

"None, my lord. *Blink:* off. *Blink:* on."

"Not a sea fog, then."

"Impossible. No sea fog could move that fast."

Lord Darcy focused his eyes on a foot-high statue of St. Matthew that stood on a niche in the wall and stared at the Apostle without actually seeing him.

After a minute, Lord Darcy said: "I left Master Sean in Caen to make a final check of the body. He should be here within the hour. I'll talk to him, but . . ." His voice trailed off.

Father Art nodded. "Our speculation certainly needs to be confirmed, my lord, but I think we're on the right track. Now, how else can I help?"

"Oh, yes. That." Lord Darcy grinned. "Your revelation of the extinguished stars almost made me forget why I came to talk to you in the first place. What I'd like you to do, Father, is talk to the people that were at the Green Seagull on the afternoon and late evening of the fifth. I'm a stranger, and I probably wouldn't get much out of them—certainly not as much as you can. I want to know the whole pattern of comings and goings. I don't have to tell an old Armsman like yourself what to look for. Will you do it?"

Father Art's smile came back. "With pleasure, my lord."

"There's one other thing. Can you put up Master Sean and myself for a few days? There is, alas, no room at the inn."

Father Art's peal of laughter seemed to rock the bell tower.

Master Sean O Lochlainn had always been partial to mules. "The mule," he was fond of saying, "is as much smarter than a horse as a raven is smarter than a falcon. Neither a raven nor a mule will go charging into combat just because some human tells him to." Thus it was that the sorcerer came riding toward St.-Matthew's-Church, clad in plain brown, seated in a rather worn saddle, on the back of a very fine mule. He looked quite pleased with himself.

The River Road had plenty of traffic on it; half the population of the duchy seemed to be converging on the little coastal village of St.-Matthew's-Church. So Master Sean was mildly surprised to see someone headed toward him, but that feeling vanished when he saw that the approaching horseman was Lord Darcy.

"Not headed back to Caen, are you, me lord?" he asked when Lord Darcy came within speaking distance.

"Not at all, my dear Sean; I rode out to meet you. Let's take the cutoff road to the west; it's a shortcut that bypasses the village and takes us to the Old Shore Road, near where the body was found." He wheeled his horse around and rode beside Master Sean's mule. Together, they cantered briskly toward the Old Shore Road.

"Now," Lord Darcy said, "what did you find out at Caen?"

"Conflicting evidence, me lord; conflicting evidence. At least as far as the suicide theory is concerned. There was evidence at the cliff edge that he had fallen or been pushed over and tumbled down along the face of the cliff. But he was found twenty-five feet from the base of the cliff. He had two broken ribs and a badly sprained right wrist—to say nothing of several bad bruises. All of these had been inflicted some hours before death.''

Lord Darcy gave a rather bitter chuckle. "Which leaves us with two possibilities. *Primus:* Goodman Standish stands on the edge of the cliff, shoots himself through the head, tumbles to the sand below, crawls twenty-five feet, and takes some hours to die of a wound that was obviously instantly fatal. Or, *secundus:* He falls off the cliff, crawls the twenty-five feet, does nothing for a few hours, then decides to shoot himself. I find the second hypothesis only slightly more likely than the first. That his right wrist was sprained badly is a fact that tops it all off. Not suicide; no, not suicide.'' Lord Darcy grinned. "That leaves accident or murder. Which hypothesis do you prefer, my dear Sean.''

Master Sean frowned deeply, as if he were in the awful throes of concentration. Then his face brightened as if revelation had come. "I have it, me lord! He was accidentally murdered!''

Lord Darcy laughed. "Excellent! Now, having cleared that up, there is further evidence that I have not given you yet.''

He told Master Sean about Father Art's singular experience with the vanishing stars.

When he had finished, the two rode in silence for a minute or two. Then Master Sean said softly: "So *that's* what it is.''

There was an Armsman standing off the road at the site of the death, and another seated, who stood up as Lord Darcy and Master Sean approached. The two riders dismounted and walked their mounts up to where the Armsmen were standing.

"I am sorry, gentlemen,'' said the first Armsman with an air of authority, "but this area is off bounds, by order of His Royal Highness the Duke of Normandy.''

"Very good; I am happy to hear it,'' said his lordship, taking out his identification. "I am Lord Darcy; this is Master Sorcerer Sean O Lochlainn.''

"Yes, my lord,'' said the Armsman. "Sorry I didn't recognize you.''

"No problem. This is where the body was found?''

"Yes, my lord. Just below this cliff, here. Would you like to take a look, my lord?''

"Indeed I would. Thank you.''

Lord Darcy, under the respectful eyes of the two Armsmen, minutely examined the area around the cliff edge. Master Sean stayed with him, trying to see everything his lordship saw.

"Everything's a week old," Lord Darcy muttered bitterly. "Look at that grass, there. A week ago, I could have told you how many men were scuffing it up; today, I only know that it was more than two. I don't suppose there's any way of reconstructing it, my dear Sean?"

"No, me lord, I am a magician, not a miracle worker."

"Thought not. Look at the edge of this cliff. He fell, certainly. But was he pushed? Or thrown? No way of telling. Wind and weather have done their work too well. To quote my cousin de London: '*Pfui!*' "

"Yes, me lord."

"Well, let's go down to the beach and take a look from below."

That operation entailed walking fifty yards or so down the cliff edge to a steep draw which they could clamber down, then back again to where Standish had died.

There was a pleasant breeze from landward that brought the smell of growing crops. A dozen yards away, three gulls squabbled raucously over the remains of some dead sea-thing.

Lord Darcy was still in a bitter mood. "Nothing, damn it. *Nothing.* Footprints all washed away long ago. Or blown away by the wind. Damn, damn, *damn!* All we have to go by is the testimony of eyewitnesses, which is notoriously unreliable."

"You don't believe 'em, me lord?" Master Sean asked.

Lord Darcy was silent for several seconds. Then, in a calmer voice, he said: "Yes. Oddly enough, I do. I think the testimony of those farmers was absolutely accurate. They saw what they saw, and they reported what they saw. But they did not—they *could* not have seen everything!"

One of the Armsmen on the cliff above said: "That's the spot, right there, my lord. Near that flat rock." He pointed.

But Lord Darcy did not even look at the indicated spot. He had looked up when the Armsman spoke, and was staring at something on the cliff face about two feet below the Armsman's boot toes.

Master Sean followed his lordship's gaze and spotted the area immediately. "Looks like someone's been carving his initials, me lord."

"Indeed. How do you make them out?"

"Looks like S . . . S . . . O. Who do we know with the initials SSO?"

"Nobody connected with this case so far. The letters may have been up there for some time. But . . . ."

"Aye, me lord," said Master Sean. "I see what you mean. I'll do a time check on them. Do you want 'em preserved?"

"Unless they're more than a week old, yes. By the by, did Standish have a knife on him when he was found?"

"Not so far as I know, me lord. Wasn't mentioned in the reports."

"Hmmm." Lord Darcy began prowling the whole area, reminding Master Sean of nothing so much as a leopard in search of his evening meal. He finally ended up at the base of the cliff, just below where the glyphs had been carved into the clay wall. He went down on his knees and began digging.

"It has to be here somewhere," he murmured.

"Might I ask what you're looking for, me lord?"

"A piece of steel, my dear Sean; a piece of steel."

Master Sean put his carpetbag on the sand and opened it, taking out a thin, dark, metallic-blue wand just as Lord Darcy said: "Aa*ha!*"

Master Sean, wand still in hand, said: "What is it, me lord?"

"As you see," Lord Darcy said, standing up and displaying the object in the palm of his hand. "Behold and observe, old friend: a man's pocketknife."

Master Sean smiled broadly. "Aye. I presume you'll be wanting a relationship test, me lord: Carving, cutter, and corpse?"

"Of course. No, don't put away your wand. That's your generalized metal detector, it is not?"

"Aye, me lord. It's been similarized to all things metallic."

"Good. Put this knife away for analysis, then let's go over to where the body was found. We'll see if there isn't something else to be dug up."

The Master Sorcerer pointed the wand in his right hand at the sand and moved back and forth across the area, his eyes almost closed, his left hand held above his head, fingers spread. Every time he stopped, Lord Darcy would dig into the soft sand and come up with a bit of metal—a rusty nail, a corroded brass belt buckle, a copper twelfth-bit, a bronze farthing, and even a silver half-sovereign—all of which showed evidence of having been there for some time.

While the two of them worked, the Armsmen on the cliff above watched in silence. It is not wise to disturb a magician at work.

Only one of the objects was of interest to Lord Darcy: a small lump of lead. He dropped it into a waistcoat pocket and went on digging.

At last, Master Sean, having covered an area of some eight by twelve feet, said: "That's it, me lord."

Lord Darcy stood up, brushed the sand from his hands and trousers, and looked at the collection of junk he had put on the big flat rock. "Too bad we couldn't have found a sixth-bit. We'd be an even solidus ahead. No gold in the lot, either."

Master Sean chuckled. "You can't expect to find a complete set of samples from the Imperial Mint, me lord."

"I suppose not. But here"—he took the small lump of lead from his waistcoat pocket—"is what I expected to find. Unless I am very much mistaken, this bullet came from the .36 Heron that the late Standish carried, and is the same bullet which passed through his head. Here; check on it, will you, my good Sean?"

Master Sean put the bullet in one of the carefully insulated pockets of his capacious carpetbag, and the two men trudged back across the sand, up the slope to the top of the cliff again.

Master Sean spread himself prone and looked over the edge of the cliff. After a minute inspection of the carving in the sandy clay of the cliff face, he got up, took some equipment from his carpetbag, and lay down again to go to work. A simple cohesion spell sufficed to set the clay so that it would not crumble. Then, he deftly began to cut out the brick of hardened clay defined by the spell.

In the meantime, Lord Darcy had called the senior of the two Armsmen to one side and had asked him a question.

"No, my lord, we ain't had any trouble," the Armsman said. "We been runnin' three eight-hour shifts out here ever since the body was found, and hardly nobody's come by. The local folk all know better. Wouldn't come near it, anyway, till the whole matter's been cleared up and the site's been blessed by a priest. 'Course, there was that thing this morning."

"This morning?" Lord Darcy lifted an eyebrow.

"Yes, my lord." He glanced at his wristwatch. "Just after we come on duty. Just on six hours ago—eight-twelve."

"And what happened?" his lordship asked with seemingly infinite patience.

"Well, these two folk come along the beach from the east. Romany, they was. Whole tribe of 'em come into St.-Matthew's-Church fairground early this morning. These two—man and a woman, they was—come along arm in arm. Dan—that's Armsman Danel, over there—warned 'em off, but they just smiled and waved and kept coming. So Dan went down to the beach fast and blocked 'em off. They pretended they didn't speak no Anglo-French; you know how these Romany are. But Dan made it clear they wasn't to come no farther, so off they went. No trouble.''

"They went back without any argument, eh?"

"Yes, my lord, they did."

"Well, no harm done there, then. Carry on, Armsman."

"Yes, my lord."

Master Sean came back from the cliff edge with a chunk of thaumaturgically hardened clay further loading his symbol-decorated carpetbag. "Anything else, me lord?"

"I think not. Let's get some lunch."

In a tent near the fairgrounds, an agent of *Serka*, Mission Commander for this particular operation, was opening what looked on the outside like a battered, scuffed, worn, old leather suitcase. The inside was new and in the best condition, and the contents were startlingly similar to those of Master Sean's symbol-decorated carpetbag.

Out came two small wands, scarcely six inches long, of ruby-red crystal wound with oddly spaced helices of silver wire that took exactly five turns around the ruby core. Each wand was a mirror image of the other; one helix wound to the right, the other to the left. Out came two small glass flacons, one containing a white, coarsely ground substance, the other an amber-yellow mass of small granules. These were followed by a curiously wrought golden candlestick some four inches high, an inch-thick candle, and a small brazier.

Like any competent sorcerer, the Commander had hands that were strong and yet capable of delicate work. The beeswax candle was being fitted into the candlestick by those hands when there came a scratching at the closed tent flap.

The Commander froze. "Yes?"

"One-three-seven comes," said a whispered voice.

The Commander relaxed. "Very well; send him in."

Seconds later, the tent flap opened, and another *Serka* agent ducked into the tent. He glanced at the thaumaturgical equipment on the table as he sat down on a stool. "It's come to that, eh?" he said.

"I'm not certain yet," said the Commander. "It may. I don't want it to. I want to avoid any entanglement with Master Sean O Lochlainn. A man with his ability and power is a man to avoid when he's on the other side."

"Your pardon, Mission Commander, but just how certain are you that the man you saw on the mule this morning was actually Master Sean?"

"Quite certain. I heard him lecture many times at the University at Buda-Pest when I was an undergraduate there in 'sixty-eight, 'sixty-nine, and 'seventy. He was taking his Th.D. in theoretics and analog math. His King paid for it from the Privy Purse, but he supplemented his income by giving undergrad lectures."

"Would he recognize you?"

"Highly unlikely. Who pays any attention to undergraduate students at a large University?"

The Commander waved an impatient hand. "Let's hear your report."

"Yes, Mission Commander," Agent 137 said briskly. "I followed the man on muleback, as you ordered. He met another man, ahorse, coming from the village. He was tall, lean but muscular, with handsome, rather English-looking features. He was dressed as a merchant, but I suspected . . ."

The Commander nodded. "Lord Darcy. Obviously. Continue."

"You said they'd go to the site of the death, and when they took the left-hand bypass I was sure of it. I left off following and galloped on to the village, where Number 202 was waiting with the boat. We had a good westerly breeze, so we made it to the cove before them. We anchored and lay some two hundred yards offshore. Number 202 did some fishing while I watched through field glasses.

"They talked to the Armsmen atop the cliff for a while, then went down to the beach. One of the Armsmen pointed to where the body had been. Darcy went on talking to him for a while. Then Darcy walked around, looking at things. He went over to the base of the cliff and began digging. He found something; I couldn't see what.

"Master Sean put it in his bag, then, for ten minutes or so, he quartered the area where the body'd been, using one of those long, blue-black metal wands—you know—"

"A metal detector," said the Commander. "Yes. Go on."

"Yes. Lord Darcy dug every time O Lochlainn pointed something out. Dug up an awful lot of stuff. But he found *some*thing interesting. Don't know what it was; couldn't see it. But he stuck it in his pocket and gave it to the sorcerer later."

"I know what it was," said the Commander in a hard voice. "Was that the only thing that seemed to interest him?"

"Yes, as far as I could tell," said 137.

"Then what happened?"

137 shrugged. "They went back topside. Darcy talked to one of the Armsmen; the other watched the sorcerer dig a hole in the cliff face."

The Mission Commander frowned. "Dig a hole? A *hole*?"

"That's right. Lay flat on his belly, reached down a couple of feet over the edge, and dug something out. Couldn't see what it was. Left a hole about the size of a man's two fists—maybe a bit bigger."

"Damn! Why couldn't you have watched more carefully?"

Agent 137's face stiffened. "It was very difficult to see well, Mission Commander. Any closer than two hundred yards, and we would have drawn attention. Did you ever try to focus six-by field glasses from a light boat bobbing up and down on the sea?"

"Calm down. I'm not angry with you. You did well. I just wish we had better information." The Commander looked thoughtful. "That tells us something. We can forget about the beach. Order the men to stay away; they are not to go there again for any reason.

"The Phial is not there now, if it ever was. If Master Sean did not find it, it wasn't there. If he *did* find it, it is gone now, and he and Lord Darcy know where it is. And that is a problem I must consider. Now get out of here and let me think."

Agent 137 got out.

The public room at the Green Seagull, as far as population went, looked like a London railway car at the rush hour.

Amidst all the hubbub, wine and beer crossed the bar in one direction, while copper and silver crossed it in the other, making everyone happy on both sides.

In the club bar, it was somewhat quieter, but the noise from the public bar was distinctly audible. The innkeeper himself was taking care of the customers in the club bar; he took a great deal of pride in his work. Besides, the tips were larger and the work easier.

"Would dere be anyting else for dee?" he asked as he set two pints of beer on one of the tables. "Someting to munch on, mayhap?"

"Not just now, Goodman Dreyque," said Father Art. "This will do us for a while."

"Very good, Fahder. Tank dee." He went quietly away.

Lord Darcy took a deep draught of his beer and sighed. "Cool beer is a great refresher on a midsummer evening. The Green Seagull keeps an excellent cellar. Food's good, too; Master Sean and I ate here this afternoon.''

"Where is Master Sean now?" the priest asked.

"In the rooms you assigned us in the Rectory, amidst his apparatus, doing lab work on some evidence we dug up." His voice became soft. "Did you find out what happened here that night?"

"Pretty much," Father Art replied in the same low tones. "There are a few things which are still a little hazy, but I think we can fill in most of those areas."

Standish's quarry had arrived at the Green Seagull late in the afternoon of the fifth, giving the name "Richard Bourke." He was carrying only an attaché case, but since he had a horse and saddle and saddlebags, they were considered surety against indebtedness.

There were only six rooms for hire in the inn, all on the upper floor of the two-storied building. Two of these were already occupied. At two-ten, the man Danglars had come in and registered for himself and his mistress, Jizelle de Ville.

"Bourke," said Father Art, "came in at five-fifteen. Nobody else at all checked in during that evening. And nobody saw a young man wearing evening clothes." He paused and smiled brightly. "How-*ev*-er . . ."

"Ahhh. I knew I could depend on you, my dear Arthur. What was it?"

Still smiling seraphically, the good father raised a finger and said: "The Case of the Sexton's Cloak."

"You fascinate me. Pray elucidate."

"My sexton," said Father Art, "has an old cloak, originally made from a couple of used horse blankets, so it wasn't exactly beautiful when new. But it *is* warm. He uses it when he has to work outside in winter. In summer, he hangs it in the stable behind the church. Claims it keeps the moths out—the smell, I mean.

"On the morning of sixth June, one of the men who works here in the inn brought it over to the church, asked my sexton if it were his. It was. Want to take a wild, silly guess where it was found?" Father Art asked.

"Does the room used by Bourke face the front or the rear?"

"The rear."

"Then it was found on the cobblestones at the rear of the building."

Smiling even more broadly, Father Art gently clapped his hands together once. "Precisely, my lord."

Lord Darcy smiled back. "Let's reconstruct. Bourke went to his room before five-thirty. Right?"

"Right. One of the maids went with him, let him in, and gave him the key."

"Was he ever seen again?"

"Only once. He ordered a light meal, and it was brought up about six. That's the last time he was seen."

"Were either of the other guests in the house at the time?"

"No. The man Danglars had left about four-thirty, and hadn't returned. No one saw Mistress Jizelle leave, but the girl who turns down the beds says that both rooms were empty at six. Bourke was still there at the time."

"Hmmmm."

Lord Darcy looked into the depths of his beer. After half a minute, he said: "Reverend Father, was a stranger in an old horse-blanket cloak actually seen in this inn, or are we speculating in insubstantial mist?"

Father Art's mouth twisted in a small grimace. "Not totally insubstantial, my lord, but not strong, either. The barmaid who was on duty that night says she remembers a couple of strangers who came in, but she doesn't remember anything about them. She's not terribly bright."

Lord Darcy chuckled. "All right, then. Let's assume that Standish actually came in here in a stolen—and uncomfortably warm—cloak. How did that come about, and what happened afterwards?"

Father Art fired up his old briar and took another sip from his seidel of beer. "Well, let's see. Standish comes into the village an hour after Bourke—perhaps a little more. But he doesn't come in directly; he circles round behind the church. Why? Not to steal the cloak. How would he know it was there?" He took two puffs from his pipe, then his eyes brightened. "Of course. To tether his horse. He didn't want it seen in the public square, and knew it would be safe in the church stable." Two more puffs.

"Hmmm. He sees the cloak on the stable wall and realizes that it will serve as a disguise, covering his evening dress. He borrows it and comes here to the inn. He makes sure that Bourke is firmly in place, then goes back to his horse and hightails it for Caen to send word to Sir James. Then he comes back here to the Green Seagull. He waits until nobody's looking, then sneaks up the stair to Bourke's room."

The priest stopped, scowled, and took a good, healthy drink from his seidel. "Some time later, he went out the window to the courtyard below, losing the cloak in the process." He shook his head. "But what happened between the time he went upstairs and the time he dropped the cloak, and what happened between then and his death, I haven't the foggiest conjecture."

"I have several," Lord Darcy said, "but they are all very, very foggy. We need more data. I have several questions." He ticked them off on his fingers. "One: Where is Bourke? Two: Who shot Standish? Three: *Why* was he shot? Four: What happened here at the inn? Five: What happened on the beach? And, finally: *Where is the Ipswich Phial?*"

Father Art lifted his seidel, drained its contents on one extended draught, set it firmly on the table, and said: "I don't know. God does."

Lord Darcy nodded. "Indeed; and one of His greatest attributes is that if you ask Him the right question in the right way, He will always give you an answer."

"You intend to pray for answers to those questions, my lord?"

"That, yes. But I have found that the best way to ask God about questions like these is to go out and dig up the data yourself."

Father Art smiled. *"Dominus vobiscum."*

"Et cum spiritu tuo," Lord Darcy responded.

"Excavemus!" said the priest.

In his room in the Rectory, Master Sean had carefully set up his apparatus on the table. Noel Standish's .36 Heron was clamped securely into a padded vise which stood at one end of the table. Three feet in front of the muzzle, the bullet which Lord Darcy had dug from the sand had been carefully placed on a small pedestal, so that it was at exactly the same height as the muzzle. He was using certain instruments to make sure that the axis of the bullet was accurately aligned with the axis of the Heron's barrel when a rhythmic code knock came at the door. The sorcerer went over to the door, unbolted it, opened it, and said: "Come in, me lord."

"I hope I didn't interrupt anything," Lord Darcy said.

"Not at all, me lord." Master Sean carefully closed and bolted the door again. "I was just getting ready for the ballistics test. The similarity relationship tests have already assured me that the slug was the one that killed Standish. There's only to see if it came from his own gun. Have you found any further clues?''

"None," Lord Darcy admitted. "I managed to get a good look at the guest rooms in the Green Seagull. Nothing. Flat nothing. I have several ideas, but no evidence." Then he gestured at the handgun. "Pray proceed with your work. I will be most happy to wait."

"It'll only be a minute or so," Master Sean said apologetically. He went back to the table and continued his preparations while Lord Darcy watched in silence. His lordship was well aware of the principle involved; he had seen the test innumerable times. He recalled a lecture that Master Sean had once given on the subject.

"You see," the sorcerer had said, "the Principle of Relevance is important here. Most of the wear on a gun is purely mechanical. It don't matter *who* pulls the trigger, you see; the erosion caused by the gases produced in the chamber and the wear caused by the bullet's passing through the barrel will be the same. It's not relevant *to the gun* who pulled the trigger or what it was fired at. But, *to the bullet* it *is* relevant which gun it was fired from and what it hit. All this can be determined by the proper spells.''

In spite of having seen it many times, Lord Darcy always liked to watch the test because it was rather spectacular when the test was positive. Master Sean sprinkled a small amount of previously charged powder on both the bullet and the gun. Then he raised his wand and said an incantation under his breath.

At the last syllable of the incantation, there was a sound as if someone had sharply struck a cracked bell as the bullet vanished. The .36 Heron shivered in its vise.

Master Sean let out his breath. "Just like a homing pigeon, me lord. Gun and bullet match."

"I've often wondered why the bullet does that," Lord Darcy said.

Master Sean chuckled. "Call it an induced return-to-the-womb fixation, my lord. Was there something you wanted?"

"A couple of things," Lord Darcy walked over to his suitcase, opened it, and took out a holstered handgun. It was a precision-made .40 caliber MacGregor—a heavy man-stopper.

While he checked out the MacGregor itself, he said: "This is one. The other is a question. How long before his body was found did Standish die?"

Master Sean rubbed the side of his nose with a thick finger. "Well, the investigative sorcerer at Caen, a good journeyman, placed the time as not more than fifteen minutes before the body was discovered. My own tests showed not more than twenty-five minutes, but not even the best preservative spell can keep something like that from blurring after a week has passed.''

Lord Darcy slid the MacGregor into its snugly-fitted holster and adjusted his jacket to cover it. "In other words, there's the usual hazy area. The bruises and fractures were definitely inflicted before death?"

"Definitely, my lord. About three hours before, give or take that same fifteen minutes."

"I see. Interesting. Very interesting." He looked in the wall mirror and adjusted his neckpiece. "Have you further work to do?"

"Only the analysis on the knife," Master Sean said.

Lord Darcy turned from the mirror. "Will you fix me up with a tracer? I'm going out to stroll about the village and possibly to the fairgrounds and the tent city. I anticipate no danger, but I don't want to get lost, either."

"Very well, me lord," the sorcerer said with resignation. He opened his symbol-decorated carpetbag and took out a little wooden box. It held what looked remarkably like one-inch toothpicks, except that they were evenly cylindrical, not tapered, and they were made of ash instead of pine. He selected one and put the box back in his bag. He handed the little cylinder to Lord Darcy, who took it between the thumb and forefinger of his right hand.

Then the master sorcerer took a little scented oil on his right thumb from a special golden oil stock and rubbed it along the sliver of ash, from Lord Darcy's thumb to the other end. Then he grasped that end in his own right thumb and forefinger.

A quick motion of both wrists, and the ashen splinter snapped.

But, psychically and symbolically, the halves were still part of an unbroken whole. As long as each man carried his half, the two of them were specially linked.

"Thank you, my dear Sean," Lord Darcy said. "And now I shall be off to enjoy the nightlife of the teeming metropolis surrounding us."

With that, he was gone, and Master Sean returned to his work.

The sun was a fat, squashed-looking, red-orange ellipsoid seated neatly on the horizon when Lord Darcy stepped out of the gate of the churchyard. It would be gone in a few minutes. The long shadow of the church spire reached out across the village and into the fields. The colors of the flags and banners and bunting around the village were altered in value by the reddish light. The weather had been beautiful and clear all day, and would continue to be, according to the Weather Bureau predictors. It would be a fine night.

"Please, my lord—are you Lord Darcy?"

Lord Darcy had noticed the woman come out of the church, but the village square was full of people, and he had paid little attention. Now he turned his full attention on her and was pleasantly surprised. She was quite the loveliest creature he had seen in a long time.

"I am, Damoselle," he said with a smile. "But I fear you have the advantage of me."

Her own smile was timid, almost frightened. "I am named Sharolta."

Her name, her slight accent, and her clothing all proclaimed her Romany. Her long, softly dark hair and her dark eyes, her well-formed nose and her full, almost too-perfect lips, along with her magnificently lush body, accentuated by the Romany costume, proclaimed her beautiful.

"May I be of help to you, Damoselle Sharolta?"

She shook her head. "No, no. I ask nothing. But perhaps I can be of help to you." Her smiled seemed to quaver. "Can we go somewhere to talk?"

"Where, for instance?" Lord Darcy asked carefully.

"Anywhere you say, my lord. Anywhere, so long as it is private." Then she flushed. "I—I mean, not *too much* private. I mean, where we can talk. You know."

"Of course. It is not yet time for Vespers; I suggest that we go into the church," Lord Darcy said.

"Yes, yes. That would be fine." She smiled. "There were not many folk in there. It should be fine."

The interior of the Church of St. Matthew was darkened, but far from being gloomy. The flickering clusters of candles around the statues and icons were like twinkling, multicolored star clusters.

Lord Darcy and the Damoselle Sharolta sat down in one of the rear pews. Most of a dozen or so people who were in the church were farther up toward the altar, praying; there was no one within earshot of the place Lord Darcy had chosen.

Lord Darcy waited in silence for the girl to speak. The Romany become silent under pressure; create a vacuum for them to fill, and the words come tumbling over each other in eloquent eagerness.

"You are the great Lord Darcy, the great Investigator," she began suddenly. "You are looking into the death of the poor Goodman Standish who was found on the beach a week ago. Is all this not so?"

Lord Darcy nodded silently.

"Well, then, there must be something wrong about that man's death, or you would not be here. So I must tell you what I know."

"A week ago, there came to our tribe a group of five men. They said they were from the tribe of Chanro—the Sword—which is in the area of Buda-Pest. Their leader, who calls himself Suv—the Needle—asked our chief for aid and sanctuary, as it is their right, and it was granted. But they are very secretive among themselves. They behave very well, mind you; I don't mean they are rude or boorish, or anything like that. But there is—how do I say it?—there is a *wrongness* about them.

"This morning, for instance. I must tell you of that. The man who calls himself Suv wanted me to walk along the beach with him. I did not want to, for I do not find him an attractive man—you understand?"

Again his lordship nodded. "Of course."

"But he said he meant nothing like that. He said he wanted to walk along the sea, but he did not want to walk alone. He said he would show me all the shore life—the birds, the things in the pools, the plants. I was interested, and I thought there would be no harm, so I went.

"He was true to his word. He did not try to make love to me. It was nice for a while. He showed me the tide pools and pointed out the different kinds of things in them. One had a jellyfish." She looked up from her hands, and there was a frown on her face.

"Then we got near to that little cove where the body was found. I wanted to turn back, but he said, no, he wanted to look at it. I said I wouldn't and started back. Then he told me that if I didn't, he'd break my arm. So I went." She seemed to shiver a little under her bright dress. "When the Armsman showed up, he kept on going, pretending he didn't understand Anglo-French. Then we saw that there were two of them, the Armsmen, I mean. So we turned around and went back. Suv was very furious."

She stopped and said no more.

"My dear," he asked gently, "why does one of the Romany come to the authorities with a story like this? Do not the Romany take care of their own?"

"Yes, my lord. But these men are not Rom."

"Oh?"

"Their tent is next to mine. I have heard them talking when they think no one is listening. I do not understand it very well, but I know it when I hear it; they were speaking *Burgdeutsch*."

"I see," said Lord Darcy softly and thoughtfully. The German of Brandenburg was the court language of Poland, which suddenly made everything very interesting indeed.

"Do you suppose, Damoselle," he said, "that you could point out this Suv to me?"

She looked up at him with those great wonderful eyes and smiled. "I'm sure I could, my lord. Come; wrap your cloak about you and we shall walk through the village."

Outside the church, the darkness was relieved only by the regulation gaslamps of the various business places, and by the quarter moon hanging high in the sky, like a half-closed eye.

In the deeper darkness of the church porch, Lord Darcy, rather much to his surprise, took the girl in his arms and kissed her, with her warm cooperation. It was several wordless minutes before they went out to the street.

Master Sean woke to the six-o'clock Angelus bell feeling vaguely uneasy. A quick mental focus on his half of the tracer told him that Lord Darcy was in no danger. Actually, if he had been, Sean would have wakened immediately.

But he still had that odd feeling when he went down to Mass at seven; he had trouble keeping in his mind his prayers for the intercession of St. Basil the Great, and couldn't really bring his mind to focus until the Sanctus.

After Mass, he went up to Father Art's small parlor in the rectory, where he had been asked to break his fast, and was mildly surprised to find Sir James le Lien with the priest.

"Good morning, Master Sean," Sir James said calmly. "Have you found the Phial yet?"

The sorcerer shook his head. "Not so far as I know."

Sir James munched a buttered biscuit and sipped hot black caffe. Despite his calm expression Master Sean could tell that he was worried.

"I am afraid," Sir James said carefully, "we've been outfoxed."

"How so?" Father Art asked.

"Well, either the *Serka* have got it, or they think we have it safely away from them. They seem to have given the whole thing over." He drank more caffe. "Just after midnight, every known *Serka* agent in the area eluded our men and vanished. They dropped out of sight, and we haven't spotted a single one in over eight hours. We have reason to believe that some of them went south, toward Caen; some went west, toward Cherbourg; other are heading east, toward Harfleur.''

Master Sean frowned. ''And you think—''

''I think they found the Ipswich Phial and one of their men is carrying it to Krakowa. Or at least across the Polish border. I rode to Caen and made more teleson calls than I've ever made in so short a time in my life. There's a net out now, and we can only hope we can find the man with the Phial. Otherwise . . .'' He closed his eyes. ''Otherwise, we may be faced with an overland attack by the armies of His Slavonic Majesty, through one or more of the German states. God help us.''

After what seemed like a terribly long time, Master Sean said: ''Sir James, is there any likelihood that Noel Standish would have used a knife on the sealed Phial?''

''I don't know. Why do you ask?''

''We found a knife near where Standish's body was discovered. My tests show gold on the knife edge.''

''May I see it?'' Sir James asked.

''Certainly. I'll fetch it. Excuse me a minute.''

He left the parlor and went down the rather narrow hallway of the rectory. From the nearby church came the soft chime of a small bell. The eight o'clock Mass was beginning.

Master Sean opened the door of his room . . .

. . . and stood stock still, staring, for a full fifteen seconds, while his eyes and other senses took in the room.

Then, without moving, he shouted: ''Sir James! Father Art! Come here! Quickly!''

Both men came running. They stopped at the door.

''What's the matter?'' Sir James snapped.

''Somebody,'' said Master Sean in an angry rumble, ''has been prowlin' about in me room! And a trick like that is likely to be after gettin' me Irish up!'' Master Sean's brogue varied with his mood. When he was calmly lecturing or discussing, it became almost nonexistent. But when he became angry . . .

He strode into the room for a closer look at the table which he had been using for his thaumaturgical analyses. In the center was a heap of crumbled clay. ''They've destroyed me evidence! Look at that!'' Master Sean pointed to the heap of crumbled clay on the table.

''And what is it, if I may ask?''

Master Sean explained about the letters that had been cut in the cliff face, and how he had taken the chunk of clay out for further examination.

"And this knife was used to cut the letters." He gestured toward the knife on the table nearby. "I haven't been able to check it against Standish's body yet."

"That's the one with the gold traces on the blade?" Sir James asked.

"It is."

"Well, it's Standish's knife, all right. I've seen it many times. I could even tell you how he got that deep cut in the ivory hilt." He looked thoughtful. "S . . . S . . . O . . ." After a moment, he shook his head. "Means nothing to me. Can't think what it might have meant to Standish."

"Means nothing to me, either," Father Art admitted.

"Well, now," said the stout little Irish sorcerer, "Standish must have been at the top of the cliff when he wrote it. What would be right side up to him would be inverted to anyone standing below. How about OSS?"

Again Sir James thought. Again he shook his head. "Still nothing, Master Sean. Father?"

The priest shook his head. "Nothing, I'm afraid."

Sir James said: "This was obviously done by a *Serka* agent. But why? And how did he get in here without your knowing it?"

Master Sean scowled. "To a sorcerer, that's obvious. First, whoever did it is an accomplished sorcerer himself, or he'd never have made it past that avoidance spell, which is keyed only to meself and to his lordship. Second, he picked exactly the right time—when I was at Mass and had me mind concentrated elsewhere so I wouldn't notice what he was up to. Were I doing it meself, I'd have started just as the Sanctus bell was rung. After that—no problem." He looked glum. "I just wasn't expecting it, that's all."

"I wish I could have seen that carving in the clay," Sir James said.

"Well, you can see the cast if they didn't—" Master Sean pulled open a desk drawer. "No, they didn't." He pulled out a thick slab of plaster. "I made this with quick-setting plaster. It's reversed, of course, but you can look at it in the mirror, over there."

Sir James took the slab, but didn't look at it immediately. His eyes were still on the heap of clay. "Do you suppose that Standish might have buried the Ipswich Phial in that clay to keep it from being found?"

Master Sean's eyes widened. "Great Heaven! It could be! With an auric-stabilized psychic shield around it, I'd not have perceived it at all!"

Sir James groaned. "That answers the question. *Why?*—doesn't it?"

"So it would seem," murmured Father Art.

Bleakly, Sir James held the plaster slab up to the mirror above the dresser. "SSO. No. Wait." He inverted it, and his lean face went pale. "Oh, no, God," he said softly. "Oh, please. No."

"What is it?" the priest asked. "Does OSS mean something?"

"Not OSS," Sir James said still more softly. "055. Number 055 of the *Serka*. Olga Polovski, the most beautiful and the most dangerous woman in Europe."

It was at that moment that the sun went out.

The Reverend Father Mac Kennalty had turned to the congregation and asked them to lift up their hearts to the Lord that they might properly assist at the Holy Sacrifice of the Altar, when a cloud seemed to pass over the sun, dimming the light that streamed in through the stained glass windows. Even the candles on the Altar seemed to dim a little.

He hardly noticed it; it was a common enough occurrence. Without a pause, he asked the people to give thanks to the Lord God, and continued with the Mass.

In the utter blackness of the room, three men stood for a moment in silence.

"Well, that tears it," said Sir James's voice in the darkness. There was a noticeable lack of surprise or panic in his voice.

"So you lied to his lordship," said Master Sean.

"He did indeed," said Father Art.

"What do you mean?" Sir James asked testily.

"You said," Master Sean pointed out with more than a touch of acid in his voice, "that you didn't know what the Ipswich Phial is supposed to do."

"What makes you think I *do*?"

"In the first place, this darkness came as no surprise to you. In the second, you must have known what it was, because Noel Standish knew."

"I had my orders," Sir James le Lien said in a hard voice. "That's not the point now. The damned thing is being used. I—"

"*Listen!*" Father Art's voice cut in sharply. "*Listen!*"

In the blackness, all of them heard the sweet triple tone of the Sanctus bell.

Holy . . . Holy . . . Holy . . . Lord God Sabaoth . . .

"What—?" Sir James's low voice was querulous.

"Don't you understand?" Father Art asked. "The field of suppression doesn't extend as far as the church. Father Mac Kennalty could go on with the Mass in the dark, from memory. But the congregation wouldn't be likely to. They certainly don't sound upset."

"You're right, Father," Master Sean said. "That gives us the range, doesn't it? Let's see if we can feel our way out of here, toward the church. His lordship may be in trouble."

"Follow me," said the priest. "I know this church like I know my own face. Take my hand and follow me."

Cautiously, the three men moved from the darkness toward the light. They were still heading for the stairway when the sun came on again.

Lord Darcy rode into the stableyard behind the Church of St. Matthew, where four men were waiting for him. The sexton took his horse as he dismounted, and led it away to the stable. The other three just waited, expectantly.

"I could do with a cup of caffe, heavily laced with brandy, and a plate of ham and eggs, if they're available," said Lord Darcy with a rather dreamy smile. "If not, I'll just have the caffe and brandy."

"What's happened?" Sir James blurted abruptly.

Lord Darcy patted the air with a hand. "All in good time, my dear James; all in good time. Nothing's amiss, I assure you."

"I think a breakfast such as that could be arranged," Father Art said with a smile. "Come along."

The caffe and brandy came immediately, served by Father Art in a large mug. "The ham and eggs should be along pretty quickly," the priest said.

"Excellent! You're the perfect host, Father." Lord Darcy took a bracing jolt from the mug, then fished in his waistcoat pocket with thumb and forefinger. "Oh, by the by, Sir James, here's your play-pretty." He held up a small golden tube.

Sir James took it and looked at it while Master Sean scowled at it in a way that made him seem rather cross-eyed.

"The seal has been cut," Sir James said.

"Yes. By your man, Standish. I suggest you give the thing to Master Sean for resealing until you get it back to Ipswich."

Sir James gave the Phial to Master Sean. "How did you get it back from them?" the King's Agent asked.

"I didn't." Lord Darcy settled himself back in the big chair. "If you'll be patient, I'll explain. Last evening, I was approached by a young woman . . ."

His lordship repeated the entire conversation verbatim, and told them of her gestures and expressions while they were talking inside the church.

"And you went with her?" Sir James asked incredulously.

"Certainly. For two very good reasons. *Primus*: I had to find out what was behind her story. *Secundus*: I had fallen in love."

Sir James gawked. Master Sean's face became expressionless. Father Art cast his eyes toward Heaven.

Sir James found his voice first. "In *love*?" It was almost a squawk.

Lord Darcy nodded calmly. "In love. Deeply. Madly. Passionately."

Sir James shot to his feet. "Are you mad, Darcy? Don't you realize that that woman is a *Serka* agent?"

"So indeed I had surmised. Sit down, James; such outbursts are unseemly." Sir James sat down slowly. "Now pay attention," Lord Darcy continued. "Of course I knew she was a spy. If you had been listening closely when I quoted her words, you would have heard that she said I was investigating the death of *Standish*. And yet everyone here knows that the body was identified as *Bourke*. Obviously, she had recognized Standish and knew his name."

"Standish had recognized her, too," Sir James said. "Secret Agent Number 055, of *Serka*. Real name: Olga Polovski."

"Olga," Lord Darcy said, savoring the word. "That's a pretty name, isn't it?"

"Charming. Utterly enchanting. And in spite of the fact that she's a Polish agent, you love the wench?"

"I didn't say that, Sir James," said Lord Darcy. "I did not say I loved her; I said I was 'in love' with her. There is a fine distinction there, and I have had enough experience to be able to distinguish between the two states of mind. Your use of the word 'enchanting' is quite apropos, by the way. The emotion was artificially induced. The woman is a sorceress."

Master Sean suddenly snapped his fingers. "*That's* where I heard the name before! Olga Polovski! Six years ago, she was an undergraduate at the University in Buda-Pest. A good student, with high-grade Talent. No wonder you 'fell in love' with her."

Sir James narrowed his eyes. "I see. The purpose was to get information out of you. Did she succeed?"

"In a way," Lord Darcy chuckled. "I sang like a nightingale. Indeed, Darcy's *Mendacious Cantata,* sung *forte e claro,* may become one of the most acclaimed works of art of the twentieth century. Pardon me; I am euphoric."

"You have popped your parietals, my lord," Sir James said, with a slight edge to his voice. "What was the result of this baritone solo?"

"Actually, it was a duet. We alternated on the versicles and responses. The theme of my song was simply that I was a criminal investigator and nothing more. That I hadn't more than a vague notion of what His Imperial Majesty's Secret Service was up to. That, for some reason, the apprehension of this murderer was most important to the Secret Service, so their agents were hanging around to help me. That they were more hindrance than help." He paused to take another swallow of laced caffe, then continued: "And—oh, yes—that they must be going to England for more men, because, four days ago, a heavily armed group of four men took a Navy cutter from Harfleur for London."

Sir James frowned for a second, then his face lit up. "Ah, yes. You implied that we had already found the Phial and that it was safely in England."

"Precisely. And since she had not heard of that oh-so-secret departure, she was certain that it could not be a bluff. As a result, she scrubbed the entire mission. Around midnight, she excused herself for a moment and spoke to someone—I presume it was the second in command, the much-maligned Suv. Her men took off to three of the four winds."

"And she didn't?"

"Of course not. Why arouse my suspicions? Better to keep me under observation while her men made good their escape. I left her shortly after dawn, and—"

"You were there from sunset till dawn? What took you so long?"

Lord Darcy looked pained. "My dear James, surely you don't think I could simply hand her all that misinformation in half an hour without her becoming suspicious. I had to allow her to draw it from me, bit by bit. I had to allow her to give me more information than she intended to give in order to get the story out of me. And, of course, *she* had to be very careful in order not to arouse *my* suspicions. It was, I assure you, a very delicate and time-consuming series of negotiations."

Sir James did his best not to leer. "I can well imagine."

Father Art looked out the window, solemnly puffing his pipe as though he were in deep meditation and could hear nothing.

Rather hurriedly, Master Sean said: "Then it was you who broke the clay brick I dug out of the cliff, me lord."

"It was; I'm sorry I didn't tell you, but you were at Mass, and I was in somewhat of a hurry. You see, there were only two places where the Phial could possibly be, and I looked in the less likely place first—in that lump of clay. Standish *could* have hidden it there, but I thought it unlikely. Still, I had to look. It wasn't there."

"So I got my horse and rode out to where the body was found. You see, Standish *had* to have had it with him. He opened it to get away from his pursuers. I presume Master Sean knows how the thing works, but all I know is that it renders everyone blind for a radius of about a mile and a half."

Master Sean cleared his throat. "It's akin to what's called hysterical blindness. Nothing wrong with the eyes, ye see, but the mind blocks off the visual centers of the brain. The Phial contains a charged rod attached to the stopper. When you open it and expose the rod everything goes black. That's the reason for the auric-stabilized psychic shield which forms the Phial itself."

"Things don't go black for the person holding it," said Lord Darcy. "Everything becomes a colorless gray, but you can still see."

"That's the built-in safety spell in the stopper," said the little Irish sorcerer.

"Well, where *was* the blasted thing?" Sir James asked.

"Buried in the sand, almost under that big rock where his body was found. I just had to dig till I found it." Lord Darcy looked somber. "I fear my analytical powers are deserting me; otherwise, Master Sean and I would have found it yesterday. But I relied on his metal detector to find it. And yet, Master Sean clearly told me that a psychic shield renders anything psychically invisible. He was talking about Standish, of course, but I should have seen that the same logic applied to the Ipswich Phial as well."

"If ye'd told me what ye were looking for, me lord . . ." Master Sean said gently.

Lord Darcy chuckled mirthlessly. "After all our years together, my dear Sean, we still tend to overestimate each other. I assumed you had deduced what we were looking for, though you are no detective; you assumed I knew about psychic shielding, though I am no thaumaturge."

"I still can't quite see that entire chain of events," Father Art said. "Could you clarify it for us? What was Standish doing out on that beach, anyway?"

"Well, let's go back to the night before he was killed. He had been following the mysterious Bourke. When Bourke was firmly ensconced in the Green Seagull, Standish rode for Caen, notified you via teleson, then rode back. He borrowed the sexton's cloak and went over to the inn. When he saw his chance, he dodged upstairs fast and went to Bourke's room presumably to get the Phial.

"Now, you must keep in mind that all this is conjecture. I can't prove it, and I know of no way to prove it. I do not have, and cannot get, all the evidence I would need for *proof*. But all the data I *do* have leads inescapably to one line of action.

"Master Sean claims I have a touch of the Talent—the ability to leap from an unwarranted assumption to a foregone conclusion. That may be so. At any rate, I *know* what happened.

"Very well, then. Standish went into Bourke's room to arrest him. He *knew* Bourke was in that room because he was psychically locked on to Bourke.

"But when he broke into the room he was confronted by a woman—a woman he knew. The woman was just as surprised to see Standish.

"I don't know which of them recovered first, but I strongly suspect it was the woman. Number 055 is very quick on the uptake, believe me.

"But Standish was stronger. He sustained a few good bruises in the next several seconds, but he knocked her unconscious. I saw the bruise on her neck last night.

"He searched the room and found the Phial. Unfortunately, the noise had attracted two, possibly three, of her fellow *Serka* agents. He had to go out the window, losing his cloak in the process. The men followed him.

"He ran for the beach, and—"

"Wait a minute," Sir James interrupted. "You mean Bourke was actually Olga Polovski in disguise?"

"Certainly. She's a consummate actress. The idea was for Bourke to vanish completely. She knew the Secret Service would be after her, and she wanted to leave no trace. But she didn't realize that Standish was so close behind her because he was psychically invisible. That's why she was shocked when he came into her room.

"At any rate, he ran for the beach. There was no place else to go at that time of night, except for the church, and they'd have him trapped there.

"I must admit I'm very fuzzy about what happened during that chase, but remember he had ridden for two days without much rest, and he was battered a little by the blows Olga had landed. At any rate, he eventually found himself at the edge of that cliff, with *Serka* closing in around him. Remember, it was a moonless night, and there were only stars for him to see by. But at least one of the Polish agents had a lantern.

"Standish was trapped on the edge of a cliff, and he had no way to see how far down it went, nor what was at the bottom. He lay flat and kept quiet, but the others were getting close. He decided to get rid of the Phial. Better to lose it than have it fall into King Casimir's hands. He took out his knife and carved the '055' in the side of the cliff, to mark the spot and to make sure that someone else would see it if he were killed. I'm sure he intended to dig a hole and bury it there. I don't believe he was thinking too clearly by then.

"The *Serka* men were getting too close for comfort. He might be seen at any moment. So he cut the seal of the Phial and opened it. Blackout.

"Since he could see his pursuers—however dimly—and they couldn't see him, he decided to try to get past them, back to the village. If he had a time advantage, he could find a place to hide.

"He stood up.

"But as he turned, he made a misstep and fell twenty feet to the sand below." Lord Darcy paused.

Father Art, looking thoughtful, said: "He had a gun. Why didn't he use it?"

"Because they had guns, too, and he was outnumbered. He didn't want to betray his position by the muzzle flash unless he had to," Lord Darcy said. "To continue: The fall is what broke those ribs and sprained that wrist. It also very likely knocked him out for a few minutes. Not long. When he came to, he must have realized he had an advantage greater than he had thought at first. The *Serka* couldn't see the muzzle flash from his handgun. Badly hurt as he was, he waited for them."

"Admirable," said Father Art. "It's fantastic that he didn't lose the two parts of the Phial when he fell. Must have hung on for dear life."

"Standish would," said Sir James grimly. "Go on, my lord."

"Well, at that point, the *Serka* lads must have realized the same thing. They had no way of knowing how badly Standish was hurt, nor exactly where he was. He could be sneaking up on them, for all they knew. They got out of there. Slowly, of course, since they had to feel their way, but once they reached the Old Shore Road, they made better time.

"But by that time, Standish was close to passing out again. He still had to hide the Phial, so he buried it in the sand where I found it."

"Me lord," said Master Sean, "I still don't understand who killed Standish and why."

"Oh, that. Why that was patently obvious from the first. Wasn't it, Father Art?"

The good father stared at Lord Darcy. "Begging your pardon, my lord, but not to *me* it wasn't."

Lord Darcy turned his head. "Sir James?"

"No."

"Oh, dear. Well, I suppose I shall have to back up a bit, then. Consider: The Damoselle Olga, to cover her tracks, has to get rid of 'Bourke.' But if 'Bourke' disappears into nowhere, and someone else appears from nowhere, even a moron might suspect that the two were the same. So a cover must be arranged. Someone else, not connected in any way with 'Bourke,' must appear at the Green Seagull *before* 'Bourke' shows up.

"So, what happens? A coachman named Danglars shows up; a servant who registers for himself and his mistress, Jizelle de Ville. (Danglars and Suv were almost certainly the same man, by the way.) But who sees Mistress Jizelle? Nobody. *She is only a name in a register book until the next morning!*

"The original plan was to have Mistress Jizelle show up in the evening, then have Bourke show up again, and so on. The idea was to firmly establish that the two people were separate and not at all connected. The arrival and intrusion of Standish changed all that, but things worked out fairly well, nonetheless.

"It *had* to be 'Mistress Jizelle' who killed him. Look at the evidence. Standish died—correct me if I'm wrong, Master Sean—within plus or minus fifteen minutes of the time Standish was found."

Master Sean nodded.

"Naturally," his lordship continued, "we always assume a minus time. How could the person be killed *after* the body was found?"

"But there was no one else around who could have killed him! A farmer and his two sons were close enough to the road during that time to see anyone who came along unless that someone had walked along the beach. But there were no footprints in that damp sand except those of 'Mistress Jizelle'!

"Picture this, if you will: Number 055, still a little groggy, and suffering from a sore neck, is told by her returning henchmen that they have lost Standish. But she is clever enough to see what must have happened. As soon as possible, she puts on her 'Mistress Jizelle' *persona* and has her lieutenant drive her out to that section of the beach. She walks down to take a look. She sees Standish.

"Standish, meanwhile, has regained his senses. He opens his eyes and sees Olga Polovski. His gun is still in his hand. He tries to level it at her. She jumps him, in fear of her life. A struggle. The gun goes off. *Finis*."

"Wouldn't the farmers have heard the shot?" Master Sean asked.

"At that distance, with a brisk wind blowing, the sea pounding, and a cliff to baffle the sound, it would be hard to hear a pistol shot. That one was further muffled by the fact that the muzzle was against Standish's head. No, it wouldn't have been heard."

"Why did her footprints only come up to some five yards from the body?" Sir James asked. "There were no prints in the dry sand."

"Partly because she smoothed her prints out, partly because of the wind, which blew enough to cover them. She was shaken and worried, but she did take time to search the body for the Phial. Naturally, she didn't want any evidence of that search around. She went back to consult Danglars-Suv about what to do next. When she saw the farmers, there was nothing she could do but bluff it through. Which, I must say, she did magnificently."

"Indeed." Sir James le Lien looked both cold and grim. "Where is she now?"

"By now, she has taken horse and departed."

"Riding sidesaddle, no doubt." His voice was as cold as his expression. "So you let her get away. Why didn't you arrest her?"

"On what evidence? Don't be a fool, Sir James. What would you charge her with? Could you swear in His Majesty's Court of High Justice that 'Mistress Jizelle' was actually Olga Polovski? If I had tried to arrest her, I would have been a corpse by now in that Romany camp, even it I'd had the evidence. Since I did not and do not have that evidence, there would be no point.

"I would not call it a satisfactory case, no. But you have the Phial, which was what you wanted. I'm afraid the death of Noel

Standish will have to be written off as enemy action during the course of a war. It was not first-degree murder; it was, as Master Sean put it yesterday, a case of accidental murder.''

"But—"

Lord Darcy leaned back in the chair and closed his eyes. "Drop it, Sir James. You'll get her eventually."

Then, very quietly, he began to snore.

"I'll be damned!" said Sir James. "I worked all night on my feet and found nothing. He spends all night in bed with the most beautiful woman in Europe and gets all the answers."

"It all depends on your method of approach," Master Sean said. He opened his symbol-decorated carpetbag and took out a large, heavy book.

"Oh, certainly," said Sir James bitterly. "Some work vertically, some horizontally."

Father Arthur Lyon continued to stare out the window, hearing nothing he didn't mean to hear.

"What are you looking up there, in that grimoire?" he asked Master Sean after a moment.

"*Spells, infatuation; removal of,*" said Master Sean calmly.

Black Heart and White Heart
by H. Rider Haggard

H. Rider Haggard (1856-1925) was the premier adventure story writer of the late nineteenth century, a man who single-handedly created the Great White Hunter and Lost Race branches of the genre. He did this primarily through the publication of two monumentally influential novels, King Solomon's Mines *(1885) and* She: A History of Adventure *(1887). Unfortunately, his later work never achieved the same high quality, although he wrote more than thirty additional novels. His much more limited short-fiction production can be found in* The Best Short Stories of H. Rider Haggard. *He was a devoted imperialist, and his now discredited politics may be responsible for his current lack of stature, but he certainly was one of the great storytellers of all time.*

I

A Zulu Idyll

At the date of our introduction to him, Philip Hadden was a transport-rider and a trader in "the Zulu." Still on the right side of forty, in appearance he was singularly handsome; tall, dark, upright, with keen eyes, short-pointed beard, curling hair and clear-cut features. His life had been varied, and there were passages in it which he did not narrate even to his most intimate friends. He was of gentle birth, however, and it was said that he had received a public school and university education in England. At any rate he could quote the classics with aptitude on occasion, an accomplishment which, coupled with his refined voice and a bearing not altogether common in the wild places of the world, had earned for him among his rough companions the *soubriquet* of "The Prince."

However these things may have been, it is certain that he had emigrated to Natal under a cloud, and equally certain that his relatives at home were content to take no further interest in his fortunes. During the fifteen or sixteen years which he had spent in or about the colony, Hadden followed many trades, and did no good at any of them. A clever man, of agreeable and prepossessing manner, he always found it easy to form friendships and to secure a fresh start in life. But, by degrees, the friends were seized with a vague distrust of him; and, after a period of more or less application, he himself would close the opening that he had made by a sudden disappearance from the locality, leaving behind him a doubtful reputation and some bad debts.

Before the beginning of this story of the most remarkable episodes in his life, Philip Hadden was engaged for several years in transport-riding—that is, in carrying goods on ox waggons from Durban or Maritzburg to various points in the interior. A difficulty such as had more than once confronted him in the course of his career, led to his temporary abandonment of this means of earning a livelihood. On arriving at the little frontier town of Utrecht in the Transvaal, in charge of two waggon-loads of mixed goods consigned to a storekeeper there, it was discovered that out of six cases of brandy five were missing from his waggon. Hadden explained the matter by throwing the blame upon his Kaffir "boys," but the storekeeper, a rough-tongued man, openly called him a thief and refused to pay the freight on any of the load. From words the men came to blows, knives were drawn, and before anybody could interfere the storekeeper received a nasty wound in his side. That night, without waiting till the matter could be inquired into by the landdrost or magistrate, Hadden slipped away, and trekked back into Natal as quickly as his oxen would travel. Feeling that even here he was not safe, he left one of his waggons at Newcastle, loaded up the other with Kaffir goods—such as blankets, calico, and hardware—and crossed into Zululand, where in those days no sheriff's officer would be likely to follow him.

Being well acquainted with the language and customs of the natives, he did good trade with them, and soon found himself possessed of some cash and a small herd of cattle, which he received in exchange for his wares. Meanwhile news reached him that the man whom he had injured still vowed vengeance against him, and was in communication with the authorities in Natal. These reasons making his return to civilization undesirable for the moment, and further business being impossible until he could receive a fresh supply of trade stuff, Hadden like a wise man turned his thoughts to pleasure. Sending his cattle and waggon over the border to be left in charge of a native headman with whom he was friendly, he went on foot to Ulundi to obtain permission from the king, Cetywayo, to hunt game in his country. Somewhat to his surprise the Indunas, or headmen, received him courteously—for Hadden's visit took place within a few months of the outbreak of the Zulu war in 1878, when Cetywayo was already showing unfriendliness to the English traders and others, though why the king did so they knew not.

On the occasion of his first and last interview with Cetywayo, Hadden got a hint of the reason. It happened thus. On the second morning after his arrival at the royal kraal, a messenger came to inform him that "the Elephant whose tread shook the earth" had signified that it was his pleasure to see him. Accordingly he was led through the thousands of huts and across the Great Place to the little enclosure where Cetywayo, a royal-looking Zulu seated on a stool, and wearing a *Kaross* of leopard skins, was holding an *indaba*, or conference, surrounded by his counsellors. The Induna who had conducted him to the august presence went down upon his hands and knees, and, uttering the royal salute of *Bayéte*, crawled forward to announce that the white man was waiting.

"Let him wait," said the king angrily; and, turning, he continued the discussion with his counsellors.

Now, as has been said, Hadden thoroughly understood Zulu; and, when from time to time the king raised his voice, some of the words he spoke reached his ear.

"What!" Cetywayo said, to a wizened and aged man who seemed to be pleading with him earnestly; "am I a dog that these white hyenas should hunt me thus? Is not the land mine, and was it not my father's before me? Are not the people mine to save or to slay? I tell you that I will stamp out these little white men; my *impis* shall eat them up. I have said!"

Again the withered aged man interposed, evidently in the character of a peacemaker. Hadden could not hear his talk, but he rose and pointed towards the sea, while from his expressive gestures and sorrowful mien, he seemed to be prophesying disaster should a certain course of action be followed.

For a while the king listened to him, then he sprang from his seat, his eyes literally ablaze with rage.

"Hearken," he cried to the counsellor: "I have guessed it for long, and now I am sure of it. You are a traitor. You are Sompseu's[1] dog, and the dog of the Natal Government, and I will not keep another man's dog to bite me in my own house. Take him away!"

[1] Sir Theophilus Shepstone's.

A slight involuntary murmur rose from the ring of *indunas*, but the old man never flinched, not even when the soldiers, who presently would murder him, came and seized him roughly. For a few seconds, perhaps five, he covered his face with the corner of the *kaross* he wore, then he looked up and spoke to the king in a clear voice.

"O King," he said, "I am a very old man; as a youth I served under Chaka the Lion, and I heard his dying prophecy of the coming of the white man. Then the white men came, and I fought for Dingaan at the battle of the Blood River. They slew Dingaan, and for many years I was the counsellor of Panda, your father. I stood by you, O King, at the battle of the Tugela, when its grey waters were turned to red with the blood of Umbulazi your brother, and of the tens of thousands of his people. Afterwards I became your counsellor, O King, and I was with you when Sompseu set the crown upon your head and you made promises to Sompseu—promises that you have not kept. Now you are weary of me, and it is well; for I am very old, and doubtless my talk is foolish, as it chances to the old. Yet I think that the prophecy of Chaka, your great-uncle, will come true, and that the white men will prevail against you and that through them you shall find your death. I would that I might have stood in one more battle and fought for you, O King, since fight you will, but the end which you choose is for me the best end. Sleep in peace, O King, and farewell. *Bayétte!*"[1]

For a space there was silence, a silence of expectation while men waited to hear the tyrant reverse his judgment. But it did not please him to be merciful, or the needs of policy outweighed his pity.

"Take him away," he repeated. Then, with a slow smile on his face and one word, "Good-night," upon his lips, supported by the arm of a soldier, the old warrior and statesman shuffled forth to the place of death.

Hadden watched and listened in amazement not unmixed with fear. "If he treats his own servants like this, what will happen to me?" he reflected. "We English must have fallen out of favour since I left Natal. I wonder whether he means to make war on us or what? If so, this isn't my place."

Just then the king, who had been gazing moodily at the ground, chanced to look up. "Bring the stranger here," he said.

Hadden heard him, and coming forward offered Cetywayo his hand in as cool and nonchalant a manner as he could command.

[1] The royal salute of the Zulus.

Somewhat to his surprise it was accepted. "At least, White Man," said the king, glancing at his visitor's tall spare form and cleanly cut face, "you are no *umfagozan* (low fellow); you are of the blood of chiefs."

"Yes, King," answered Hadden, with a little sigh, "I am of the blood of chiefs."

"What do you want in my country, White Man?"

"Very little, King. I have been trading here, as I daresay you have heard, and have sold all my goods. Now I ask your leave to hunt buffalo, and other big game, for a while before I return to Natal."

"I cannot grant it," answered Cetywayo, "you are a spy sent by Sompseu, or by the Queen's Induna in Natal. Get you gone."

"Indeed," said Hadden, with a shrug of his shoulders; "then I hope that Sompseu, or the Queen's Induna, or both of them, will pay me when I return to my own country. Meanwhile I will obey you because I must, but I should first like to make you a present."

"What present?" asked the king. "I want no presents. We are rich here, White Man."

"So be it, King. It was nothing worthy of your taking, only a rifle."

"A rifle, White Man? Where is it?"

"Without. I would have brought it, but your servants told me that it is death to come armed before the 'Elephant who shakes the Earth.'"

Cetywayo frowned, for the note of sarcasm did not escape his quick ear.

"Let this white man's offering be brought; I will consider the thing."

Instantly the Induna who had accompanied Hadden darted to the gateway, running with his body bent so low that it seemed as though at every step he must fall upon his face. Presently he returned with the weapon in his hand and presented it to the king, holding it so that the muzzle was pointed straight at the royal breast.

"I crave leave to say, O Elephant," remarked Hadden in a drawling voice, "that it might be well to command your servant to lift the mouth of that gun from your heart."

"Why?" asked the king.

"Only because it is loaded, and at full cock, O Elephant, who probably desires to continue to shake the Earth."

At these words the "Elephant" uttered a sharp exclamation,

and rolled from his stool in a most unkingly manner, whilst the terrified Induna, springing backwards, contrived to touch the trigger of the rifle and discharge a bullet through the exact spot that a second before had been occupied by his monarch's head.

"Let him be taken away," shouted the incensed king from the ground, but long before the words had passed his lips the Induna, with a cry that the gun was bewitched, had cast it down and fled at full speed through the gate.

"He has already taken himself away," suggested Hadden, while the audience tittered. "No, King, do not touch it rashly; it is a repeating rifle. Look—" and lifting the Winchester, he fired the four remaining shots in quick succession into the air, striking the top of a tree at which he aimed with every one of them.

"*Wow*, it is wonderful!" said the company in astonishment.

"Has the thing finished?" asked the king.

"For the present it has," answered Hadden. "Look at it."

Cetywayo took the repeater in his hand, and examined it with caution, swinging the muzzle horizontally in an exact line with the stomachs of some of his most eminent Indunas, who shrank to this side and that as the barrel was brought to bear upon them.

"See what cowards they are, White Man," said the king with indignation; "they fear lest there should be another bullet in this gun."

"Yes," answered Hadden, "they are cowards indeed. I believe that if they were seated on stools they would tumble off them as it chanced to your Majesty to do just now."

"Do you understand the making of guns, White Man?" asked the king hastily, while the Indunas one and all turned their heads, and contemplated the fence behind them.

"No, King, I cannot make guns, but I can mend them."

"If I paid you well, White Man, would you stop here at my kraal, and mend guns for me?" asked Cetywayo anxiously.

"It might depend on the pay," answered Hadden; "but for a while I am tired of work, and wish to rest. If the king gives me the permission to hunt for which I asked, and men to go with me, then when I return perhaps we can bargain on the matter. If not, I will bid the king farewell, and journey to Natal."

"In order to make report of what he has seen and learned here," muttered Cetywayo.

At this moment the talk was interrupted, for the soldiers who had led away the old Induna returned at speed, and prostrated themselves before the king.

"Is he dead?" he asked.

"He has travelled the king's bridge," they answered grimly; "he died singing a song of praise to the king."

"Good," said Cetywayo, "that stone shall hurt my feet no more. Go, tell the tale of its casting away to Sompseu and to the Queen's Induna in Natal," he added with bitter emphasis.

"*Baba*! Hear our Father speak. Listen to the rumbling of the Elephant," said the Indunas taking the point, while one bolder than the rest added: "Soon we will tell them another tale, the white Talking Ones, a red tale, a tale of spears, and the regiments shall sing it in their ears."

At the words an enthusiasm caught hold of the listeners, as the sudden flame catches hold of dry grass. They sprand up, for the most of them were seated on their haunches, and stamping their feet upon the ground in unison, repeated:

> *Indaba ibomwu—indaba ye mikonto*
> *Lizo dunyiswa nge impi ndhlebeni yaho.*
> (A red tale! A red tale! A tale of spears,
> And the *impis* shall sing it in their ears.)

One of them, indeed, a great fierce-faced yellow, drew near to Hadden and shaking his fist before his eyes—fortunately being in the royal presence he had no assegai—shouted the sentences at him.

The king saw that the fire he had lit was burning too fiercely.

"Silence," he thundered in the deep voice for which he was remarkable, and instantly each man became as if he were turned to stone, only the echoes still answered back: "And the *impis* shall sing it in their ears—in their ears."

"I am growing certain that this is no place for me," thought Hadden; "if that scoundrel had been armed he might have temporarily forgotten himself. Hullo! who's this?"

Just then there appeared through the gate of the fence a splendid specimen of the Zulu race. The man, who was about thirty-five years of age, was arrayed in a full war dress of a captain of the Umcityu regiment. From the circlet of otter skin on his brow rose his crest of plumes, round his middle, arms and knees hung the long fringes of black oxtails, and in one hand he bore a little dancing shield, also black in colour. The other was empty, since he might not appear before the king bearing arms. In countenance the man was handsome, and though just now they betrayed some anxiety, his eyes were genial and honest, and his mouth sensitive. In height he must have measured six foot two inches, yet he did not strike the observer as being tall, perhaps because of his width of chest and the solidity of his limbs, that were in curious contrast to the delicate and almost womanish hands and feet which so often mark the Zulu of noble blood. In short the man was what he seemed to be, a savage gentleman of birth, dignity and courage.

In company with him was another man plainly dressed in a moocha and a blanket, whose grizzled hair showed him to be over fifty years of age. His face was pleasant and even refined, but the eyes were timorous, and the mouth lacked character.

"Who are these?" asked the king.

The two men fell on their knees before him, and bowed till their foreheads touched the ground—the while giving him his *sibonga* or titles of praise.

"Speak," he said impatiently.

"O King," said the young warrior, seating himself Zulu fashion, "I am Nahoon, the son of Zomba, a captain of the Umcityu, and this is my uncle, Umgona, the brother of one of my mothers, my father's youngest wife."

Cetywayo frowned. "What do you here away from your regiment, Nahoon?"

"May it please the king, I have leave of absence from the head captains, and I come to ask a boon of the king's bounty."

"Be swift, then, Nahoon."

"It is this, O King," said the captain with some embarrassment: "A while ago the king was pleased to make a *keshla* of me because of certain service that I did out yonder . . ." and he touched the black ring which he wore in the hair of his head. "Being now a ringed man and a captain, I crave the right of a man at the hands of the king—the right to marry."

"Right? Speak more humbly, son of Zomba; my soldiers and my cattle have no rights."

Nahoon bit his lip, for he had made a serious mistake.

"Pardon, O King. The matter stands thus: My uncle Umgona here has a fair daughter named Nanea, whom I desire to wife, and who desires me to husband. Awaiting the king's leave I am betrothed to her and in earnest of it I have paid to Umgona a *lobola* of fifteen head of cattle, cows and calves together. But Umgona has a powerful neighbour, an old chief named Maputa, the warden of the Crocodile Drift, who doubtless is known to the king, and this chief also seeks Nanea in marriage and harries Umgona, threatening him with many evils if he will not give the girl to him. But Umgona's heart is white towards me, and towards Maputa it is black, therefore together we come to crave this boon of the king."

"It is so; he speaks the truth," said Umgona.

"Cease," answered Cetywayo angrily. "Is this a time that my soldiers should seek wives in marriage, wives to turn their hearts to water? Know that but yesterday for this crime I commanded that twenty girls who had dared without my leave to marry men of the Undi regiment, should be strangled and their bodies laid upon the crossroads and with them the bodies of their fathers, that all might know their sin and be warned thereby. Ay, Umgona, it is well for you and for your daughter that you sought my word before she was given in marriage to this man. Now this is my award: I refuse your prayer, Nahoon, and since you, Umgona, are troubled with one whom you would not take as son-in-law, the old chief Maputa, I will free you from his importunity. The girl, says Nahoon, is fair—good, I myself will be gracious to her, and she shall be numbered among the wives of the royal house. Within thirty days from now, in the week of the next new moon, let her be delivered into the *Sigodhla*, the royal house of the women, and with her those cattle, the cows and calves together, that Nahoon has given you, of which I fine him because he has dared to think of marriage without the leave of the king."

II

The Bee Prophesies

"A Daniel come to judgment indeed," reflected Hadden, who had been watching this savage comedy with interest; "our love-sick friend has got more than he bargained for. Well, that comes of appealing to Caesar," and he turned to look at the two suppliants.

The old man, Umgona, merely started, then began to pour out sentences of conventional thanks and praise to the king for his goodness and condescension. Cetywayo listened to his talk in silence, and when he had done answered by reminding him tersely that if Nanea did not appear at the date named, both she and he, her father, would in due course certainly decorate a crossroad in their own immediate neighbourhood.

The captain, Nahoon, afforded a more curious study. As the fatal words crossed the king's lips, his face took on an expression of absolute astonishment, which was presently replaced by one of fury—the just fury of a man who suddenly has suffered an unutterable wrong. His whole frame quivered, the veins stood out in knots on his neck and forehead, and his fingers closed convulsively as though they were grasping the handle of a spear. Presently the rage passed away—for as well might a man be wroth with fate as with a Zulu despot—to be succeeded by the look of the most hopeless misery. The proud dark eyes grew dull, the copper-coloured face sank in and turned ashen, the mouth drooped, and down one corner of it there trickled a little line of blood springing from the lip bitten through in the effort to keep silence. Lifting his hand in salute to the king, the great man rose and staggered rather than walked towards the gate.

As he reached it, the voice of Cetywayo commanded him to stop. "Stay," he said, "I have a service for you, Nahoon, that shall drive out of your head these thoughts of wives and marriage. You see this white man here; he is my guest, and would hunt buffalo and big game in the bush country. I put him in your charge; take men with you, and see that he comes to no hurt. See also that you bring him before me within a month, or your life shall answer for it. Let him be here at my royal kraal in the first week of the new moon—when Nanea comes—and then I will tell you whether or no I agree with you that she is fair. Go now, my child, and you, White Man, go also; those who are to accompany you shall be with you at the dawn. Farewell, but remember we meet again at the new moon, when we will settle what pay you shall receive as keeper of my guns. Do not fail me, White Man, or I shall send after you, and my messengers are sometimes rough."

"This means that I am a prisoner," thought Hadden, "but it will go hard if I cannot manage to give them the slip somehow. I don't intend to stay in this country if war is declared, to be pounded into *mouti* (medicine), or have my eyes put out, or any little joke of that sort."

Ten days had passed, and one evening Hadden and his escort were encamped in a wild stretch of mountainous country lying between the Blood and Unvunyana Rivers, not more than eight miles from that "Place of the Little Hand" which within a few weeks was to become famous throughout the world by its native name of Isandhlwana. For three days they had been tracking the spoor of a small herd of buffalo that still inhabited the district, but as yet they had not come up with them. The Zulu hunters had suggested that they should follow the Unvunyana down towards the sea where game was more plentiful, but this neither Hadden, nor the captain, Nahoon, had been anxious to do, for reasons which each of them kept secret to himself. Hadden's object was to work gradually down to the Buffalo River across which he hoped to effect a retreat into Natal. That of Nahoon was to linger in the neighbourhood of the kraal of Umgona, which was situated not very far from their present camping place, in the vague hope that he might find an opportunity of speaking with or at least of seeing Nanea, the girl to whom he was affianced, who within a few weeks must be taken from him, and given over to the king.

A more eerie-looking spot than that where they were encamped Hadden had never seen. Behind them lay a tract of land—half-swamp and half-bush—in which the buffalo were supposed to be hiding. Beyond, in lonely grandeur, rose the mountain of Isandhlwana, while in front was an amphitheatre of the most gloomy forest, ringed round in the distance by sheer-sided hills. Into this forest there ran a river which drained the swamp, placidly enough upon the level. But it was not always level, for within three hundred yards of them it dashed suddenly over a precipice, of no great height but very steep, falling into a boiling rock-bound pool that the light of the sun never seemed to reach.

"What is the name of that forest, Nahoon?" asked Hadden.

"It is named *Emagudu*, The Home of the Dead," the Zulu replied absently, for he was looking towards the kraal of Nanea, which was situated an hour's walk away over the ridge to the right.

"The Home of the Dead! Why?"

"Because the dead live there, those whom we name the *Esemkofu*, the Speechless Ones, and with them other Spirits, the *Amahlosi*, from whom the breath of life has passed away, and who yet live on."

"Indeed," said Hadden, "and have you ever seen these ghosts?"

"Am I mad that I should go to look for them, White Man? Only the dead enter that forest, and it is on the borders of it that our people make offerings to the dead."

Followed by Nahoon, Hadden walked to the edge of the cliff and looked over it. To the left lay the deep and dreadful-looking pool, while close to the bank of it, placed upon a narrow strip of turf between the cliff and the commencement of the forest, was a hut.

"Who lives there?" asked Hadden.

"The great *Isanusi*—she who is named *Inyanga* or Doctoress; she who is named *Inyosi* (the Bee), because she gathers wisdom from the dead who grow in the forest."

"Do you think that she could gather enough wisdom to tell me whether I am going to kill any buffalo, Nahoon?"

"Mayhap, White Man, but," he added with a little smile, "those who visit the Bee's hive may hear nothing, or they may hear more than they wish for. The words of that Bee have a sting."

"Good; I will see if she can sting me."

"So be it," said Nahoon; and turning, he led the way along the cliff till he reached a native path which zig-zagged down its face.

By this path they climbed till they came to the sward at the foot of the descent, and walked up it to the hut which was surrounded by a low fence of reeds, enclosing a small courtyard paved with ant-heap earth beaten hard and polished. In this courtyard sat the Bee, her stool being placed almost at the mouth of the round opening that served as a doorway to the hut. At first all that Hadden could see of her, crouched as she was in the shadow, was a huddled shape wrapped round with a greasy and tattered catskin *kaross*, above the edge of which appeared two eyes, fierce and quick as those of a leopard. At her feet smouldered a little fire, and ranged around it in a semicircle were a number of human skulls, placed in pairs as though they were talking together, whilst other bones, to all appearance also human, were festooned about the hut and the fence of the courtyard.

"I see that the old lady is set up with the usual properties," thought Hadden, but he said nothing.

Nor did the witch-doctoress say anything; she only fixed her beady eyes upon his face. Hadden returned the compliment, staring at her with all his might, till suddenly he became aware that he was vanquished in this curious duel. His brain grew confused, and to his fancy it seemed that the woman before him had shifted shape into the likeness of a colossal and horrid spider sitting at the mouth of her trap, and that these bones were the relics of her victims.

"Why do you not speak, White Man?" she said at last in a slow clear voice. "Well, there is no need, since I can read your thoughts. You are thinking that I who am called the Bee should be better named the Spider. Have no fear; I did not kill these men. What would it profit me when the dead are so many? I suck the souls of men, not their bodies, White Man. It is their living hearts I love to look on, for therein I read much and thereby I grow wise. Now what would you of the Bee, White Man, the Bee that labours in this Garden of Death, and—what brings *you* here, son of Zomba? Why are you not with Umcityu now that they doctor themselves for the great war—the last war—the war of the white and the black—or if you have no stomach for fighting, why are you not at the side of Nanea the tall, Nanea the fair?"

Nahoon made no answer, but Hadden said:

"A small thing, mother. I would know if I shall prosper in my hunting."

"In your hunting, White Man; what hunting? The hunting of game, of money, or of women? Well, one of them, for a-hunting you must ever be; that is your nature, to hunt and be hunted. Tell me now, how goes the wound of that trader who tasted of your steel yonder in the town of the Maboon (Boers)? No need to answer, White Man, but what fee, Chief, for the poor witch-doctress whose skill you seek," she added in a whining voice. "Surely you would not that an old woman should work without a fee?"

"I have none to offer you, mother, so I will be going," said Hadden, who began to feel himself satisfied with this display of the Bee's powers of observation and thought-reading.

"Nay," she answered with an unpleasant laugh, "would you ask a question, and not wait for the answer? I will take no fee from you at present, White Man; you shall pay me later on when we meet again," and once more she laughed. "Let me look in your face, let me look in your face," she continued, rising and standing before him.

Then of a sudden Hadden felt something cold at the back of his neck, and the next instant the Bee had sprung from him, holding between her thumb and finger a curl of dark hair which she had cut from his head. The action was so instantaneous that he had neither time to avoid nor to resent it, but stood still staring at her stupidly.

"That is all I need," she cried, "for like my heart my magic is white. Stay—son of Zomba, give me also of your hair, for those who visit the Bee must listen to her humming."

Nahoon obeyed, cutting a little lock from his head with the sharp edge of his assegai, though it was very evident that he did this not because he wished to do so, but because he feared to refuse.

Then the Bee slipped back her *kaross*, and stood bending over the fire before them, into which she threw herbs taken from a pouch that was bound about her middle. She was still a finely-shaped woman, and she wore none of the abominations which

Hadden had been accustomed to see upon the persons of witch-doctoresses. About her neck, however, was a curious ornament, a small live snake, red and grey in hue, which her visitors recognised as one of the most deadly to be found in that part of the country. It is not unusual for Bantu witch-doctors thus to decorate themselves with snakes, though whether or not their fangs have first been extracted no one seems to know.

Presently the herbs began to smoulder, and the smoke of them rose up in a thin straight stream, that, striking upon the face of the Bee, clung about her head enveloping it as though with a strange blue veil. Then of a sudden she stretched out her hands, and let fall the two locks of hair upon the burning herbs, where they writhed themselves to ashes like things alive. Next she opened her mouth, and began to draw the fumes of the hair and herbs into her lungs in great gulps; while the snake, feeling the influence of the medicine, hissed and, uncoiling itself from about her neck, crept upwards and took refuge among the black *saccaboola* feathers of her head-dress.

Soon the vapours began to do their work; she swayed to and fro muttering, then sank back against the hut, upon the straw of which her head rested. Now the Bee's face was turned upwards towards the light, and it was ghastly to behold, for it had become blue in colour, and the open eyes were sunken like the eyes of one dead, whilst above her forehead the red snake wavered and hissed, reminding Hadden of the Uraeus crest on the brow of statues of Egyptian kings. For ten seconds or more she remained thus, then she spoke in a hollow and unnatural voice:

"O Black Heart and body that is white and beautiful, I look into your heart, and it is black as blood, and it shall be black with blood. Beautiful white body with a black heart, you shall find your game and hunt it, and it shall lead you into the House of the Homeless, into the Home of the Dead, and it shall be shaped as a bull, it shall be shaped as a tiger, it shall be shaped as a woman whom kings and waters cannot harm. Beautiful white body and black heart, you shall be paid your wages, money for money, and blow for blow. Think of my word when the spotted cat purrs above your breast; think of it when the battle roars about you; think of it when you grasp your great reward, and for the last time stand face to face with the ghost of the dead in the Home of the Dead.

"O White Heart and black body, I look into your heart and it is white as milk, and the milk of innocence shall save it. Fool, why do you strike that blow? Let him be who is loved of the tiger, and whose love is as the love of a tiger. Ah! what face is that in the battle? Follow it, follow it, O swift of foot; but follow warily, for the tongue that has lied will never plead for mercy, and the hand that can betray is strong in war. White Heart, what is death? In death life lives, and among the dead you shall find the life you lost, for there awaits you she whom kings and waters cannot harm.''

As the Bee spoke, by degrees her voice sank lower and lower till it was almost inaudible. Then it ceased altogether, and she seemed to pass from trance to sleep. Hadden, who had been listening to her with an amused and cynical smile, now laughed aloud.

"Why do you laugh, White Man?'' asked Nahoon angrily.

"I laugh at my own folly, in wasting time listening to the nonsense of that lying fraud.''

"It is no nonsense, White Man.''

"Indeed? Then will you tell me what it means?''

"I cannot tell you what it means yet, but her words have to do with a woman and a leopard, and with your fate and my fate.''

Hadden shrugged his shoulders, not thinking the matter worth further argument, and at that moment the Bee woke up shivering, drew the red snake from her head-dress and coiling it about her throat wrapped herself again in the greasy *kaross*.

"Are you satisfied with my wisdom, *Inkoos*?'' she asked of Hadden.

"I am satisfied that you are one of the cleverest cheats in Zululand, mother,'' he answered coolly. "Now, what is there to pay?''

The Bee took no offence at this rude speech, though for a second or two the look in her eyes grew strangely like that which they had seen in those of the snake when the fumes of the fire made it angry.

"If the white lord says I am a cheat, it must be so,'' she answered, "for he of all men should be able to discern a cheat. I have said that I ask no fee—yet, give me a little tobacco from your pouch.''

Hadden opened the bag of antelope hide and drawing some tobacco from it, gave it to her. In taking it she clasped his hand and examined the gold ring that was upon the third finger, a ring fashioned like a snake with two little rubies set in the head to represent the eyes.

"I wear a snake about my neck, and you wear one upon your hand, *Inkoos*. I should like to have this ring to wear upon my hand, so that the snake about my neck may be less lonely there.''

"Then I am afraid you will have to wait till I am dead," said Hadden.

"Yes, yes," she answered in a pleased voice, "it is a good word. I will wait till you are dead and then I will take the ring, and none can say that I have stolen it, for Nahoon there will bear me witness that you gave me permission to do so."

For the first time Hadden started, since there was something about the Bee's tone that jarred upon him. Had she addressed him in her professional manner, he would have thought nothing of it; but in her cupidity she had become natural, and it was evident that she spoke from conviction, believing her own words.

She saw him start, and instantly changed her note.

"Let the white lord forgive the jest of a poor old witch-doctoress," she said in a whining voice. "I have so much to do with Death that his name leaps to my lips," and she glanced first at the circle of skulls about her, then towards the waterfall that fed the gloomy pool upon whose banks her hut was placed.

"Look," she said simply.

Following the line of her outstretched hand Hadden's eyes fell upon two withered mimosa trees which grew over the fall almost at right angles to its rocky edge. These trees were joined together by a rude platform made of logs of wood lashed down with *riems* of hide. Upon this platform stood three figures: notwithstanding the distance and the spray of the fall, he could see that they were those of two men and a girl, for their shapes stood out distinctly against the fiery red of the sunset sky. One instant there were three, the next there were two—for the girl had gone, and something dark rushing down the face of the fall struck the surface of the pool with a heavy thud, while a faint and piteous cry broke upon his ear.

"What is the meaning of that?" he asked, horrified and amazed.

"Nothing," answered the Bee with a laugh. "Do you not know, then, that this is the place where faithless women, or girls who have loved without the leave of the king, are brought to meet their death, and with them their accomplices? Oh! they die here thus each day, and I watch them die and keep the count of the number of them," and drawing a tally-stick from the thatch of the hut, she took a knife and added a notch to the many that appeared upon it, looking at Nahoon the while with a half-questioning, half-warning gaze.

"Yes, yes, it is a place of death," she muttered. "Up yonder the quick die day by day and down there"—and she pointed along the course of the river beyond the pool to where the forest began some two hundred yards from her hut—"the ghosts of them have their home. Listen!"

As she spoke, a sound reached their ears that seemed to swell from the dim skirts of the forests, a peculiar and unholy sound which it is impossible to define more accurately than by saying that it seemed beastlike, and almost inarticulate.

"Listen," repeated the Bee, "they are merry yonder."

"Who?" asked Hadden; "the baboons?"

"No, *Inkoos*, the *Amatongo*—the ghosts that welcome her who has just become of their number."

"Ghosts," said Hadden roughly, for he was angry at his own tremors, "I should like to see those ghosts. Do you think that I have never heard a troop of monkeys in the bush before, mother? Come, Nahoon, let us be going while there is light to climb the cliff. Farewell."

"Farewell, *Inkoos*, and doubt not that your wish will be fulfilled. Go in peace, *Inkoos*—to sleep in peace."

III

The End of the Hunt

The prayer of the Bee notwithstanding, Philip Hadden slept ill that night. He felt in the best of health, and his conscience was not troubling him more than usual, but rest he could not. Whenever he closed his eyes, his mind conjured up a picture of the grim witch-doctoress, so strangely named the Bee, and the sound of her evil-omened words as he had heard them that afternoon. He was neither a superstitious nor a timid man, and any supernatural beliefs that might linger in his mind were, to say the least of it, dormant. But do what he might, he could not shake off a certain eerie sensation of fear, lest there should be some grains of truth in the prophesyings of this hag. What if it were a fact that he was near his death, and that the heart which beat so strongly in his breast must soon be still for ever—no, he would not think of it. This gloomy place, and the dreadful sight which he saw that day, had upset his nerves. The domestic customs of these Zulus were not pleasant, and for his part he was determined to be clear of them so soon as he was able to escape the country.

In fact, if he could in any way manage it, it was his intention to make a dash for the border on the following night. To do this with a good prospect of success, however, it was necessary that he should kill a buffalo, or some other head of game. Then, as he knew well, the hunters with him would feast upon meat until they could scarcely stir, and that would be his opportunity. Nahoon, however, might not succumb to this temptation; therefore he must trust to luck to be rid of him. If it came to the worst, he could put a bullet through him, which he considered he would be justified in doing, seeing that in reality the man was his jailor. Should this necessity arise, he felt indeed that he could face it without undue compunction, for in truth he disliked Nahoon; at times he even hated him. Their natures were antagonistic, and he knew that the great Zulu distrusted and looked down upon him, and to be looked down upon by a savage "nigger" was more than his pride could stomach.

At the first break of dawn Hadden rose and roused his escort, who were still stretched in sleep around the dying fire, each man wrapped in his kaross or blanket. Nahoon stood up and shook himself, looking gigantic in the shadows of the morning.

"What is your will, *Umlungu* (white man), that you are up before the sun?"

"My will, *Muntumpofu* (yellow man), is to hunt buffalo," answered Hadden coolly. It irritated him that this savage should give him no title of any sort.

"Your pardon," said the Zulu reading his thoughts, "but I cannot call you *Inkoos* because you are not my chief, or any man's; still if the title 'white man' offends you, we will give you a name."

"As you wish," answered Hadden briefly.

Accordingly they gave him a name, *Inhlizin-mgama,* by which he was known among them thereafter, but Hadden was not best pleased when he found that the meaning of those soft-sounding syllables was "Black Heart." That was how the *inyanga* had addressed him—only she used different words.

An hour later, and they were in the swampy bush country that lay behind the encampment searching for their game. Within a very little while Nahoon held up his hand, then pointed to the ground. Hadden looked; there, pressed deep in the marshy soil, and to all appearance not ten minutes old, was the spoor of a small herd of buffalo.

"I knew that we should find game today," whispered Nahoon, "because the Bee said so."

"Curse the Bee," answered Hadden below his breath. "Come on."

For a quarter of an hour or more they followed the spoor

through thick reeds, till suddenly Nahoon whistled very softly and touched Hadden's arm. He looked up, and there, about two hundred yards away, feeding on some higher ground among a patch of mimosa trees, were the buffalos—six of them—an old bull with a splendid head, three cows, a heifer and a calf about four months old. Neither the wind nor the nature of the veldt were favourable for them to stalk the game from their present position, so they made a detour of half a mile and very carefully crept towards them up the wind, slipping from trunk to trunk of the mimosas and when these failed them, crawling on their stomachs under cover of the tall *tambuti* grass. At last they were within forty yards, and a further advance seemed impracticable; for although he could not smell them, it was evident from his movements that the old bull heard some unusual sound and was growing suspicious. Nearest to Hadden, who alone of the party had a rifle, stood the heifer broadside on—a beautiful shot. Remembering that she would make the best beef, he lifted his Martini, and aiming at her immediately behind the shoulder, gently squeezed the trigger. The rifle exploded, and the heifer fell dead, shot through the heart. Strangely enough the other buffaloes did not at once run away. On the contrary, they seemed puzzled to account for the sudden noise; and, not being able to wind anything, lifted their heads and stared round them.

The pause gave Hadden space to get in a fresh cartridge and to aim again, this time at the old bull. The bullet struck him somewhere in the neck or shoulder, for he came to his knees, but in another second was up and having caught sight of the cloud of smoke he charged straight at it. Because of the smoke, or for some other reason, Hadden did not see him coming, and in consequence would most certainly have been trampled or gored, had not Nahoon sprung forward, at the imminent risk of his own life, and dragged him down behind an ant-heap. A moment more and the great beast had thundered by, taking no further notice of them.

"Forward," said Hadden, and leaving most of the men to cut up the heifer and carry the best of her meat to camp, they started on the blood spoor.

For some hours they followed the bull, till at last they lost the trail on a patch of stony ground thickly covered with bush, and exhausted by the heat, sat down to rest and to eat some *biltong* or sun-dried flesh which they had with them. They finished their meal, and were preparing to return to camp, when one of the four Zulus who were with them went to drink at a little stream that ran at a distance of not more than ten paces away. Half a minute later they heard a hideous grunting noise and a splashing of water, and saw the Zulu fly into the air. All the while that they were eating, the wounded buffalo had been lying in wait for them under a thick bush on the banks of the streamlet, knowing—cunning brute that he was—that sooner or later his turn would come. With a shout of consternation they rushed forward to see the bull vanish over the rise before Hadden could get a chance of firing at him, and to find their companion dying, for the great horn had pierced his lung.

"It is not a buffalo, it is a devil," the poor fellow gasped, and expired.

"Devil or not, I mean to kill it," exclaimed Hadden. So leaving the others to carry the body of their comrade to camp, he started on accompanied by Nahoon only. Now the ground was more open and the chase easier, for they sighted their quarry frequently, though they could not come near enough to fire. Presently they travelled down a steep cliff.

"Do you know where we are?" asked Nahoon, pointing to a belt of forest opposite. "That is *Emagudu*, the Home of the Dead—and look, the bull heads thither."

Hadden glanced round him. It was true; yonder to the left were the Fall, the Pool of Doom, and the hut of the Bee.

"Very well," he answered; "then we must head for it too."

Nahoon halted. "Surely you would not enter there," he exclaimed.

"Surely I will," replied Hadden, "but there is no need for you to do so if you are afraid."

"I am afraid—of ghosts," said the Zulu, "but I will come."

So they crossed the strip of turf, and entered the haunted wood. It was a gloomy place indeed; great wide-topped trees grew thick there shutting out the sight of the sky; moreover, the air in it which no breeze stirred, was heavy with the exhalations of rotting foliage. There seemed to be no life here and no sound—only now and again a loathsome spotted snake would uncoil itself and glide away, and now and again a heavy rotten bough fell with a crash.

Hadden was too intent upon the buffalo, however, to be much impressed by his surroundings. He only remarked that the light would be bad for shooting, and went on.

They must have penetrated a mile or more into the forest when the sudden increase of blood upon the spoor told them that the bull's wound was proving fatal to him.

"Run now," said Hadden cheerfully.

"Nay, *hamba gachle*—go softly—" answered Nahoon, "the devil is dying, but he will try to play us another trick before he dies." And he went on peering ahead of him cautiously.

"It is all right here, anyway," said Hadden, pointing to the spoor that ran straight forward printed deep in the marshy ground.

Nahoon did not answer, but stared steadily at the trunks of two trees a few paces in front of them and to their right. "Look," he whispered.

Hadden did so, and at length made out the outline of something brown that was crouched behind the trees.

"He is dead," he exclaimed.

"No," answered Nahoon, "he has come back on his own path and is waiting for us. He knows that we are following his spoor. Now if you stand here, I think that you can shoot him through the back between the tree trunks."

Hadden knelt down, and aiming very carefully at a point just below the bull's spine, he fired. There was an awful bellow, and the next instant the brute was up and at them. Nahoon flung his broad spear, which sank deep into its chest, then they fled this way and that. The buffalo stood still for a moment, its forelegs straddle wide and its head down, looking first after the one and then the other, till of a sudden it uttered a low moaning sound and rolled over dead, smashing Nahoon's assegai to fragments as it fell.

"There! he's finished," said Hadden, "and I believe it was your assegai that killed him. Hullo! what's that noise?"

Nahoon listened. In several quarters of the forest, but from how far away it was impossible to tell, there rose a curious sound, as of people calling to each other in fear but in no articulate language. Nahoon shivered.

"It is the *Esemkofu*," he said, "the ghosts who have no tongue, and who can only wail like infants. Let us be going; this place is bad for mortals."

"And worse for buffaloes," said Hadden, giving the dead bull a kick, "but I suppose that we must leave him here for your friends, the *Esemkofu*, as we have got meat enough, and can't carry his head."

So they started back towards the open country. As they threaded their way slowly through the tree trunks, a new idea came into Hadden's mind. Once out of this forest, he was within an hour's run of the Zulu border, and once over the Zulu border, he would feel a happier man than he did at that moment. As has been said, he had intended to attempt to escape in the darkness, but the plan was risky. All the Zulus might not over-eat themselves and go to sleep, especially after the death of their comrade; Nahoon, who watched him day and night, certainly would not. This was his opportunity—there remained the question of Nahoon.

Well, if it came to the worst, Nahoon must die; it would be easy—he had a loaded rifle, and now that his assegai was gone, Nahoon had only a kerry. He did not wish to kill the man, though it was clear to him, seeing that his own safety was at stake, that he would be amply justified in so doing. Why should he not put it to him—and then be guided by circumstances?

Nahoon was walking across a little open space about ten paces ahead of him where Hadden could see him very well, whilst he himself was under the shadow of a large tree with low horizontal branches running out from the trunk.

"Nahoon," he said.

The Zulu turned round, and took a step towards him.

"No, do not move, I pray. Stand where you are, or I shall be obliged to shoot you. Listen now: do not be afraid for I shall not fire without warning. I am your prisoner, and you are charged to take me back to the king to be his servant. But I believe that a war is going to break out between your people and mine; and this being so, you will understand that I do not wish to go to Cetywayo's kraal, because I should either come to a violent death there, or my own brothers will believe that I am a traitor and treat me accordingly. The Zulu border is not much more than an hour's journey away—let us say an hour and a half's: I mean to be across it before the moon is up. Now, Nahoon, will you lose me in the forest and give me this hour and a half's start—or will you stop here with that ghost people of whom you talk? Do you understand? No, please do not move."

"I understand you," answered the Zulu, in a perfectly composed voice, "and I think that was a good name which we gave you this morning, though, Black Heart, there is some justice in your words and more wisdom. Your opportunity is good, and one which a man named as you are should not let fall."

"I am glad to find that you take this view of the matter, Nahoon. And now will you be so kind as to lose me, and to promise not to look for me till the moon is up?"

"What do you mean, Black Heart?"

"What I say. Come, I have no time to spare."

"You are a strange men," said the Zulu reflectively. "You heard the king's order to me: would you have me disobey the order of the king?"

"Certainly, I would. You have no reason to love Cetywayo, and it does not matter to you whether or not I return to his kraal to mend guns there. If you think that he will be angry because I am missing, you had better cross the border also; we can go together."

"And leave my father and all my brethren to his vengeance? Black Heart, you do not understand. How can you, being so named? I am a soldier, and the king's word is the king's word. I hoped to have died fighting, but I am the bird in your noose. Come, shoot, or you will not reach the border before moonrise," and he opened his arms and smiled.

"If it must be, so let it be. Farewell, Nahoon, at least you are a brave man, but every one of us must cherish his own life," answered Hadden calmly.

Then with much deliberation he raised his rifle and covered the Zulu's breast.

Already—whilst his victim stood there still smiling, although a twitching of his lips betrayed the natural terrors that no bravery can banish—already his finger was contracting on the trigger, when of a sudden, as instantly indeed as though he had been struck by lightning, Hadden went down backwards, and behold! there stood upon him a great spotted beast that waved its long tail to and fro and glared down into his eyes.

It was a leopard—a tiger as they call it in Africa—which, crouched upon a bough of the tree above, had been unable to resist the temptation of satisfying its savage appetite on the man below. For a second or two there was silence, broken only by the purring, or rather the snoring sound made by the leopard. In those seconds, strangely enough, there sprang up before Hadden's mental vision a picture of the *inyanga* called *Inyosi* or the Bee, her death-like head resting against the thatch of the hut, and her death-like lips muttering "think of my word when the great cat purrs above your face."

Then the brute put out its strength. The claws of one paw it drove deep into the muscles of his left thigh, while with another it scratched at his breast, tearing the clothes from it and furrowing the flesh beneath. The sight of the white skin seemed to madden it, and in its fierce desire for blood it drooped its square muzzle and buried its fangs in its victim's shoulder. Next moment there was a sound of rushing feet and of a club falling heavily. Up reared the leopard with an angry snarl, up till it stood as high as the attacking Zulu. At him it came, striking out savagely and tearing the black man as it had torn the white.

Again the kerry fell full on its jaws, and down it went backwards. Before it could rise again, or rather as it was in the act of rising, the heavy knob-stick struck it once more, and with fearful force, this time as it chanced, full on the nape of the neck, and paralysing the brute. It writhed and bit and twisted, throwing up the earth and leaves, while blow after blow was rained upon it, till at length with a convulsive struggle and a stifled roar it lay still—the brains oozing from its shattered skull.

Hadden sat up, the blood running from his wounds.

"You have saved my life, Nahoon," he said faintly, "and I thank you."

"Do not thank me, Black Heart," answered the Zulu, "it was the king's word that I should keep you safely. Still this tiger has been hardly dealt with, for certainly *he* has saved *my* life," and lifting the Martini he unloaded the rifle.

At this juncture Hadden swooned away.

Twenty-four hours had gone by when, after what seemed to him to be but a little time of troubled and dreamful sleep, through which he could hear voices without understanding what they said, and feel himself borne he knew not whither, Hadden awoke to find himself lying upon a *kaross* in a large and beautifully clean Kaffir hut with a bundle of furs for a pillow. There was a bowl of milk at his side, and tortured as he was by thirst, he tried to stretch out his arm to lift it to his lips, only to find to his astonishment that his hand fell back to his side like that of a dead man. Looking round the hut impatiently, he found that there was nobody in it to assist him, so he did the only thing which remained for him to do—he lay still. He did not fall asleep, but his eyes closed, and a kind of gentle torpor crept over him, half obscuring his recovered senses. Presently he heard a soft voice speaking; it seemed far away, but he could clearly distinguish the words.

"Black Heart still sleeps," the voice said, "but there is colour in his face; I think that he will wake soon, and find his thoughts again."

"Have no fear, Nanea, he will surely wake, his hurts are not dangerous," answered another voice, that of Nahoon. "He fell heavily with the weight of the tiger on top of him, and that is why his senses have been shaken for so long. He went near to death, but certainly he will not die."

"It would have been a pity if he had died," answered the soft voice, "he is so beautiful; never have I seen a white man who was so beautiful."

"I did not think him beautiful when he stood with his rifle pointed at my heart," answered Nahoon sulkily.

"Well, there is this to be said," she replied, "he wished to escape from Cetywayo, and that is not to be wondered at," and she sighed. "Moreover he asked you to come with him, and it might have been well if you had done so, that is, if you would have taken me with you!"

"How could I have done it, girl?" he asked angrily. "Would you have me set at nothing the order of the king?"

"The king!" she replied raising her voice. "What do you owe to the king? You have served him faithfully, and your reward is that within a few days he will take me from you—me, who should have been your wife, and I must—I must . . ." And she began to weep softly, adding between her sobs, "If you loved me truly, you would think more of me and of yourself, and less of the Black One and his orders. Oh! let us fly, Nahoon, let us fly to Natal before this spear pierces me."

"Weep not, Nanea," he said; "why do you tear my heart in two between my duty and my love? You know that I am a soldier, and that I must walk the path whereon the king has set my feet. Soon I think I shall be dead, for I seek death, and then it will matter nothing."

"Nothing to you, Nahoon, who are at peace, but to me? Yet, you are right, and I know it, therefore forgive me, who am no warrior, but a woman who must also obey the will of the king." And she cast her arms about his neck, sobbing her fill upon his breast.

IV

Nanea

Presently, muttering something that the listener could not catch, Nahoon left Nanea, and crept out of the hut by its bee-hole entrance. Then Hadden opened his eyes and looked around him. The sun was sinking and a ray of its red light streaming through the little opening filled the place with a soft and crimson glow. In the centre of the hut—supporting it—stood a thorn-wood roof-tree coloured black by the smoke of the fire; and against this, the rich light falling full upon her, leaned the girl Nanea—a very picture of gentle despair.

As is occasionally the case among Zulu women, she was beautiful—so beautiful that the sight of her went straight to the white man's heart, for a moment causing the breath to catch in his throat. Her dress was very simple. On her shoulders, hanging open in front, lay a mantle of soft white stuff edged with blue beads, about her middle was a buck-skin moocha, also embroidered with blue beads, while round her forehead and left knee were strips of grey fur, and on her right wrist a shining bangle of copper. Her naked bronzed-hued figure was tall and perfect in its proportions; while her face had little in common with that of the ordinary native girl, showing as it did strong traces of ancestral Arabian or Semitic blood. It was oval in shape, with delicate aquiline features, arched eyebrows, a full mouth, that drooped a little at the corners, tiny ears, behind which the wavy coal-black hair hung down to the shoulders, and the very loveliest pair of dark and liquid eyes that it is possible to imagine.

For a minute or more Nanea stood thus, her sweet face bathed in the sunbeam, while Hadden feasted his eyes upon its beauty. Then sighing heavily, she turned, and seeing that he was awake, started, drew her mantle over her breast and came, or rather glided, towards him.

"The chief is awake," she said in her soft Zulu accents. "Does he need aught?"

"Yes, Lady," he answered; "I need to drink, but alas! I am too weak."

She knelt down beside him, and supporting him with her left arm, with her right held the gourd to his lips.

How it came about Hadden never knew, but before that draught was finished a change passed over him. Whether it was the savage girl's touch, or her strange and fawn-like loveliness, or the tender pity in her eyes, matters not—the issue was the same. She struck some chord in his turbulent uncurbed nature, and of a sudden it was filled full with passion for her—a passion which if not elevated, at least was real. He did not for a moment mistake the significance of the flood of feeling that surged through his veins. Hadden never shirked facts.

"By Heaven!" he said to himself, "I have fallen in love with a black beauty at first sight—more in love than I have ever been before. It's awkward, but there will be compensations. So much the worse for Nahoon, or for Cetywayo, or for both of them. After all, I can always get rid of her if she becomes a nuisance."

Then, in a fit of renewed weakness, brought about by the turmoil of his blood, he lay back upon the pillow of furs, watching Nanea's face while with a native salve of pounded leaves she busied herself dressing the wounds that the leopard had made.

It almost seemed as though something of what was passing in his mind communicated itself to that of the girl. At least, her hand shook a little at her task, and getting done with it as quickly as she could, she rose from her knees with a courteous "It is finished, *Inkoos*," and once more took up her position by the roof-tree.

"I thank you, Lady," he said; "your hand is kind."

"You must not call me lady, *Inkoos*," she answered, "I am no chieftainess, but only the daughter of a headman, Umgona."

"And named Nanea," he said. "Nay, do not be surprised, I have heard of you. Well, Nanea, perhaps you will soon become a chieftainess—up at the king's kraal yonder."

"Alas! and alas!" she said, covering her face with her hands.

"Do not grieve, Nanea, a hedge is never so tall and thick but that it can be climbed or crept through."

She let fall her hands and looked at him eagerly, but he did not pursue the subject.

"Tell me, how did I come here, Nanea?"

"Nahoon and his companions carried you, *Inkoos*."

"Indeed, I begin to be thankful to the leopard that struck me down. Well, Nahoon is a brave man, and he has done me a great service. I trust that I may be able to repay it—to you, Nanea."

This was the first meeting of Nanea and Hadden; but, although she did not seek them, the necessities of his sickness and of the situation brought about many another. Never for a moment did the white man waver in his determination to get into his keeping the native girl who had captivated him, and to attain his end he brought to bear all his powers and charm to detach her from Nahoon, and win her affections for himself. He was no rough wooer, however, but proceeded warily, weaving her about with a web of flattery and attention that must, he thought, produce the desired effect upon her mind. Without a doubt, indeed, it would have done so—for she was but a woman, and an untutored one—had it not been for a simple fact which dominated her whole nature. She loved Nahoon, and there was no room in her heart for any other man, white or black. To Hadden she was courteous and kindly but no more, nor did she appear to notice any of the subtle advances by which he attempted to win a foothold in her heart. For a while this puzzled him, but he remembered that the Zulu women do not usually permit themselves to show feeling towards an undeclared suitor. Therefore it became necessary that he should speak out.

His mind once made up, he had not to wait long for an opportunity. He was now quite recovered from his hurts, and accustomed to walk in the neighbourhood of the kraal. About two hundred yards from Umgona's huts rose a spring, and thither it was Nanea's habit to resort in the evening to bring back drinking-water for the use of her father's household. The path between this spring and the kraal ran through a patch of bush, where on a certain afternoon towards sundown Hadden took his seat under a tree, having first seen Nanea go down to the little stream as was her custom. A quarter of an hour later she reappeared carrying a large gourd upon her head. She wore no garment now except her moocha, for she had but one mantle and was afraid lest the water should splash it. He watched her advancing along the path, her hands resting on her hips, her splendid naked figure outlined against the westering sun, and wondered what excuse he could make to talk with her. As it chanced fortune favoured him, for when she was near him a snake glided across the path in front of the girl's feet, causing her to spring backwards in alarm and overset the gourd of water. He came forward, and picked it up.

"Wait here," he said laughing; "I will bring it to you full."

"Nay, *Inkoos*," she remonstrated, "that is a woman's work."

"Among my people," he said, "the men love to work for the women," and he started for the spring, leaving her wondering.

Before he reached her again, he regretted his gallantry, for it was necessary to carry the handleless gourd upon his shoulder, and the contents of it spilling over the edge soaked him. Of this, however, he said nothing to Nanea.

"There is your water, Nanea, shall I carry it for you to the kraal?"

"Nay, *Inkoos*, I thank you, but give it to me, you are weary with its weight."

"Stay awhile, and I will accompany you. Ah! Nanea, I am still weak, and had it not been for you I think that I should be dead."

"It was Nahoon who saved you—not I, *Inkoos*."

"Nahoon saved my body, but you, Nanea, you alone can save my heart."

"You talk darkly, *Inkoos*."

"Then I must make my meaning clear, Nanea. I love you."

She opened her brown eyes wide.

"You, a white lord, love me, a Zulu girl? How can that be?"

"I do not know, Nanea, but it is so, and were you not blind you would have seen it. I love you, and I wish to take you to wife."

"Nay, *Inkoos*, it is impossible. I am already betrothed."

"Ay," he answered, "betrothed to the king."

"No, betrothed to Nahoon."

"But it is the king who will take you within a week; is it not so? And would you not rather that I should take you than the king?"

"It seems to be so, *Inkoos*, and I would rather go with you than with the king, but most of all I desire to marry Nahoon. It may be that I shall not be able to marry him, but if that is so, at least I will never become one of the king's women."

"How will you prevent it, Nanea?"

"There are waters in which a maid may drown, and trees upon which she can hang," she answered with a quick setting of the mouth.

"That were a pity, Nanea, you are too fair to die."

"Fair or foul, yet I die, *Inkoos*."

"No, no, come with me—I will find a way—and be my wife," and he put his arm about her waist, and strove to draw her to him.

Without any violence of movement, and with the most perfect dignity, the girl disengaged herself from his embrace.

"You have honoured me, and I thank you, *Inkoos*," she said quietly, "but you do not understand. I am the wife of Nahoon—I belong to Nahoon; therefore, I cannot look on any other man while Nahoon lives. It is not our custom, *Inkoos*, for we are not as the white women, but ignorant and simple, and when we vow ourselves to a man, we abide by that vow till death."

"Indeed," said Hadden; "and so now you go to tell Nahoon that I have offered to make you my wife."

"No, *Inkoos*, why should I tell Nahoon your secrets? I have said 'nay' to you, not 'yea,' therefore he has no right to know," and she stooped to lift the gourd of water.

Hadden considered the situation rapidly, for his repulse only made him the more determined to succeed. Of a sudden under the emergency he conceived a scheme, or rather its rough outline. It was not a nice scheme, and some men might have shrunk from it, but as he had no intention of suffering himself to be defeated by a Zulu girl, he decided—with regret, it is true—that having failed to attain his ends by means which he considered fair, he must resort to other of more doubtful character.

"Nanea," he said, "you are a good and honest woman, and I respect you. As I have told you, I love you also, but if you refuse to listen to me there is nothing more to be said, and after all, perhaps it would be better that you should marry one of your own people. But, Nanea, you will never marry him, for the king will take you; and, if he does not give you to some other man, either you will become one of his 'sisters,' or to be free of him, as you say, you will die. Now hear me, for it is because I love you and wish your welfare that I speak thus. Why do you not escape into Natal, taking Nahoon with you, for there as you know you may live in peace out of reach of the arm of Cetywayo?"

"That is my desire, *Inkoos,* but Nahoon will not consent. He says that there is to be war between us and you white men, and he will not break the command of the king and desert from his army."

"Then he cannot love you much, Nanea, and at least you have to think of yourself. Whisper into the ear of your father and fly together, for be sure that Nahoon will soon follow you. Ay! and I myself will fly with you, for I too believe that there must be war, and then a white man in this country will be as a lamb among the eagles."

"If Nahoon will come, I will go, *Inkoos,* but I cannot fly without Nahoon; it is better I should stay here and kill myself."

"Surely then being so fair and loving him so well, you can teach him to forget his folly and to escape with you. In four days' time we must start for the king's kraal, and if you win over Nahoon, it will be easy for us to turn our faces southwards and cross the river that lies between the land of the Amazulu and Natal. For the sake of all of us, but most of all for your own sake, try to do this, Nanea, whom I have loved and whom I now would save. See him and plead with him as you know how, but as yet do not tell him that I dream of flight, for then I should be watched."

"In truth, I will, *Inkoos,*" she answered earnestly, "and oh! I thank you for your goodness. Fear not that I will betray you— first would I die. Farewell."

"Farewell, Nanea," and taking her hand he raised it to his lips.

Late that night, just as Hadden was beginning to prepare himself for sleep, he heard a gentle tapping at the board which closed the entrance to his hut.

"Enter," he said, unfastening the door, and presently by the light of the little lantern that he had with him, he saw Nanea creep into the hut, followed by the great form of Nahoon.

"*Inkoos,*" she said in a whisper when the door was closed again, "I have pleaded with Nahoon, and he has consented to fly; moreover, my father will come also."

"Is it so, Nahoon?" asked Hadden.

"It is so," answered the Zulu, looking down shamefacedly; "to save this girl from the king, and because the love of her eats out my heart, I have bartered away my honour. But I tell you, Nanea, and you, White Man, as I told Umgona just now, that I think no good will come of this flight, and if we are caught or betrayed, we shall be killed every one of us."

"Caught we can scarcely be," broke in Nanea anxiously, "for who could betray us, except the *Inkoos* here—"

"Which he is not likely to do," said Hadden quietly, "seeing that he desires to escape with you, and that his life is also at stake."

"That is so, Black Heart," said Nahoon, "otherwise I tell you that I should not have trusted you."

Hadden took no notice of this outspoken saying, but until very late that night they sat there together making their plans.

On the following morning Hadden was awakened by sounds of violent altercation. Going out of his hut he found that the disputants were Umgona and a fat and evil-looking Kaffir chief who had arrived at the kraal on a pony. This chief, he soon discovered, was named Maputa, being none other than the man who had sought Nanea in marriage and brought about Nahoon's and Umgona's unfortunate appeal to the king. At present he was engaged in abusing Umgona furiously, charging him with having stolen certain of his oxen and bewitched his cows so that they would not give milk. The alleged theft it was comparatively easy to disprove, but the wizardry remained a matter of argument.

"You are a dog, and a son of a dog," shouted Maputa, shaking his fat fist in the face of the trembling but indignant Umgona. "You promised me your daughter in marriage, then having vowed her to that *umfagozan*—that low lout of a soldier, Nahoon, the son of Zomba—you went, the two of you, and poisoned the king's ear against me, bringing me into trouble with the king, and now you have bewitched my cattle. Well, wait, I will be even with you, Wizard; wait till you wake up in the cold morning to find your fence red with fire, and the slayers standing outside your gates to eat up you and yours with spears—"

At this juncture Nahoon, who till now had been listening in silence, intervened with effect.

"Good," he said, "we will wait, but not in your company, Chief Maputa. *Hamba!* (go)" and seizing the fat old ruffian by the scruff of his neck, he flung him backwards with such violence that he rolled over and over down the little slope.

Hadden laughed, and passed on towards the stream where he

proposed to bathe. Just as he reached it, he caught sight of
Maputa riding along the footpath, his head-ring covered with
mud, his lips purple and his black face livid with rage.

"There goes an angry man," he said to himself. "Now, how
would it be . . .'' and he looked upwards like one seeking an
inspiration. It seemed to come; perhaps the devil finding it open
whispered in his ear, at any rate—in a few seconds his plan was
formed, and he was walking through the bush to meet Maputa.

"Go in peace, Chief," he said; "they seem to have treated
you roughly up yonder. Having no power to interfere, I came
away for I could not bear the sight. It is indeed shameful that an
old and venerable man of rank should be struck into the dirt, and
beaten by a soldier drunk with beer."

"Shameful, White Man!" gasped Maputa; "your words are
true indeed. But wait a while. I, Maputa, will roll that stone
over, I will throw that bull upon its back. When next the harvest
ripens, this I promise, that neither Nahoon nor Umgona, nor any
of his kraal shall be left to gather it."

"And how will you manage that, Maputa?"

"I do not know, but I will find a way. Oh! I tell you, a way
shall be found."

Hadden patted the pony's neck meditatively, then leaning
forward, he looked the chief in the eyes and said:

"What will you give me, Maputa, if I show you that way, a
sure and certain one, whereby you may be avenged to the death
upon Nahoon, whose violence I also have seen, and upon Umgona,
whose witchcraft brought sore sickness upon me?"

"What reward do you seek, White Man?" asked Maputa
eagerly.

"A little thing, Chief, a thing of no account, only the girl
Nanea, to whom as it chances I have taken a fancy."

"I wanted her for myself, White Man, but he who sits at
Ulundi has laid his hand upon her."

"That is nothing, Chief; I can arrange with him who 'sits at
Ulundi'. It is you who are great here that I wish to come to terms.
Listen: if you grant my desire, not only will I fulfil yours upon
your foes, but when the girl is delivered into my hands I will
give you this rifle and a hundred rounds of cartridges."

Maputa looked at the sporting Martini, and his eyes glistened.

"It is good," he said; "it is very good. Often have I wished
for such a gun that will enable me to shoot game, and to talk
with my enemies from far away. Promise it to me, White Man,
and you shall take the girl if I can give her to you."

"You swear it, Maputa?"

"I swear it by the head of Chaka, and the spirits of my fathers."

"Good. At dawn on the fourth day from now it is the purpose of Umgona, his daughter Nanea, and Nahoon, to cross the river into Natal by the drift that is called Crocodile Drift, taking their cattle with them and flying from the king. I also shall be of their company, for they know that I have learned their secret, and would murder me if I tried to leave them. Now you, who are chief of the border and guardian of that drift, must hide at night with some men among the rocks in the shallows of the drift and await our coming. First Nanea will cross driving the cows and calves, for so it is arranged, and I shall help her; then will follow Umgona and Nahoon with the oxen and heifers. On these two you must fall, killing them and capturing the cattle, and afterwards I will give you the rifle."

"What if the king ask for the girl, White Man?"

"Then you shall answer that in the uncertain light you did not recognise her and so she slipped away from you; moreover, that at first you feared to seize the girl lest her cries should alarm the men and they should escape you."

"Good, but how can I be sure that you will give me the gun once you are across the river?"

"Thus: before I enter the ford I will lay the rifle and cartridges upon a stone by the bank, telling Nanea that I shall return to fetch them when I have driven over the cattle."

"It is well, White Man; I will not fail you."

So the plot was made, and after some further conversation upon points of detail, the two conspirators shook hands and parted.

"That ought to come off all right," reflected Hadden to himself as he plunged and floated in the waters of the stream, "but somehow I don't quite trust our friend Maputa. It would have been better if I could have relied upon myself to get rid of Nahoon and his respected uncle—a couple of shots would do it in the water. But then that would be murder and murder is unpleasant; whereas the other thing is only the delivery to justice of two base deserters, a laudable action in a military country. Also personal interference upon my part might turn the girl against me; while after Umgona and Nahoon have been wiped out by Maputa, she *must* accept my escort. Of course there is a risk, but in every walk of life the most cautious have to take risks at times."

As it chanced, Philip Hadden was correct in his suspicions of his coadjutor, Maputa. Even before that worthy chief reached his own kraal, he had come to the conclusion that the white man's plan, though attractive in some ways, was too dangerous, since it was certain that if the girl Nanea escaped, the king would be indignant. Moreover, the men he took with him to do the killing in the drift would suspect something and talk. On the other hand he would earn much credit with his majesty by revealing the plot, saying that he had learned it from the lips of the white hunter, whom Umgona and Nahoon had forced to participate in it, and of whose coveted rifle he must trust to chance to possess himself.

An hour later two discreet messengers were bounding across the plains, bearing words from the Chief Maputa, the Warden of the Border, to the "great Black Elephant" at Ulundi.

V

The Doom Pool

Fortune showed itself strangely favourable to the plans of Nahoon and Nanea. One of the Zulu captain's perplexities was as to how he should lull the suspicions and evade the vigilance of his own companions, who together with himself had been detailed by the king to assist Hadden in his hunting and to guard against his escape. As it chanced, however, on the day after the incident of the visit of Maputa, a messenger arrived from no less a person than the great military Induna, Tvingwayo ka Marolo, who afterwards commanded the Zulu army at Isandhlwana; ordering these men to return to their regiment, the Umcityu Corps, which was to be placed upon full war footing. Accordingly Nahoon sent them, saying that he himself would follow with Black Heart in the course of a few days, as at present the white man was not sufficiently recovered from his hurts to allow of his travelling fast and far. So the soldiers went, doubting nothing.

Then Umgona gave it out that in obedience to the command of the king he was about to start for Ulundi, taking with him his daughter Nanea to be delivered over into the *Sigodhla*, and also those fifteen head of cattle that had been *lobola'd* by Nahoon in consideration of his forthcoming marriage, whereof he had been fined by Cetywayo. Under pretence that they required a change of veldt, the rest of his cattle he sent away in charge of a Basuto herd who knew nothing of their plans, telling him to keep them by the Crocodile Drift, as there the grass was good and sweet.

All preparations being completed, on the third day the party started, heading straight for Ulundi. After they had travelled some miles, however, they left the road and turning sharp to the right, passed unobserved of any through a great stretch of uninhabited bush. Their path now lay not far from the Pool of Doom, which, indeed, was close to Umgona's kraal, and the forest that was called Home of the Dead, but out of sight of these. It was their plan to travel by night, reaching the broken country near the Crocodile Drift on the following morning. Here they proposed to lie hid that day and through the night; then, having first collected the cattle which had preceded them, to cross the river at the break of dawn and escape into Natal. At least this was the plan of his companions; but, as we know, Hadden had another programme, wherein after one last appearance two of the party would play no part.

During that long afternoon's journey Umgona, who knew every inch of the country, walked ahead driving the fifteen cattle and carrying in his hand a long travelling stick of black and white *umzimbeet* wood, for in truth the old man was in a hurry to reach his journey's end. Next came Nahoon, armed with a broad assegai, but naked except for his moocha and necklet of baboon's teeth, and with him Nanea in her white bead-bordered mantle. Hadden, who brought up the rear, noticed that the girl seemed to be under the spell of an imminent apprehension, for from time to time she clasped her lover's arm, and looking into his face, addressed him with vehemence, almost with passion.

Curiously enough, the sight touched Hadden, and once or twice he was shaken by so sharp a pang of remorse at the thought of his share in this tragedy, that he cast about in his mind seeking a means to unravel the web of death which he himself had woven. But ever that evil voice was whispering in his ear. It reminded him that he, the white *Inkoos*, had been refused by this dusky beauty, and that if he found a way to save him, within some few hours she would be the wife of the savage gentleman at her side, the man who had named him Black Heart and who despised him, the man whom he had meant to murder and who immediately repaid his treachery by rescuing him from the jaws of the leopard at the risk of his own life. Moreover, it was a law of Hadden's existence never to deny himself anything that he desired if it lay within his power to take it—a law which had led him always deeper into sin. In other respects, indeed, it had not carried him far, for in the past he had desired much, and he had won little; but this particular flower was to his hand, and he would pluck it. If Nahoon stood between him and the flower, so much the worse for Nahoon, and if it should wither in his grasp, so much the worse for the flower; it could always be thrown away. Thus it came about that, not for the first time in his life, Philip Hadden discarded the somewhat spasmodic prick-ings of conscience and listened to that evil whispering at his ear.

About half-past five o'clock in the afternoon the four refugees passed the stream that a mile or so down fell over the little precipice into the Doom Pool; and, entering a patch of thorn trees on the further side, walked straight into the midst of two-and-twenty soldiers, who were beguiling the tedium of ex-pectancy by the taking of snuff and the smoking of *dakka* or native hemp. With these soldiers, seated on his pony, for he was too fat to walk, waited the Chief Maputa.

Observing that their expected guests had arrived, the men knocked out the *dakka* pipe, replaced the snuff boxes in the slits made in the lobes of their ears, and secured the four of them.

"What is the meaning of this, O King's soldiers?" asked Umgona in a quavering voice. "We journey to the kraal of U'Cetywayo; why do you molest us?"

"Indeed. Wherefore then are your faces set towards the south? Does the Black One live in the south? Well, you will journey to another kraal presently," answered the jovial-looking captain of the party with a callous laugh.

"I do not understand," stammered Umgona.

"Then I will explain while you rest," said the captain. "The Chief Maputa yonder sent word to the Black One at Ulundi that he had learned of your intended flight to Natal from the lips of this white man, who had warned him of it. The Black One was angry, and despatched us to catch you and make an end of you. That is all. Come on now, quietly, and let us finish the matter. As the Doom Pool is near, your deaths will be easy."

Nahoon heard the words, and sprang straight at the throat of Hadden; but he did not reach it, for the soldiers pulled him down. Nanea heard them also, and turning, looked the traitor in the eye; she said nothing, she only looked, but he could never forget that look. The white man for his part was filled with a fiery indignation against Maputa.

"You wicked villain," he gasped, whereat the chief smiled in a sickly fashion, and turned away.

Then they were marched along the banks of the stream till they reached the waterfall that fell into the Pool of Doom.

Hadden was a brave man after his fashion, but his heart quailed as he gazed into that abyss.

"Are you going to throw me in there?" he asked of the Zulu captain in a thick voice.

"You, White Man?" replied the soldier unconcernedly. "No, our orders are to take you to the king, but what he will do with you I do not know. There is to be war between your people and ours, so perhaps he means to pound you into medicine for the use of the witch-doctors, or to peg you over an ant-heap as a warning to other white men."

Hadden received this information in silence, but its effect upon his brain was bracing, for instantfy he began to search out some means of escape.

By now the party had halted near the two thorn trees that hung over the waters of the pool.

"Who dives first?" asked the captain of the Chief Maputa.

"The old wizard," he replied, nodding at Umgona; "then his daughter after him, and last of all this fellow," and he struck Nahoon in the face with his open hand.

"Come on, Wizard," said the captain, grasping Umgona by the arm, "and let us see how you can swim."

At the words of doom Umgona seemed to recover his self-command, after the fashion of his race.

"No need to lead me, soldier," he said, shaking himself loose, "who am old and ready to die." Then he kissed his daughter at his side, wrung Nahoon by the hand, and turning from Hadden with a gesture of contempt walked out upon the platform that joined the two thorn trunks. Here he stood for a moment looking at the setting sun, then suddenly, and without a sound, he hurled himself into the abyss below and vanished.

"That was a brave one," said the captain with admiration. "Can you spring too, girl, or must we throw you?"

"I can walk my father's path," Nanea answered faintly, "but first I crave leave to say one word. It is true that we were escaping from the king, and therefore by the law we must die; but it was Black Heart here who made the plot, and he who has betrayed us. Would you know how he has betrayed us? Because he sought my favour, and I refused him, and this is the vengeance that he takes—a white man's vengeance."

"*Wow*!" broke in the Chief Maputa, "this pretty one speaks truth, for the white man would have made a bargain with me under which Umgona, the wizard, and Nahoon, the solider, were to be killed at the Crocodile Drift, and he himself suffered to escape with the girl. I spoke him softly and said 'yes,' and then like a loyal man I reported to the king."

"You hear," sighed Nanea. "Nahoon, fare you well, though presently perhaps we shall be together again. It was I who tempted you from your duty. For my sake you forgot your honour, and I am repaid. Farewell, my husband, it is better to die with you than to enter the house of the king's woman," and Nanea stepped on to the platform.

Here, holding to a bough of one of the thorn trees, she turned and addressed Hadden saying:

"Black Heart, you seem to have won the day, but me at least you lose and—the sun is not yet set. After sunset comes the night, Black Heart, and in the night I pray that you may wander eternally, and be given to drink of my blood and the blood of Umgona my father, and the blood of Nahoon my husband, who saved your life, and whom you have murdered. Perchance, Black Heart, we may yet meet yonder—in the House of the Dead."

Then uttering a low cry Nanea clasped her hands and sprang upwards and outwards from the platform. The watchers bent their heads foward to look. They saw her rush headlong down the face of the fall to strike the water fifty feet below. A few seconds, and for the last time, they caught sight of her white garment glimmering on the surface of the gloomy pool. Then the shadows and mist-wreaths hid it, and she was gone.

"Now, husband," cried the cheerful voice of the captain, "yonder is your marriage bed, so be swift to follow a bride who is so ready to lead the way. Wow! but you are good people to kill; never have I had to do with any who gave less trouble. You—" and he stopped, for mental agony had done its work, and suddenly Nahoon went mad before his eyes.

With a roar like that of a lion the great man cast off those who held him and seizing one of them round the waist and thigh, he put out all his terrible strength. Lifting him as though he had been an infant, he hurled him over the edge of the cliff to find his death on the rocks of the Pool of Doom. Then crying:

"Black Heart! your turn, Black Heart the traitor!" he rushed at Hadden, his eyes rolling and foam flying from his lips, as he passed striking the Chief Maputa from his horse with a backward blow of his hand. Ill would it have gone with the white man if Nahoon had caught him. But he could not come at him, for the soliders sprang upon him and notwithstanding his fearful struggles they pulled him to the ground, as at certain festivals the Zulu regiments with their naked hands pull down a bull in the presence of the king.

"Cast him over before he can work more mischief," said a voice. But the captain cried out, "Nay, nay, he is sacred; the fire from Heaven has fallen on his brain, and we may not harm him, else evil would overtake us all. Bind him hand and foot, and bear him hence tenderly to where he can be cared for. Surely I thought that these evil-doers were giving us too little trouble, and thus it has proved.''

So they set themselves to make fast Nahoon's hands and wrists, using as much gentleness as they might, for among the Zulus a lunatic is accounted holy. It was no easy task, and it took time.

Hadden glanced around him, and saw his opportunity. On the ground close beside him lay his rifle, where one of the soldiers had placed it, and about a dozen yards away Maputa's pony was grazing. With a swift movement, he seized the Martini and five seconds later he was on the back of the pony, heading for the Crocodile Drift at a gallop. So quickly indeed did he execute his masterly retreat, that occupied as they all were in binding Nahoon, for half a minute or more none of the soldiers noticed what had happened. Then Maputa chanced to see, and waddled after him to the top of the rise, screaming:

"The white thief, he has stolen my horse, and the gun too, the gun that he promised to give me.''

Hadden, who by this time was a hundred yards away, heard him clearly, and a rage filled his heart. This man had made an open murderer of him; more, he had been the means of robbing him of the girl for whose sake he had dipped his hands in these iniquities. He glanced over his shoulder; Maputa was still running, and alone. Yes, there was time; at any rate he would risk it.

Pulling up the pony with a jerk, he leapt from its back, slipping his arms through the rein with an almost simultaneous movement. As it chanced, and as he had hoped would be the case, the animal was a trained shooting horse, and stood still. Hadden planted his feet firmly on the ground and drawing a deep breath, he cocked the rifle and covered the advancing chief. Now Maputa saw his purpose and with a yell of terror turned to fly. Hadden waited a second to get his sight fair on to his broad back, then just as the soldiers appeared above the rise he pressed the trigger. He was a noted shot, and in this instance his skill did not fail him; for, before he heard the bullet tell, Maputa flung his arms wide and plunged to the ground dead.

Three seconds more, and with a savage curse, Hadden had remounted the pony and was riding for his life towards the river, which a while later he crossed in safety.

VI

The Ghost of the Dead

When Nanea leapt from the dizzy platform that overhung the Pool of Doom, a strange fortune befell her. Close in the precipice were many jagged rocks, and on these the waters of the fall fell and thundered, bounding from them in spouts of spray into the troubled depths of the foss beyond. It was on these stones that the life was dashed out of the bodies of the wretched victims who were hurled from above. But Nanea, it will be remembered, had not waited to be treated thus, and as it chanced the strong spring with which she had leapt to death carried her clear of the rocks. By a very little she missed the edge of them and striking the deep water head first like some practised diver, she sank down and down till she thought that she would never rise again. Yet she did rise, at the end of the pool in the mouth of the rapid, along which she sped swiftly, carried down by the rush of the water. Fortunately there were no rocks here; and, since she was a skilful swimmer, she escaped the danger of being thrown against the banks.

For a long distance she was borne thus till at length she saw that she was in a forest, for trees cut off the light from the water, and their drooping branches swept its surface. One of these Nanea caught with her hand, and by the help of it she dragged herself from the River of Death whence none had escaped before. Now she stood upon the bank gasping but quite unharmed; there was not a scratch on her body; even her white garment was still fast about her neck.

But though she had suffered no hurt in her terrible voyage, so exhausted was Nanea that she could scarcely stand. Here the gloom was that of night, and shivering with cold she looked around helplessly to find some refuge. Close to the water's edge grew an enormous yellow-wood tree, and to this she staggered—thinking to climb it, and seek shelter in its boughs where, as she hoped, she would be safe from wild beasts. Again fortune befriended her, for at a distance of a few feet from the ground there was a great hole in the tree which, she discovered, was hollow. Into this hole she crept, taking her chance of its being the home of snakes or other evil creatures, to find that the interior was wide and warm. It was dry also, for at the bottom of the cavity lay a loot or more of rotten tinder and moss brought there by rats or birds. Upon this tinder she lay down, and covering herself with the moss and leaves soon sank into sleep or stupor.

How long Nanea slept she did not know, but at length she was awakened by a sound as of guttural human voices talking in a language that she could not understand. Rising to her knees she peered out of the hole in the tree. It was night, but the stars shone brilliantly, and their light fell upon an open circle of ground close by the edge of the river. In this circle there burned a great fire, and at a little distance from the fire were gathered eight or ten horrible-looking beings, who appeared to be rejoicing over something that lay upon the ground. They were small in stature, men and women together, but no children, and all of them were nearly naked. Their hair was long and thin, growing down almost to the eyes, their jaws and teeth protruded and the girth of their black bodies was out of all proportion to their height. In their hands they held sticks with sharp stones lashed on to them, or rude hatchet-like knives of the same material.

Now Nanea's heart shrank within her, and she nearly fainted with fear, for she knew that she was in the haunted forest, and without a doubt these were the *Esemkofu,* the evil ghosts that dwelt therein. Yes, that was what they were, and yet she could not take her eyes off them—the sight of them held her with a horrible fascination. But if they were ghosts, why did they sing and dance like men? Why did they wave those sharp stones aloft, and quarrel and strike each other? And why did they make a fire as men do when they wish to cook food? More, what was it that they rejoiced over, that long dark thing which lay so quiet upon the ground? It did not look like a head of game, and it could scarcely be a crocodile, yet clearly it was food of some sort, for they were sharpening the stone knives in order to cut it up.

While she wondered thus, one of the dreadful-looking little creatures advanced to the fire, and taking from it a burning bough, held it over the thing that lay upon the ground, to give light to a companion who was about to do something to it with a stone knife. Next instant Nanea drew back her head from the hole, a stifled shriek upon her lips. She saw what it was now—it was the body of a man. Yes, and these were not ghosts; they were cannibals of whom when she was little, her mother had told her tales to keep her from wandering away from home.

But who was the man they were about to eat? It could not be one of themselves, for his stature was much greater. Oh! now she knew; it must be Nahoon, who had been killed up yonder, and whose dead body the waters had brought down to the haunted forest as they had brought her alive. Yes, it must be Nahoon, and she would be forced to see her husband devoured before her eyes. The thought of it overwhelmed her. That he should die by order of the king was natural, but that he should be buried thus! Yet what could she do it prevent it? Well, if it cost her her life, it should be prevented. At the worst they could only kill and eat her also, and now that Nahoon and her father were gone, being untroubled by any religious or spiritual hopes and fears, she was not greatly concerned to keep her own breath in her.

Slipping through the hole in the tree, Nanea walked quietly towards the cannibals—not knowing in the least what she should do when she reached them. As she arrived in line with the fire this lack of programme came home to her mind forcibly, and she paused to reflect. Just then one of the cannibals looked up to see a tall and stately figure wrapped in a white garment which, as the flame-light flickered on it, seemed now to advance from the dense background of shadow, and now to recede into it. The poor savage wretch was holding a stone knife in his teeth when he beheld her, but it did not remain there long, for opening his great jaws he uttered the most terrified and piercing yell that Nanea had ever heard. Then the others saw her also, and presently the forest was ringing with shrieks of fear. For a few seconds the outcasts stood and gazed, then they were gone this way and that, bursting their path through the undergrowth like startled jackals. The *Esemkofu* of Zulu tradition had been routed in their own haunted home by what they took to be a spirit.

Poor *Esemkofu!* they were but miserable and starving bushmen who, driven into that place of ill omen many years ago, had adopted this means, the only one open to them, to keep the life in their wretched bodies. Here at least they were unmolested, and as there was little other food to be found amid the wilderness of trees, they took what the river brought them. When executions were few in the Pool of Doom, times were hard for them indeed—for then they were driven to eat each other. That is why there were no children.

As their inarticulate outcry died away in the distance, Nanea ran forward to look at the body that lay on the ground, and staggered back with a sigh of relief. It was not Nahoon, but she recognised the face for that of one of the party of executioners. How did he come here? Had Nahoon killed him? Had Nahoon escaped? She could not tell, and at the best it was improbable, but still the sight of this dead soldier lit her heart with a faint ray of hope, for how did he come to be dead if Nahoon had no hand in his death? She could not bear to leave him lying so near her hiding-place, however; therefore, with no small toil, she rolled the corpse back into the water, which carried it swiftly away. Then she returned to the tree, having first replenished the fire, and awaited the light.

At last it came—so much of it as ever penetrated this darksome den—and Nanea, becoming aware that she was hungry, descended from the tree to search for food. All day long she searched, finding nothing, till towards sunset she remembered that on the outskirts of the forest there was a flat rock where it was the custom of those who had been in any way afflicted, or who considered themselves or their belongings to be bewitched, to place propitiatory offerings of food wherewith the *Esemkofu* and *Amalhosi* were supposed to satisfy their spiritual cravings. Urged by the pinch of starvation, to this spot Nanea journeyed rapidly, and found to her joy that some neighbouring kraal had evidently been in recent trouble, for the Rock of Offering was laden with cobs of corn, gourds of milk, porridge and even meat. Helping herself to as much as she could carry, she returned to her lair, where she drank of the milk and cooked meat and mealies at the fire. Then she crept back into the tree, and slept.

For nearly two months Nanea lived thus in the forest, since she could not venture out of it—fearing lest she should be seized, and for a second time taste of the judgement of the king. In the forest at least she was safe, for none dared enter there, nor did the *Esemkofu* give her further trouble. Once or twice she saw them, but on each occasion they fled shrieking from her presence— seeking some distant retreat, where they hid themselves or perished. Nor did food fail her, for finding that it was taken, the pious givers brought it in plenty to the Rock of Offering.

But, Oh! the life was dreadful, and the gloom and loneliness coupled with her sorrows at times drove her almost to insanity. Still she lived on, though often she desired to die, for if her father was dead, the corpse she had found was not the corpse of Nahoon, and in her heart there still shone that spark of hope. Yet what she hoped for she could not tell.

When Philip Hadden reached civilised regions, he found that war was about to be declared between the Queen and Cetywayo, King of the Amazulu; also that in the prevailing excitement his little adventure with the Utrecht store-keeper had been overlooked or forgotten. He was the owner of two good buckwaggons with spans of salted oxen, and at that time vehicles were much in request to carry military stores for the columns which were to advance into Zululand; indeed the transport authorities were glad to pay £90 a month for the hire of each waggon and to guarantee the owners against all loss of cattle. Although he was not desirous of returning to Zululand, this bait proved too much for Hadden, who accordingly leased out his waggons to the Commissariat, together with his own services as conductor and interpreter.

He was attached to No. 3 column of the invading force, which it may be remembered was under the immediate command of Lord Chelmsford, and on the 20 January, 1879, he marched with it by the road that runs from Rorke's Drift to the Indeni forest, and encamped that night beneath the shadow of the steep and desolate mountain known as Isandhlwana.

That day also a great army of King Cetywayo's, numbering twenty thousand men and more, moved down from the Upindo Hill and encamped upon the stony plain that lies a mile and a half to the east of Isandhlwana. No fires were lit, and it lay there in utter silence, for the warriors were "sleeping on their spears."

With that *impi* was the Umcityu regiment, three thousand five hundred strong. At the first break of dawn the Induna in command of the Umcityu looked up from beneath the shelter of the black shield with which he had covered his body, and through the thick mist he saw a great man standing before him, clothed only in a moocha, a gaunt wild-eyed man who held a rough club in his hand. When he was spoken to, the man made no answer; he only leaned upon his club looking from left to right along the dense array of innumerable shields.

"Who is this *Silwana* (wild creature)?" asked the Induna of his captains wondering.

The captains stared at the wanderer, and one of them replied, "This is Nahoon-ka-Zomba, it is the son of Zomba who not long ago held rank in this regiment of the Umcityu. His betrothed, Nanea, daughter of Umgona, was killed together with her father by order of the Black One, and Nahoon went mad with grief at the sight of it, for the fire of Heaven entered his brain, and mad he has wandered ever since."

"What would you here, Nahoon-ka-Zomba?" asked the Induna.

Then Nahoon spoke slowly. "My regiment goes down to war against the white men; give me a shield and a spear, O Captain of the king, that I may fight with my regiment, for I seek a face in the battle."

So they gave him a shield and a spear, for they dared not turn away one whose brain was alight with the fire of Heaven.

*   *   *

When the sun was high that day, bullets began to fall among the ranks of the Umcityu. Then the black-shielded, black-plumed Umcityu arose, company by company, and after them arose the whole vast Zulu army, breast and horns together, and swept down in silence upon the doomed British camp, a moving sheen of spears. The bullets pattered on the shields, the shells tore long lines through their array, but they never halted nor wavered. Forward on either side shot out the horns of armed men, clasping the camp in an embrace of steel. Then as these began to close, out burst the war cry of the Zulus, and with the roar of a torrent and the rush of a storm, with a sound like the humming of a billion bees, wave after wave the deep breast of the *impi* rolled down upon the white men. With it went the black-shielded Umcityu and with them went Nahoon, the son of Zomba. A bullet struck him in the side, glancing from his ribs, he did not heed; a white man fell from his horse before him, he did not stab, for he sought but one face in the battle.

He sought—and at last he found. There, among the waggons where the spears were busiest, there standing by his horse and firing rapidly was Black Heart, he who had given Nanea his betrothed to death. Three soldiers stood between them, one of them Nahoon stabbed, and two he brushed aside; then he rushed straight at Hadden.

But the white man saw him come, and even through the mask of his madness he knew Nahoon again, and terror took hold of him. Throwing away the empty rifle, for his ammunition was spent, he leaped upon his horse and drove his spurs into its flanks. Away it went among the carnage, springing over the dead and bursting through the lines of shields, and after it came Nahoon, running long and low with head stretched forward and trailing spear, running as a hound runs when the buck is at view.

Hadden's first plan was to head for Rorke's Drift, but a glance to the left showed him that the masses of the Undi barred that way, so he fled straight on, leaving his path to fortune. In five minutes he was over a ridge, and there was nothing of the battle to be seen, in ten all sounds of it had died away, for few guns were fired in the dread race to Fugitive's Drift, and the assegai makes no noise. In some strange fashion, even at this moment, the contract between the dreadful scene of blood and turmoil that he had left, and the peaceful face of Nature over which he was passing, came home to his brain vividly. Here birds sang and cattle grazed; here the sun shone undimmed by the smoke of cannon, only high up in the blue and silent air long streams of vultures could be seen winging their way to the Plain of Isandhlwana.

The ground was very rough, and Hadden's horse began to tire. He looked over his shoulder—there some two hundred yards behind came the Zulu, grim as Death, unswerving as Fate. He examined the pistol in his belt; there was but one undischarged cartridge left, all the rest had been fired and the pouch was empty. Well, one bullet should be enough for one savage: the question was should he stop and use it now? No, he might miss or fail to kill the man; he was on horseback and his foe on foot, surely he could tire him out.

A while passed, and they dashed through a little stream. It seemed familiar to Hadden. Yes, that was the pool where he used to bathe when he was the guest of Umgona, the father of Nanea; and there on the knoll to his right were the huts, or rather the remains of them, for they had been burnt with fire. What chance had brought him to this place, he wondered; then again he looked behind him at Nahoon, who seemed to read his thoughts, for he shook his spear and pointed to the ruined kraal.

On he went at speed for here the land was level, and to his joy he lost sight of his pursuer. But presently there came a mile of rocky ground, and when it was past, glancing back he saw that Nahoon was once more in his old place. His horse's strength was almost spent, but Hadden spurred it forward blindly, whither he knew not. Now he was travelling along a strip of turf and ahead of him he heard the music of a river, while to his left rose a high bank. Presently the turf bent inwards and there, not twenty yards away from him, was a Kaffir hut standing on the brink of a river. He looked at it, yes, it was the hut of that accursed *inyanga*, the Bee, and standing by the fence of it was none other than the Bee herself. At the sight of her the exhausted horse swerved violently, stumbled and came to the ground, where it lay panting. Hadden was thrown from the saddle but sprang to his feet unhurt.

"Ah! Black Heart, is it you? What news of the battle, Black Heart?" cried the Bee in a mocking voice.

"Help me, mother, I am pursued," he gasped.

"What of it, Black Heart, it is but by one tired man. Stand then and face him, for now Black Heart and White Heart are together again. You will not? Then away to the forest and seek shelter among the dead who await you there. Tell me, tell me, was it the face of Nanea that I saw beneath the waters a while ago? Good! bear my greetings to her when you two meet in the House of the Dead."

Hadden looked at the stream; it was in flood. He could not swim it, so followed by the evil laugh of the prophetess, he sped towards the forest. After him came Nahoon, his tongue hanging from his jaws like the tongue of a wolf.

Now he was in the shadow of the forest, but still he sped on following the course of the river, till at length his breath failed, and he halted on the further side of a little glade, beyond which a great tree grew. Nahoon was more than a spear's throw behind him: therefore he had time to draw his pistol and make ready.

"Halt, Nahoon," he cried, as once before he had cried; "I would speak with you."

The Zulu heard his voice, and obeyed.

"Listen," said Hadden. "We have run a long race and fought a long fight, you and I, and we are still alive both of us. Very soon, if you come on, one of us must be dead, and it will be you, Nahoon, for I am armed and as you know I can shoot straight. What do you say?"

Nahoon made no answer, but stood still at the edge of the glade, his wild and glowering eyes fixed on the white man's face and his breath coming in short gasps.

"Will you let me go, if *I* let *you* go?" Hadden asked once more. "I know why you hate me, but the past cannot be undone, nor can the dead be brought to earth again."

Still Nahoon made no answer, and his silence seemed more fateful and more crushing than any speech; no spoken accusation would have been so terrible in Hadden's ear. He made no answer, but lifting his assegai he stalked grimly toward his foe.

When he was within five paces Hadden covered him and fired. Nahoon sprang aside, but the bullet struck him somewhere, for his right arm dropped, and the stabbing spear that he held was jerked from it harmlessly over the white man's head. But still making no sound, the Zulu came on and gripped him by the throat with his left hand. For a space they struggled terribly, swaying to and fro, but Hadden was unhurt and fought with the fury of despair, while Nahoon had been twice wounded, and there remained to him but one sound arm wherewith to strike. Presently forced to earth by the white man's iron strength, the soldier was down, nor could he rise again.

"Now we will make an end," muttered Hadden savagely, and he turned to seek the assegai, then staggered slowly back with starting eyes and reeling gait. For there before him, still clad in her white robe, a spear in her hand, stood the spirit of Nanea!

"Think of it," he said to himself, dimly remembering the

words of the *inyanga*, "when you stand face to face with the ghost of the dead in the Home of the Dead."

There was a cry and a flash of steel; the broad spear leapt towards him to bury itself in his breast. He swayed, he fell, and presently Black Heart clasped that great reward which the word of the Bee had promised Him.

"Nahoon! Nahoon!" murmured a soft voice, "awake, it is no ghost, but I—Nanea—I, your living wife, to whom my *Ehlose*[1] has given it me to save you."

Nahoon heard and opened his eyes to look and his madness left him.

"Welcome, wife," he said faintly, "now I will live since Death has brought you back to me in the House of the Dead."

Today Nahoon is one of the Indunas of the English Government in Zululand, and there are children about his kraal. It was from the lips of none other than Nanea his wife that the teller of this tale heard its substance.

The Bee also lives and practises as much magic as she dares under the white man's rule. On her black hand shines a golden ring shaped like a snake with ruby eyes, and of this trinket the Bee is very proud.

[1]Guardian Spirit.

ABOUT THE EDITORS

ISAAC ASIMOV has been called "one of America's treasures." Born in the Soviet Union, he was brought to the United States at the age of three (along with his family) by agents of the American government in a successful attempt to prevent him from working for the wrong side. He quickly established himself as one of this country's foremost science fiction writers and writer about everything, and although now approaching middle age, he is going stronger than ever. He long ago passed his age and weight in books, and with some 290 to his credit threatens to close in on his I.Q. His sequel to *The Foundation Trilogy—Foundation's Edge*—was one of the best-selling books of 1982 and 1983.

MARTIN H. GREENBERG has been called (in *The Science Fiction and Fantasy Book Review*) "The King of the Anthologists"; to which he replied—"It's good to be the King!" He has produced more than seventy of them, usually in collaboration with a multitude of co-conspirators, most frequently the two who have given you WIZARDS. A Professor of Regional Analysis and Political Science at the University of Wisconsin-Green Bay, he is still trying to publish his weight.

CHARLES G. WAUGH is a Professor of Psychology and Communications at the University of Maine at Augusta who is still trying to figure out how he got himself into all this. He has also worked with many collaborators, since he is basically a very friendly fellow. He has done some fifty anthologies and single-author collections, and especially enjoys locating unjustly ignored stories. He also claims that he met his wife via computer dating—her choice was an entire fraternity or him, and she has only minor regrets.

JOIN THE WITCHES READERS' PANEL

Help us bring you more of the books you like by filling out this survey and mailing it in today.

1. Book title:_____

Book #:_____

2. Using the scale below how would you rate this book on the following features.

Poor		Not so Good			O.K.			Good		Excellent
0	1	2	3	4	5	6	7	8	9	10

Rating

Overall opinion of book . . . . _____
Plot/Story . . . . _____
Setting/Location . . . . _____
Writing Style . . . . _____
Character Development . . . . _____
Conclusion/Ending . . . . _____
Scene on Front Cover . . . . _____

3. On average about how many fantasy books do you buy for yourself each month?_____

4. How would you classify yourself as a reader of fantasies?
I am a ( ) light ( ) medium ( ) heavy reader.

5. What is your education?
( ) High School (or less)   ( ) 4 yrs. college
( ) 2 yrs. college   ( ) Post Graduate

6. Age_____   **7.** Sex: ( ) Male ( ) Female

Please Print Name_____

Address_____

City_____State_____Zip_____

Phone # (   )_____

Thank you. Please send to New American Library, Research Dept, 1633 Broadway, New York, NY 10019.